Charlotte's Story

ALSO BY LAURA BENEDICT

NOVELS

Bliss House

Devil's Oven

Calling Mr. Lonely Hearts

Isabella Moon

ANTHOLOGIES

Surreal South '11

Surreal South '09

Surreal South: An Anthology of Short Fiction

Charlotte's Story

A BLISS HOUSE NOVEL

LAURA BENEDICT

PEGASUS CRIME

NEW YORK LONDON

CHARLOTTE'S STORY

Pegasus Books LLC
80 Broad Street, 5th Floor
New York, NY 10004

First Pegasus Books cloth edition October 2015

Interior design by Maria Fernandez

ISBN: 978-1-60598-878-8

10 9 8 7 6 5 4 3 2 1

Printed in the United States of America
Distributed by W. W. Norton & Company, Inc.

For Monica and Teresa,
my sisters, my friends

Far safer, of a midnight meeting
External ghost,
Than an interior confronting
That whiter host.

—EMILY DICKINSON

Charlotte's Story

Chapter 1

1957: The End of Time

We came to the end of time on a bright October afternoon. I had
finished a second glass of champagne even though I thought three
o'clock in the afternoon was a ridiculous time to be drinking wine.
But that's what we were doing because Press said we'd been too sad
for too long and needed cheering. We were the only adults in the
house for the first time in two months since his mother, Olivia, had
died. The wine was the color of hay bathed in sunshine, sparkling
in the filtered afternoon light of the salon. All the furnishings in
the substantial room—the ornate European furniture, the gilt-
edged mirrors and antique carpets—spoke of my mother-in-law's
preference for stateliness over comfort, and I had never dared to
even slip my shoes off inside it. Now Bliss House and its orchards
and woods were ours, and the birthright of our two children, Eva and
Michael. I was mistress of Bliss House, but I didn't quite feel it yet,
and wondered if I ever would.

Press took the bottle of Perrier-Jouet—his favorite, and what his mother had served at our wedding party—from the ice bucket to pour me a third glass.

"We shouldn't, Press. Really, we shouldn't." Secretly, I wanted more, but I protested because I thought I should. It was in my nature. Or, more rightly, in my bourgeois upbringing. (Bourgeois as in *NOCD—Not our class, darling,* as the thoughtlessly raised Yankee girls at Burton Hall, my college, used to say.) I was taught that people who drank in the afternoons were useless, and probably drunks.

In answer, Press bent to touch his lips to my neck, tickling the tender skin beneath my right ear, and I felt the roughness of the late-day growth of his beard. With an agonizing slowness that I knew was intentional, his lips found my mouth and he kissed me deeply in a way that implied both hunger and possession.

Had Bliss House still belonged to his mother, he certainly never would have kissed me with such passion outside the privacy of our bedroom.

When he stood again, he was smiling and I was self-conscious of the flush that consumed my torso, neck, and face. Even my ears felt hot. The glass refilled, I drank as deeply as I dared, given the frantic bubbles. Press knew me well enough to know that my protest that we shouldn't drink any more had held self-censure but not conviction. I was exhausted from caring for the children, and the wine was tempting.

There is a haze around that afternoon that I'll never be able to dispel, and I can't remember if I truly could smell the scent of the roses just outside the room. The screens were still in the French doors that opened onto the gardens: a boxwood maze with a tall statue of the goddess Hera with her peacock at its center, and geometric rows of cultivated rose bushes. It was only early October and, because the climate in central Virginia is not overly harsh, the roses would continue to bloom through the earliest days of

November. Their scent is strongest around four or five o'clock when the hum of the bees finishing their day's work is most hypnotic. But I choose to believe that I did smell the roses. Some small recompense for the hell that was about to be unleashed on us.

Press sat down on the hassock in front of the tufted slipper chair into which I had sunk and lifted my feet onto his lap.

I laughed and tried to pull away, but he held my heels firmly.

"Preston Bliss, what are you doing?" I'd teased him in the past about not liking to touch my feet. In fact, he didn't much like anyone's feet—not even the baby's, which I was kissing and playing with all the time. But now he was sliding off one of my shoes, and then the other, so that my feet were bare in his hands. Some women wore stockings daily throughout the 1950s, but that day they seemed unnecessary, given that the staff had the day off and we weren't planning to leave the house. He massaged my feet for a few moments, making me giggle as he stroked the arch of my foot with his smooth, uncallused fingers (he was a gentleman, a lawyer, and had never become as interested in working the estate's orchards as his mother had imagined he should be). The house was so quiet that my laughter filled the room, and I quickly covered my mouth as though someone might hear. Olivia hadn't minded laughter, but the room spoke so much of her that she might have been with us, watching from one of the enormous wing chairs stationed near the fireplace like guardians at the entrance to an ashen cave, instead of in the graveyard of St. Anselm's Episcopal church buried beside her husband.

With a quick, gentle squeeze of each foot, Press tucked my feet beside him on the hassock.

"Did you know that you're a queen, my love?" Leaning forward, he touched my hair.

I shook my head, already a bit silly with champagne. He'd greeted me with the first glass after I'd finished putting the children's toys away. "I'm just the. . . ." I considered for a moment.

My mother-in-law had been the queen of Bliss House, and Eva Grace, napping in her trundle bed in the nursery a few feet from one-year-old Michael's crib, was certainly the princess. Where did that leave me? My pedigree was respectable, as Virginia pedigrees went. My father was a Carter, even though he owned an office-supply store, and my mother's family had moved from Pennsylvania to Virginia before the Revolutionary War. But I was just plain Charlotte Frances Carter, daughter of a merchant from Clareston, Virginia, and hadn't *come from money* as Preston had. There were people—people in my own family, in fact—who weighted pedigree far more significantly than money, and believed that Olivia had encouraged our marriage because pedigree was something that she and the Bliss family lacked. But my aunts hadn't really understood Olivia. She hadn't cared at all about such things.

I felt languorous, even a little sleepy, and I suspected that I was about to make a fool of myself, but I didn't care. Press hadn't been himself, but more opinionated, tense, and somehow bolder since Olivia's death, and I'd been so occupied with the children that I was happy to have this playful, attentive Press to myself.

"I'm more like the daughter of a baronet. I don't know what that would be. A baronetess?"

"No. You're a queen. My mother adored you, and she always told me that I didn't treat you nearly as well as you should be treated."

His words made me happy. That day I was still such a girl, and the wine—at first surprisingly bitter, yet pleasing on my tongue— had given me the feeling of being on a honeymoon again. His watchful brown eyes still regarded me with a proprietary sense of both pride and indulgence that I identified as true love. At thirty-one, he was four years older than I and, when the weather was fine, kept himself trim with early-morning rowing on the James. I've described him as compact, and while his shoulders were square and facial features quite blunt, he was not a small man. He was only an inch shorter than my unladylike height of five feet, nine inches. His "golden goddess," he called me, as though I were Kim Novak or a blond Bergman.

He kissed me again, his hand covering the back of my bare neck, his fingers sliding up into my hair. (I'd had my hair cropped stylishly short to keep Michael from constantly pulling on it.) Tired as I was, I couldn't help but respond. I had been a virgin when we married, and my attraction to Press showed no signs of abating. He was deeply sensual. I saw his effect on other women, too, though I never questioned his faithfulness. Later you may wonder at my naïveté, but try not to judge me too harshly.

I almost stopped him as he unbuttoned the cotton blouse so beautifully ironed by Marlene, our housekeeper, and slipped his hand inside. But I remembered that we were alone. The house was ours, and our children were asleep, and the birds were noisy outside the open window, and the champagne was pleasing on our twining tongues.

Finally he pulled back and stood to help me from the chair. When I tried to stifle an unexpected yawn, he smiled. I giggled like a teenager. I was as in love with him at that moment as I ever had been. His faintly olive skin was also flushed, and I only felt a tiny amount of the embarrassment that I would have felt a few weeks before at being half-undressed in such a public room, the doors open to both the garden and Bliss House's enormous central hall. I felt brave and desirable and voraciously needful of what we were about to do there. As he led me to the largest sofa (brocade chrysanthemums in varying shades of blue—I've long since gotten rid of it), I tripped, dizzy with heat and wine, but he caught and steadied me.

I had a fleeting thought, wondering if it would always be like this, but I knew the children would soon wake, and the staff and Nonie, the woman who had raised me and was our children's nanny, would return, and our lovemaking would again be confined to my bedroom or his. But then the thought was gone, and I asked for more to drink. Press laughed and said there was no more for me, but that he had something else I'd like, and I thought him terribly wicked.

He lay down on the sofa, which was beneath a far window, and I remember looking at his mouth as he pulled me onto him, and there was something strange about the set of his lips—something hard and unfamiliar that made me think of the bitterness of the champagne. Then he parted them and kissed me again, and I closed my eyes and molded my body against his. But there is no trace of the next few hours left in my memory. It was as though we had reached the farthest border of some island of time and could not go on.

When I opened my eyes again, it was dusk, and the light of a single lamp groped pitifully in the overwhelming dark of the big room. My best friend Rachel knelt beside me, and Press stood in the shadows beyond her, his face solemn. He was holding Michael, who was sucking his thumb as he rested his head against his father's shoulder.

Rachel's face was wet with tears.

Chapter 2

The Children's Grove

I could feel the eyes of all of Old Gate on us once again. Once again I was grateful for the dense veil draped over the front of the black silk hat I'd bought for Olivia's funeral. Its netting was more difficult to see out of than that of more delicate veils, but it also meant that it was harder to see behind it. Of course, friends and acquaintances alike wanted to see my face. Death had come to Bliss House again so quickly, and their eyes were hungry for its effect on us. If I had been thinking hard about it, I might have hated them all on that achingly clear, horrid October morning. But I wasn't thinking about them. I was beyond thinking; I existed in a state that barely recognized words or even other people. Eva was dead, and I was the one responsible.

As Father Aaron's voice droned in the background, I watched a fly drift from rose to rose on Eva's tiny *oh, God, impossibly tiny* white coffin. They were fat yellow roses from the garden at Bliss House, the garden where I'd pushed her as a baby in the big English pram that had once held Preston, the garden whose recently replanted maze had grown just tall enough to hide her as she ran away from Nonie and me—had it been only a few days earlier?—her laughter ringing shrill and joyful in the fall sunshine.

The fly finally alighted, crawling over a single spotless petal, stopping every few seconds to rub its front feet together. Feeding or washing. Defecating. Defiling. *Defiling!*

Unable to bear it any longer, I lunged forward to sweep the thing away, off of my baby's coffin, breaking the rhythm of Father Aaron's godly imprecations, giving gathered Old Gate confirmation of my pain. My pain and my shame. The armful of stems, which the florist had loosely tied together with a white ribbon, flew off the coffin and scattered at the feet of the priest. Preston grabbed me from behind, wrapping one arm about my waist and firmly staying my upraised arm with his other hand.

As he pulled me away from the grave, I heard a feral keening that might have been mistaken for the call of some terrified animal. But of course it was my own cry. I can still hear it in my mind when Bliss House is restless in its silence and I think of that day. I collapsed back onto Press.

"Charlotte, Charlotte." His voice was a fierce whisper in my ear. Was he admonishing or comforting me? Now I think it was something else entirely.

Nonie, seated behind us with Michael on her lap, released an uncharacteristic sob. Michael was blessedly silent.

Press led me back to my chair and helped me sit down. A part of me wanted to tell him about the fly, to explain, but the words wouldn't come. People talk of the numbness of grief, but I wasn't numb. I felt as though the outermost layer of my skin had been peeled away so that the halting breaths and pitying gazes of everyone around us chafed me like dried thistles. In the end, it was my father who calmed me, taking my hand gently as though he knew how much any touch would hurt. Father

Aaron continued the burial liturgy, condemning my daughter to darkness.

⌒

By the time we crossed the graveyard, my black high heels sinking into the soft ground as we made our way toward the line of cars waiting along Church Street, I was calmer. All was muted and quiet, and time had still not returned to its normal pace. A single white cloud hung motionless in the sky above our heads, and even the chiming of the quarter-hour from the carillon at the Presbyterian church at the end of the block seemed too long and slow. My father was at my side; Press walked a few steps ahead, his head down, the hems of his pants wearing a thin line of morning damp from the brown and gold leaves strewn over the dying grass. He seemed to be watching the ground. I couldn't know if he had chosen to leave me to the care of my father, or just couldn't bear to walk by my side. He had assured me again and again that he didn't blame me for Eva's death, but how could I be certain? Though he had been the one to leave the house while the children napped and I slept—drunk with champagne—how could he have known that I wouldn't wake before the children? That Eva would get out of bed and try to give herself a bath? In my heart, I knew I was at fault. I clung to my father's hand. A lifeline.

Far behind us in the Children's Grove, the gravediggers had begun to shovel dirt into Eva's grave. I wanted to run back to them to help. Or, better, to do it myself.

Were there places in the world where mothers were the ones who buried their children? Clearing the ground of grass and leaves as though readying it for a garden, hauling away the stones, cleaving the naked dirt with a spade, the force of it driven by their wordless pain? There could be no better way to use that pain, that sharp, relentless, endless pain that sat like a rock in my gut and pulsed its poison throughout my body. Eva's grave had been dug that morning (Or the day before. I didn't know, didn't want to know.), but I could at least help to cover her. Hide the bright, white coffin away in the sheltering earth. Who better to lay a child to sleep than her own mother?

My father's hand tightened around mine as though he'd heard my thoughts and might keep me from turning back.

The Children's Grove, with its pensive army of stone and marble cherubs guarding rows of small graves, had been my choice. Preston had wanted Eva buried in the gated section of the cemetery reserved long ago for the Bliss family; but even fighting from the depths of my guilt, I had won. She would sleep in the company of the twenty or so children who had died in a flu epidemic of forty years earlier, along with the several more who had been buried there since. Eva had loved being with other children and had adored Michael too. It was the right place for her.

I stumbled on a hole that had been covered by leaves, and my father steadied me.

"Are you sure you're up to having all these people back at the house, Lottie?" He kept his voice low, no doubt to keep Press from hearing. Although he was always friendly with Press, they were never truly close. Neither of them ever spoke to me about it, but I suspect it was a mutual choice.

There was no question of canceling the wake. It was the tradition of the family to open the house to anyone who wanted to come and visit after a funeral. And there had been several funerals tied to Bliss House in the eighty years of its existence.

"Marlene will have everything ready. It doesn't matter, Daddy. I don't care."

The truth was that I really *didn't* care. Eva was dead. Let them stare. Let them wonder. Let them eat our food and gossip about us. It was both the cost and privilege of living at Bliss House, the house my father had once called "that worrisome place."

Chapter 3

Death, Endless Death

Press's face and shoulders were canted over the steering wheel as though he might make the Cadillac sedan—which he'd bought for me when Michael was born—go faster. Several people had approached us before we reached the car, delaying our departure, and he had stood rudely fingering his keys, tolerating their condolences. I hadn't wanted to speak with them either, and had just nodded at first, hoping they would finish so we could return to the house and get the whole thing over with. I suppose I fell back on my training, trying to be polite even though I felt dead inside.

Press—at least this new Press—was very different from me. He wasn't often rude, but his air of natural privilege had intensified. Months earlier, before Olivia's funeral, he had shocked me by saying that he didn't give a damn about the feelings of the people who kept calling and coming by to tell us how sorry they were. Father Aaron had told us grief might expose itself in unexpected ways, and, as the weeks progressed, I found myself even a little excited by Press's unpredictability.

"Without Olivia in the house, he can be his own man now, Lottie. That's a good thing for you both," my father had said.

Still, I was certain that eventually Press would again become the kind, funny, pleasant man I'd married. I did see that man again, briefly, that golden afternoon in the salon, but then he was gone forever.

When Augie Shaw, Olivia's lawyer, went over her will with us, we learned that Olivia had specifically left half of Bliss House and the surrounding land to me, along with a substantial gift of money and jewelry. I had seen a flash of real surprise in Press's eyes. Then he had smiled—but only with his lips. There was no doubt to whom he believed Bliss House really belonged.

By the time Eva died, his singular obsession was Bliss House.

~

"Terrance and Marlene are already at the house, Press. I'm sure Daddy and Nonie are there by now too." I spoke quietly, unsure of how much to say, how to balance my own grief with my concern for him. It felt awkward, as though I were relearning how to talk, how to think.

Nonie and Michael had gone ahead in my father's Hudson Hornet so Nonie could give Michael lunch and then put him down for his nap. You might wonder that I let Michael out of my sight now that he was my only child. It's not that I didn't love Michael as much as Eva, or that I didn't worry that I could easily lose him as well. Michael has a goodness about him that's much like his sister's. A natural smile. An eagerness to please. He was with the two people whom I trusted most in the world and, given what had happened to Eva, I trusted them far more than I trusted myself.

Press didn't respond, but watched the road, his hands restless on the wheel.

⌢

When Rachel Carstairs—though she was just pretty Rachel Webb, my roommate at Burton Hall College in 1950—told me about the man from Old Gate she wanted me to meet, she warned me that he wasn't exactly handsome. But I'd immediately found Hasbrouck Preston Bliss oddly charming and funny. I had met enough handsome, not-very-smart boys at college mixers. I wanted something more.

"Press is so much fun, Charlotte. You won't believe how much fun he is, and he's crazy for pretty blondes. The perfect person to bring you out of your shell. You deserve some happiness, darling, and you know as well as I do that you don't want to spend your life slaving away as an art teacher or whatever it is that you think you're going to do." Such a speech from anyone who wasn't Rachel would've sounded vapid and, perhaps, cruel, but it was the sort of thing that Rachel—her dark eyes wide and slyly innocent—could say with utter seriousness. "Plus, he's been moaning for the past two years that he wants to get married and stop knocking around that huge house with just his mother and those creepy servants. Well, *I* think they're creepy, anyway."

I'd never thought of myself as having a shell, and was slightly offended, but then Rachel was always on me to get out and socialize and to stop studying so much. I was what well-meaning adults called "bookish." (The teenage Michael is like me in that way.) So Rachel brought me home to Old Gate and threw Preston and me together at her mother's Thanksgiving Saturday open house.

In the early afternoon, the younger guests gathered in the pool house where there were shuffleboard, pool and ping-pong tables, a long, mirrored bar, and a real juke box with flashing yellow and green lights. Despite all the activity around us—twenty or thirty people had already arrived, and a few couples were even dancing—Rachel wasn't interested in anything but introducing me to Press, and led me by the hand as I followed her slight form across the room. She was even more diminutive than usual in her close-fitting Chinese silk pajamas, dramatic red and embroidered with gold chrysanthemums. Her glamorous figure, rich black hair coiffed into a sleek chignon, piquant nose and mouth beneath enormous brown eyes meant that she could get away with wearing just about anything. I'd first thought that my own dress, an ivory sheath with appliqués of dark green vines along the hem and deep décolletage, was too elegant for an open house, but Rachel had encouraged me, and now I was glad. The flat shoes felt wrong—I'd been reluctant to wear high heels because Rachel had told me Press was about my height—but overall I was pleased by the effect. Maybe I sound vain. Maybe I *am* vain, even still. But there is only one time in a girl's life when she is twenty-one and confident in the knowledge that she is healthy and attractive. Confident, too, that nothing truly bad could ever happen to her. She hasn't been tested.

I glanced at myself in the mirror behind the bar to see that my upswept blond hair was perfectly set, and more than one man was watching my—well, *our*—progress across the room.

We stopped in front of two men sitting on barstools, their heads close in earnest discussion. One of the men, who turned out to be Jack Carstairs, was even more blond than I, his ice-white hair clipped short on the sides, but molded with a sleek, flawless wave that angled neatly away from his forehead. Even though he was seated, I could tell he was tall by the way he hunched down to speak to the man with him. If I was more than seven inches taller than Rachel, then he was at least a foot taller. Perhaps also noticing our approach in the mirror, he turned to watch us, a hint of annoyance flitting briefly across his striking, angular face. Though I was curious about Press, I caught myself staring at Jack. The irises of his blue eyes were alarmingly light, and I wondered for a moment if he were an albino—a kind of person I'd heard about but had never seen. His skin had a cool, pinkish-white cast, but his eyes were definitely blue. His clothes were neat to the point of fastidiousness and his hair had surely taken many minutes to perfect. Rachel had mentioned Jack many times, and hadn't said he was a homosexual, but I had heard that homosexual men were often very particular about their appearance. (When Rachel married him a few years later, I remembered my silent speculation and had a laugh at myself.)

But it was the other man whom Rachel addressed, and who finally arrested my attention.

"Press! You and Porky Pig need to stop talking right this minute."

Jack's eyes narrowed slightly. "Rachel, you bitch." He turned his gaze to me, frankly looking me up and down. There was the merest hint of approval in his unusual eyes. "What will your friend think?"

"Why, she'll think you're a perfect love, even though you used to be big as a house. Didn't he used to be big as a house?" She rested a hand prettily on Press's leg. "You remember you told me how he got a wad of icing stuck up his nose at your birthday party when you were kids?" Then she turned to me, rolled her eyes. "He made such a fuss, crying and carrying on, that he couldn't breathe and his mama had to take him home."

Press smiled and put a hand on her shoulder. "Jack was wrong to call you a bitch. Dogs are bitches. You're just a brat."

Rachel gave him an exaggerated pout.

"See? You love me." She held her face close to his so he could kiss her cheek. His hand slipped down, lingering on her back, and for the first time I found myself wondering if there had ever been anything between them. It took me by surprise to realize that I had already begun to think of Press as belonging to me.

When Rachel formally introduced us, I felt my face and neck go hot. I offered my hand and hoped that he wouldn't feel it shaking, because I could feel just the slightest tremor in it. Even though the college Rachel and I attended educated only women, it had many male professors, and, of course, I'd known boys at home and met others at dances. But this felt new. Different. Preston Bliss, though he was only four years older than Rachel and me, was truly a man.

Getting off the stool, he stood up, and I was immediately glad I'd worn the flats. His eyes weren't quite even with mine, and I soon learned he was five feet eight to my five feet nine. My reaction must have shown in my eyes because—after a tightening of his jaw that was so slight that I might have imagined it—he gave me a broad smile and enveloped my hand in his.

"Charlotte, I'm Preston. But please call me Press. Everyone does." His cool, rather soft hand gripped mine with firm pressure.

Perhaps it was just because they weren't quite even with mine that I noticed his thick eyebrows first. If he'd been a female friend of Rachel's, she would've long ago attacked them with her vicious tweezers. (I had been one of her victims, but even now my brows are as fair as my hair, and so she didn't torment me often. Also, she was a bit near-sighted and was too vain to wear her glasses.) Press's hair, dark like his brows, was coarse with aggressive, barely tamed natural waves. He faced me with an unabashed frankness that showed in his brown eyes, which didn't leave mine for a second. His skin was more olive than I had expected. Maybe it was something about his being young and wealthy and Virginian that had made me think he would be more like the fair, patrician-looking Jack Carstairs.

Press's nose was rather large and his lashes brown and thick. His chestnut wool jacket hung neatly over darker brown pants and almost hid a deep-green sweater vest. His shirt was white, his tie the color of a yellowed autumn leaf. Jack's more conservative gray wool jacket and regimental tie seemed rather dull in comparison.

Glancing away at Rachel for the briefest of moments, Press then looked back at me and said, "You're much prettier than Rachel led me to believe. Like a fashion model."

Jack guffawed, spewing Coca-Cola (which I later learned was probably spiked with bourbon) onto the bar.

Rachel was unfazed. "Just dance with the girl, Press. You don't have to marry her this minute."

As though it had been planned, Nat King Cole's *Somebody Loves Me* dropped with a click onto the turntable in the jukebox and began to play.

Lifting my veil, I surveyed my red-splotched face in the Cadillac's visor mirror. I hadn't used mascara that morning, only a bit of powder out of habit and a few indifferent dabs of a muted pink lipstick. Using the lipstick had thrown me into fresh tears. Eva had raided my dressing table for it only the week before to draw lopsided stars on Michael's cheek.

"Angel kisses," she'd called them, with a little lisp in her lilting voice. Nonie had scolded her, but I couldn't help but laugh. She was so much more cheerful, more adventurous than I had been as a child, raised as I was only by the watchful Nonie and my father. Whenever I put on lipstick, it is always Nonie's voice in my head, telling me that only fast girls wore makeup, and only bounders required it of their wives. *Bounders*, as though we weren't living in the 1950s but in some 19th-century novel in which all men are dangerous and all women damsels in distress.

I rolled the car window down halfway to get some air, telling myself I wouldn't start crying again, wouldn't make another scene as I had at the cemetery. I had only to get through the next couple of hours. Then I could cry. Then it wouldn't matter.

The heat from the outside was stifling and quickly dispelled the weak cold generated by the clicking air conditioner.

"Dammit, what now? Charlotte, can you see anything?"

A long line of cars was stopped in the middle of the shady tunnel of trees leading to Bliss House. I could just see the buttery yellow brick of the house and a crisp blue patch of sky at the end of the lane.

Press got out with an agitated sigh, leaving the car idling, his suit jacket lying on the seat.

Was I supposed to follow him?

As he made his way through the line of cars, I strained to see him out the front window. There were mourners in the road, mostly women looking bewildered and upset, and a larger group of people gathered near the trees.

I shut off the car, and the air conditioner ticked to a stop.

Forgetting to pull the veil back over my face, I slipped back into the patent leather heels I had unconsciously taken off during the drive home, and started out the passenger door. Because it had been a wet fall, I checked to make sure I wasn't getting out into mud, and pulled my foot back immediately when I detected a sudden movement in the grass feathering the edge of the lane. In another second I might have missed the flick of the black snake's tail as the snake made for the cover of the trees. Is there any woman whose senses don't sharpen when she sees a snake? *And you will bite her heel—she will curse you.* When you live in the country, there are injunctions against killing snakes in the wild. Especially black snakes. But I hate them. Pulling the door shut, I slid across the front seat and got out on the other side. Beneath my feet, the lane's pale mix of crushed seashells and small stones was warm and uneven. In minutes, my shoes would be gloved with a fine, pearly dust.

A few dozen feet away in the grass, a closed carriage—yes, a very few eccentric families drove them with their horses on a Sunday afternoon, or on special occasions, and I suppose a funeral is a special occasion—was overturned in the grass along the right side of the lane. Just beyond the line of oak trees, a horse, detached from the carriage, rose on its rear legs, crying out, its eyes rolling white. Its flank shone with blood, and my heart broke for the poor animal. But it seemed more frightened than injured, and two men were doing their best to calm it and keep hold of the swinging reins.

Press clambered atop the wrecked carriage and was helping another man wrestle a wheel away from where it had collapsed against the carriage door. He normally wasn't a person given to quick action, or any kind of physical labor, and so the scene felt even more strange to me. With the loud cries of the horse, I couldn't hear if there were sounds coming from inside. As I got closer, I could see one gray head resting, motionless, in the shoebox-sized rear window of the carriage. Alarmed, I called out Press's name.

Nearly everyone in the crowd turned to look at me. Press shouted, "Take everyone to the house, Charlotte. Quickly."

I knew I should obey immediately, but I was paralyzed by the unnaturalness of the scene. I had to see. Had to know.

The carriage belonged to close friends of Press's, Zion and Helen Heaster, an older couple who had retired to Old Gate after living in New York City for most of their lives. Zion was a playwright, Helen an actress who had started out as a Ziegfeld girl and later became famous—or so Press had told me—for playing Lady Macbeth. I rarely saw the two of them; but Press saw them often, as Zion was the unofficial head of the local theatre group he and Rachel and Jack belonged to. If they were badly hurt, Press would be devastated.

Perhaps it was the heady, oppressive heat of midday, or the terror of the horse that filled me with sudden dread, but I had a terrible feeling that Zion and Helen were already dead. That the accident had happened on the day of Eva's funeral somehow made it seem even more likely to me. First Olivia, and now three more deaths so close together. How much were we supposed to bear?

Had Michael and Nonie made it safely to the house? What if the horse had bolted in front of my father's car?

In the distance, I heard more car doors slamming. Voices.

What is it? What can it be? Why are we stopped?

Farther up the lane, the guests who had arrived but hadn't yet gone inside the house were wandering back toward the accident. They were going the wrong way, and I knew Press was expecting me to head them off. Tearing myself away, I walked toward one of the groups of women gathered in the lane, well away from the men and the damp grass.

Rachel, immediately recognizable in a feather-trimmed black hat, black silk swing top, and narrow skirt, saw me and broke off from the group. No matter that she was halfway through her ninth month of pregnancy—she always looked as though she'd stepped out of the pages of *Vogue* or *Harper's Bazaar*.

"Oh, Charlotte. They're saying something spooked the horse. It nearly strangled itself."

I touched her hand. "Rachel, you know it's Zion and Helen in the carriage?"

Rachel's brown eyes widened. She started past me toward the carriage, but I wrapped my hand around her arm before she could get away.

"Oh, God. It can't be them! Helen said they were taking the car." As she strained toward them, she almost pulled me off my feet. I was stronger and wouldn't let her go.

"There's nothing we can do. Let Press and the men handle it."

"But Helen!" Her voice broke in a sob. Rachel was as close to the Heasters as Press was, almost as close to Helen as she was to her own mother. "Do you think they're dead? Oh, God, what if they're dead?"

Now the people near us were staring at Rachel instead of the carriage.

It was a strange role reversal. Rachel was usually the brave, confident one of the two of us, always ready with advice on how to handle Olivia or keep Press happy. It was the second time in a week I'd seen her cry—the first was as she'd knelt beside me the day Eva died. As I drew her closer to me, I felt the violent shaking of her childlike shoulders. Jack had even told her that she should stay home from the funeral, that the upset wasn't good for the baby she was carrying. I looked around but didn't see him. Rachel rarely listened to him, anyway.

I knew Press wanted me to get everyone up to the house, but I had to know if Zion and Helen were still alive.

Press was lifting aside the carriage's broken door. His face, which he had so carefully shaved that morning, dripped with perspiration. When the door was open all the way, one of the other men held it back, and Press thrust one arm and much of his upper body into the carriage's interior. The crowd was silent.

Press was an actor, and a pretty good one—oh, yes, a very good one. I'd seen him onstage in community theatricals: *Our Town, Pygmalion, The Merry Wives of Windsor.* At first it had been hard to reconcile the man I saw every morning with the man in false beards and heavy makeup who showed up as Falstaff or the obstreperous Henry Higgins. It wasn't just his face that changed, but the way he walked, and his gestures. When we traveled to see plays in D.C. or New York, I watched a change come over him as his eyes followed the actors. He had a hunger for the stage, a hunger to be someone else. I couldn't help but think he imagined himself to be onstage that day.

When he looked up from the interior of the carriage, darkness like a shadow crossed his face. But there was no movement in the russet oak leaves hanging overhead or in the near-cloudless sky. I held my breath, just like everyone else who was waiting. We were rapt, and during those few seconds he was the center of our world. He lowered his eyes and slowly shook his head. As though on cue, a man shouted "No!" and a murmur of dismay rippled through the crowd.

Rachel went rigid. "No," she echoed. Her legs gave way and she collapsed to the ground in a spicy flush of Lanvin's *My Sin.*

Before I could kneel down, Jack appeared seemingly from nowhere and gently pushed me aside so he could revive her. The concern on his face was very real. As much as Rachel complained about him, he was always solicitous of her. He carried her back to my Cadillac, which was closer than their car, and drove ahead to the house to get her out of the heat.

I probably should have gone with them. But Jack was a doctor and could do more for her than I could. Once again falling back on my training—to be polite and, yes, an obedient wife—I recovered myself and encouraged the crowd to move toward the house.

Chapter 4

Bliss House

Bliss House sits at the end of its lane, restful, like a journey's end. Tall and straight, yellow-bricked and black against the sky, it wears its soft slate mansard roof as a man in a formal summer suit might wear a comfortable cap. The two shallow wings off either side of the house aren't wide enough to imply any welcoming embrace. Press had told me it had been a wildly expensive house when it was built by his grandfather, Randolph Bliss, in the 1870s, designed by a black Frenchman named Hulot, whom he'd hired as a kind of slap in the face to his defeated neighbors. It's very unlike the other grand houses in the area, having both a ballroom and a full theater on the third floor, and no columns or sweet porticoes or climbing ivy. When he first saw it, my father called it one of the ugliest houses he'd ever seen, but fortunately not in front of Press or his mother.

I don't think of Bliss House as ugly.

I empathize with Bliss House. It is tall and ungainly, and a bit unsuited to its watercolor rural surroundings, just like me. It's not that I'm not at home in the country. But Old Gate is a kind of gateway to the wilds of western Virginia, and Bliss House might have been a happier house if it had been built on the eastern side of the state, where I was born. A region filled with people of wider experience, more sophisticated tastes.

There is romance at Bliss House. Its gardens are formal, but lush. Even the herb garden tucked around the back, with its circle on circle of tightly pressed stones and thick rings of soil filled with flowering herbs, was designed with an eye toward beauty, as well as usefulness. And then there is the dome set high in the center of the three-story front hall: a scene of the starry sky, just before full dark, as though the architect had left the roof off. Depending on the light outside, the stars may seem to almost disappear; but in the evening, even in the reflected light of the great chandelier, the stars emerge bearing their own vibrant light. Press and Olivia and even the servants never seemed to notice the stars change, which annoyed me. But I know what I have seen.

I have said that it is tradition for anyone from the town to be allowed to call at the house after a funeral, but the tradition didn't just apply to funerals. Olivia had held a garden party every late spring when the azaleas bloomed, and another at the New Year. Guests always arrived with a cautious air of excitement and barely disguised curiosity. For a while, I was like them, but once I moved in, I began to resent their crude interest. We were not creatures on display for their prurient observation. Bliss House has a reputation for unnatural death and for the supposed presence of the lingering dead, but most of what people imagine and gossip about is untrue (yet what they don't know is far more horrific). The family has seen more than its share of tragedy. Rachel had even prodded me about it, telling me that everyone in Old Gate believed that Randolph Bliss, who had come to Virginia from Long Island, had committed some crime and caused the house to be cursed before the first brick was laid.

"It's infamous," she said. "When you're married, we can have fabulous séances and talk to all the people who died there." We'd both been a little drunk on the crème de menthe she'd brought from her parents' house after Thanksgiving break—the break during which I'd met Press. But after the wedding, she never mentioned it, let alone suggested a séance.

⁓

I believed in ghosts long before I moved into Bliss House.

⁓

I was six years old.

Practical Nonie had me collecting sticks in the back yard and putting them in the giant red wheelbarrow placed near the garage. Two days earlier, there had been a tropical storm that had hung about for days offshore, sweeping one narrow arm inland for just a few hours, bringing down several trees and power lines in our little town in eastern Virginia. I was hot and cross and plagued by the mosquitoes that had appeared quickly after the rain. The air was languid, making my hair stick to my neck and my romper to my back, and though I was not usually rebellious, I'd taken off my shoes in spite of Nonie's admonition that I should not. What I really wanted to be doing was eating the red velvet cake that she was making in the kitchen for my father's birthday, and so I was doing my chore reluctantly, trying to see how slowly I could walk across the grass to the wheelbarrow.

I'd picked up a particularly large stick and was dragging it behind me, pretending I was a horse put to work like Black Beauty, when the wind picked up and the air turned markedly cooler. It was as sudden as if there had been some loud horn or thunderclap to announce it, and I stopped walking, wondering if there *had* been a sound. First I looked into the sky, but then my eyes came to rest on a woman standing at the other side of the yard, beside the wheelbarrow. She was a girl, really, and wore a belted robe the color of lemon custard whose hem played lightly around her bare feet. I was surprised but also terribly impressed that she was outside with bare feet, just like me. When she smiled and held out her hand, I realized she was the girl in all the pictures in my father's bedroom, and in the one beside my bed. I knew her as *Mother*, but of course I'd been barely four years old when she died, and her voice, her touch, the way her face really looked, had faded from my mind. Her blond hair hung in untidy waves above her shoulders, and she was inhumanely pale. But I felt no fear.

Dropping the stick, I hurried toward her, the grass cold and wet on my feet. The wind was loud in my ears, and it turned to a kind of static as though it were coming from a badly tuned radio. But as I got closer, I realized with some disappointment that she wasn't looking at me, but beyond me. When I looked back over my shoulder, I stumbled and fell, sprawling onto the grass and its minefield of small, sharp sticks. I lay there breathing hard, waiting, half-hoping she would come to help me up.

Then the wind was gone, and Nonie was standing over me.

"You'd best get up, or you'll be covered with chiggers."

I stood still, watching the empty space where my mother had been, as Nonie brushed the dirt from my romper and legs and tut-tutted about little girls who should listen and keep their shoes on when they were told.

Somehow I knew not to say anything about my mother to Nonie, but that night I told my father.

"Did she look happy?" he asked.

It took me a minute to answer. Could ghosts be happy or unhappy? "Yes. I think so. I don't know why."

He smiled at that but didn't offer any kind of explanation.

I was ten years old before I overheard the truth about my mother. Already at school, a rotten older boy named Scott had cornered me in the coatroom and told me that my mother had hanged herself in our garage, but I called him a liar and ran away. He had given voice to my own deepest fears. My father would never park the car in the garage, but kept a small bass boat he rarely used in there on a trailer. The rest of the space was filled with old tools and the equipment he used to keep our lawn looking neat. A few weeks after Scott's revelation, two of my father's older sisters, my aunts, were washing the dinner dishes in the kitchen, which looked out on the garage. When I heard one of them, Ruth, say my mother's name, I stopped just outside the doorway.

"He should've torn that down right after it happened. Gives me the willies just to look at it, and Lord knows the neighbors must want it gone. I'd faint dead away if I had to go in there." The second aunt, Beth (for Rehobeth, a name I found strange and exotic), told her to lower her voice.

"If Charlotte doesn't remember what happened, then it doesn't matter. It's only a garage. Roman says he can live with it, and that should be good enough for us, shouldn't it? It's *his* shame, and he has to suffer it. We're not going to change him now." She made a *tsk-tsk* sound that she used often to express her disapproval—and she disapproved of many things. Although she was the prettiest of my father's three sisters, at thirty-eight her scowls had already creased her brow and set deep lines into either side of her unpainted lips. "We can only pray that she doesn't have her mother's unstable nature. Here, pass me that pan to dry."

"If I had found *our* mother like that, I would've gone stark raving mad."

It took me some moments to understand what they were saying—that *I* had been the one to discover my mother, dead. Leaning against the wall outside the kitchen, I ceased to hear their words, but only the low tones of their voices. When my father found me there, he asked me if anything was wrong, but I told him I wasn't feeling well and wanted to go to bed. I finally met his eyes, and he looked at me a long time. Perhaps he was hearing more of what my aunts were saying. I could not. Would not. But I could see he knew that I'd found out.

He let me go on to bed.

Despite my aunts' opinions, I've never felt shame over what my mother did. Only sadness that she would leave us so callously. It was, perhaps, some strange kind of blessing that I can't remember that day, that I had no remembered image of my mother, dead in her yellow robe, her limp body hanging in our garage. My only memory is of her standing outside on that strange, hot, windy day, holding out her hand to me. I never told Rachel or even Press. (Though I'm certain he found out.) Holding the knowledge close to my heart, I hoped it would make me a better mother to my own children.

My mother has never come to me in Bliss House. Until the day of Eva's funeral, I had never experienced more than the occasional sense of something fluttering at the edge of my field of vision. An unexpected chill in a well-heated room.

Finally almost all the women who had been at the funeral were gathered on the wide terrace running along the front of the house. Someone—probably Terrance, our houseman, or one of the day women acting at Terrance's instruction—had distributed a number of umbrellas and a few antique parasols that Olivia kept in storage.

One group stood in the thin band of shade at the edge of the forsythia bushes in the center of the circular drive as though they might draw some coolness from its tangle of shaggy branches. I could have told them that the only shade to be had from it was deep in the bowels of the overgrown mess.

Only a few months earlier, Shelley, the orchardkeeper's shy younger sister who was very fond of the children, had given Eva a real bunny for Easter, and I had to crawl inside the forsythia to find it when it escaped from its hutch near the entrance to the garden maze. The bunny had darted inside to hide, alarmed by his sudden freedom. While the outside of the bushy mass was covered in yellow flowers, there were no leaves or flowers on the gnarled trunks of the bushes, and branches arched and dipped overhead, slapping me gently as I crawled, calling nervously for the bunny. It was a dark cathedral redolent of dirt and rotting leaves, and I was glad Eva hadn't come with me. It was a place to escape to, a secret, empty place in the vast outdoors. When I finally emerged with the bunny, I was stunned to find that Eva had gone into the house, leaving Michael asleep in the grass, and doubly stunned to see that, by my watch, I'd been inside for nearly twenty minutes.

My heart pounded. What might have happened to him? I told no one what I'd done. Had I simply been . . . entranced? I'm still not sure.

Now I felt the same sense of living out of time, of having missed something. The accident had stolen my attention, pushing my grief away for a little while. I'd met my father on the lane as he hurried back to the overturned carriage: Michael and Nonie were safe in the house. Press was far down the lane, doing his part. If Olivia had been alive, she would've already made sure that everyone was inside, calmed and fed and given lemonade or sweet iced tea or sherry.

I quietly cleared my throat.

"Let's all go inside, shall we? There are cold drinks in the dining room, and we can wait for news."

The women stopped talking and all turned to stare silently at me. For a moment I worried that I hadn't actually spoken. Hoping they'd follow, I approached the front door where Terrance waited. I gave him a small smile.

What shall I tell you, now, about Terrance? He was our houseman, tall and gaunt and of indeterminate age, with slight folds in the lids of his dark eyes that made me wonder if someone in his family had come from somewhere in Asia. He no longer had a single hair on his head or face—no brows or lashes, not even a single hair growing from one of the many moles dotting his face and neck. His clothes—including his jacket and, in winter, his pullover V-neck sweater—were always black, except for his white standard-collar shirt. He had worked for the family his entire life, and was as much a part of Bliss House as its cherry moldings and priceless carpets and motes of dust floating in the shafts of sunlight coming from the windows around the dome. Terrance simply *was*. Yet that day, I had no idea at all how much a part of Bliss House he truly was.

Is?

Waiting for the women to respond, I caught a movement over near the patio.

Someone stood inside the glass French doors, watching from the dining room. It was a woman, but I couldn't quite make out her face. Then she moved slightly, and, in a reflected flash of light, I saw the faded blond hair, the thick stroke of silver at the hairline that seemed to exist to highlight the long, pinkish scar just above her eye. Her mouth was wide and thin, firm with intent.

Olivia.

Heedless of both Terrance and the women around me, I hurried into the cool embrace of the front hall. As my eyes adjusted, I found that there were five or six people who hadn't come back outside on hearing of the accident, standing in the middle of the hall, beneath the dome. I didn't have the presence of mind to greet them, and if they were offended, I couldn't help it.

I knew before I went into the dining room that Olivia wouldn't really be standing by the window, or anywhere else. But perhaps there would be some vestige, something moved or disturbed. If it were possible for anyone to come back from death on the strength of her ties to a particular place, Olivia would be that person. Every room was stamped with some piece of artwork, some fabric, some piece of furniture that had been hers, or whose history she knew. Her face was on a number of portraits. I hadn't yet changed anything in either her bedroom or morning room, even though she had left all of her personal belongings to me. Bliss House itself had belonged to her. So why would she leave in death?

The dining room wasn't empty, but there was no Olivia, and I surprised myself by feeling disappointed rather than relieved.

Marlene, our housekeeper, looked up from the table where she was putting out a stack of linen luncheon napkins from the press in the butler's pantry. I thought she was around fifty years old at the time, but even at twenty-seven I was a poor judge of the age of anyone who might be over thirty. In truth, Marlene was barely forty then, but she hadn't bothered to cover the premature gray mixed into her brown hair, and her eyes were dark but not wide or lively. Beneath the short sleeves of her black, summer wool dress, her arms were fleshy and loose. There was a kind reserve in her eyes that I appreciated, even though what she said next brought me up short.

"Mrs. Bliss would have me put out more sherry. Because of the accident."

How many more times would I have to hear similar suggestions beginning with the words *Mrs. Bliss would have*? Grief and the possible presence of Olivia couldn't quell my own self-consciousness and irritation.

"Sherry, and Scotch too, I think," I told her, my voice sounding breathless even to me. "The men may want something strong."

She went back to arranging the napkins on the Sheraton sideboard, which, like the baronial dining table, was overladen with food—ham biscuits, gelatin molds and tomato aspics, deviled eggs, peach and apple pies and crumbles, fruit salad, fried chicken, and fried chicken livers—that people had been bringing to the house for two days, and with more that Marlene and her helpers had made.

31

The dining room was Marlene's purview. Not mine. I didn't like the room at all, and almost never used the steep, narrow stairs in the minuscule hallway between the dining room and kitchen, even though they were the closest to the second-floor nursery.

The dining-room walls—twelve feet high like those of the rest of the rooms on the first floor—were completely covered with a mural of staring eyes. Not human eyes, but the eyes of peacock feathers that were so precisely drawn that they looked like they'd been painted from the memory of a terrible dream. Press had told me he'd been made to count them once as a punishment for some infraction he couldn't now recall. How many eyes did he say there were? More than a thousand, I think. What a thing to do to a child!

But it wasn't just the walls. There, drooping in a grand crystal vase that someone in the family had brought from some long-ago European trip, was a lush armful of peacock feathers that begged to be touched. Stroked. The coronas around their opaque pupils glimmered gold.

All those eyes. Had they witnessed Olivia's return? My mind was restless, and I was so shaken that I believed I could feel my blood pulsing through my veins.

If Olivia could come back, why not Eva?

Chapter 5

A Sign

For nearly two weeks after the frantic strangeness of the day of Eva's funeral, I stayed close to my bedroom, tethered by guilt and grief. The day itself lives in my memory in a series of tableaux: the fly on Eva's flowers, the gray, bloody head against the carriage window, the terrified horse, Olivia's face in the French doors. But isn't that what our memories are? We walk down a long hallway, opening doors into rooms whose permanent contents wait to surprise or comfort or horrify us. I lay in my bed, not wanting to breathe, remembering brushing Eva's teeth before bedtime, checking her for ticks when we returned from walking on the deer trail in the woods, her pleased laughter when, at two years old, she stuck her hand in a bowl of noodles and wiped them in her hair. Strangely, I even lingered over Eva in her bath, singing the Eensy Weensy Spider as she tried to string bubbles along the inner wall of the tub as though they would make a spider's web.

She'd awoken from her nap that day as I slept downstairs, and tried to draw herself a bath in the bathroom off the nursery. Press said she had turned off the water and hadn't yet undressed, but must have tumbled in, hitting her head. By the time he took me up to see her, he had laid her on her bed and taken Michael from the bedroom. Yet sometimes in my dreams I saw her in the water face down, yet somehow alive. I wouldn't—couldn't—imagine her otherwise.

Even though my dreams were tortured, I slept. To my shame, I rarely thought of the Heasters, and my dreams were filled with only Eva.

I knew it was only a matter of time before Nonie would force me from my bed. I could only remain there as long as she was willing to chase after Michael, whom I made sure to see at least once a day. Even though I couldn't trust myself to be left alone with him, I knew better than anyone that he shouldn't be allowed to think that I had abandoned him completely.

Waking to sunshine, I could hear Press moving around in his bedroom. (Does it surprise you that we had separate bedrooms? That was the family's tradition, and I quickly got used to having my privacy whenever I wished. I loved my room with its pale green-and-white dogwood-blossom wallpaper, thick wool green-and-tan carpet, and sumptuous white bedding. I realize now how considerate Olivia had been by updating the bathroom and redecorating the bedroom before I moved in.) He was probably getting ready for work, which I should describe as *work, such as it was*. He kept a law office in Old Gate proper, handling the affairs of a few of his mother's old friends, but he mostly dealt with the details of the Bliss estate.

He'd told me the night before that he was going to work, and that he was visiting Rachel and Jack afterwards, if I didn't mind. There had been something, too, about a memorial for Helen and

Zion, but I hadn't really listened. Or cared. I assumed that he just wanted to get away from my sadness.

I wondered, silently, how he could move so quickly and go on with living. Wasn't it his sadness, too?

"Charlotte?" His voice was muffled by the door connecting our rooms, but I heard both my name and the soft knock.

I didn't answer. Everything could continue to go on without me, and I had no desire to see him. I couldn't yet let go of my self-blame. It was mine. My guilt, and my shame. I wasn't willing to share.

Nonie was with Michael, and Marlene and Terrance would mind the house as they always did. There would be a breakfast tray outside my room, left there at 8:30 by Terrance if I hadn't appeared in the dining room earlier. Nothing compelled me to move from where I lay. Eva was gone, no matter what I did or didn't do.

Press came quietly into the room. Standing beside my bed, he was a shadow blocking the sharp light of early fall that filtered through my eyelids. His cologne, the *Floris No. 89* he'd begun wearing after his trip to New York to see plays with Jack and Rachel (I'd had terrible morning sickness with Michael and couldn't go), was overpowering in the still air. I kept my eyes closed. Finally, he bent to kiss my cheek, brushing my hair lightly with his fingertips.

He walked across my room, not back to the door, but toward my tall dresser.

I opened my eyes just a little to see him raise the bottle of sleeping drops that Jack had brought to me after Eva died up to the light of the window. Jack was a firm believer in the power of pharmaceuticals, and always said that there was no reason anyone should suffer if there was a drug to help. I shut my eyes again quickly.

I knew Jack had meant well, but I hadn't taken the drops in over a week. I was certain that if Olivia could come back, then Eva could too. I just wanted to see her one more time. It had to be possible. I worried that the drops might make me sleep so deeply that I might miss her in the night.

I didn't know who to pray to in order to see my child again. Not God. God didn't govern Bliss House. After years of being immune to whatever link Bliss House had to the dead, Bliss House had shown me Olivia. There had to be more. It *had* to show me more.

Press left the room, shutting the door quietly behind him.

"Michael, go to Mother." Nonie's voice.

I opened my eyes to a different light.

My one-year-old son gave a shrill crow of pleasure as he ran across the carpet to my bed.

Had I fallen back asleep? Yes. I'd fallen asleep with a prayer on my lips.

"Eva."

In a dream, she'd been in the kitchen, standing on a stool beside Olivia, her yellow curls tied back out of her face with a Wedgwood blue velvet ribbon I'd never seen before. Olivia, who had long ago taught Marlene all the recipes she'd learned herself as a girl, seldom went into the kitchen except to give instructions or to catalogue the pantry's contents. ("Even the best staff makes mistakes," she'd once confided to me. "They become careless, and get cheated or become too generous with the family's things. It's rarely malicious, but they need to remember whose things they are minding.") This dream-Olivia was stirring something into the kitchen's enormous crockery mixing bowl, and I could hear her murmur to Eva, who was watching, rapt. I had almost heard what she was saying, but Nonie's voice had broken the dream. It was gone.

"What is it?"

My tone must have irritated Nonie, because she responded with a forceful "I've brought Michael. It's time you got up."

Michael, oblivious to the tension, gave another small shriek and clambered up the bed stairs to my four-poster. His blond head was damp and his cheeks were bright pink. They'd obviously been outside for a walk.

"Mmmm. Mamamamama." He fell over onto my stomach and collapsed with a grunt.

I felt the heat of his little body through the sheet. I sighed.

"What time is it?"

Nonie stood, watchful, beside the bed. As always, she was neat and impeccably dressed, despite the fact that she spent her days with small children. She wore rich browns and tans and, given that her hair was a warm caramel color, she gave the impression of always being ready for fall. Today, the abstract elephant-and-leaf pattern of her short-sleeved cotton shirtdress was whimsical—for her, anyway—but the dress was carefully tailored, with a matching belt that cinched her still-tidy waist. Other than long walks, I never knew Nonie to take much exercise. She kept herself covered when she was outside, so her fifty-something face beneath her delicately striped brown eyeglasses was virtually unlined. She'd been in her mid-twenties when she came to help raise me, and while her beakish nose and assertive jaw kept her from being conventionally pretty, the harsh angles of her face had softened over the years so that she seemed much less intimidating on first glance than she had when I was little. Of course, I'd grown to love her too.

"I'm about to put him down for his afternoon nap."

I winced as Michael tried to stand up on my thigh, unsteady in his hard-soled white walkers. I took one of his hands, and he wrapped his fingers around one of mine and squeezed as he righted himself. He was so determined, always persevering even when something challenged him.

Everything had seemed to come more easily to Eva, as though she knew that nothing was too difficult for her to do or try.

"You're hurting Mother, Michael. Get down." Nonie's voice was still sharper than I'd heard it in a long while, and Michael looked back at her so that he almost lost his balance. But I pulled him toward me so he would fall onto me instead of onto the bed, or perhaps the floor.

"Why are you frightening him?"

In fact, Michael looked more surprised than frightened, and quickly resumed trying to balance on me. I didn't care that it hurt. I was finally happy to have him with me. Something had changed, just a little. It wasn't the desperate kind of feeling I'd had every time I'd seen him over the past weeks.

"I understand your husband will be staying in town to have dinner with Rachel and Jack. Maybe you should dress and join him, Lottie."

I didn't respond at first. I knew I should go and spend time with Rachel. She was surely still very upset about Helen and Zion. That I didn't care much for them shouldn't have influenced my decision to stay home, but it did.

"They'll understand. They'll be talking a lot about Helen and Zion. I don't need to be there."

Nonie was finally quiet. I knew she meant well. I also knew that, like me, she hadn't cared much for the Heasters. When they came to the house, she stayed in her room and listened to the radio or watched the television we had bought her for her fiftieth birthday (Press thought it was fine to indulge Nonie, but he believed televisions were foolish and plebeian and wouldn't own one). She referred to them as "those New York people" and was unimpressed with Zion's booming voice and full, leonine hair and the way Rachel and Jack and Preston hung on his every word. Also in the silence between us was the knowledge that she had been out of town when Eva died. Her guilt, I knew, was comparable to my own. But she had still cared for Michael when I couldn't. No real grandmother could have done better.

I did get up and dress and wash my face a few minutes after she took a very wound-up, sleepy Michael back to the nursery. Time was still slow. But when I left my room, I saw through eyes that hadn't cried that day.

In the hallway, I was assaulted by the smell of decaying flowers: lilies and roses and carnations, sent or brought to the house even days after Eva's funeral. They were scattered in vases downstairs and on the second-floor gallery, which was where the family's bedrooms were. Press's and my bedrooms, the nursery, and Nonie's room were all on the eastern side of the house. Olivia's rooms and two guest rooms were directly opposite, across the wide expanse of the hall, which was open to the third floor and the ceiling's dome. I stood looking over the gallery railing, remembering how the church had also smelled heavily of flowers during Eva's church service.

The hall and gallery walls—upstairs and down—were covered with paintings. There were many portraits, mostly Bliss family members, but a few from Olivia's family as well, including one of her stern, plain-faced parents. As I went down the front stairs, I stopped, arrested by the portrait we'd had done of a two-year-old Eva and me that was hung above the landing near the bottom of the stairs. It was a very feminine painting, set in the rose garden with the maze blurred in the background, and full of the colors of late spring. In contrast, we wore ivory dresses: a tea gown for me, a simple silk dress piped in pink for Eva, who sat at my feet, her hand resting on a stuffed white peacock wearing a gold crown. I hadn't wanted it in the painting, but Press's friend J. C. Jaquith had had it sent from F.A.O. Schwartz in New York, and it pleased Press that it was a peacock and that Eva loved it, so I had relented. I didn't like the way its head was tilted, as though its sharp orange beak were about to strike our daughter on the knee, but Press had laughed and said the artist was just having a joke.

Why had Olivia wanted it here in the hall, rather than in the salon or in one of the sunnier rooms? She'd never said, but had had it hung while I was out of the house, in time for a dinner party she was giving in honor of the painting's completion. She'd had me dress Eva in the dress from the portrait, even though it was, by then, a bit too small. Press had beamed, holding Eva like a prize, as we stood beneath the painting for the assembled guests. Eva had smiled placidly and even clapped her hands along with the guests. I was anxious, not liking the attention, the stares of Olivia's Historical Society friends and bridge partners and their husbands.

Now I wondered if I could bear to look at the portrait every day. As I passed it in the afternoon sunlight, I ran my fingertips over the edge of the frame. It was hung too high for me to touch the textured paint strokes that made up my daughter's face.

I found Marlene in the kitchen making bread for our dinner. She had twisted her hair into its usual chignon, and wore a full white apron over her dark gray dress.

"I'd like all the funeral flowers removed, Marlene. Have any more notes arrived?"

She looked up, startled, the half-smile I'd seen on her lips before she'd heard me fading into a look of surprise.

"No, Miss Charlotte. Mr. Preston may have met the postman on his way into town. There's been no mail delivered here today."

Both Marlene and Terrance called Press by the familiar *Mr. Preston*, and referred to me as *Miss Charlotte* at, I suspected, Olivia's original direction. It had occurred to me to ask them to start calling me Mrs. Bliss, but I wasn't sure I was ready for them to. And since I'd seen Olivia on the day of the funeral—for certainly it *was* Olivia—it also felt strangely presumptuous.

"Mr. Preston won't be here for dinner tonight."

"Yes, ma'am. He mentioned that."

I left Marlene and went to the dining room where all the peacock eyes seemed to watch me. The thought that Olivia might be watching as well made me feel strangely shy.

Moving past the enormous cabinet filled with the silver pieces that Terrance was forever polishing, I went to stand exactly where I'd seen Olivia behind the glass. Outside the window, the October sunshine beckoned, but I closed my eyes against it. Olivia and I hadn't been close, but we shared a love for Press and the children, and she was always kind to me. Though I hadn't had the chance or inclination to explore them yet, she had specifically left all of her personal belongings—the contents of her bedroom and morning room—to me.

Did it feel just a bit cooler here than in the rest of the dining room? There had to be a reason why she wanted me to see her. I was certain that I would have heard immediately if anyone else had caught sight of her. Bliss House was notorious enough that anyone who had direct experience of some strange occurrence there was unlikely to keep it a secret. God only knew, they must have still been talking about the deaths of the Heasters in the drive.

I thought that perhaps I already knew the reason Olivia had appeared only to me. She was here to help me keep Eva close, perhaps even guide me to her.

"Olivia." I whispered so that Marlene wouldn't hear. "Help me."

I opened my eyes. Outside the doors, a breeze ruffled the delicate blood-red leaves of the miniature Japanese maples Olivia had planted as accents around the patio. How odd, that provincial Olivia would pick something so boldly exotic to decorate the outside of Bliss House.

I waited, listening to the faint sounds of Marlene in the kitchen and my own breathing. After a few minutes, I began to feel the slightest bit foolish. I wanted to believe, to trust that Olivia was with me. But it felt a little unnatural. Or perhaps I was afraid.

It occurred to me that I might get closer to Olivia by looking through her things. It was my right, yes? No one would ask why.

They belonged to me. Marlene had already been hinting that she would get Terrance to pack up whatever clothing of Olivia's I wanted to give away and take it to the Presbyterian thrift store in town.

As though reading my mind, Marlene called me from the dining room's kitchen entrance.

Turning at the sound of her voice, I was just in time to see one of the glass patio doors swing violently open, as though by a strong wind, and hit the corner of a chair placed against the wall. Two of the door's panels shattered, scattering shards of glass onto the carpet below.

Chapter 6

Domestic Bliss

Up to that point in my life, I was no liar. My father could look at my face and know in an instant that I was about to tell him an untruth.

"Don't tell me what you think you want to say, Lottie. I see in your eyes it's not the truth." My mother was just like me, he said. And I have her eyes: bright blue and guileless.

But I learned to lie. If there is shame in that fact, I don't feel it.

The previous day, I'd been sufficiently shaken by the incident with the door that I hadn't ventured into Olivia's room, and neither had I wanted to return to the dining room. Because Press was out, I had Terrance bring supper up to the nursery. Nonie, Michael, and I ate in companionable chaos, with Michael delighting in being able to climb off and on his small chair at the child-sized nursery table any time he wanted. Even Nonie was amused with him, though I could tell she wasn't trying to show it. I felt more content in the nursery, closer to Eva's things that still sat on their shelves and in their drawers, and closer to her. I could miss her here, but the pain was almost bearable because she seemed so close.

When Press had finally come home, I was already asleep. He didn't enter my room—not then, and not in the morning—so it had been more than a day since we'd spoken. Was I wrong to prefer it that way? I couldn't reconcile his swift return to normality with the physical ache in my chest that rose every time I put my hand on the nursery door, or looked at the cushioned booster seat we'd had made so Eva could sit at the dining-room table with us like a big girl, or at the lonesome playhouse beside the stone path leading to the swimming pool, or nearly every time I breathed in the air that she would never breathe again. What was wrong with him?

When I came downstairs in the morning to make sure I hadn't dreamed the incident with the broken glass, Press was there, sitting at the table. His head was bent over a book—probably recommended to him by Zion, who had often sent him home with philosophy and theater books. When he looked up, I saw his skin was flush with color and health: he'd been out rowing on the James with Jack at dawn. So, that had resumed as well.

He smiled. Before he rose from his chair, there was a second's hesitation and I heard the faint ring of a bell in the kitchen. He had rung for Terrance by pressing the bell beneath the carpet with his foot.

"Don't get up." But I was too late. Press was out of his chair, taking long, quick strides to reach me.

I took a tiny step backwards, unprepared for the sheer gravity of his presence, the air of *Floris* and the outdoors about him. He wasn't deterred, and inwardly I cringed in advance of his touch. But instead of folding me in his arms as I feared he might, he merely put one arm around my shoulders and guided me to my chair.

"Have you had your coffee, my love?"

As though to answer for me, Terrance came through the kitchen door carrying a cup and saucer, sugar bowl, and creamer on a tray. Press took his coffee black.

I murmured a *thank you* to Terrance, who poured my coffee and refilled Press's. He went back to the kitchen.

"Guess who was awake when I looked in on him at 5:15 this morning?"

"Was he?"

"Hard at work, trying to get himself out of the crib."

"Where was Nonie? Did you take him out?"

Press looked briefly hurt as though I thought he couldn't be trusted with Michael on his own. He wasn't far wrong. But he didn't bristle.

"Nonie was right behind me." He smiled. "That woman has ears like a bat."

I stirred two lumps of sugar into my coffee.

"That's her job."

Press seemed eager—too eager—to be helpful or, perhaps, kind. If noticing Eva's things caused a knot in my chest, Press's presence was tightening it. I knew my discomfort with him wasn't necessarily rational, but I still wondered if I would ever feel differently.

My eyes rested on the door whose missing panels of glass Terrance had temporarily replaced with tight-fitting squares of wood. Press followed my eyes, saw where I was looking.

"Terrance is arranging a repair. Marlene tells me we had some nasty wind yesterday. Did you hear it?"

So Marlene hadn't mentioned that I'd been in the room.

"Oh, my. What a shame." Not a lie. Not quite.

Marlene and I both knew that there hadn't been any kind of wind. After the door flew open, the air had remained completely still, and the door rested, motionless, against the chair it had hit. We'd stared at the broken glass glistening on the floor, stunned.

As we watched, a dowdy moth the color of parchment careened in from the garden as though blinded by the sunlight, and landed on one of the larger shards of glass. All was silent, so I clearly heard Marlene draw a sharp, startled breath. After a moment, the moth stacked its wings on its back so that it looked like a tiny chunk of wood, and didn't move again.

Marlene's face had undergone a swift change, from surprise to purposefulness.

"I'll clean this up." Then she disappeared into the kitchen, presumably to get a broom and dustpan.

We would never speak of it to each other.

To Press, I said the first word that came into my mind: "October." As though that were all the explanation anyone needed for door panes shattering, Press nodded and closed his book. *A Handbook of Acting* by Madame Eva Alberti was written in faded gold on the red cover. *Eva.* The writer's name caught me short. Was Press reading it where I could see it just to be cruel? No, it wasn't possible. I looked away. Surely I was being too sensitive.

Terrance returned with a soft-boiled egg in a china cup and a piece of buttered toast on a Minton porcelain plate decorated with dragons and birds. Usually the sight of the beautifully painted design pleased me, but I could only think of how fascinated Eva had been with them.

"You're going to work today?"

Press cleared his throat, giving me the impression he was about to say something he thought was important.

"Yes, but first I'm driving into Lynchburg."

Lynchburg was the nearest city to Old Gate, though we often found ourselves going up to Charlottesville if we needed to shop for something unusual. Maybe the prejudice was because we frequented The Grange, the resort hotel just outside Charlottesville. Lynchburg seemed a rougher place to me than Charlottesville, even though both were historic university towns. Press often teased me that I was prejudiced because I was from the eastern part of the state.

"The crematory has Zion and Helen's ashes ready. Someone needs to pick them up."

"Can't they just send them?"

He smiled, a look of mock incredulity on his suntanned face. "You're not suggesting they put Zion and Helen in the mail, are you? I can't see Helen standing for that."

"I meant by car. Delivery." I felt myself redden. "Why do *you* have to go?"

He put his hand over mine, and I surprised myself by not immediately pulling away.

"I shouldn't have brought it up. Have I upset you?"

So much death.

"There's no family? Wasn't there a nephew? I thought I remembered Helen mentioning one." Zion and Helen were committed atheists who had directed—in the will that Press had made up for them—that they be immediately cremated after death, without interment. There had been no funeral.

"We wrote to him at the address in Helen's address book, but we never got an answer."

We. I wasn't sure whom he meant, but I guessed it was Rachel and Jack or maybe some of the others in the group. I didn't want to think about Zion and Helen anymore.

"How is Rachel?"

After asking, I took a bite of toast that was rich with melted butter from the dairy that delivered to us every weekday, but it felt oily and unpleasant in my mouth. No food tasted good to me, and I thought it might never again. I returned the toast to the plate and sipped my coffee to wash away the feel of it.

"She's distressed. Still upset about Helen. And Zion, of course. Why don't you go and see her? The baby's weighing her down. She says she can hardly sit for five minutes."

"I remember feeling like that with Michael."

"You stood through dinner three nights in a row. I thought we were going to have to build you your own special table that reached up to *here*." He held one hand about a foot over the table. "Remember how Eva. . . ." He stopped.

He was about to say that Eva had wanted to stand to eat, too.

⟋

She'd been fine in her own chair the first two evenings that I'd had to stand as we ate in the dining room, but on the third evening she began to rock her entire little body as though she would topple the little seat off the chair.

"Mommy! I want to eat with you."

I was already horribly uncomfortable and self-conscious. The baby—Michael—had dropped several inches inside me, yet had one foot pressing hard against my upper ribcage. It was painful and I felt as though I might burst with the pressure. Olivia had suggested that I might be more comfortable if Terrance brought a tray to my room, and that Press could even join me if I liked. But the truth was that I could barely sit at all. And though I'd persuaded Nonie to leave Richmond, where she was living with her sister, she hadn't yet arrived. I wanted to stay at the table to look after Eva, and I wondered silently if Olivia thought Terrance could do that as well. (Eva chattered frequently at Terrance, who was always polite in response. But she never made him smile. Nothing made Terrance smile.)

"Stop, Eva." Resting a hand on one side of the seat, I held on to her with the other. "You need to sit still." She had gotten food in her hair and all down one side of her face, something she hadn't done in many months.

"Unnnnnnhhhhh, no!" Arching her back, she lifted her face to the ceiling and gave the seat another jerk so that she almost forced it, as well as the chair it sat on, over backwards. But I caught it as it tipped. When I tried to resettle her in her seat, making sure the strap affixed to it was secure, she hit at me with the flat of her tiny rounded palm.

Reflexively I fell back. Even though she was two and a half, she had never been one to throw tantrums. And she'd never hit anyone. She opened her mouth, yelling, and I glanced over at Press. He shrugged.

At the head of the table, Olivia, who had never once interfered in our raising of Eva, pushed back her chair and got up. Crossing the few feet of Oriental carpet between us, she stood over Eva, not saying a word. Press and I stared. Eva's cry faltered.

I opened my mouth to speak, then closed it.

Olivia rested a hand on Eva's now-damp forehead. Eva stared up at the only grandmother she would ever know. She hiccuped.

"Oh, for heaven's sake." Olivia pulled back the chair and picked off the stray peas that had fallen into Eva's lap from her plate. Then she undid the strap I'd just tightened and lifted her granddaughter, not seeming to mind that the rice decorating Eva's pinafore would surely transfer to her own beige silk blouse and oxblood tweed skirt.

"The poor child has a fever, Charlotte. Look how she's rubbing her ear. She probably has an infection."

"No. She can't. I'm sure she's getting too old."

Eva laid her head on Olivia's shoulder. She put her thumb in her mouth and whimpered discontentedly. I could see now that her eyes were glazed. I was already feeling like I was betraying her by bringing a new baby into our little family, and here I hadn't even noticed that she was sick.

Now, Press stood up. "Let me take her, Mother."

"No, I will." I held open my arms. "I'll take her upstairs."

Olivia shook her head. Terrance had appeared silently a few feet behind her, but she seemed to know he was there. (That Olivia had Terrance there in the house at all was a strange and remarkable thing. But I did not know that then, and still wonder how she had tolerated him.)

"Bring some warm, wet cloths to the nursery, Terrance. Also get the medicine dropper and mineral oil from my bathroom. And pour a cognac." There was a hint of a smile at the corners of her mouth, and in her hazel eyes. "That's for me," she said. "Finish your dinners."

As she left the room, Eva waved a limp *good-bye* with a hand slung over her grandmother's shoulder.

I was too tired, too surprised to argue or go after them. Later, I peeked into the nursery to see Olivia sitting in the rocking chair with Eva cuddled against her and sucking her thumb as Olivia read her a story. Leaving quietly before Eva could spot me, I heard Olivia's pleasant voice behind me, reading the tale of Hansel and Gretel and the evil witch who lived in the gingerbread house.

Michael was born within twenty-four hours, and Nonie arrived at the house the next day.

"I miss her." Press squeezed my hand. "You know how much I miss her, Charlotte. How can you not know?"

But we let her die. I wanted to scream the words, but I wasn't going to cause a scene. Still, I wouldn't comfort him. He would have to find his own comfort if that's what he was really looking for. I changed the subject.

"You're going to the office when you get back from Lynchburg?" In truth, I didn't care what time he came home. I wanted Bliss House to myself—Marlene, Terrance, Nonie, and Michael notwithstanding.

His thick brows came together almost imperceptibly. I wasn't going to make forgiveness easy, if I forgave him at all.

"Wills," he said. "Two new ones on my desk."

It took our child's death to remind their owners, I thought. How appropriate. If the same thought occurred to him, he didn't say.

He lifted my hand to his lips and kissed the palm of it tenderly, the way he had often done when we were first married. "I won't be late tonight. What will you do today?"

I knew I should go and see Rachel. She hadn't done anything wrong, and had even called the house sometime during the past weeks. But I wasn't in the mood to talk to her. I loved Rachel, but she required a lot of attention and energy, and I had always been one to give it. Both were in limited supply for me that day.

Without much of a plan, I had dressed in comfortable slacks and a navy blue cardigan. I had even put on a light coat of lipstick and a dash of mascara to give an impression of some kind of normality. It wasn't that I was lying about the way I was feeling. Not really. I only wanted to be functional. A part of me was still in my bed upstairs, unable to move. To breathe. But there was nothing I could learn by staying there. Nothing would ever change—or at least nothing would change in the way I needed it to.

"I may start going through your mother's things." I didn't mention that I had almost begun the day before, and really hadn't known that's what I was going to do until I said it. But as I did, I knew it was right.

Chapter 7

Olivia's Room

Press had tried to encourage me. "Have some fun. Pretend it's a treasure hunt."

Nothing in my life had felt less like a treasure hunt.

Before approaching Olivia's room (was I procrastinating?), I went to the nursery and found Michael sleeping on Eva's trundle bed, breathing heavily. Nonie led me out of the room, whispering that she'd found him awake and with Preston in the room just before dawn, but he'd gone back to sleep.

"Press didn't wake him," I said automatically. "He found him trying to get out of his crib."

Nonie didn't respond, but went on as though I hadn't spoken.

"We rocked in the chair for a while, and he just climbed right down and went over there." She gestured to Eva's bed. "The poor thing closed his eyes and went right back to sleep."

I had to look away so Nonie wouldn't see the tears in *my* eyes.

Grief comes to people in different ways. Even children.

Michael had few real words, yet, but nearly every day since she died he'd searched all around the nursery and wherever else he was in the house for Eva. I wondered how long it would be before he got used to her not being there. The few weeks she'd been gone were like a lifetime for a one-year-old.

"Let him sleep as long as he wants."

Nonie gave a small sigh that told me she disagreed. She had kept both Eva and Michael on a strict schedule. But if anything justified a break in the schedule, it was Michael's need for his sister.

I kissed her on the cheek. She was so dear to me, and she'd loved both of my children. "He might be getting sick. I'll listen for him if you want to go down and get some breakfast."

She looked skeptical, but it was all I had to offer her. It didn't occur to me then to speculate about what might have awakened him. It was much later, when he was five years old, that his night terrors began. As we went out, I left the nursery door open halfway so I might hear him when he woke.

⁓

I hadn't spent much time in Olivia's room when she was alive, and now, when all her things belonged to me, I felt like an intruder. Beginning a few days after her death, I'd told Marlene and Terrance to keep the door to her bedroom closed. Seeing the door open had chilled me every time I came out of my own bedroom and looked across the gallery.

Olivia's was an oddly Victorian room, cluttered and crowded compared to the rest of the house, which was full of antiques and precious things but had more of a sense of air and light to it.

Even the wallpaper was dense with cherry blossoms, and for the first time I made the connection between it and the hand-painted cherry trees on the wallpaper of the ballroom on the third floor. That motif was Oriental, with repeated images of an old man and a beautiful Japanese girl. But like the theater, the ballroom was rarely used—not even for Olivia's annual New Year's Eve party. "Wasted space," was how she had referred to it. "And the devil to heat in the winter." (I envisioned it as something more than wasted space. I imagined transforming it into a big, friendly winter playroom where the children could run around on snowy days; but that idea, of course, had been put on hold. I hadn't even mentioned it to Press.)

The last time I'd been in the bedroom was with Marlene, to retrieve the brooch and necklace that Olivia had left to her.

I found that I couldn't look directly at Olivia's massive four-poster, canopied bed—the bed she had died in—though it stayed in my field of vision wherever I went in the room. Press had asked a few weeks earlier if I wanted Olivia's room for myself; or if not, did I think Eva would like it. It was the largest bedroom in the house, with a beautiful view of the rose garden and the hills beyond. Perhaps I was superstitious, but I told him I would never sleep in it, and that it was too big a room for a little girl. No matter how we changed it, it would always be Olivia's room to me.

But that morning I was glad to be surrounded by Olivia's things. I got to work—well, not really work, though I was pretending even to myself that I was there to start cleaning things out. What I wanted was to be close to Olivia, to let her know I was listening, even though the idea of actually communicating with her frightened me, and the sense of her presence I'd had on the day of the funeral had faded. If it hadn't been for the broken glass in the dining room, I wondered if I would have continued to imagine that she might help me at all.

Because of our difference in size (and also because the idea of wearing her things seemed macabre and strange to me), I had no use for the rows of shoes and clothes in the tall French armoire and closet. Olivia's tweed luncheon suits, day dresses, and cocktail dresses were plentiful and expensive, but not gaudy. At least ten evening gowns had been hung in the closet, carefully shrouded in linen bags, along with a mink coat and a number of fox, ocelot, and mink pieces. There were several pairs of wool pants I'd seen her in on the coldest days if she was staying home, and a single pair of worn dungarees. Olivia administered the orchards, and knew plenty about cultivation and horticulture, but she managed to run the farm in sensible shoes and slacks or tweed skirts. Unlike Press and me, she didn't ride. I'd always wondered about that, but she appeared not to care about horses at all.

Her bathroom was neat as a pin. For a woman in her fifties, she had remarkably few unguents and perfumes. It might have been the bathroom of a particularly tidy guest. In all the years I'd lived with Olivia, I had only been in her bathroom twice, to get aspirin. In fact, I'd never really known Olivia to have a bodily function beyond a sneeze or cough until just before she died. Press had told me he'd never once heard her break wind, or seen her rinse her mouth when she brushed her teeth. Everything was done in the privacy of her room or bathroom. Olivia once overheard him joke that moments after he'd shot out of her fully clothed body, she'd bathed, changed, and had Terrance bring her a cocktail before the doctor even arrived for his delivery. Instead of getting angry or embarrassed, Olivia had just shaken her head and told him that, no, he'd been born at eight in the morning, and she never had cocktails before five in the afternoon.

I almost tripped on a framed photograph that had fallen, face down, onto the carpet in front of the commode table that held Olivia's two mahogany jewelry caskets.

I picked it up, but had to take it to the window to get a better look because it was so faded. It had always been on the table, but I had never looked at it closely.

A very young Olivia sat in a wicker chair in the garden, with her husband, Michael Searle Bliss, who looked even younger, standing beside her. His slender hand rested tentatively on her shoulder.

He seemed uncomfortable, perhaps too hot in his stiff collar and three-piece suit. His cheeks wore a residue of pink that was visible even in the faded colors of the photograph. (That it was in color was a kind of miracle in itself. It must have cost a small fortune to have it done.) Olivia's simple ankle-length dress of yellow, flower-patterned silk, was fresh and contemporary for its time, though the large black bow at the waist gave it a playful look that wouldn't at all have suited the conservative, sophisticated woman I'd known. But it worked for the girl with the attentive eyes and plain features in the photo. The camera's distance made her scar seem insignificant.

They were an interesting couple. It was difficult to imagine Olivia being so young, and even stranger to know that her husband would be dead before they were married a year. He didn't look old enough to be married at all, and his mild features—high cheek-bones, sloping shoulders, and slight limbs—had little in common with my husband's. Their coloring was the same, and the thickness of the eyebrows was something like Press's, but the resemblance ended there. The family resemblance was slightly stronger when I compared Press to his father's portrait hanging in the library.

I replaced the photograph between the jewelry boxes, which were full to overflowing. Many of her more extravagant pieces were horn or antique platinum or yellow gold. Intricate Art Nouveau pins and necklaces with flower and scroll motifs. Fanciful enamel and jeweled birds, insects, and animals that had a whimsy about them that seemed unlike Olivia.

As I suspected, there were several peacock-themed pieces, including an enameled white jeweled peacock with a clasp that, when opened, released a small and very sharp gold blade. It surprised me, but I wasn't hurt, and I made a mental note to put it up somewhere that Michael couldn't reach it. The largest piece was a vibrant blue male peacock with a citrine crown, his tail tapered, not fanned. His head was in profile so that only one gold-rimmed eye was visible, and that was a single dark emerald that had the winking clarity of a diamond. The brooch was both ugly and curiously attractive at the same time. Thinking it might be a conversation piece that would look good on my fall coat, I slipped it into my pocket, feeling a bit like a thief.

Looking at the jewelry, I realized I had no idea what to do with it all. I had both my mother's and my own simple jewelry, which, along with Olivia's, would have eventually gone to Eva. Press had a cousin who lived in the area; yet, although he was a Bliss, he and Press weren't close. But the cousin did have a young daughter, Jane, who should probably receive some of Olivia's things. I closed the caskets. Where once I had marveled at their contents, now those contents weighed on me as though they were a part of some dragon's cursed hoard. I would deal with them later.

Perhaps it was my own laziness or the fact that I was already overwhelmed, but I decided to tell Marlene that she could have whatever clothes of Olivia's she wanted, and that she should pack the rest and have Terrance take them to the thrift store. I wondered who I would later see in Olivia's clothes. I did set aside Olivia's many lovely hand-tatted lace and fine linen handkerchiefs. She had collected them since she was a girl, and she was especially proud of them. They had been among the first things she'd taken time to show me after I moved into the house, and she had insisted that I borrow one of the oldest and most fragile to carry on my wedding day.

Press might have thought differently, but as far as I was concerned, everything else in the room could stay exactly as it was for all time. But I decided that the door should remain open. I didn't want to be afraid of it anymore.

Thus emboldened, I went through the narrow door connecting the bedroom to Olivia's morning room.

Unlike the bedroom, the morning room wasn't crowded with bric-a-brac, but it had plenty of furniture. A pair of chairs and a low table in front of the fireplace, a large writing desk and another chair, a couple of tables along the walls, and a chaise longue in front of the windows, with another small table and a floor lamp beside it. While there was plenty of furniture, Olivia hadn't entertained much in this room. Only her closest friends ever saw it.

The walls were covered, from the chair railing to the ceiling, with paintings of children. Most were reproductions of quite famous works: Leighton's strange and dignified *May Sartoris*, Bouguereau's *Temptation*, Renoir's *Young Girl with Parasol*, and his *Mlle Irène Cahen d'Anvers*. Mary Cassatt's *Young Girl at a Window* was the most poignant. Despite the 19th-century dress, the girl, so serious and intent, reminded me of the Olivia in the photograph. This was how Olivia might have looked as a pensive teenage girl, unaware that she would be the sole mistress of Bliss House for nearly her entire adult life. What would her thoughts have been?

What had mine been, coming to Bliss House? I hadn't imagined that Olivia would die before she was even sixty years old and that I would be in her morning room without her.

I avoided the neat desk with its bulging letter holder. She'd suddenly taken to her bed in the days just before she died, refusing to let anyone be with her except Terrance and Marlene. Press had told me not to worry, that she very occasionally had spells when she retired completely to her room, but that it hadn't happened in a long time. Jack confided that he thought she'd become too dependent on the chloral hydrate drops her elderly internist had prescribed for her occasional sleeplessness and might have begun to mix them with alcohol. But no one even whispered the word "suicide." It had been a terrible accident, Jack and the internist assured us. To spare the family any public embarrassment, her death had been recorded as simple cardiac arrest. It was, the internist said, what had certainly killed her in the end.

That it had been an accident was what I chose to believe. Olivia wasn't a moody, unpredictable sort of person. And I could never have faced the knowledge that both my children's grandmothers had been selfish enough to commit suicide.

Beneath the watchful eyes of all those children, I opened the door to the room's single enormous closet. I felt around for a light switch, but there was only a dangling beaded chain attached to an exposed bulb.

The naked light was harsh, the closet as big as one of the bedrooms in the servants' area at the back of the house. All three walls were lined with crowded but neatly ordered shelves. Close by was a row of china-faced dolls in old-fashioned dresses, and a toy monkey with movable limbs and wide, mischievous eyes. Curious, I touched its fur, but drew my hand back quickly. The fur was real. I shuddered. The dolls were less alarming; but, wary now, I did not touch their hair. Other shelves contained dishes and baskets, and stacks of framed embroidered samplers with traditional aphorisms and bible quotes. The stitching was careful but not practiced. I wondered if Olivia had done them herself as a girl. I knew no needle arts. Rachel's mother had taught her to smock, and she was always at work on some project.

I had to stand on tiptoe to get a better look at what was on the top shelf, and then wished I hadn't.

Even with the glare from the bulb, I could see what the dusty, glass-domed display cases arranged there held: lifelike arrangements of taxidermy birds—a juvenile owl, finches, bluebirds, a woodpecker, butterflies and moths, and the delicate skeleton of what had probably been a tiny monkey (it appeared to be eating a crab).

I was both fascinated and disgusted. But there was nothing here that needed to be immediately gotten rid of. Had the taxidermy animals belonged to Olivia? Perhaps they had been here even before she arrived.

Below the dolls on a lower shelf was a row of wooden boxes labeled with ranges of letters: A–F, G–L, M–R, S–V, W–Z. Sliding out the S–V from its place, I found that it contained rows of heavy glass slides. I had used slide projectors in college, but these slides were much larger and thicker. Holding one to the light, I saw an 18th-century sailing ship that tilted in the water as though it were sinking. There were several more of ships—some in color, some in black and white. But after the ships, I pulled out several more of snakes—a cobra in a pen, a black snake like an ebony "S" separating a plot of vibrant, painted green grass. I might have stayed there all day, holding the curious slides up to the light, examining one after the other. They were obviously quite old and were like tiny windows into the past. I had no projector on which to show them right now, but they were here, waiting for me, any time I wanted to look. When Michael was a little older, I was sure he would like them too. I returned the box to the shelf.

Satisfied that I hadn't missed anything critical, I had almost turned to leave when I noticed a large covered object on the floor at the opposite end of the closet. Given the taxidermy creatures and the dolls, I might have been afraid to approach it, but the heavy drape was tailored and the thing beneath seemed to have geometric proportions rather than organic.

I touched it, and a feeling of warmth swept over me as though the drape hid some sort of heater. Before I could pull off the cover, I heard a shout from outside the room. Leaving the light on and the closet door behind me open, I ran from the morning room and into the bedroom and out. Below me, Nonie was hurrying up the stairs, calling Michael's name. Across the gallery, Michael had worked his arm and shoulder into the narrow space between two of the gallery uprights and had nearly worked his head through. Covering my mouth to keep from screaming at him and scaring him, I ran past the staircase and past Nonie, who was running up the stairs, puffing heavily.

Michael seemed not to notice either of us, and gave a start when I grabbed him. Perhaps I hurt him when I jerked him from between the uprights, because he began to scream and pound at me, pushing me away as I tried to hold on to him. His body was damp with sweat and exertion. He'd been trying very hard to get through the uprights, having no understanding that success would have meant certain death for him. I looked down into the hall where Marlene and Terrance stared up at us. When Nonie reached me, she stood, breathless, holding on to the railing for support. I didn't want to look at her face, knowing I would see blame there. Justified blame.

After Michael was calm, I took him downstairs and gave him a late breakfast. Within fifteen minutes, he was happily smearing oatmeal on his high-chair tray, laughing. I kept him close to me the rest of the morning.

Chapter 8

Confidences

Rachel and I sat in big wicker chairs on the screened porch of the 18th-century farmhouse she shared with Jack. It was one of the oldest houses in the county, built not long after Old Gate was officially established as a town. Ignoring pleas from her mother, as well as the Old Gate Historical Society, Rachel had insisted on building onto its original 1,200 square feet, adding a spacious sunny kitchen and sitting room, two more bedrooms, and a long porch along the back. But it had been well done. Jack had gone along with the build as he did with everything that Rachel wanted. He was too busy in his medical practice to object too much.

Beyond the porch, a simple garden with a winding path sloped downward to meet the rest of the property. It was too shaded for roses, but there were now-spent rhododendrons and hydrangeas, holly bushes—almost trees, really—and some lemon balm. Beds of harebells, wild bleeding hearts, and hostas of all sizes hugged the path. Rachel's mother, Holly, had crowded beds of giant hostas in her yard and was always dividing and giving them away. Beyond the garden, the path led to a sizable pond half-surrounded by cattails and weedy yellow brush gone to seed. The pond was stocked with bass, though Jack had little time to fish, and had a small flock of white geese that lived there year-round. The path then wandered out to the barn, which had been roughly renovated to accommodate the theater group and the occasional large party.

With her basket of smocking notions beside her chair, and a square of bright green fabric on her lap, Rachel looked relaxed and content in her sleeveless purple maternity blouse over a smart black cotton sateen skirt. As always, she was in full makeup, but her hair was pulled into a ponytail as though she were still a teenager. She looked oddly innocent, for Rachel.

In college she'd been a troublemaker, sneaking out for dates, smoking in our dorm room. She hadn't cared. As long as she was having fun, anything was okay with her. After she and Jack married, she calmed considerably. She still loved to throw parties, though she complained that—outside of the theater group—Old Gate was full of boring people who did boring things. I hoped the baby she was carrying would satisfy her need for activity.

I'd come, as Press had suggested, to see how she was doing. As selfish as Rachel was (I loved her but had no illusions about her ideas of her own importance), even she could not have expected me to visit any sooner after Eva's death. I sympathized with her, though. She was probably lonesome, just waiting for the baby to come.

It had been hard to leave Michael after the incident with the railing. But God knew he was safer alone with Nonie than he was with me. Early in the afternoon, as he was about to go down for his nap, I'd wanted to lie down on Eva's trundle bed until he fell asleep, but Nonie had taken my arm and led me quietly out of the nursery.

"You don't want to suffocate him, Lottie. Go and visit Rachel the way you planned. Stay as long as you like. I'll watch him."

What went unspoken was that *I* was the one who hadn't been watching that morning.

A light rain was falling, dropping through the nearby trees like quiet music. Somewhere beneath the fallen leaves, a lone, late-in-the-season cricket chirruped for a mate. There was nothing odd or frightening about the farmhouse. No local legends of ghosts. No unexplained deaths. Even though I was used to Bliss House, I was comfortable here, which was probably why I felt relaxed enough to tell Rachel about seeing Olivia the day of Eva's funeral. I had to tell someone, and I couldn't tell Nonie. She would've made me lie down until the notion passed.

"You poor baby. How frightening." Rachel touched my hand after I'd told her everything. If she noticed that it was trembling slightly, she didn't say. Behind us in the kitchen, I could hear her new housekeeper, Sarah, readying the tea tray.

"You told Press, didn't you? What did he say?"

"Of course I didn't tell him. He'd think I was insane. Rachel, you know I wouldn't make something like that up, don't you? You can't tell him I told you, either."

Rachel shook her head.

"I've said a hundred times that house is haunted, silly. And how like Olivia to keep hanging around. The old. . . ." She caught herself and gave me a wicked little smirk. "What are you going to do?" Then her face changed and she put her hand to her belly. "The beast is kicking again. Such a little stinker already. Jack's sure it's a girl, but I told him I heard that intelligent men father girls. So, it's pretty much guaranteed to be a boy, right?" She laughed, amused by her own joke. "Want to feel?"

That was Rachel. Impulsive. Playfully cruel. Maybe she was being genuine, but I was still sensitive because of Eva. I didn't know what I would do if she gave birth to a baby girl just weeks after Eva's death. The thought sickened me.

"No. I—"

Before I could finish, she grabbed my hand and laid it on the swell of her stomach. She watched my face expectantly as though waiting for me to comment on a fabulous new hat or pair of shoes she'd just purchased.

Beneath the fabric of her blouse, I felt the rolling pressure of a shoulder or knee of the baby as it squirmed in her womb. She was due within weeks, and the baby was stunningly active, given how large it was inside her. At the same point in both of my pregnancies, my children had been still for such long periods that I'd lain awake at night, alert for any kind of movement and fearful that they had died. Press had humored me, putting his face against my naked belly, listening. Telling me he felt and heard things that I suspected he really hadn't.

I nodded and tried a smile. Rachel was satisfied.

"Do you want me to come over and scare Olivia away? Or we could do an exorcism. You've got Father Aaron. Don't priests do that sort of thing?"

"Please don't be mean. I shouldn't have told you. You must think I'm an idiot."

"You know how Olivia was about me. She thought all Jews stole babies and ate them or something."

I objected, even though I knew she wasn't far from wrong. I hadn't known Olivia before World War II, but the inhuman treatment of the German and Polish Jews in the war obviously hadn't made any kind of impression on her. Sensible about so many things, she was shamelessly anti-Semitic.

"She was old-fashioned. But I never heard her say one unpleasant thing about you."

Rachel made a scoffing sound. Then she turned in her chair to call into the house.

"Sarah. Where's that tea? And bring out some of those ladyfingers you baked this morning."

Sarah was new because Rachel didn't keep housekeepers long. I assumed she wore them out with her demands. It never occurred to me then that some of them might not want to work for her because of her Jewish background. Jack wasn't Jewish, or any other faith that I knew of. I wondered how they would raise the baby, but I didn't ask.

"Maybe I don't want Olivia to go away. Maybe she's trying to tell me something."

Rachel leaned forward as best she could. "That does sound a little crazy, honey. Are you sure you're all right?" Her dark eyes were serious. "Press told me he didn't think you were doing very well."

I looked down at my hands in my lap, noticing how bitten and ragged several of the nails on my left hand were. I didn't remember biting them. It was an old, old habit, one that Nonie had broken me of when I was seven or eight.

"I don't think about her every minute, the way I have been."

"No one would blame you if you did, Charlotte. No one blames you for anything." She paused. "You don't have to pretend with me. She was your precious angel."

There was no stopping the tears then. I didn't really want comfort from anyone, because I knew there was no real comfort anywhere. Eva was *my* child. Press couldn't understand. Not really. Not Nonie, not even my best friend could comprehend the depth of the empty space inside me. It was a nameless, endless chasm that could never be filled—not with air or water or tears, and certainly not words of any kind. Rachel let me cry and just held my hand, occasionally squeezing it. Outside the screens, the rain fell harder, drowning out the sound of my sobs.

I don't know how long we sat like that. Five minutes, or an hour. When I think back, I realize that, for many reasons, it must have been a Herculean effort for Rachel. My handkerchief was limp and wet, and the area behind my eyes felt washed out and scratchy. Finally, the sound of the rain was the only sound left.

Weeks earlier, I couldn't have imagined myself crying as I had in front of her. And certainly not in front of the more distant friends and acquaintances who had been at the cemetery. Death had changed me; but, despite her initial hysteria over the Heasters at the house, it had not changed Rachel. She was her cool, unemotional self. The silence between us turned quickly awkward.

"Do you want me to call Press to take you home?"

"God, no. There's no reason." I ran the handkerchief carefully below each eye, remembering that I'd put on a small amount of mascara, though I doubted there was any left.

"What can I do? Do you want me to drive you? I can still fit behind the wheel." She patted her stomach. There seemed to be more baby than there was of Rachel.

Once again I tried to smile but couldn't quite make it happen.

"Nonie will wonder where I am," I lied. "I should go."

I got up to leave just as Sarah was cautiously putting down a tray with iced tea and a plate full of ladyfingers drizzled with raspberry syrup on the low table in front of us. No doubt she'd been waiting in the kitchen for me to stop crying. Had she been listening, as well? My sobbing was just more fodder for the Old Gate gossip mill.

"Sarah, wrap up the ladyfingers for Mrs. Bliss to take with her. Her husband will love them. Here, help me up, will you?"

Sarah was lean and hollow-eyed, younger than most of Rachel's housekeepers. The arm she held out to Rachel looked strong, like she was used to heavy work.

"Yes, ma'am."

As we walked to the front door, Rachel kept her hand around my waist. We embraced on the front step and exchanged kisses. Before I turned away, I lifted the little bag. "Maybe I'll let Michael have a bite of one. They smell wonderful. Thank you."

We parted, but she called out to me just as I reached the car. "Wait. I meant to ask you what you thought about Halloween. Isn't Press brilliant for suggesting it?"

I must have looked puzzled, because she rolled her eyes and sighed. "Press is such an idiot. He told you about the memorial for

Helen and Zion, yes? He said we'd do it in your theater on Halloween. They would've loved that."

⁓

There is nowhere on earth more beautiful in the fall than
the hills around Old Gate, the colors of the trees violent against the
dulling earth beneath them. But I didn't see them as I drove
back to Bliss House. They could've been purple or black as night
or in flames, as much impression as they made on me.

I wove through town, past the library and the courthouse, past the
new furniture store that had opened in May with a celebration that
had included a brass band and a clown handing out balloons. I had
driven Nonie and Eva into town to hear the band, and Eva had gone
right up to the clown who, truth be told, was not a very good one,
with makeup that didn't completely hide his day-old beard, and a thin
piece of rope binding one of his giant red shoes. The other children
hung back, wary. But not Eva. She challenged the clown with her
smile and asked for a second balloon for Michael, who bounced in
my arms, excited by the music.

The memory of how Eva had looked up at the clown, her arm
lifted to reach the balloon's string (Had the balloon been yellow or
red? It seemed critical that I remember, and I could not.), was so
strong that I also drove past the stop sign on Market Street without
stopping.

With the great blaring of another car's horn, I came to myself
in time to keep from rear-ending a car that had stopped on the
other side of the intersection. My window was open and I hadn't
turned on the radio, so I heard the man who had almost hit me
yelling at me as he continued through the intersection. My mouth
went dry.

Carefully, with a small wave, I drove around the stopped car.
Just as I reached the edge of town, I heard a police siren behind me.

The sidewalks and curbs had run out, so I pulled over to the shoulder in front of a lot where a new Baptist church was being built.

Not all the county deputies were known to me, but in my sideview mirror I saw Dennis Mueller, the son of Karla Mueller who did my hair every Thursday, get out of the black-and-white patrol car. He had his mother's squarish face and light-brown hair. My vanity hadn't yet returned, but I touched the ends of my own hair where it brushed my ear. I hadn't been to see her in weeks. At least it was Dennis, and not his boss, Sheriff Hugh Walters, who was a close friend of both Press's and mine. I hadn't seen him since the funeral, and although he'd been kind, I hoped not to see him again anytime soon.

I rolled down my window.

"I'm so sorry, Dennis. I don't know why I didn't stop. I must have been thinking about getting home." My second lie of the afternoon.

"It was dangerous the way you went through that intersection, Mrs. Bliss. Someone might have been hurt."

He was so young, only out of high school three or four years.

"I understand. Of course. What do you need?" I fumbled in my purse for my license.

When I gave it to him, he only glanced at it before returning it to me. The rain had stopped, but there were still a few drops scattered over his midnight-blue cap.

"That's all right, Mrs. Bliss. I'm not going to give you a ticket today. Just be more careful. We've had more than our share of wrecks in the county lately."

"That's very nice of you. I promise to be more careful."

We fell silent for a moment. I was about to ask him to say hello to his mother for me when he spoke again. He pushed his hat back just a bit on his head.

"I sure was sorry to hear about your daughter, ma'am. My mother was very upset, too. She said she was a sweet little girl."

69

I smiled in spite of myself. "She gave Eva her first haircut. I don't think anyone else could have done it as well."

Dennis Mueller nodded. He looked sad and uncomfortable.

"She's given a lot of kids their first haircut. Sometimes the little girls' daddies come in, complaining that their wives brought the girls in without telling them first. You'd be surprised how many of them don't want their daughters' hair cut at all."

I didn't know quite what to say, but knew he was trying to be friendly.

"I know this isn't any of my business, ma'am, but everyone says you were at home that Monday it happened."

As his words sank in, my heart started to pound. Were they thinking of prosecuting me, after all? Hugh had told us not to worry. He considered it an accident and didn't see any reason for there to be an inquest.

"I. . . ." The words wouldn't come. As I sat there, several cars passed by, but I was oblivious as to who was inside.

He spoke hurriedly. "I only ask, Mrs. Bliss, because I thought I saw you and your husband turn up your driveway in a hurry that afternoon. I was on my way out of town to a welfare check at the other end of the county, and your husband's car went by pretty fast. Not so fast as I would've necessarily pulled him over, but pretty fast. But, pardon me, everyone was saying that you were home by yourself when it happened."

"I don't understand."

He looked down at the ground like an abashed child. "It's not like you're someone who would leave a couple of little kids alone in that house. I wondered when the sheriff told us, that's all. I told him, but he said I was wrong. I just wanted to be sure."

"That she didn't die alone?"

"Yes, ma'am."

It was like Karla Mueller to have a son who noticed things. She knew everything about everyone, and could tell if you were having a bad day the moment you put your hand on the doorknob of her shop.

"No, Dennis. I was in the house. I'm the one who was responsible."

"But I was sure I saw you late that afternoon, ma'am."

"It must have been my friend, Rachel, coming to the house with my husband." Though I had never thought to ask why she had already been there when I awoke. Of course it had been the farthest thing from my mind after I learned what had happened to Eva.

He watched me a moment as though trying to decide if I was telling the truth. If I hadn't been in a mild state of shock from the suddenness of his question, I might have accused him of being rude. He had said "that house." I realized that he wasn't as concerned with what *I* had or hadn't done as he was that it had happened at *that house.*

Chapter 9

Suspicions

As I came up the shadowy drive, my heart gave a little jump when I saw Nonie, head down and slightly bent at the waist, pulling Michael in Eva's Radio Flyer wagon. Nonie's coat, the color of a gold chrysanthemum, and the red wagon were cheerful splashes against the hay-colored grass and brown-red leaves of the oaks. Eva had liked to pull her dolls in the wagon while Michael rode in his stroller, but one day she had insisted that she be allowed to have Michael in the wagon instead of her dolls. Press and I had watched as she pulled the heavy wagon, her little face reddening beneath her curls, as she pretended it was no effort at all.

"See? It's easy, Mommy."

Press had laughed behind his hand, but I whispered for him to stop. It seemed so important to her that we be impressed.

Before reaching them, I stopped the car and turned off the ignition. When I rolled down the window, I heard raindrops falling from leaf to leaf as though it were still raining. Nonie wore a scarf over her hair, and she'd put a cap and light jacket on Michael. She didn't believe in keeping children indoors all day, no matter what the weather.

"He saw the wagon and would have absolutely nothing to do with his stroller. Fussed like a banshee." Nonie glanced back at Michael, who was waving a giant yellow maple leaf that had blown over from beyond the driveway.

"You gave in? That's not the Nonie I know." But of course she knew he was missing Eva. Though she was always strict, she was also genuinely kind. "Doesn't that hurt your back? The handle's so short."

"Not all of us are troubled with generous height, Lottie. Sometimes I think you forget that," she teased. She looked down at Michael. "You'd better hope you have your mother's height, Michael. Or she'll make fun of you too, one day."

I laughed, surprising myself. It felt natural, and I was momentarily grateful to her. Poor Michael had seen plenty of tears and sadness and was likely to see more.

"Your husband is home."

"So early?"

"It's not as though he keeps a schedule, is it? There was a decorator's van here a little while ago. But it's gone now."

"Decorator?"

Nonie shrugged. "I have no idea."

I blew Michael a kiss and reminded Nonie to come inside if it began to rain again. She nodded, humoring me, and they moved on. I waited until they were well past me before I restarted the car.

⌒

I parked in front of the house and left the keys in the ignition. There were some things that Terrance took care of that I very much appreciated, and parking the cars in the garage for us was one of them. The original carriage house had burned around the turn of the century, and the inside of the new carriage house set off to the east of the house was a gray, grim place, with cinderblock bays for three cars and an unused apartment built above. But the bays themselves, though plain, had exposed beams and dark corners. I'd once looked up—I'm not sure what led me to do it—to see a copperhead curling along one of the beams, and I hadn't wanted to go in there again.

As Terrance opened the front door of Bliss House for me, I suddenly remembered the black snake in the lane. Had that been what spooked the Heasters' horse? It had to be. I wondered if anyone else had seen it, or if I was the only one. Only Zion and, perhaps, Helen would know. Helen would have been frightened of the snake. She was a woman of the city and, given the way she'd talked about the inadequacies of Old Gate, I had the impression that she was never truly comfortable here. Of course, they had lived in Old Gate proper, in a cluttered cottage with several cats. I doubted they had a snake problem.

"Good afternoon, Miss Charlotte." Terrance nodded.

I turned back to look down the lane for Nonie and Michael, worried that they might come across the same snake. Certainly the black snake was harmless and would hurry into the grass if it weren't already hiding there. If it didn't hide, I would be more worried for it than I would for Michael and the very protective, stick-wielding Nonie.

"Hello, Terrance. Can you tell me where Mr. Preston is?"

⌒

There was a fire laid in the library, even though it was probably still over seventy degrees outside. Press stood at the desk, a Scotch in one hand. The ice cubes were still large, so he probably hadn't had it very long. My father didn't understand why a man would put ice in a single malt, but then he still didn't understand why some grown men didn't bother to take their hats off when they went into buildings.

More than any other room in Bliss House, the library, with its smell of old books, polished wood, and low afternoon light, suited Preston. Even though his body was quite athletic, he had an old-fashioned, almost antique look about him, and his strong features made him seem almost roguish. His face would be right at home in the portrait gallery of some Old World museum: Amsterdam, perhaps. Or Rome.

"You went out!" He put his drink down on the desk beside a small pile of open boxes and strode across the room to me. "I'm so glad, my love. How is Rachel?"

"She sent you these." I was determined to speak to him about the memorial plans, but knew it was always best to approach him carefully about things we might disagree about. I definitely thought having the memorial at the house was inappropriate. I turned my head so he could kiss me on the cheek, then handed him the small paper bag, which was spotted with grease from the butter in the ladyfingers.

He opened it and looked inside. "These smell damned good. That new housekeeper of hers . . . what's her name? Cynthia? Susan? I can't keep up. She's a decent cook. Jack and I both told Rachel she needs to be nice to this one."

Setting the bag on a table, he took out a ladyfinger and popped two-thirds of it into his mouth. "Damned good," he said with his mouth still a little full. "Do you want one?"

"They're for you. But you might save part of one for Michael."

"Of course. If you think Nonie will let him have one." He said this with a look of mischief in his eyes.

I had loved this playful Preston. I was still drawn to him, even though there was a wall inside me then that didn't want to let him pass. He was not the way back to Eva.

"What's in the boxes? I didn't see any mail on the table in the hall."

He glanced back at the desk.

"Want a drink? It's after five."

I wondered how far a drink would go to dispel the wall inside me, but wasn't tempted. The last champagne I'd drunk had made me sleep so deeply that I'd let my daughter drown.

"Water is fine. Ice too, please."

While Press poured my water, I went to look in the open boxes on the desk. Both were full of rich velvet fabric. Midnight blue, deep scarlet, ruby red with shiny gold threads woven through it. Green with outlines of large, abstract stars, also in gold. I lowered one of the cardboard lids. "J. C. Jacquith Designs, NYC" was neatly hand-lettered on the return label. I took out one of the fabric pieces and carried it to the window to get a better look. The velvet was lush, but the gold threads were sharp as though they were made of actual metal and caught at my fingertips.

"What are these for?"

I wasn't a fool. I already knew what they were for.

"Samples that J.C. sent down weeks ago. I was getting ready to throw them away. The curtains up in the theater are moth-eaten. It's Mother's fault for letting them get to that state."

There was a note card that had fallen between the two boxes. I picked it up. The paper was heavy stock and scented—something peppery and arresting. The note was dated more than two months earlier, only a week or so after Olivia had died.

"Darling Press, Again, I'm just crushed about your dear old mummy. I hope you're still holding up like the brick that you are. Here are the samples I promised. The red velvet with the gold is what they've put in the studio at Carnegie. Too much? Maybe! Call with the measurements. I'll bring them down and supervise installation myself. It's going to be spectacular! Love to you and Precious Bride—J."

The paper's scent was vivid, like J.C. herself. I'd found her intimidating with her expensive tailored clothes, bold, interested gaze, and exaggerated gestures. She had a habit of holding her hand out to men to be kissed, and they usually obliged without hesitation. Their reward was a smile full of blazingly white large teeth. J.C. wasn't beautiful or even particularly pretty. But she had what Nonie called "go-to-hell style."

"Why are we replacing the curtains? No one ever sees them." I was being disingenuous, so the words felt predictably clumsy.

It was a longstanding disagreement between Press and his mother. Like the ballroom, she believed the theater to be a waste of space and resources, but had refused to let Preston use it. By the time we were married, the discussions had all been exhausted, leaving me to hear only "she's irrational about the theater" from Press, and "a home is no place for theatrical productions" from Olivia. It didn't matter to Olivia that Preston's group only wanted to rehearse. They held their infrequent performances in the auditorium of Fellowes Academy, a nearby private girls' boarding school, and had done them there since Zion and Helen had started the group fifteen years earlier.

Press handed me my water. "You and Marlene can continue using my mother's menus from now until the end of time, if you like. We can even keep her bedroom as a shrine."

At those words, I wondered for a moment if he somehow knew what I was thinking about Olivia's room. And that Olivia was still here—somewhere.

His heavy eyebrows lifted, lightening his face. It was a look he got when he was truly excited. "But the house is ours to do with as we choose, isn't it? Now that Zion and Helen are gone, I'd like to take the group in a new direction. This place. . . ." He swept his arm, I assumed to indicate the house. "Bliss House is so much more than my mother would ever let it be. Now it's *ours*, Charlotte. Everyone in the group adores you, my darling. I've been telling you for months, you should come and at least read with us. You'd be terrific on stage. Helen was always saying that you and your killer cheekbones belonged up there."

When Press introduced Helen to me at our engagement party, Helen had reached up and taken my face in her tiny hands that sparkled with stacks of expensive rings and given my cheeks a not-so-gentle squeeze.

"Look at those cheekbones, Zion! This is a girl born to play Brunhild, yes? But do you sing, my dear?"

Even though the group didn't do musicals, that line, "But do you sing, my dear?" became a kind of joke between Press and me.

"I don't think so. I'll leave the theater to you and Rachel." Sometimes Press was like a particularly winning child whose pleas I found hard to resist no matter what my mood. But the wall was up. Even if I felt my emotions, my body responding to him, I wouldn't be drawn from my purpose. My grief.

"Then come and play with us. We'll be at loose ends without Zion and Helen. Helen kept us going."

"Come and *play* with you?" Even the word *play* felt repellent in my mouth. "What are you saying? Our baby girl hasn't been dead a month. What do you think you're doing?"

He put a hand on my arm. Angry, I shook it off and picked up the note from the desk.

"When is J.C. coming? Have you already arranged it?"

"She'll be here the day after tomorrow."

"Jesus, Press. How could you not tell me about this?" I searched his eyes looking for understanding, waiting for him to tell me that he hadn't meant to hurt me. "You need to tell her not to come!"

"It's just a few days. She'll be here, and the work will be done, then everyone will be gone. I've already had the outside stairway to the theater repaired, and the workmen will use that."

How had I not heard? Not noticed? I vaguely remembered voices, hammering, but just barely. It must have taken days to repair the towering, dangerously narrow wood-and-iron stairway that hugged the western side of the house as though it didn't want to be seen. It was a leftover from the days when Randolph Bliss had invited in the locals to see minstrel shows and even the occasional traveling preacher, though the rumors were that the family secretly mocked them. Someone from the town had fallen from the top of the stairs years before, but I didn't know the details.

"And then? Don't lie to me. Rachel told me about the memorial."

"Lie to you? Darling, we aren't the only ones who lost something precious. There are a dozen people living in or near Old Gate who loved Helen and Zion like parents. It's only right that they be able to come together and mourn them properly." He reached out for my arm again, but hesitated.

I was glad he stopped, because I might have hit him or flung myself at him. Still, I could hardly speak. My jaw was clenched so tightly, the words barely escaped.

"They don't have to do it here."

Behind my thoughts, my rage, I heard a rustling somewhere. From outside the room? No. From the nearby wall, or perhaps the fireplace. I thought of rats. They were a constant problem in the orchard's storage buildings. But I didn't want to look away from Press.

"Charlotte, they died here."

"They died in the drive."

"It's still our home. Our house. Bliss House isn't just the house—it's everything we own. That I own. I have an obligation."

The rustling got louder. Press glanced away for just a second toward the fireplace.

"It's just a room. You can have it in town at the auditorium. Or if they hadn't been goddamn heathens, you could do it in a church like you would for normal people. You act like it matters, giving them some kind of service. They're probably in hell, anyway."

My breath came short and my body was flushed with heat. The sounds from the fireplace were louder, more violent, as though the chimney were about to collapse. I wasn't sure how much longer we could ignore them.

In my heels I was almost two inches taller than Press, but his body filled the space in front of me and I could feel the force, the presence of him overwhelming me.

Then he smiled. It wasn't the same smile that so often charmed me. This was like someone else's cruel smile. It was the first time I had ever felt even a little afraid of him.

We turned as the sounds from the fireplace erupted into a chaos of flying embers and terrible shrieks. Yellow-hot sparks and tiny chunks of burning wood littered the hearth and carpet. Alarmed, I fell back. Press pushed me roughly aside to grab the brass-handled broom hanging near the wood caddy and quickly swept the burning embers back into the fireplace. But the sparking continued, fueled by the vicious tangle of whatever was now wrestling in the fireplace. Rancid tendrils of smoke unfurled around us.

Press thrust the broom at me, shouting "Use this! Keep the fire off the carpet."

I took it without question and hurried to the farthest bits of red smoldering on the antique Yomut carpet. Press had taken the poker and shovel and was gingerly trying to handle the creature— or creatures—scattering the fire. The shrieking was fading, and it would surely end in death. Press suddenly jumped aside, and some mad, flaming *thing* shot past him and into the room.

I screamed.

A trail of embers dropped to the floor, melting into the carpet. The thing hit a row of shelved books, and it, too, fell to the floor, floundering.

The library door opened. Terrance, with more speed than I could imagine him capable of, grabbed the brown cashmere throw blanket from where it sat on a chair and tossed it on the thing. I watched as the throw lifted and fell, lifted and fell, until it shuddered to a stop.

Whatever was left in the fireplace gave a loud *pop* and whistled finally into silence.

"Miss Charlotte, let me." Marlene took the broom from me. In the flurry, I'd forgotten the smoldering bits of wood on the carpet. Fortunately, most had burned themselves out.

I went to the fireplace where Press stood looking down into the scattered logs. Among the squarish chunks of spent firewood, something long and twisted lay draped like a thick piece of rope. As I watched, it moved slowly as though it were trying to turn itself over. Then it was still.

"Snake." Preston jabbed at it. "Not a very big one." He turned, pointing the poker at where Terrance stood across the room. "I believe that was a raven."

Terrance had picked up the other creature in the ruined blanket. He folded back the edge so we could see the limp body of the bird.

Chapter 10

The Magic Lantern

Dense silver clouds from the previous day hung over the house all through the night, pressing against the windows as though they would come inside. The bedroom itself was cast in gray as I rose groggily from my bed in the steely morning light to retrieve my robe from the closet. Before I could put it on, I doubled over in a fit of coughing. My hands still smelled of smoke, even though I had scrubbed them, and Terrance and Marlene had left all the windows on the first floor open until well after nine the previous night.

We'd had a damp, rather dismal dinner in the dining room. Press made a weak joke about Marlene serving us roasted raven, but when neither Nonie nor I laughed, he looked down at his plate and was uncharacteristically reticent for the rest of the meal.

"I'm going for a walk," he said when we were finished. "Care to join me?"

Given the argument we'd had just two hours earlier, I thought he was being sarcastic. I was surprised to see that his face was serious.

"I don't think so."

I could feel Nonie's eyes on us. Had she heard the argument in the library? Bliss House was big, and sound didn't travel well through its walls. Or perhaps she was just being her discreet self.

Press nodded and excused himself. As he left the room, he ran a hand over Michael's head, making him squawk with pleasure.

"Daddy!"

Press went through the kitchen door, which meant he was probably going to the mudroom for his boots and thus would presumably be walking in the orchards rather than on the lane. It felt strange not to care that he was upset with me. My head was too full of the screams of the bird, and the look of Press's smile. I wasn't sure what either meant. I felt confused and angry.

Five hours later, while the rest of the house was sleeping, I found myself still awake, unable to settle. Terrified that I would be awake until dawn—Bliss House, no matter how familiar it feels, is no place to wander or wonder in the loneliest part of the night—my resolve not to take the sleeping medication that Jack had prescribed gave out, and I put several drops in some water and drank it. Not long after, I fell into a dreamless, uninterrupted sleep.

After breakfast in my room, I started down the gallery to the nursery, stopping in front of Press's door to listen. Nothing. Was he even inside? I put my hand on the doorknob, but then didn't turn it.

In the nursery, I found Michael again sleeping later than usual. The shades were still drawn, and the weak daylight barely showed around their edges. Standing over my son's crib, I let my hand hover a bare inch above his damp forehead, not touching so he wouldn't wake. His mouth was open, and his breath made a little hum as he exhaled. I longed to trace the sweet curve of his tiny lips. Before Eva was gone, I had prayed that he would be kind and smart. But now I only prayed that he would live.

Eva's trundle bed across the room was made up with its ruffle-edge coverlet and sham over its single pillow. On it, I could see the outlines of the rubber-faced Lassie dog my father had given her and Buttercup, one of her favorite dolls. The rest of her toys lived on shelves, safe from Michael's curious, careless hands. She had let him play frequently with the Lassie, not minding that he would pull it to the floor, laughing, then drop onto it with a loud *oomph*, and laugh some more. There was no reason now not to let him play with everything. But it didn't seem right. I felt protective of her things, as though they'd become mine. Or as though she might come back and want them.

Leaving Marlene in Olivia's bedroom to sort through clothes, I went into the morning room and shut the door between us. Marlene had been solemn, but I could tell she was pleased when I'd told her she could take whatever clothes she wanted for herself before sending the rest into town for the thrift store. She and Olivia were about the same size, and as she held up one dress after another in front of the mirror, she looked like a different woman. I rarely saw her out of her shapeless, uniform-style dresses. But when I suggested that it would be fine with me if she wore other, more comfortable clothes—Olivia's or her own—when we weren't entertaining, she had looked offended.

"Is there something wrong with my dresses, Miss Charlotte?"

"Of course not. I just thought you might be—I don't know, Marlene—bored." Realizing I'd made some kind of mistake, I immediately tried to take it back and apologized. (Something Press would've frowned on, I knew.) "I'm sorry. I didn't mean anything by it."

"Mrs. Bliss never objected. Did Mr. Preston say something?" Frown lines creased her soft, pleasant brow.

I shook my head. "Please forget I said anything at all. It's not really my business what you wear." My departure from the room was probably quicker than was strictly decorous. I couldn't help but be embarrassed. Along with everything else that had happened, it was going to be a long time before I got used to dealing with Marlene and Terrance by myself. But Terrance worried me more than Marlene. I was awkward with her, yes, but I found him puzzling. He had started taking his instructions, I assumed, from Press. Or perhaps he had been here so long that he didn't need any instruction at all.

The morning room, on the west side of the house, was even less bright than my own bedroom this early in the day. As I opened the windows, I could see beyond the garden and into the changing trees whose colors moped against the pearly gray of the sky. By the end of the month, we would be able to see all the way out to the swimming pool that sat in a small clearing in the trees. It was a strange place for a swimming pool. Olivia hadn't wanted it in view of the house and gardens, and I suspected it had something to do with her sense of personal modesty. The shade that covered it meant that the well water that filled it rarely got above the frigid temperature it had been when in the ground. In the fall, the pool filled with leaves that had to be dredged out by the part-time gardener. When my eyes lighted on Eva's little playhouse on the path, I turned back to the room.

All around me, the children in the portraits stared or looked away, depending on where the portraits were hung. Why so many

85

children? Most of them girls. Yet Press, Olivia's only child, had been a boy. I wondered if she had been disappointed to not have a girl instead. Had Eva filled that need for her? I certainly hadn't been any kind of daughter to her.

There had been times when I'd wished for a closer relationship with her, but I was shy, and Olivia, while kind and generous, had been as emotionally distant with me as she was with Press. How strange it must have been for the two of them, living in Bliss House all those years together. If Press had been closer to her, I suspect I might have felt more encouraged. They were always polite but distant with each other, as though she were a fond aunt and he a dutiful nephew.

It made me happy that she had seemed to want to be closer to Eva. That past spring, she'd begun to let Eva occasionally come into the morning room when she was having her late-morning tea. I had looked across the hall one morning to see Eva tapping politely on the morning-room door, waiting until Olivia answered. Had Olivia shown her the toys in the closet? Eva had never said, but I knew that if I had been the inquisitive four-year-old my daughter was, I couldn't have resisted asking what was behind the door. I'm certain she would've been frightened of the hideous taxidermy animals. I should have asked Press if he knew where they'd come from, but I never did.

With the windows open, the room quickly turned humid. October rain didn't yet mean it was cold outside. Still, it was pleasant—particularly during that time of day, before the sun bled through the windows. I decided that if the room were ever to be mine, I would have to change it. The wallpaper and the paintings felt oppressive. Yet even though I felt watched, overwhelmed, I also felt a sense of belonging. All those years, I'd been an outsider in Olivia's small world, and now it was my world. It felt right that Eva had spent time there too.

But what I'd come into the room for was not in the room itself, but in the closet.

I had opened the windows and looked outside. I had looked at the portraits. I had thought much about my daughter and the former owner of the room. Why was I hesitating? I knew the thing that waited for me in the closet was important. Olivia had meant for me to find it. I didn't know what was under the drape, but when I'd touched it, a kind of current had run through my body. Yes, Olivia had meant for me to find it.

Despite the dustiness of the articles on the shelves, the fitted drape was pristine. I lifted it away, folded it, and carefully put it aside. A small brass plaque on the side of the antique projector I'd revealed read PALMER'S MAGIC LANTERN.

Terrance removed a table lamp and a set of porcelain dogs from a small drop-leaf table that was against the wall, and set them on the desk.

"Mrs. Olivia Bliss liked to use the lantern in the evening sometimes. I'm sorry to say that we no longer have the screen, Miss Charlotte, but I can hang a sheet on the wall for you."

"Where did the slides come from? There are so many." I stood in the open doorway of the closet, looking at the boxes. Like the lantern itself, the individual boxes were heavy, but the boxes weren't so heavy that I couldn't carry them myself. I lifted one from the shelf.

"Family, I believe." That was the only answer I got from him.

He moved the table into the middle of the room and took down the paintings from the facing wall. Despite his slenderness and age, he didn't struggle at all with the projector in the way that I had. I could only lift it an inch from the floor. As he carried it to the table, I stayed near him, my arms held out in a pantomime of helpfulness. When it was settled, he breathed forcefully—it might have been a sigh. I wasn't sure.

"Shall I put the sheet up for you tonight, Miss Charlotte?"

I glanced wistfully at the tall windows. It hadn't gotten any grayer outside, but then it wasn't turning sunny, either.

"I can put it up right away if you like. The curtains can be closed."

While I usually tried not to be any more trouble than I needed to be, my desire to see the slides overrode any thoughts of Terrance's inconvenience. He did, after all, work for me. I smiled.

"I'd like that, thank you. Will you show me how to use it?"

Chapter 11

Another World

Virginia history is in my blood. I didn't have to read much about it in books, because much of my family, particularly my father's sisters, talked about it as though it had happened in their lifetimes. Neighbors and acquaintances identified themselves by their links to the Revolutionary or the Civil War, and there were a few people still alive who had witnessed the latter. One of my very distant uncles had served under General Washington, and as Virginians my family's loyalties were hardly split when it came to the Civil War—or The Recent Unpleasantness, as one of my aunts liked to call it. As a child, all my school holidays were spent tromping around battlefields with my father: New Market, Fredericksburg, Fort Sumter, Shiloh, Gettysburg, Malvern Hill.

But college showed me so much more. We took bus trips to Washington, D.C., and New York City. We prowled through museums and great houses. We stood quietly in artists' studios, letting the smell of oil paint permeate our skin while we listened to artists tell their stories as they worked. (Painters have a reputation as introverts, but the ones I met were full of information—gossip and history and opinions of the world that were remarkably observant. And they loved an audience.) Back at school, I reveled in my art and art history classes. Painting or drawing, and often sitting in the dark auditorium staring up at slides of the artwork that wasn't readily available to us. Artwork from the Louvre and Florence and Amsterdam. Of course, many of the girls at school had traveled extensively and found the classes dull. But that was never true for me.

As I sat in Olivia's morning room, the curtains drawn, a cooling pot of tea nearby, I tried to remember the way I'd felt at school: calm but ready for something new. I closed my eyes, resting in the quiet, listening to the electrical hum of the projector. Had my last days of calm really been before I'd married Press and come to this place? If anyone had asked me weeks or even a few years earlier, surely I would have said that I was happy. I loved my children. I loved Press. Didn't I love him? Now I just felt like I didn't know him. He had always given me everything I needed. If I had suspected him of being selfish, it wasn't that he had kept things that were rightfully mine for himself. With me he was always generous—even if he wasn't quite with others.

A few hours earlier, I had wondered what he would think of my being in this room, looking at these old slides. I doubted that he would care. As much as he professed to love us, and loved Bliss House, he was so often elsewhere. But I belonged where I was, and had a feeling that he wouldn't believe me if I told him how the room itself seemed to sigh with pleasure, grateful to have me there.

Anxious not to spoil the aura of adventure about what I was doing, I chose sections of slides to view at random, rather than begin with the box labeled A–F.

Terrance had given me careful instructions, and I handled the slides gingerly, doing my best not to touch the housing that had turned dangerously warm when the bulb was lighted.

I almost wept at the beauty of those first images. It was Paris—
a place I'd never been. Press had promised that we would go,
someday. More than ten years after the last World War, it was a
popular place for honeymoons. Jack and Rachel had gone, and
Rachel had come back with a trunk full of expensive, perfectly
tailored dresses and suits.

These images were more than a half century old, even from the
1890s and earlier. There were, of course, the obligatory shots of
the Eiffel Tower, the Arc de Triomphe, the palace at Versailles, the
stately Louvre with its parade of windows and chimneys. Carefully
framed shots that must have been taken by professional photogra-
phers, then hand-colored. The skies were a perfect blue, the stone of
Notre Dame a sallow cream, down to the shadowy arches fanning
into the doors of its western face. Such rich, extravagant color, as
though the photographer had invented each blue, each bit of yellow
in the cathedral windows and dabbed red in the flag or on a man's
cap just in that moment, just for that picture. Was it real? No. It was
day, and no doubt the colors would be dull in the sunlight from the
outside. But this was a fantasy world. The perfect colors gave each
location a kind of fairytale quality as though they were in a Paris
that never rained, that was never smudged with coal smoke or grit.

The streets of this Paris were nearly empty of people and car-
riages. No cars. The focus was on the architecture, the structures'
forms and lines.

The flowers in the Jardin du Luxembourg in front of the palace
were like jewels, the grass beyond a fervent green, the palace solid
and settled in its landscape like a dowager queen.

There were landscapes, too, of beaches and a mountainous area
that was nothing like our nearby Blue Ridge. These mountains
looked less populated, with the occasional tidy valley village nestled
between them. Pristine mountain lakes, again colored a luminous
blue, against forests of near-black pine trees and jagged gray rock
faces. No people. How happy could I be, standing in the shallows

of one of these remote lakes, listening to the birds, small fish fluttering around my ankles? Alone.

I had never lived alone for more than a week at a time. The idea at once thrilled and frightened me. Olivia had never lived alone until her husband died. Nor had my own mother or Nonie. We were all, always, attached to men. Fathers or husbands or employers or children. Could I ever live on my own, given the chance? Was I strong enough?

Yet even as I sat there alone, I wasn't seeking solitude, but Olivia.

Going back to the first box, I found an alphabet series. These weren't photographs, but illustrations of animals, each paired with a number from one to twelve. Holding them up to the light before putting them in the machine, I wasn't alarmed, and thought they might be fun for Michael to look at. Even the first one—eight Adders on Ladders (the ladders forming the letter A)—seemed odd, but clever. But when I reached seven Cavorting Cockroaches forming the letter C on the shirtfront of a horrified little boy, and then got to four Murderous Marmosets with exaggerated claws extended, teeth bared and silvery fur dangerously spiked, I stopped looking for more. Had Press been forced to see these hideous slides? They were the stuff of nightmares.

I was relieved to come to several slides of an enormous meadow dotted with hot-air balloons, probably the beginning or end of a race, shot from a hillside. Three teenaged boys in clothes from a generation past stood in the foreground, leaning on one another, watching the balloons. One of the boys looked back over his shoulder squinting at the camera, his shoulder hiding the lower part of his jaw as though he didn't want his whole face to be seen. I wondered how long he had stared at the photographer to make his face so clear in the image. Unlike the other boys, he wore no cap, and with his narrowed eyes and lanky black hair he reminded me of one of a pair of twins I'd known in primary school. Boys who had tormented even older children, pelting them with rocks from behind an old shed that sat on the road near the school. It was rumored that they had once tied the tails of two cats together just to watch them fight. As I stared at the boy's unpleasant face, one of his eyelids dropped in a lascivious wink.

I gasped, disbelieving. But then he was still again. Beyond him, the two other boys then seemed to come to life. The second boy, the one with white-blond hair, turned his head slowly to look at the third boy. He inclined his forehead so that it rested against the hair just above the third boy's ear. I knew that profile, that tall forehead and the permanent look of hauteur. But that hauteur melted as he tenderly nuzzled the third boy's cheek and the lobe of his ear. I knew I should look away. I knew that what I was seeing couldn't possibly be real. And yet, when the third boy suddenly turned to face the second and roughly grabbed the back of the white-blond head, and kissed him with sudden violence, I knew the feel of that kiss, the fullness of those lips against mine. I put my hand to my throat and closed my eyes, terrified.

At a tap on the door, I opened my eyes. The teenagers on the screen had returned to being anonymous figures who certainly didn't at all resemble my husband and his best friend.

What was wrong with me that I'd imagined such a thing? Something I couldn't have even conceived of in my most secret thoughts?

"Charlotte?" Nonie opened the door from the hall a few inches. "Are you asleep?"

Embarrassed, I tried to keep my voice light. "Of course I'm not asleep. I don't need a nap."

"Are you coming down to dinner?"

Dinner? I looked around the dim room. There was no clock, and I didn't remember seeing a clock. Glancing at the curtains closed over the window, I could see the light had faded significantly.

"What time is it?"

"Why are the lights off? What are you doing in here?" Nonie used a voice I hadn't heard in a long time. I felt seven years old.

I moved to switch off the lantern, but my hand brushed the searing housing instead and I cried out.

Nonie rushed inside, bringing in a soft unfocused light from the hallway with her. Then she pressed the wall switch, flooding the room with light. I brought my injured hand to my eyes.

"I'm not doing anything wrong, if that's what you're thinking." I spoke harshly without meaning to.

Nonie ignored me, anyway. "Let me see." She took my wrist and inspected the burn. "The aloe plant is in the butler's pantry. We'll put some on it when we go down." Looking at me closely, she let go of my wrist and touched the sleeve of my blouse. I couldn't remember shedding my sweater.

"You're soaking. It's like a furnace in here." She looked around. "What's that smell? Like something burning."

I waved my hand. "Me?" I said, trying to be funny to make up for my harshness.

Her eyes rested on the lantern and the boxes of slides piled beside it.

"I meant to show you this," I said. "You said you hadn't seen one in a long time."

She shook her head. "Not since I was twenty or so. Though even by then, not many people used them, except for. . . ."

"Except for what?"

A flush of heat came over Nonie's face. Whether from the temperature of the room, or what she was about to say, I wasn't sure. It *was* awfully warm. Sweat had gathered in a rivulet between my breasts, and the seams of my blouse under my arms were wet.

"You need to come downstairs, but you don't want to come to the table like that. I'll go lay something out for you." She started out of the room.

"But what do you mean? Tell me."

Nonie turned in the doorway. "Just be careful what you look at in there. But I suppose Olivia Bliss was probably not the kind of person to own *those* sorts of pictures."

"Oh."

I finally understood. She meant just the sort of pictures I'd just seen: people like Press and Jack doing unspeakable things. But I couldn't have seen what I had seen. They were slides, not films. It wasn't possible. They were just innocent pictures.

She sighed. "I'll go lay out your clothes. Hurry. Your husband's already at the table with Michael."

"Press is home?"

"You don't think I would leave Michael by himself in the dining room, do you?"

"Did he say anything?"

"He just came in. Terrance gave him a Scotch, and he asked where you were. I thought it best that I come find you."

Press was home, and I'd been pulled back into my life. I looked at the boxes of slides and the cooling lantern. What were these things, and what did it all mean?

I carefully unplugged the lantern from the wall socket and tucked the cord beneath the table so no one might trip on it. I wasn't sure I wanted to ever turn the thing on again.

Chapter 12

Enchantment

Mommy.

What mother doesn't wake when her child whispers her name? When it comes in the night, a whisper is more alarming than a cry. Grateful that I hadn't taken the sleeping drops, I threw back the covers and felt for my robe. Finding it near the end of the bed, I put it on, forgetting for just a moment that Eva wasn't really there whispering for me. But from the depths of my disappointment came the realization that *someone* had called for me.

There was enough moonlight to see my way across the room. My door, which was always closed when I slept, stood open to the gallery.

Mommy.

Footsteps outside my room. Light, running footsteps. Thinking it might be Michael looking for me, I started down the gallery to the nursery fully awake, my heart quickened by the voice.

Mommy. Mommy. Mommy.

Was it Eva's voice? It was young. Feminine. I wanted it to be Eva, but there was something teasing in the sound.

It seemed to come from everywhere. First, a few feet ahead of me. Now, near the back stairs. Then from the hall below. Above me, the stars painted on the dome were mute, the chandelier a silhouette in the moonlight from the clerestory windows. I knew that everyone in Bliss House was asleep, but the night around me felt wakeful, as though something were going on behind one of the closed bedroom doors. Only Olivia's bedroom door was open, and, beside it, a faint light shone beneath the morning-room door. As I watched, the light faded and brightened, like a stuttering flame. Had Eva awakened me to warn me of a fire? It seemed possible.

I was close to Press's door but, afraid of appearing foolish, I chose not to wake him right away. And if it really were Eva, what would I do? God help me, I couldn't bear the thought of sharing her with him. He didn't deserve her.

I crossed the gallery and, taking a deep breath to calm the pounding of my heart (pounding, yes—even though I would never be afraid of my own child), I put my hand on the shining brass knob of the morning-room door. To say it was cold was an understatement, like saying a 104-degree day was a little warm. I drew my hand back and pressed it to my mouth, breathing into it to lessen the sting. When I reached for the knob again, I used the sleeve of my robe, but it made little difference. As soon as the knob was free of its catch, I pushed the door open with my shoulder. Even through my robe I could feel that the door itself was like a block of ice. The hinges—always kept oiled by the dedicated Terrance—complained of the cold as well.

I hesitated before I went inside, remembering the image of the teenage boys. But Eva had called me, so I had to go on.

Inside? How to tell you. . . .

The morning room was transformed. Frigid with cold. No. Not just cold, but with a frost that hid the true nature of every surface, as though every object had been fitted with a glittering pavé of tiny diamonds. Shaken and uncertain, I turned to look behind me into the hallway. I was still in the house and hadn't been swept into some dream place or other universe.

I stepped inside, hoping to see Eva. Will you believe me when I tell you that the door closed slowly behind me? I was so stunned by what I was seeing, I didn't see it close but only heard it catch, softly, as though it had been shut with great care. Had it slammed, I might have screamed. That would have brought Press, and perhaps Terrance and Marlene and Nonie, running to find me. It might have changed everything that happened later: I might never have seen what Olivia wanted to show me, and perhaps no one else would have died that dreadful October.

There was no Eva. But all around me, despite the cold, which was oddly flat and without sting, was the smell of roses. Not the fresh, ethereal scent of newly opened buds, but roses whose scent was fecund almost to the point of rot. I covered my mouth with my hand.

The light still flickered erratically, as in an old film. I saw the reflection in the windows first because the curtains had been pulled aside. Who had done that? Terrance, perhaps, thinking I would not be back in the room that night? I crossed the room to the chaise longue beneath the windows and picked up the folded mohair blanket that Olivia had kept there for reading on cool days. Frost crystals flew about like sprites as I shook the blanket in the air and then wrapped it around me. Clutching it close against the cold, I saw my own shape in the glass, surrounded by a bright halo. A delicate layer of frost covered the glass, but when I touched it I found the surface smooth. The frost seemed to be on the other side of the mirror.

You're wondering about the source of the light. I didn't want to look at it, because I knew what it was and I was afraid. I think I knew what it was even before I crossed the gallery.

The sheet that Terrance had hung was filled with light from the lantern, which sat silently on its table, untouched by the frost. The sheet itself was also dull in comparison to everything around it—even the paintings had been turned into winterscapes.

You might think that I was brave to remain in that enchanted, terrifying room. There have been things that I've done, things I've had to contend with as mistress of Bliss House, that I never would have imagined I could live through. But I am a mother and was a mother then. There is something sacred about being a mother. Not necessarily holy, but at least unique in the sense that there is nothing else in the world to compare to it. I have read stories about men in battle dying for one another, their intimacy a creation of their vulnerability in the face of a common enemy. But the danger needn't be great for a mother to feel an intense need to protect her child, and it doesn't matter to her if her actions appear irrational to someone on the outside. They are rational within the universe created by the bond between her and her child. Even her fear of death is secondary to the possibility of her child suffering for even one moment out of a single day. A single hour.

Eva had suffered. Was she still suffering? I only knew that I hadn't been there when she had needed me most. I had compromised the bond between us. I had failed her, and I was desperate for her to forgive me. I wanted another chance.

Wrapping the blanket more tightly around me, I brushed the frost from the seat of the upholstered chair Terrance had moved in front of the makeshift screen earlier in the day, and sat down with my legs tucked under me for warmth. I didn't speculate on why it was so cold, remembering the cold draft where Olivia had stood in the dining room. If it was cold, I reasoned, Olivia was near.

Chapter 13

Olivia Revealed

She *was* there, of course, on the screen. Waiting for me.

This was a younger Olivia than the one in the photo in her room or the portrait in the salon. A girl I might have shared secrets with at Burton Hall, or sat next to on the bus going downtown, our white-gloved hands folded on our laps. A teenaged Olivia, her smooth blond hair parted in the exact center of her head, and two braids twisted into tight spirals that covered her ears. She wore a simple green linen shirtwaist and a familiar look of unwavering confidence. A challenge in her eyes and the open curves of her brows—one of which was ever so slightly lifted. How will you explain yourself to me? Why should I be interested? Seated, her right elbow rested casually on the chair's arm, one of her two long necklaces caught up to dangle from her fingers. It was a perfect picture, except for the angry scar from an accident that she'd had as a child above her right brow.

It surely wasn't possible, but she leaned forward a few inches and beckoned to me. I breathed in sharply.

Watch, Charlotte. Listen.

Olivia's voice, low and relaxed—the same voice she used when reading Eva a story—but coming from far, far away so that I also had to lean forward to hear.

I feared I had gone mad, or might be dreaming, but the cold told me otherwise.

The necklaces dropped from her slender fingers, and she held out her hand.

You must know, Charlotte.

Yes, now I was terribly afraid—not of Olivia herself, but of the fact of what was happening. She was reaching out to me. Did I dare? I rose from the chair, careful not to trip on the blanket. She waited, her hazel eyes more patient than I'd ever known them to be in life. *In life. Surely this was life too.* Her presence was warm. Surreal. Perfect.

I barely felt the cold on my feet as I crossed the few feet of carpet to where she waited. I reached for her hand.

~

It is my betrothal day. Me, Olivia. I can hardly believe it.

My father has not spoken to me for four days, and my mother won't stop talking. I steal a glance at her as she tries to flirt with the attractive dark-eyed boy sitting across from us who looks like he has been kept in a broom closet his entire life, and I want to beg her to be quiet because she sounds like a fool. Look at the boy, Michael Searle Bliss: Did you ever see a boy who was so polite and neat? He's kind to my mother, but I wonder if he isn't patronizing her. Being patronized is the thing she likes best, aside from a coconut blancmange. It makes me want to scream, but she has made her way in the world by pretending to let others advise her while making sure that she gets exactly what she wants. What she wants now is for me to be married and away from the house.

My father and his anger simmer beside me. His fingers grip the knees of his brown wool pants so tightly that his knuckles are white. The lawyer—who, like the tall ugly man with moles on his face and neck, arrived wearing an old-fashioned Homburg even though it's nearly eighty degrees outside—keeps trying to engage him in conversation from where he stands behind Michael Searle's chair. You would think by now that the man would understand that my mother is in charge in this matter.

I've never been alone with Michael Searle Bliss, who is always called by both his first and middle names. He has written me letters—long, rather interesting letters telling me about Virginia and the town of Old Gate, where he lives with his mother, Lucy. Although he is only a year younger than I, the letters are as enthusiastic as if they'd been written by a child. When these letters come, my mother reads them first, but I do not care just as I don't care whom I marry anymore.

There is money enough for me to live on when my parents are dead, but my mother is determined that I should marry. Although I won't complain, as it is the only way I won't have to listen to her constant harping about my stubbornness, my posture, my table manners, anymore. I have only the vaguest idea of how she settled on Michael Searle. It had something to do with our mothers being very distant cousins. Why this rich boy would have any interest in a scarred girl who cares more about accounting for her father's acreage and livestock than throwing parties or running a house, I'm sure I don't know.

But it is why my father is angry. He imagined I would act as the son he never had, taking over the management of his land when he got too old. My father is an abrasive man. He alienated the only other suitor I ever had, calling his Irish family "mackerel-eating papists" during a dinner at which he drank too much wine. Though I suspected he wasn't really as drunk as he pretended. If he were kinder, and my mother less ambitious, I might have stayed with them forever.

I know I should listen to what they're saying. I hear my name, though no one talks to me directly. But the room is hot and I dislike the way the tall, ugly man stares at a point just above my head, as though I am invisible.

There are parties to celebrate our upcoming wedding. More of them are in Raleigh than in Virginia because Michael's mother is still in mourning and is, anyway, rather reclusive. Michael Searle and I smile dimly through them while my mother comments behind her hand about the quality of the wine being served. Many people's stockpiles put by before the Volstead Act are running low, and so the quality is uneven. She embarrasses me, and I try to keep her away from Michael Searle. I've become protective of him, somehow, as though he were a younger brother rather than my betrothed. The parties are a torment. He is a dreadful dancer, and so we sit watching the others. He urges me on, encouraging me to dance with the other young men who politely ask, but I become sad for him when I see him sitting, alone, wearing his mourning armband and smoking cigarette after cigarette. I wonder that he doesn't have any friends. Of course, so many of the young men our age went off to war and died. Perhaps his friends have all died. I do not ask.

At the parties, regardless of the quality of the wine (or gin or bourbon), everyone drinks heavily. Nothing so coarse as bathtub gin—though I have been to hidden roadside taverns, much to the chagrin of my father and the shame of my mother. Michael Searle and I have a fondness for champagne. I think, sometimes, that I would like to drink champagne until I drown in it.

~

Three weeks before the wedding, Michael's mother disappears from Bliss House, and her body is found deep in the woods. When Michael calls to tell me, I try to convince him that my mother and I should come up to help him and be with him. But he tells me it's better that I don't. When I do see him, there is a new sadness in his eyes and he tells me that he has found morphine in her room, that everyone thinks she died of a heart attack, but he fears she was an addict. It's deeply shocking, and I cannot reconcile his words with the kind woman who had already welcomed me as a daughter and pressed several pieces of her elegant jewelry on me. I have heard of people becoming slaves to morphine and opium, but I have never known anyone personally. My father wants to call off the wedding because her death is a bad omen, but my mother says that I must decide. I tell her that there is no reason at all that I shouldn't marry Michael Searle, though I'm not sure if I am marrying him because I care about him, or because I pity him.

The wedding is my mother's day. Her triumph is twofold: that, at twenty-four, I am still a virgin; and I will marry into great wealth. My bosom friend from childhood, Margaret, who is lately married herself, has tears in her eyes as I hand my fragrant sweet pea and rose bouquet to her to hold at the altar.

Michael Searle finally comes to me our first night on the SS Leviathan. On the train, and at the hotel in New York, we had separate rooms. I didn't understand, and was too shy to ask why. My less-than-demonstrative parents have always shared a bedroom, a bed. I'm not naïve. I raised rabbits to sell for meat. I have seen cows and bulls in the fields. My dearest Margaret told me what happened on her wedding night, how she'd been alarmed at first, but then was happy. So very happy.

I fear I will never have children.

He asks me at dinner if he can come to my cabin. We wear our traveling clothes, still, as is the custom for the first night of a voyage. My costume is from Paris, a gift from Michael Searle's mother, who was so much more stylish than my own mother. I wear the peacock brooch she gave me as well. Very precious. Very expensive. I think it impressed my mother, as so many things about the Bliss family do.

We sit side by side on the banquette, looking out at the room at all the guests. I scorn my mother because of her affection for rich things, but I am dazzled by the long ropes of pearls, the beauty of the women, so many so daring in their very short dresses. I have finally bobbed my hair, against my father's wishes. But I am a married woman and I have left his house forever.

Michael Searle touches my hand beneath the table. He has kissed me more than once. Timid but lovely kisses that, indeed, rouse something in me even though I don't swoon when I see him, as dear Margaret tells me she does whenever she has been separated from her Roger for more than a day. When Michael Searle slides his hand onto my thigh beneath the table, I reach for it, scandalized but thrilled, and I find it trembling beneath mine. "May I come to your cabin tonight?" he whispers. "Please?" His breath hints of the bourbon he's poured into our Coca-Colas from his flask (the ship is dry, and we have both bourbon and wine hidden in our trunks) and cigarette smoke, which by no means repels me. I am a secret smoker like so many of my friends. He didn't know it about me until I asked him for a cigarette on the train. We are strangers in so many ways.

Michael Searle is shy and kind. He never bullies or shames me. Is it any wonder that I was happy to leave my father's house, even to enter some other form of bondage?

Each of the preceding nights, I'd put on the delicate ivory silk nightgown and feather-trimmed robe my mother bought for my trousseau. Waiting. Eventually I fell asleep, to awaken to a faint knock on my door from the train matron or the hotel maid, suggesting breakfast. This night, I have sprinkled it with a bit of the precious Chanel No. 5 Michael Searle gave me for my birthday.

Now that it will happen, I am nervous. My stomach and my head feel light, as though I haven't eaten dinner at all. When the light tap comes on the door, I startle.

Michael Searle is calmer, much less agitated than he was at dinner. And also, like me, perhaps a little drunk. We sit on the tiny sofa beneath the porthole and drink wine, talking about the dinner, the music, what we will do when we get to England and Paris. The Great War has been over for several years, but neither of us has been to Europe and we aren't sure what to expect.

Finally, the pauses between our words, our sentences, become longer. I am relaxed and begin to feel myself flag. I want something to happen. The thing that made Margaret giggle as we sat in the Hotel Baltimore in Raleigh, having tea at the table near the fountain.

The single lamp beside the bed suddenly dims, startling us both, and we laugh. Michael Searle gets up and turns it off. I can see him in shadow. I am no longer so nervous.

"Olivia." His voice is a whisper, but I hear sadness in it. "I'll try to make you happy. Forgive me if I can't. Will you forgive me?"

I don't know how to answer. I have never thought too much of being happy. After my accident, I became used to being pointed at and whispered about. I became brave and aloof instead of frightened in the face of unpleasantness. Thank God for dear Margaret! She sees beyond my face. My bravado. But the house—Bliss House—that is now ours together frightens me. On my visits, Michael Searle showed me all of it, from the servants' rooms to the places he'd hidden to play as a lonely little boy (How could he be otherwise? He had few friends, he told me.) to the roof with its magnificent view and strange collection of tiny shacks. At night, lying alone in one of the bedrooms near the back stairs, I heard sobbing and laughter and footsteps coming from the third floor when everyone else was asleep and there were no other guests besides my mother. She heard nothing, and so the sounds must not exist. They must not matter.

"We have to choose to be happy, Olivia. You know it as well as I."

I choose to trust him.

I have never been naked in front of a man before, and my mother has hinted that it isn't necessary if I don't want it to be that way. But the wine makes me bold, and although he looks politely away, I notice a small tremble on his lips that I can see even in shadow. I take off my robe and untie the front of my gown so that it hangs open, partially exposing my breasts.

Michael lays his blue velvet smoking jacket over the back of the chair. I am surprised to see that beneath it, he wears a long old-fashioned nightshirt tucked into his pants. But who am I to judge? I know so little about men.

Margaret has told me enough that I believe my mother wrong—that I should not simply bear what will happen to me, and that I should touch him in ways similar to the ways in which he touches me. He is tender enough, lightly pushing my gown away so that it falls from me. Kissing my shoulder, the crook of my elbow, my wrist. Approaching me gently. Kissing me deeply, bringing more than a flutter of a response to my body.

How does he know what to do? I had taken his trembling for fear. But had it been desire? Anticipation?

He helps me onto the bed. We can feel the vibration of the ship, hear the constant hum of the engines. He lies atop me but not so that he puts his full weight on me, and takes my face in his hands. He wears no scent but smells faintly of perspiration and the ship's lavender soap. We've never spoken of my scar. Sometimes, in fact, I even forget that it is there. Now he puts his lips to it and I feel his breath on my face. No man, not even the young Irish boy who cared for me, had ever kissed that most tender place. Something inside me breaks: the embarrassment, the fear, the years of my mother looking hopefully at my male friends, praying that one might take pity on me and marry me. It wasn't that I believed I was ugly or unlovable. It was the sense that I had disappointed. Always disappointed. It almost made me bitter.

Almost.

Each night of the crossing, and in England, before we arrive in Paris, he comes to me. Touches me. His lips on my face, my breasts. His hands running over my body, searching. Searing me. Causing me to put my hand to my mouth so the others on our corridor won't hear.

But he never removes his nightshirt, and he gently pushes my hands away or stops me with a kiss when I try to do it for him.

"Wait," he says. "Soon."

I wait. I want to write to Margaret to ask her what to do, but the post would take too long. By the time a letter reaches her we will be leaving Paris. Waiting is all I can do.

Before another ship returns us to New York a month later, I am in love with this gentle man who makes me laugh and makes me wait. I find myself looking for his face if we are separated in a crowd, or if I leave my room to go down to breakfast before he has left his room. He knows so much. His dark eyes are intelligent and he knows the histories of so many of the pieces of art we see, he knows the cities from studying maps in books, he talks of the places where we will travel later. He knows all about the war, and tells me Germany will never, ever truly give up.

I love him. I trust him.

God forgive him.

⁓

The brief, damp touch of a small hand on my face woke me. I opened my eyes in startlingly bright sunlight to find Eva standing beside me. She looked as pitiful as I had ever seen her, her eyes and face drooping with exhaustion. And she was wet. Her pink cotton playsuit clung to her achingly thin body, exposing the outline of her delicate ribs. Droplets of water emerged from her clinging curls before gathering into rivulets and running into the gray hollows of her cheeks. She wore the same blue velvet ribbon in her hair that I'd seen in my dream, but now it was limp and hung loosely. I tried to reach for her, to smooth the water off of her face, but my arms felt stiff as though invisibly bound and I sobbed in frustration, fearful that she would go away before I could hold her again.

"Eva, baby."

But she was backing away from me, carefully, placing one dirty white sandal behind the other as though following some invisible line.

"No, stay!"

My arms and legs wouldn't move when I tried to reach for her. Even my voice felt mired in my throat. When she turned and ran, I was afraid she would collide with the room's heavy furniture and hurt herself. But of course the dead can't be hurt.

Her footsteps echoed in the vast hall as she disappeared.

Thrashing against whatever was binding me, I finally pulled free, only to fall to the floor.

Opening my eyes again, I saw that the door to the hallway was shut. I understood that I had probably been dreaming.

The fall had hurt; I lay on my side, the mohair blanket wound around my body. My mouth was so dry, I could hardly open it. One arm was caught beneath me, and my free hand clutched a limp sprig of goldenrod.

Disengaging myself from the blanket, I stood up. My bones felt hollow and my muscles ached. Limping from stiffness, I went to the lantern and laid the sprig of goldenrod beside it. The sheet on the wall was blank and dingy gray in the weak morning light.

I was filled with pity for Olivia. For myself. I rested my fingers on the cold lantern and looked down. My heart seemed to stop for an eternity.

The plug lay untouched, exactly where I had left it the evening before.

Chapter 14

Escape

I approached the morning cautiously, wondering if I would ever feel quite complete again. My experience with Olivia had depleted me, leaving the inside of my head feeling as though it had been scrubbed out with lye or something equally caustic. When I looked in the mirror, it seemed to me that I was paler than usual. My hair badly needed a trim. It was Tuesday, my usual day at the hairdresser's, but I couldn't imagine going into the beauty shop and facing all the inquisitive, sympathetic women who would surely be there. Did it matter how I looked? Not to me. I was beginning to think that it didn't matter to Press, either, and perhaps hadn't mattered to him in a long while.

No. That wasn't fair of me to think or say. Not then. When I thought back to the months and years before Olivia died, I was certain he had once loved me deeply. Not with an unreserved passion, but he'd loved me enough. At least that's how I remember our time together. The passion between us—physical as well as emotional—had been real. Our plans for our future had been real.

Now there was hammering and laughter and the smell of cigarette smoke from the theater on the third floor, a sign that all was no longer wonderful between us. It was as though he had chosen a different future.

"He's grieving," Nonie had told me. "Maybe this is his way." But her voice hadn't held any conviction. Just as she knew when I was lying, I knew when she was trying to make me feel better.

By the time I'd showered and eaten breakfast, taken a walk with Michael, and spent an hour looking at books with him in the nursery, I knew I was just putting off the moment when I would go back into the morning room. For I *would* go back there.

In the kitchen, I mentioned to Marlene and Terrance that J. C. Jaquith would be arriving the next day, and that they should get a guest room ready, and that we would probably be having a small dinner party. As I explained, I could see from the tolerant looks on their faces that Press had already told them. They were humoring me: "Flowers in the guest room, Miss Charlotte? Beef for dinner, as Mr. and Mrs. Carstairs will be dining?" They obviously considered Press to be the one who was really in charge, not me. Had Terrance been like that with Olivia and Press's father before he died? I tried to imagine the gentle Michael Searle going behind Olivia's back, making arrangements for guests. I wished I had known him. I wished Olivia had let me know her better.

⌒

"Charlotte Bliss, where are you?" Always unpredictable, Rachel had let herself in the front door with a great, undignified shout.

I was sitting briefly in Nonie's room, where she was watching a daytime talk program on one of the two television channels we could receive, with Michael playing with blocks on the floor nearby. Her room was close to the nursery at the front of the house, and the door was open, so Rachel's entry was clearly audible. Nonie raised her eyebrows, but I couldn't help but smile.

Would Rachel have announced herself that way if Olivia had been alive? Absolutely not. If Press had been home? Maybe. But it heartened me that she thought I wouldn't mind.

I leaned over the gallery railing.

"Here we are, Rachel."

She peered up at me.

When she saw my drab day dress, she waved a dismissive hand. "What are you wearing? You all look like one of those sad ladies in a vacuum cleaner advertisement. The *before* picture—you know, when she's all covered up in dust bunnies and baby goo."

I smiled. "You're too kind." Seeing her enormous stomach again, I thought I'd better go down to meet her, rather than ask her to come up. I hurried downstairs.

"You look wonderful. As always. You're glowing." I kissed her cheek.

Rachel looked down and lightly touched the pouf of fuchsia below the empire waist of her top.

"Balls! I am not. I'm hardly showing at all." She grinned at her own joke.

In truth, Rachel was almost always glowing. It was only when she was sick with the flu or some other malady that she didn't look her best. Even then, she simply looked wan, like the exotic heroine of a dime-store novel.

I noticed Terrance standing respectfully at the entrance to the dining room. All morning, I'd been wrestling with the desire to ask him about Michael Searle and Olivia.

"Yes, Terrance?"

"Shall I prepare some iced tea, ma'am? A plate of cakes in the morning room?"

The lantern was still set up in the morning room, and the thought of Rachel seeing it worried me. What would she say about it? I had told her about seeing Olivia, but she would truly think me insane if I described what I'd seen only hours earlier. And I would never in a million years tell her what I'd seen between the boys who looked like Jack and Press.

"How about the salon?" I looked at Rachel.

"Just bring them up to milady's room, Terrance. I'm going to get this beastly girl into some proper clothes and take her away for a civilized lunch. I may not even bring her back until tomorrow. How's that for a scandal?"

"Very good, Miss Rachel."

Terrance returned to the kitchen.

"Rachel, I can't go anywhere. I really don't want to see anyone." Except for my brief visit to her house, I hadn't been out since the funeral. The idea of being around a crowd caused my gut to seize with panic. Not only was it too soon, but there would be the stares. I was the woman who had gotten drunk and let her daughter die.

"Don't say no, Charlotte. Do it for me. Please?" She took my hand. "Soon I'll be stuck in the house forever. Please? Just for a few hours." Her eyes were pleading, like a child's.

It was a typically selfish rationale, and I almost told her so. "It's too soon. Nonie doesn't feel well today. Michael is such a handful." Yet another lie. It was getting easier. The excuse that Nonie didn't feel well had simply sprung to my lips.

"Marlene is here. You've let Marlene watch the—" Here, she stumbled. Rachel, who hardly ever misspoke, had been about to say "the children." Recovering quickly, she lowered her voice. "I'll speak to Marlene if you want me to. You know she won't mind."

First she had told Terrance that he should take tea to my bedroom, and now she was about to make decisions about with whom Michael should be left. I wasn't in the mood to deal with her bossiness, but

113

somewhere I found the patience to deal with her pleasantly. I tried again to distract her.

"You should take your mother to lunch. What's she doing? You said she was anxious about the baby. Being a grandmother."

Rachel rolled her eyes. "Jesus, Charlotte. She's been practicing her *bubbe* act since I got my first period. Yesterday she decided that the baby's not going to be a boy after all and came back from Lynchburg with a car full of everything pink. She's completely wrong, of course. You have to save me from her."

I glanced up at the gallery, thinking about the morning room. If I left, would I miss my chance to see more? Would Olivia abandon me?

Misunderstanding, Rachel grabbed my hand and held it in both of hers. "Let's get you changed. You know getting away for a while is the best thing." She brought my hand to her lips to give it a quick kiss. "Let's go, darling."

The day was glorious. We wound long silk scarves—mine white, Rachel's a vibrant orange—around our hair and left for The Grange with the windows of the Thunderbird all the way down. Nonie had looked surprised; but when she saw that I was dressed for going out, she shooed me out of the nursery before I could change my mind. Michael had looked up from his blocks and gave me a tight-lipped, dutiful kiss. A few minutes later, as Rachel circled the Thunderbird out of the driveway, I put my head out the window to see Nonie standing behind Michael in the window as he waved *good-bye*.

As we left the lane, heading for town, I felt my heart lighten. I was still anxious, but I was neither at the house without Eva, nor was I yet faced with other people staring at me. Judging me. I was also filled with affection for Rachel—this Rachel. She was the bright, light, fun Rachel I had loved for so long. Most of her pregnancy she'd been cross, complaining that Jack was treating her like an invalid. I wasn't sure how she was feeling about Helen and Zion, but this wasn't the time to ask. She had obviously pushed it away for the time being. Resting my head on the back of the Thunderbird's white leather seat, I felt the sunshine on my face, and let the wind tug at the layers of sadness that had accumulated since Olivia's and Eva's deaths.

When we were finally through Old Gate and on the two-lane highway that would take us within a mile of the old hotel, Rachel slowed a bit and told me to look in the glove box. Inside, I found a leather-covered flask I hadn't seen since our college days, and a pack of Marlboros.

"Good Lord. It's not even lunchtime yet."

"Terrance fed us, right? It's not like we're drinking on an empty stomach. Besides, all I can drink is brandy these days. Everything else makes me throw up."

Alcohol had made me sick during both of my pregnancies. Press had teased me, saying I was a big strong girl and was just pretending to be delicate, but he'd been wrong.

I opened the flask and held it out to Rachel. She drank in small sips, then handed it back to me. "This makes me happy! I'm so glad to get you away."

Lifting the flask to my lips, I tilted it but put my tongue against the opening so that I barely tasted the brandy at all. But I wanted it, God help me. Where was my resolve to never again touch the stuff that had led to Eva's death? And we were on our way to The Grange, which was the social center of our part of the state—a place where I was known. A place where they would all know what had happened to Eva. I might shame myself. Shame Press.

I drank as deeply as I could, given the scorching the stuff gave my throat, and ended by having a coughing fit, holding the flask far away from me so it wouldn't spill. Rachel laughed, saying I drank like a girl.

What a strange thrill it was to be drinking in the open air in the middle of the day, as though we were teenagers again. When my coughing calmed and I could swallow again, I took another, less ambitious drink.

"Light me a cigarette, honey." Rachel gave a little wave toward the glove box. Using the Thunderbird's automatic lighter, I lit a cigarette for Rachel and passed it to her. We weren't driving terribly fast, but the wind caught at the smoke, pulling it in a disappearing stream from Rachel's mouth almost as soon as she exhaled.

"No ciggy for you? You want some of mine?" Rachel held the lipstick-stained end of hers toward me.

"No. Right now, I'm happy." And I almost was. It was the closest I'd come to feeling happy in a long time.

Chapter 15

The Grange

The Grange Hotel was like an oasis in the wilderness, built a decade after the Revolutionary War as an inn for travelers headed across what was then the enormous state of Virginia to points west. But there'd been some change in the road, an exorbitant toll put up by a farmer who owned a small part of the land the road passed through, and his neighbors saw an opportunity and rerouted the road. The hotel suffered from the lack of traffic and the appearance of other, more modern inns, and was bankrupted more than once. But when the Civil War came, it was commissioned to house wounded Confederate officers and spruced up. During the post-war depression it sank back into ignominy, then was finally rescued by a syndicate that included Press's grandfather. I'd witnessed Olivia being treated with a particular kind of reverence when we were there with her. But for the first couple of years of my marriage, the waiters either continued not to recognize me, or pretended not to recognize me when I was there on my own, until I signed the check with "House Account No. 12."

There were only 250 house accounts. Rachel's family didn't even have one. Press said they probably wouldn't ever get one anyway because they were Jewish, and while I could believe it, it made me sad that—after the terrible war in Europe—any Americans could be so cruel.

Bolstered by the brandy, we browsed the hotel's tiny village of shops. Rachel couldn't try any clothes on but pushed several dresses on me with the help of the saleswoman.

"It'll be Thanksgiving before I'm wearing anything but tents. *You* might as well have some fun."

I did talk her into a black-dyed mink headband, as well as a pair of new fawn evening gloves that she would want for New Year's Eve. I bought two dresses, both of which needed to be altered and would be delivered to the house. But when I got to the window display of the children's shop, I froze. It was filled with winter dresses: infant dresses with frothed lace and tiny matching bloomers, larger dresses in silver and bright pink and green, all with crinolines, and a simple red wool skater's dress, covered with white embroidered snowflakes and white triangles inset around the skirt that would show only when the girl wearing it walked or skated. I couldn't stop myself from staring at the skater's dress. It would be just a little too big for Eva this winter, but it was so charming that I would have bought it to put away for next year.

Next year.

"What is it?" Rachel had dawdled in front of the jewelry concession next store, but caught up to me. After an awkward moment, she said "Let's go eat. I'm hungry."

When she tried to take my arm, I moved away. Maybe it was the brandy that made me want to fight the dreadful longing that filled me when I looked at the skater's dress. I only knew that I had to go inside.

Rachel let me go, but didn't follow.

The woman behind the counter was making price tags, and looked up and smiled automatically. I knew her. When she saw who I was, her smile slipped just a bit. She'd met Eva when I'd brought her shopping.

"Mrs. Bliss. It's so nice to see you."

Don't ask about her. Don't mention her name.

"What can I help you with today?" Her voice was artificially bright. Did she see something in my face? *This is what a murderer might look like.*

I glanced around the store, knowing I'd made a mistake in coming in. I wasn't ready to be there, but it was too late to turn and go. My eyes passed quickly over the boys' clothes. My palms had begun to sweat. Now I had to buy something to prove to us both that I could be here. To prove that I wasn't guilty.

"Picture books. I need picture books." My need for them was sudden and desperate, and I hurried over to the book display. The saleswoman's heels clicked over the varnished hardwood floor as she tried to keep pace.

"We have some new ones coming in a few weeks for Christmas. Here's one about construction that has lots of trucks and building equipment." Her hand hovered over the table, searching. So she remembered Michael, though I hadn't ever brought him in to the shop. "And there's a new Beatrix Potter edition as well." Picking up the oversize anthology of the Potter stories, she held it out to me and I thumbed through it, not really looking at the pictures. I knew them already. Eva had been fascinated by Mrs. Tiggywinkle, certain that she needed to have her own hedgehog as soon as possible. She had even asked Nonie if she could find a helpful hedgehog like Mrs. Tiggywinkle to fill in for her when she went on vacation. I closed it and handed it back to her. It wouldn't hurt for Michael to have his own copy, and the pictures were a good size to work from if I decided to decorate the walls of the ballroom when we renovated it.

119

"This is fine. And you have the truck book?"

She held up a second oversized book called *Things We Build*, with a bulldozer on the front.

"I'll take them both." I looked around. "And this." I picked up a large snowy lamb with a yellow ribbon around its neck from a nursery-rhymes display.

When the books were wrapped in paper and tied with a ribbon bearing the hotel's name, she slid the sales ticket across the desk. I felt her watching me as I wrote down our account number and signed. Did she see my hand shaking? I made myself write slowly, neatly. When I was done, it looked as though someone else had forged my signature.

"Oh, do you want the lamb in a box? I'm so sorry. I forgot to ask."

"No. Just let me have it."

"Are we done? I'm famished." Rachel had finally appeared. Even though she was due any day, she hadn't picked up anything for the baby. Sometimes I wondered just how happy she was about the pregnancy. Now she came up behind me. "What did you get?"

I held the lamb out to her, forcing myself to smile. "For the baby."

She looked as though she didn't understand for a moment, then gave me a sweet, slightly patronizing smile in return.

"You are the silliest person, Charlotte. We can't take that to lunch with us. But you're a dear." She touched my arm to bring me closer and, lifting herself to her full height, bussed my cheek. Taking the lamb, she gave it back to the saleswoman. "Wrap it up and have it put in my car with her other things."

She took my hand and led me from the shop.

I was tired and feeling as though I might cry at any moment. "Maybe we should just go home." Without the lamb, my arms felt strangely empty.

"You're joking!" Now she took my arm instead of just my hand. "I'm starving to death, and we're not leaving here until we get something decent to eat."

～

We ate down the hill at the hotel's Racquet Club café rather than in the massive formal dining room. The café was friendlier and more relaxed, with waitresses in white dresses and aprons instead of men in formal livery as in the dining room.

My head had begun to hurt a little and the sun streamed bright around our table, which was right beside a pair of open French doors. There were several sets of women's doubles going on the nearby tennis courts, and a man and woman playing alone on the most distant one.

Our waitress, a bubbly young woman whose dark ponytail looked as though it would burst from its bun at any moment, set down a glass of brandy and a separate club soda for Rachel, and an iced tea for me.

"Why did you just get iced tea?" she asked, after the waitress left the table. "Are you mad because I didn't get all gooey over that dear lamb you bought? I only wanted a day away from all the baby talk. Jack won't shut up about it." She sighed. "You'd think he invented babies."

"I'm not mad. I just haven't understood why you're not more excited. I loved being pregnant."

"That's fine for you. But listen to this: Jack doesn't even want me—" she stopped, closing her eyes for a few seconds and taking a deep breath. "Jack doesn't particularly want me having sex with the baby inside me. How stupid is that? He's afraid it will know what's going on, or something."

I remember thinking how strange it was that Jack would have that concern, given that he was a doctor. Self-conscious about how many times Press and I had had sex with both of my pregnancies, I didn't respond.

"I bet that doesn't stop Press." Rachel leaned forward, whispering. "He's not afraid of anything, is he?"

"Rachel!"

She gave me a knowing smile. "Come on. You can tell *me*."

When I wouldn't tell her what she wanted to know, she launched into a litany of what clothes she would buy once she was back down to what she called a *normal* size. From there she complained about her mother's obsession with the baby. I waited, but she never brought up the Heasters. It was as though they had never existed. Nonie had come close to calling Rachel outright selfish many times. I couldn't, because she was one of the few people I loved and trusted.

I'd been unable to hold on to the small sense of happiness I'd had in the car, but Rachel's chatter made it easy for me to just sit and be glad of the sunshine.

Finally the waitress brought our order, and I moved the subject away from babies and bodily functions.

"A while ago, I had this idea. It might sound a little crazy."

"If you want me to stop you from doing something crazy, you're talking to the wrong person. You know that." Rachel took a large, unladylike bite of her club sandwich. Her brandy was gone, and I suspected she was a bit drunk.

"Well, I read this piece in *Harper's Bazaar* about how people are transforming all those big old mansions in New York into more family-friendly houses. You know, modernizing them."

"And you want to change Bliss House into apartments?"

"No. But one family turned a ballroom into a giant playroom. Children can ride bikes inside, or they can use pogo sticks or roller-skate. One ballroom was even big enough to have a bowling alley installed. And, of course, most of them don't have any windows, so they don't get broken. I wonder why that is."

She shook her head. "I can't see Press wanting to do that. He's already redoing the theater, right? I'm not going to be stuck out with the bugs in my barn forever. He promised! And the idea of roller-skating and whatnot in a ballroom—particularly *that* creepy ballroom—is a little weird, Charlotte. You know Press got himself locked in there for hours once when he was a boy? He never told me what really happened, but it shook him up."

Press had told me about being locked in the ballroom, but he'd made it sound like a joke. I didn't think Rachel knew what she was talking about.

"Well, it really is partly my ballroom, too."

"Maybe." Rachel sounded doubtful. "What about Olivia? Since she's come back, don't you think she'll be pissed off?" Now she had a look of mischief in her eyes.

"No, I don't." I'd begun to feel that the Olivia I was coming to know probably wouldn't have minded whatever I wanted to do with the house.

The café had become more crowded. One of the doubles teams had been seated, and the rest of the patrons looked to have just come off the golf course. It was almost two o'clock. Michael would be going down for his nap. *And Eva should be telling Nonie she was too old to nap, that big girls should be allowed to stay up and play.*

We stopped discussing the house and had moved on to town gossip, a much safer topic. Finally, Rachel told me that the Heasters' nephew had shown up out of the blue with an appraiser, and then movers, to clear out the house.

"I had no idea. Did you even talk to him?"

Rachel shook her head. "Press said he talked to him on the telephone, and that he didn't think he'd be back for the memorial. There's just something wrong with some families."

A pair of shadows fell across the table. "What families?"

Rachel and I looked up to see Press—in tennis whites, his tan face and arms shining with a thin sheen of perspiration—with a woman standing close beside him.

He put his hand on my shoulder and kissed the top of my head.

123

"What a nice surprise, darling! Ladies, you remember J.C., don't you?"

J. C. Jacquith was as tall as I remembered, and skeleton-thin. She was more deeply tanned than even Press and had her chin-length ebony black hair (last time I'd seen her, her hair had been yellow-blonde) pulled back with a white eyelet band that matched the placket on her blouse. Instead of a traditional white tennis skirt, she wore high-waisted shorts that ended only five or six inches down her thin but muscular thighs. Was she ten, perhaps twelve years older than Press? I wasn't sure. Her nose and lips were patrician-thin, but her eyes—above her precipitous cheekbones—were large, the shocking gold color of a big cat's.

"Is there room for us, girls?" J.C.'s drawl was low and slightly nasal. "I'm desperate for a cold drink. Preston ran me ragged during that last set. I think I even perspired a little." She gave a laugh that might have been meant to be a giggle, but she had no facility for giggling. Her voice was nearly as deep as a man's.

Press signaled for the waitress to set two more places at the table, and pulled out the chair closest to him for J.C. to sit down. He also handed her the fine white cardigan that he'd obviously been carrying for her and obliged when she asked him to put it around her shoulders. As exhausted as she said she was, she'd found time to apply a fresh layer of thick, shining red lipstick.

"All these fans." She waved a hand toward the ceiling. "I get absolutely chilled. Don't you?" She was looking at Rachel, who looked back at her with obvious distaste. When Rachel didn't respond, I jumped in.

"It's been very pleasant this afternoon."

Rachel's gaze shifted to Press, who was seating himself in the fourth chair. Finally she spoke.

"I had *no idea* you were going to be here, Press, you naughty thing." She looked at me. "Did you know?"

I shook my head. *No, I hadn't known.*

Press surprised us all when he turned to me and said "Darling, I told you. You must have forgotten."

"You didn't." When had he said something? We'd barely spoken in days. "I would have remembered."

"There's no need to get upset, darling. It's not important."

Rachel and J.C. looked at me, each with something dangerously close to pity in their eyes. I wanted to run from the room.

J.C. laughed, breaking the moment. "I'm just thrilled that I get to see Precious Bride again, Press. You keep her hidden away down at that house of yours. He should let you out more, darling. You're absolutely delicious." She was staring at me with those fierce gold eyes, and I suddenly had an image of her biting into me—my arm, my cheek—licking me to tenderize me first, like a real cat with her prey.

"You know I haven't been hiding her. We've had a difficult few months." Press lightly touched my hand as if to emphasize the gravity of his words. "By tomorrow afternoon you'll be down in Old Gate with us."

The afternoon had taken a bizarre turn, and I deeply regretted leaving Bliss House. I thought of the security of the morning room, the warm mohair blanket.

The waitress stood waiting quietly by the table, and we were interrupted for a few moments. Rachel ordered a second drink, but this time just a plain club soda.

When the waitress was gone, J.C. turned her gaze toward Rachel. Rachel, who was always the center of attention in every room she entered, now looked tiny and insignificant. It was as though she were the moon, and J. C. Jacquith were the sun, which had decided to descend from the sky, flaming everything in its path.

"We've met before, haven't we?" J.C. held out her hand to Rachel. "I'm thinking your name is Roberta? Or perhaps Ruth?" She turned to Press and smiled. "You'd think I'd be better with names, wouldn't you, with my job. I mean, it's my lifeblood,

125

making sure I remember who people are." She turned back to Rachel expectantly.

While I was happy to have the attention drawn away from me, it was a horrible moment.

Now we were all watching Rachel. Her hands were squeezed into fists on either side of her plate, but her face was unnaturally calm. I knew she was deeply angry.

"My name is Rachel, you bitch. I'm sure you'll remember it now."

She gave J.C. a toothy, insincere smile, then turned her eyes to Press.

~

J.C. had pretended to be wildly amused at Rachel's response, but the rest of the lunch was tense. Rachel eventually mellowed somewhat, but I made her let me drive back to Old Gate, telling her my stomach was upset and that being a passenger would make it worse. I blamed her behavior on the hormones, but I really felt there was something else going on. She was quiet the whole way home, resting her head against the top of the seat just as I had done earlier with so much pleasure. But there was no pleasure in her face.

When we reached Bliss House, I asked her to come inside.

She didn't answer, but got out of the car and came around to the driver's-side door. I got out with my packages and stood by as she adjusted herself behind the wheel. When she had the door shut again, she looked up at me. I'd thought her more than a little drunk when we left the hotel, but there in front of the house she seemed dead sober.

"Don't be naïve, Charlotte. You know he's fucking that stick, don't you?"

Rachel was prone to cursing, so it wasn't her coarse language that disturbed me. It was that she'd given voice to my own thoughts. What had Press been doing at The Grange alone with

J.C.? Again I saw him settling her sweater across her shoulders. He hadn't mentioned that he would be seeing her, and he had invited her to the house without consulting me. It all made a sick, strange sort of sense.

Only once had I ever imagined him unfaithful with another woman. (I found the idea that he might have had some physical knowledge of another man—Jack—so repellent that I had banished it to the darkest recesses of my mind.) And, strangely enough, that woman had been Rachel. But it had been only for that one moment, on the day we'd been introduced, long before I had any claim on him.

"Don't be silly. She's just a friend." I tried to sound more con-vinced than I felt.

"Were you even watching her today?"

"I don't know why you're so worried about her."

Rachel's smile was just short of a sneer. It wasn't a pretty look for her. "Well, he hasn't been doing it with you, has he? I bet he's not." There was something ugly in her tone that I couldn't quite identify.

"Just go home, Rachel. You wouldn't be saying this if you weren't tired." It all felt too real at that moment. Too close. I wanted her to leave.

"Ah. I didn't think so."

Without another word, she put the car into gear. As she drove away, the Thunderbird's tires crunching on the driveway, I realized that the emotion I'd heard in her voice sounded a lot like jealousy.

Chapter 16

Judgment

Michael crawled around on the library carpet, alternately playing with a stack of blocks and looking at some of his picture books. Press sat in a chair near the fire, nursing his after-dinner port. He stared into the flames, barely glancing at the old script in his lap. Was he thinking about J.C.? I'd begun to wonder why he hadn't married her, or at least someone like her. Someone wealthy and independent. I hated how dowdy and insignificant I felt beside her.

I sat on a floor cushion near Michael, feeling Eva's absence. This was the time when Eva would sit on Press's lap and show him pictures she'd drawn during the day, or the things she'd collected on one of her walks with Nonie or me. She worked hard to keep his attention, serious about whatever she was showing him. Many times I'd seen him look past her, distracted, as she nattered on about the animals she'd drawn, the stories she'd made up or adapted from her favorite books. Had he loved her enough? He had wanted children, but sometimes I wondered if he really *saw* them. While he was occasionally stern, he was never mean. But neither did he play with them. It was as though they were part of his life, part of the house. They were expected.

I should have known better than to bring up my idea for the ballroom that night. Or any night. While my guilt over Eva's death colored everything I said or did, at that moment I was irritated about J.C.'s coming visit and the scene at the hotel. I wanted some kind of reaction from Press, some sign that *I* mattered, that our family mattered.

It took several minutes to explain what I wanted, and Press watched me carefully and with a strange curiosity in his eyes, as though I were speaking a foreign language that he didn't quite understand.

When I finished, he looked over at Michael, who had taken advantage of my inattention and removed a page of one of his books and begun to chew on it. His lips were stained with spots of brown ink.

"Michael!" I hurriedly swept my finger through his wet mouth to get all the paper out. When I finished, he grinned and said, "Eccccchhhh."

Press watched silently while I took care of Michael. When Michael was quiet, I asked him what he thought about my idea.

He laughed. "Charlotte, you're talking about a permanent change. There's no repairing it. It's a seventy-five-year-old classical ballroom! You have half a dozen other rooms you could turn into a playroom. He *has* a nursery, and an entire estate to play on."

"We don't even use the ballroom, and the theater will be finished any day."

He stopped. "Oh, I see. This is because you're jealous about the theater?" He shook his head. "Darling, don't you think that's a bit immature?"

A retort about grown adults remodeling an entire theater just to create a more comfortable space in which to waste time came to my lips, but Nonie's frequent admonition about my picking my battles kept me circumspect.

"It's not just about Michael. He'll have little friends. It would be for them to have a big room to play in when the weather is nasty. And I have so many ideas for how it might look. I've missed my art so much, Press." I had been an art history major in college, but I painted as well. I wasn't terribly good, but had, at least, sold a couple of pieces to strangers at the senior art fair.

"I'll think about it. You can run it by J.C. if you want. See what she thinks should be done with it." He paused. "But with just one child in the house, it doesn't really make sense, does it?" He spoke quietly, as though not wanting to point out my error in judgment too forcefully. Anyone watching us would think that he was being tender. With the firelight just beyond him, his eyes were darker than ever. I couldn't read them, but I didn't need to.

I looked down and absently smoothed Michael's hair where his head rested on my leg. He was contentedly sucking his thumb and reaching out with the other hand to play with the buttons of my cardigan.

It was a brutal question, and one that I couldn't answer.

"Time for you to go on up to Nonie, big guy." Press rose swiftly from his chair. He wasn't a particularly lithe man, but his movements were athletic and oddly graceful. Sweeping our sleepy boy from the floor, he perched him on his shoulder.

"Tell your mama good night."

Michael waved, opening and closing his small fist. "Mama."

"Good night, darling. Go right to sleep for Nonie."

When they were gone, I sat for a moment staring into the fire in the same way Press had. He was right, of course. And he was right to point it out, even if it hurt. I believed I deserved far worse treatment. With tears in my eyes, I picked up the bits of paper from the book's torn page. Balling the mess in my hand, I tossed it on the burning logs. The paper curled and smoked and quickly turned to blackened ash, indistinguishable from the rest of the burnt wood.

Then I went to the library table where I'd laid the oversize edition of Beatrix Potter stories whose images I had planned to copy and put on the walls. The strange, friendly little community of animals was a perfect bridge from Eva to Michael. Something they both might have loved. I sank down in Press's chair and turned the pages beneath the warm yellow lamplight.

I was turning the pages blindly, comforted by their familiarity, when Press came back a few minutes later. Surprised, I closed the book and looked up at him.

His footsteps dragged a bit. He had probably rowed early in the morning, and then there had been tennis with J.C. at the Racquet Club. I wondered how things were going to be between us. Would he ever really forgive me? He had told me again and again—every time I needed to hear it—that he didn't blame me for Eva's death. I couldn't quite believe him. If the situation had been reversed, if I had come home to find one of our children crying in his crib and the other child drowned in a bathtub, I would not have forgiven him.

I would have killed him.

The realization shocked me, but as I watched him going about the room, returning books to the shelves and neatening his papers on the desk, I knew it was true. He had to despise me. It would explain why he would break our marriage vows and seek out the company of another woman.

Was that why he'd lied about telling me he'd be at the club?

"Press."

"What is it? I'm going to bed."

I twisted in my chair to look up at him. "I wanted to ask you why you said you'd told me you were going to be at the club. You never told me that."

He frowned, his heavy brows coming together. He ran one hand through his rough hair.

"Charlotte, I told you this morning."

I sat up straighter.

"I didn't even see you this morning. You were gone when I got up."

Now he came back over to my chair. He got down on one knee, and he looked so serious that I had the strangest feeling he was about to propose to me again. Taking my hand, he squeezed it.

"I was on my way downstairs to go rowing and went in to check on you. But when you weren't in your room, I found you in Mother's morning room. On that fainting sofa by the window." He gestured across the room as though we were there instead of the library. "When I covered you with the blanket, you opened your eyes. Really, you seemed like maybe you'd been awake for hours. You said you were looking at slides?"

"I guess I fell asleep." What else had I said to him?

"Charlotte, you said you were waiting for Eva. What did you mean?"

Why couldn't I remember? Then it came out in a rush before I had a chance to reconsider.

"She did come to me. She was here, Press. And oh, God, she looked so miserable."

He touched my face. I couldn't bear the look of pity in his eyes. "You're torturing yourself. Don't do this. You know she's not here."

"She is. She touched me." I remembered her cold fingers on my face, how the chill had lingered even after she'd left the room. "You know it's possible."

"Stop, Charlotte. You and I both know you must have dreamed it. I know you miss her, but this is just cruel. To both of us."

I looked away. It was exactly what I'd known he would say.

"Charlotte."

"I'm sorry. I don't want to talk about it. It was a mistake."

He came around the chair. "Listen. Of course you dream about her. No one's going to blame you for that."

When I didn't answer, he scowled. "You should stay away from that lantern. Some of those pictures scared the hell out of me when I was a kid. I'm not surprised they gave you bad dreams. But I am surprised you didn't go back to your room to sleep. I thought you didn't like Mother's rooms."

"I said I was tired." Truly, I had no memory of going to the sofa or of falling asleep.

"Well, be careful." He stood up, then bent to kiss the top of my head. "That old lantern is dangerous. Mother was always worried that it might start a fire."

I watched after him as he opened the library door and left, leaving the door open behind him. The draft from the hall pulled at the fire, drawing out a few tiny embers that spent themselves in the air above the hearth. No, I should never have told him about Eva. It bothered me that I could remember every detail of what Olivia had shown me, but couldn't remember talking to him that morning. Had he really been there? The detail about putting the blanket over me seemed to make sense. But there certainly hadn't been any danger of the lantern catching on fire. That much I knew for certain.

Chapter 17

Counted Losses

The next day dawned clear and autumn-bright. If I had known what hell that day would bring, I might have barricaded myself along with Nonie and Michael in my bedroom the night before and not come out for several days, living on whatever Terrance (oh, perhaps not Terrance, now!) left at the door for us to eat. As it happened, I'd shut my bedroom door and undressed and put on my gown and robe, thinking I would go back into the morning room. But when I looked at my bed, an intense weariness came over me, and it was all I could do to keep my eyes open long enough to pull back the sheet and shut off the light. If I dreamed, I can't remember. But I woke with a strange sense of urgency, as though I'd slept too long and had gone to bed with something undone. Really, wasn't it the same urgency I'd felt every moment since Eva had drowned? I hadn't been there to stop her, to keep her from the tub. *Not now, darling. Bath tonight, before pajamas. There you go, darling. Run and play.* How many more mornings would I wake with that same question? *What have I left undone? Who will suffer?*

In the mirror, I was a different woman from the one I'd been a few weeks earlier. My face was puffy from oversleep, and the skin at my jaw looked slack, as though I were forty-seven instead of twenty-seven. Was my mouth harder? Less soft and appealing? I tried to think of how Press might see me now. Of course Rachel had been right about Press and J.C.; she had no reason to lie.

The door between our bedrooms was closed. On a mild day like this one, he often played tennis or golfed, but J.C. would be arriving in the afternoon. Press had assured me that she didn't need a thing that he and Terrance and Marlene couldn't provide, and that she would be there mostly to work on the theater. *Mostly.* I tried to imagine J.C. rolling up the sleeves of one of her expensive silk blouses to take up a paintbrush with the crew already at work in the ballroom, exposing her too-long, too-thin, insectile arms. A female praying mantis towering over the workers, biting the heads off of each one after—*Oh, God, what was I thinking?*

Even before Rachel and I had gotten out the door of the Racquet Club, Rachel had said "Do *not* trust her." Behind us, Press and J.C. were finishing their lunch. I glanced back to see J.C. lifting a glass of red wine to her lips, an act that had, indeed, made drinking red wine at lunch look unseemly.

Enough.

I ate a quick breakfast and showered and dressed, giving a thought to my clothes in the same way that Rachel had encouraged me the day before. Grief had made me thinner and pale, and, in truth, a part of me didn't care what I wore. But there was also a warning voice in my head that told me to dress carefully. With that in mind, I slid into a pair of bright pink slacks and a soft white cardigan with pearl buttons of which Eva had been particularly fond. There was still a similar one in Eva's middle drawer that she would have insisted on wearing when she saw mine.

It was always going to be like this. Always *What would Eva have said? What would she have liked?* I ran my lipstick over my lips almost in defiance, thinking: *I must do this now. I must bear it. I must remember.*

My fault.

⌒

I was in the nursery when the telephone outside Olivia's room rang. We had four telephones: one in the kitchen, one in the front hall, one in the second-floor gallery, and one in the library. Nonie was outside, hanging Michael's laundry (she insisted on doing it herself in the wringer washer in the mudroom). The call went unanswered, and when the ringing started again, I put Michael on my hip and hurried to answer it.

Buck Singleton, my father's best friend of thirty years, was on the other end of the line.

On hearing my voice, he immediately launched into what he'd called to say.

"Charlotte? Darlin', your daddy was crossing the street the same way he does every day to get to the store—you know he never goes up to the corner—and a car came out of nowhere and clipped him, knocked him over. There weren't any witnesses that we know of, but the car didn't stop. I didn't even see any brake marks on the street."

For a moment, I couldn't speak. My father was two years younger than Olivia had been when she died, but he was in excellent health, and even though it wasn't rational, a part of me had believed he would stay exactly the same as he was the day Preston and I married.

"Are you there, Charlotte? Did you hear what I said? He asked me to call you, but to not get you upset. He said he doesn't want you to come, but his leg is broken along with a couple of ribs. No one saw him hit, but they found him right away."

"Have you seen him? How is he?"

In my arms, Michael began to tug on the handset, saying "Unh unh unh!"

In the confused moments that followed, I learned that my father was, indeed, in the hospital, but was conscious. Buck had promised to call me but was supposed to discourage me from coming. His wife, Callie, who occasionally helped at my father's office-supply store, had said she would look after the store and cook any meals he needed.

"But someone needs to be there with him," I told Buck. "I'll come. Tomorrow, if we can't get the train today." I knew my aunts would certainly want to help, and that if they went instead of me, the stress would slow his healing considerably.

Buck demurred. "He won't be happy about it, honey. He was adamant he doesn't want you to leave that baby boy of yours. Is that who I hear?"

"Then I'll bring him with me." Even as I said it, I knew it wasn't a good idea. But together Nonie and I could certainly take care of both my father and Michael.

"We'll get things ready on this end. You let us know when you get here."

Michael let out a howl when I hung up the telephone without letting him have the handset. I held him closer, kissing him on the forehead.

"That wasn't very nice. It wasn't your turn to talk on the telephone today." I shifted him. "How would you like to see Grandpa?"

It wasn't enough to interrupt his swelling tantrum. Already his full cheeks had bloomed with pink and his eyes filled with angry tears.

Needing to find Nonie, I carried a squirming Michael back to the nursery and put him in his crib to cry out his tantrum alone. As I shut and locked the door, I felt a swell of anxiety. Failure. If I couldn't even handle a toddler, how useful could I be to my injured father? Someone had hit him and left him helpless and broken in broad daylight on a Clareston street. I closed my eyes.

Helpless. Alone. Just like Eva.

I heard Nonie's soft footsteps on the stairs and went to meet her.

"What is it? Where's Michael?" Seeing my face, her gray eyes filled with fear.

"Everything's all right." I laid my hand on her arm, wanting to believe I was telling the truth.

Sometimes when I spoke in the hall, with the dome high above me, I felt as though I were speaking in a church or some other public building dedicated to worship or some arcane philosophy. It was suddenly a house that was no longer benign and simply grand—it breathed with purpose. But *what* purpose, if not for shelter and perhaps to be an ostentatious display of wealth? Surely I should know. In that moment, the house's *being* felt so tangible to me that I lowered my voice almost to a whisper so that Nonie had to lean close to hear.

"Tell me, girl." Nonie covered my hand with hers and squeezed so hard that it hurt.

"Daddy's going to be all right, but he's in the hospital."

"Oh, good Lord." Nonie swayed on her feet. I caught her and led her away from the stairs to an upholstered bench outside the morning room. "Is it his heart? What is it?"

Nonie, usually so composed, her responses measured, looked stricken with physical pain. She had been heartbroken when Eva died, and poured her grief into caring for Michael and for me, keeping our lives as normal as possible. But what I'd just told her had hurt her in a different way.

"It was a traffic accident. Someone hit him with their car but then drove away. He has a broken leg, and Buck told me some of his ribs are broken. But he's in the hospital and awake enough to tell everyone not to worry about him. You know how he is."

"I know how he is," Nonie echoed. Now her voice was almost a whisper. Looking down, she took off her glasses and laid her hands on her knees. Her breath was halting. "He's going to be all right."

"We'll go right away, of course. You and Michael and I. There's no reason for Press to go. And that J.C. woman will be here any minute." I chose not to add, "They would probably prefer to be alone, anyway." But I couldn't stop myself from thinking it.

Nonie took her handkerchief from her dress pocket and pressed it to her face.

"Nonie?"

She wouldn't look at me, but she kept her eyes cast down to her lap and was quietly sobbing. Around us, the hall was as bright as it ever got during the day, bathing the walls in pale gold, showing motes of dust in the beams from the windows around the dome. The stars had faded in the morning sun.

"He's going to be all right," I said more firmly. "Nonie, what's wrong?"

When she finally looked up at me, I saw something unexpected in her eyes. She looked sorry. Apologetic.

I had known Nonie most of my life. I knew she had come from a family of teachers, and that her father had died of meningitis, that she had never been married, and that her mother lived with Nonie's sister, Moriah, who taught history in Richmond. I knew she loved deviled eggs, got tearful on hearing "Silent Night" at Christmas, voted in every election, and that she knew I had—until I went to college and she briefly went to work for another Clareston family—sometimes raided the secret stash of sugar-dusted raspberry hard candies she kept in her sweater drawer. And at that moment I knew that she loved my father.

We sat, silent except for a few delicate, retreating sniffs from Nonie as she composed herself.

In the background, Michael had stopped screaming and was now just calling for Nonie as loudly as he could. Already he was learning to try to play us against each other. A clever boy. But Nonie didn't yet get up.

"Does he know?" I said, quietly.

A denial rose to her lips, but she thought better of it and nodded.

The idea that two of the people I loved and imagined I knew best in the world had such a profound secret shocked me more than the telephone call from Buck had. I wanted to ask her how long she'd loved him, and if he loved her as well. But I already knew the answer. My father was always solicitous of her, always made sure she was comfortable and had what she needed. Whenever she came into the room, he smiled. Why had I not seen it? How difficult it must have been for the two of them to live in the same house for so long, with me, and not show affection. Or had it happened later, after I left? The child inside me felt a little wounded and unsettled, but I knew it was right.

It was 1957, and the world had changed a lot since I was a child, but I suspected it hadn't changed enough to sanction a public relationship between my father and Nonie, no matter how light her blackness was. To me, they were just two people who had been alone for a very long time.

"He'll need help," I said. "Someone to do for him."

"For a while," Nonie said.

"Yes, for a while."

She stood, and I could feel her embarrassment as a palpable thing between us. Not shame. Just her natural reserve reasserting itself, a reluctance to acknowledge that it was she who was experiencing a surge of emotion. She had always taken care of me, and it had never been the other way around.

"Nonie. . . ."

She stopped me. "We won't speak of this, Charlotte. I'll go and start packing Michael's things."

I took a deep breath, hardly believing what I was about to say. It didn't feel right to intrude on my father's and Nonie's privacy. And I didn't really want to leave Bliss House with Olivia and Eva so close. Not with J.C. about to descend.

"Michael's not going, and I'm not going."

As soon as I said the words, I felt the house relax. Almost sigh. I touched the wall beside the morning-room door and felt its velvety warmth. Yes, I was jealous and worried about my marriage, but it was more that I could see my absence as creating an emptiness. Who or what might take my place? I belonged there.

"It makes much more sense for you to go to Clareston without me. Michael is liable to trip Daddy or bother him when he's resting. Terrance can take you to the train station after lunch. I'll call Buck and ask him to pick you up." While it would have been faster for Terrance just to drive her the two and a half hours to Clareston, I knew she wouldn't have been comfortable alone with him in a car for that long. I didn't blame her. Terrance rarely said a dozen words on a talkative day.

She touched my cheek. The fleeting tenderness in her eyes was quickly replaced by her usual sensible determination even before she started for her bedroom.

My heart pounded as though I were taking some great risk. I don't know why. It was probably the most mature decision I'd ever made up to that point in my life.

I watched her walk away with urgency in her step, carrying herself even straighter than usual, if such a thing were possible. She was already like a different person to me. Not a stranger, but a woman with a different role. Still Nonie, but Nonie in love. What was she to my father? She had come to us Naomi Meriwether Jackson, a capable young woman with strong, safe hands and a firm but gentle manner. How unlike my fragile poet of a mother, a woman so fragile that she hanged herself in our garage for me to find. It was Nonie who had come in and set us both to rights, put me on a schedule and brought order to my life. Now she would mend my father.

I told myself that she would come back, even though I wasn't sure I believed it. And she eventually did, with my father. But it was under circumstances I couldn't even have imagined that morning.

Chapter 18

Violation

Knowing that leaving Michael alone a few minutes longer wouldn't cause him any harm (perhaps I was delaying, not wanting to face the fact that once Nonie was gone, I would be his only caretaker), I went into the morning room. Someone, probably Terrance, had neatened it. The slide boxes were stacked in alphabetical order and there was a short crystal vase filled with fresh yellow roses—the kind Olivia preferred to have in her rooms—on the desk. The blanket was folded on the chaise longue, and on top of it sat a large pillow with a striped silk cover and long red tassels. It hadn't been there before, but I remembered seeing it on the sofa in Olivia's room. Had Terrance left it for me, knowing I'd fallen asleep there? It looked inviting, but the idea that Terrance, inscrutable and blank to me, was not only following but anticipating my actions was disturbing. In fact, I felt I could lie down and sleep more. Perhaps for days. How easily I might have pulled the curtains and slipped back into Olivia's world, with her sensual (a trait passed on to Press, I believed, though he was much more aggressive), attractive husband, and the aura of deep apprehension I felt around the Olivia of my . . . what? Dreams? Hallucinations?

Above me, I could hear the faint movements of the men working on the theater. Muffled voices and boots on the uncarpeted floor. But there was something coming from Olivia's room as well. Not exactly a sound, but an overwhelming wave of such deep dread that it was like a warning to run away from that place as quickly as I could move. Perhaps I was becoming inured to uncertainty, and even pain, because instead of running away, I went to the closed door.

The doorknob was frigid, stinging my fingers.

(Over the many years I've had to think about that day, I've wondered why Olivia—or the house itself—chose that time to reveal such a horror to me. If it was Olivia, then surely she'd known that my need to see it was urgent. But if it was the house, which, I know now, has a kind of mind of its own, then it picked that time because I was vulnerable: my father was badly injured, and Nonie was leaving me. I was losing everything. And if it were true that the house wanted to hurt me, the question of *why* remains. It had given me such happiness and yet was taking it away with dizzying speed.)

There was no frost as there had been in the morning room, but the air was just as cold, and again smelled nauseatingly of dead roses. A single lamp burned on a bedside table, and though I knew it was quite late in the morning, in this room it was night. The furniture was the same, the fabrics on the bed and the curtains different. There were four other people in the room, completely unaware that I was watching.

Here is revulsion made real. I must show you this so you will know what evil is possible in the world. Sadly, it was only the beginning of my education.

Olivia—looking much the same as she had two nights earlier—lay against her pillows, her blond hair loosened, her face a luminous white so that her scar shone above her brow as though it were a fresh wound. The sheets were pushed to the end of the bed so that she was obscenely exposed, her gown drawn carelessly to her hips, her slender legs parted, but straight and stiff. She did not cover herself, but hugged her arms around her own chest, staring at the man climbing onto the bed with her. There was a look in her eyes that I can only describe as resigned horror, as though she knew what was about to happen, but also knew she couldn't change it.

The man was not Michael Searle.

This man's face sagged with age, but more: his face was pitted with scars and purple sores. Sparse white, greasy tufts of hair were scattered over his emaciated head, and even though I could only see his profile, I saw that his eye was filmy with cataracts and suspected he was almost blind. His skeletal, knobbed hands protruded like nocturnal alien creatures from the sleeves of his elaborate dressing gown and fumbled, clumsy, as he felt his way onto the bed.

Until that moment, Press was the only man I'd seen fully naked, and when this man loosened the gown from his body and let it drop to the bed, I almost looked away. But the unreal nature of what I saw had me transfixed. It was an ancient man's body, a body that had obviously once been robust (witness the folds of skin hanging about his gut and hips and under his arms), but was now wasted. His entire body looked hairless, and it was dotted with more irregularly shaped purple bruises and sores. There was a palpable air of malice in the angle of his body and the hunger in his face, which I'd never sensed from another human. But his malice gave him no physical strength. He wavered in the lamplight, and there was a small movement from one of the other two people who weren't near the bed, but he righted himself.

No one spoke.

Understanding what he was about to do, I covered my mouth with my hands. *Poor Olivia!* Why didn't she scream?

She didn't reach out for him, but neither did she try to get away. When she closed her eyes, I was glad. But as the man started to lower himself onto her, he collapsed, and Olivia's cries were muffled as though I were hearing them through deep water. As the man steadied himself, he spoke to her. She shook her head, and I both saw and heard her vehement, frightened *No!*

Balancing himself carefully on one bony arm, he slapped her face.

There was a gasp from one of the two men watching from the shadows. Michael Searle pressed forward in an attitude of aggression, his face twisted with anguish, but the expressionless man behind him held him fast.

I recognized that bald, narrow head, the taut, mole-dotted skin.

The scene on the bed was over in a very few minutes. I've told you enough, and if I described the sounds that came from that hideous creature that had molested the silent, stoic Olivia, you wouldn't forgive me. I have long tried to forget them.

At a signal from the old man, Terrance disengaged himself from Michael Searle. He helped the old man down from the bed and into his dressing gown and a pair of slippers. Then Terrance did an astonishing thing: he picked the old man up and carried him across the room as though he were bearing a large child. The old man's head nodded onto his chest, but when they reached Michael Searle, his thin, cracked lips broke into a smile of lascivious satisfaction. Michael Searle looked down at his feet, his body shaking violently. Before the old man and Terrance were out of the room, Michael Searle retched miserably on the floor.

Olivia, who had barely moved during the ordeal, sat up to lean forward. In the room's paltry light, she looked small among the bank of pillows, even younger than she had sitting between her parents. I would have expected to see hate or disgust in her eyes when she looked at the man who hadn't been able to protect her. But I only saw pity.

The door shut with a soft *click*, the way it always did when Terrance left a room.

The scene before me disappeared, and the room looked just as it had the day before.

Except.

In the corner beyond Olivia's jewelry table, I saw Eva. Her hair dripping, her mouth sad, the pink playsuit clinging to her little body. My heart broke to think she might have witnessed that which I'd just seen.

"Eva, baby." I held out my hand to her. She didn't move, but in seconds she was gone again.

With her withdrawal—and the disappearance of all I had seen—I felt a great ebbing of my strength. My legs felt weak, but I did not faint. Where my strength had been, there was only tremendous weariness. I sank onto a delicate bentwood chair beside the door between the two rooms and waited.

Sitting there, I began to doubt what I'd seen. I had no proof that Olivia's rape had been anything more than a hallucination. Was I so desperate to excuse myself for what had happened to Eva that I was able to imagine the unimaginable? Perhaps what Press seemed to suspect was true: grief and guilt were poisoning my mind.

The sounds of the house eventually returned. Distant footsteps, voices above me and on the outdoor stairs not far from the morning room's windows. The door from Olivia's room into the hall was closed now, though it had been open when I was in the gallery with Nonie. Somehow it was a relief. Proof that someone had closed the door—and I was sure that that someone had been Terrance, either in this time or the time I'd seen. It didn't matter which. It felt to me like time was folding in on itself. Its passage marked nothing on Bliss House.

And if all those things had indeed been real?

Terrance. How could Terrance have participated in such a horror? If confronted, would he use the excuse of war criminals everywhere? *I was just doing my job.* (I had an idea who the other man, the one who had taken Olivia, was, but it was too terrible to comprehend at that moment.) But to confront Terrance, or even to demand that he be forced from the house, I would have to tell Press what I'd seen and how I'd seen it. Press had already told Rachel that I wasn't doing well. Who else had he been talking to about me? Tales of visions would only make things worse.

I was beginning to understand why Bliss House was so feared. The things that happened here couldn't leave. They lasted forever within these walls, repeating, repeating, and repeating themselves forever, with each repetition deepening the torment of the souls trapped here.

I closed my eyes and leaned back in the chair, resting my head against the wall. I could feel the pulse of the house in my head.

Eva was still here.

If all of those things were true, then Eva would always be here in Bliss House. I could never leave.

I can barely describe how difficult it was to rouse myself from that chair in Olivia's room and go on with the day. Even as I picked up my smiling, innocent son from his crib, I held him gingerly as though I might defile him with what I had witnessed. Suddenly grateful for his purity, I squeezed him to me and covered his head with noisy kisses until he began to struggle. I never wanted to let him go. With a feeling of manic joy, I took him to Nonie's room and we watched her finish her packing. I wanted to be with the two of them forever, protected from everything ugly and vile by their sweetness. As we said our *good-byes* in the front drive, Terrance waited, holding open the passenger-side door of the Ford that he and Marlene used. Oh! How hard it was to look at that falsely benign face. To know that he'd been party to Olivia's rape.

Yes! That was the word, for although she hadn't run, it had been obvious that it was against her will. *Rape* was a word that was rarely spoken by people I knew. There was Titian's painting, *Rape of Europa*, and so many versions of the *Rape of the Sabine Women*. But the word didn't mean the same thing: Olivia hadn't been abducted. She'd been brutally violated. Her injuries weren't just physical. They were soul-deep.

"You're not to worry." Nonie's face was serious but she was distracted, already thinking of my father and what awaited her in Clareston. "Everything will be fine, Lottie."

I knew she was speaking of my father, but I prayed that she also meant that things would be fine for us at the house. They didn't feel fine, and now she wouldn't be with me. I couldn't tell her what was happening even if I wanted to. After giving Michael a quick kiss and receiving a wetter one from him, she sat back and Terrance shut her in the car. We waved after her until the car disappeared down the drive, leaving us alone.

Inside, I took Michael into the library to call Press at the office, but his telephone rang and rang. I hung up, thinking. Then I dialed Rachel's number.

My stomach tightened for no good reason that I could think of when she answered in a breathless voice and told me that yes, Press had dropped by. But I relaxed when she said she would go and get him from the kitchen where he was making a late breakfast for Jack. It was the one meal Press could make for himself, and Rachel hated to cook. I guessed Jack had been at the hospital overnight.

"Will you tell him he needs to come home? Something's happened."

Chapter 19

J. C.

J. C. Jacquith was driven down from The Grange in one of the hotel's private cars, deposited on our doorstep, and entered Bliss House on a pungent wave of *Caron Poivre*, wearing a slender and stiff-as-meringue dark green cotton dress trimmed in black. Her sunglasses, wide-brimmed hat, and heels were all black as well. I came into the hall in time to see her purse her garnet-red lips to share an enthusiastic kiss with Preston, who held her by the shoulders to—I assume—steady her.

"I always forget what a terrifying drive it is down to this place, Press." She slumped comically. "That boy driving the car seemed to think it was some kind of rally race. I'm positively dizzy."

Before Press could respond, she noticed me coming in from the dining room.

"Look, it's the Precious Bride! Darling, aren't you just as fresh as a country daisy?" She teetered over to me and kissed the air on either side of my face.

I tensed, but she gave no sign that she noticed.

Terrance came silently in behind us, and J.C. had a bright *hello, you old cad* for him, as well. "That boy just left my bags on the step like I'm some kind of hobo. Will you be an angel and bring them in for me?"

"Put her in the yellow room, Terrance." I did my best not to look at him. Though he was some thirty years older, he was the same man who had stood by while Olivia was tortured and humiliated.

I turned to J.C. "The sun won't wake you in the morning."

She was our first real guest since Olivia's funeral and, despite my dislike for her, I'd easily slipped into Olivia's former role as hostess. Press, who hadn't yet spoken, lifted an eyebrow. I don't know why he was surprised. Had he thought taking care of guests would be his job? The western side of the house was still very warm in the afternoons, but there wasn't anywhere for her on our side of the house, unless I tucked her away in the bedroom beside the ballroom on the third floor. But that would've taken more overt rudeness than I could make myself exercise.

"Aren't you a *love*! Press must've told you I'm like one of those vampire creatures. I'm *completely* allergic to mornings." Her tone was one of exaggerated gratitude, like that of an Austen character whose words might be construed either as impossibly obsequious or crudely sarcastic. I hadn't been around J.C. enough to tease out the difference. As she followed Terrance upstairs, she kept up a running stream of commentary on the paneling, the paintings, the dome, the furniture. Terrance only nodded or shook his head in response. I watched her stop dead in front of Olivia's room, and Terrance paused to wait. Had she heard something? Sensed something? Press had mentioned once that she fancied herself to have psychic sensitivities. Finally, she restarted her chatter and moved on.

As Terrance put her bags in the yellow room, she leaned out just a bit over the balcony and blew a kiss to the two of us as though she knew we'd been watching. I watched Press's face. He looked pleased, but I had no idea what he was thinking.

Twenty minutes later, after she'd changed into more casual clothes, she and Press disappeared into the theater to talk to the decorators.

I didn't see them again until we were all dressed for dinner, except at a distance. After a long conference in the theater, they went out in the army surplus Jeep Olivia had acquired a decade earlier to use on the farm, Press in shirtsleeves and a Panama hat, and J.C. in a studiously country casual outfit of khaki slacks and a bright orange belted safari jacket. One of her beautifully manicured hands held tight to the window frame of the Jeep as they left the rocky driveway; the other secured her own scarf-tied straw hat. I chanced to be in the butler's pantry, near the window, as the Jeep bounced onto the rutted farm road and passed the springhouse on the way to the orchards. It had been months since I'd been out onto the farm. Even when I dropped by the orchardkeeper's house with extra food or to visit with his sister, Shelley, who kept house for him, I preferred to leave the farm by the driveway and go around to the paved road that led to the tenant houses. Later, when I became more involved with the orchard operations, I changed my habits.

After Michael went down for his nap, I called the hospital to check on my father, but he was sleeping and I hung up feeling sad and empty. I was tired. Exhausted, really. But I didn't want to sleep or particularly be alone.

Press had held me for a moment after he rushed home and I told him what had happened, and I felt the wall I'd put up between us shift the slightest bit. But I pulled away when he began to insist that I follow Nonie to Clareston. I almost told him about seeing Eva and Olivia, that I couldn't possibly leave the house, leave them behind for that long, but I stopped myself. He seemed surprised when I refused, and I knew he was wondering what was wrong.

151

"Whatever you think best, Charlotte. I just worry that your father will be disappointed."

Another unkind observation. I was getting used to his small cruelties, and couldn't help but think again that he simply wished me out of the house while J.C. was there.

Taking my garden basket and some clippers, I went out the mudroom door to the herb garden, thinking I would trim back the oregano and thyme's fall growth. I stood for a moment with my eyes closed, comforted by the warmth of the sunshine on my face. Just the day before, I'd been driving with Rachel in the Thunderbird and walking the pristine grounds of The Grange, but that seemed like days or even months ago.

We had part-time gardeners who handled the bigger gardens, but tending the herb garden was one of the few activities Olivia and I routinely shared. Marlene had been doing her best to keep up with what I hadn't been up to doing in those past months, but she had many other jobs to do.

It was a formal hexagonal garden, the herbs separated into individual beds. Each bed had a permanent wood-burned marker, so if I wasn't sure about something, I could look it up in one of the books in the family library. Marlene wasn't a very adventurous cook and only used the oregano, thyme, rosemary, seasonal basil, and occasionally the sage. There was also peppermint for iced tea, and of course the lavender that Olivia put into the sachets that were nested in drawers and linen presses all over the house. I was no seamstress, but I was sure I could refill the hand-stitched sachets with dried lavender when it came time the next summer.

I had trimmed the thyme and had a small pile of pruned lavender stems in the garden cart when I looked up to see a man in paint-stained blue coveralls standing silently on the porch a couple of dozen feet away from where I knelt.

He was older than most of the workmen I'd seen coming and going from the theater, perhaps even older than the foreman, who looked about fifty. (But then, so many people over thirty seemed to be "about fifty" when I was young.) His paint-stained coveralls were old-fashioned, with straps like a farmer's overalls; and though his shirt was a brilliant, unstained white, there was a smell of turpentine and ash about him. Not woodsmoke but coal, as though he worked around coal fires.

"Yes? Can I help you? The entrance to the theater is on the other side of the house."

"I was told to ask for the missus. Ain't you the missus?"

"I'm Mrs. Bliss."

"You have a job for me?"

"Oh, you must be here about the ballroom." I was surprised, but suddenly excited. Press had said he would think about it. I wondered if, somehow, J.C. had been involved in his decision to let me go ahead with the playroom. It didn't matter. I was just glad.

The man nodded. "You tell me what color you want, and I'll take care of it for you." When he smiled, he showed only the very front of his teeth as though his mouth wouldn't open easily. His leathery skin appeared stretched tight over his face and head, like Terrance's. I wasn't certain, but he also seemed to be bald beneath his painter's cap. Perhaps I should forgive myself for being naïve, but I noticed and then promptly ignored the lifeless aspect of his watery blue eyes. I wanted what I wanted, and what I wanted right then was something good to happen.

I stood up, took off my gardening glove, and offered my hand.

He was enormously tall, his hand surprisingly soft and much cooler than my own. Again, the painful half-smile.

"Abram, ma'am."

The color. With a flash of irritation, I realized that I might have asked J.C. for suggestions about the exact color I was looking for. If only he'd brought a brochure or some kind of samples.

"I want the walls to be white. Not bright white, but softer. Like. . . ." I closed my eyes searching for a word. An image.

"Like new butter? Or cow's cream?"

Cow's cream was the exact image that had come to my mind. Staring into the milk pitcher on my grandmother's kitchen table after her neighbor had brought some Jersey cow's milk over for our dinner as a treat for me, the cream floating on top like a soft, shapeless continent.

"How did you know?"

"Everyone wants cream. It's a very popular color."

Of course it was. I was reassured.

We went into the house through the mudroom, but the kitchen and hallways were empty. Marlene and Terrance were absent. Upstairs, even the theater was quiet behind its closed pocket doors.

I turned on the lights in the ballroom and we were immersed in the reflection of the lights on the dark red wallpaper with its stern, identical men and beautiful Japanese women. Abram ran his hand over the wallpaper. "You want this paper painted over?"

I bristled. It was only wallpaper.

"I do. Is that a problem?"

His hand dropped from the wall.

"I can do that."

"You can get rid of those, too? And patch the ceiling?" I pointed to the giant metal circles screwed into the ceiling.

"Yes, ma'am. I can do that too."

Chapter 20

The Dinner Party

Dinner that night was a fairly tame affair with Rachel and Jack for company, and the sheriff, Hugh Walters, to round out the table. Even though we were technically in mourning (a tradition that had fallen away more and more since I was a girl), I'd suggested a slightly larger party because I didn't relish the idea of spending empty hours with J.C. and Press. But Press had vetoed the idea quickly.

"She's not worried about being entertained. I really want you to take the time to get to know her better. I'm sure you could be wonderful friends. I'll make sure Rachel, Jack, and Hugh are here."

I'd been doubtful. Rachel and J.C. at the same table again? Despite the formidable nature of Bliss House, I wasn't sure it could remain standing.

I was wrong. The evening was unseasonably warm, so, after Michael was down for the night, we ate on the patio outside the dining room, our faces softened by the light of several torches.

155

Press had brought a record player out and put on a stack of records that began with Tony Bennett, a favorite of mine. J.C. and Rachel exchanged a few very civil words, but otherwise J.C. dominated the conversation with gossipy New York stories that the men seemed to find very funny. Not surprisingly, Rachel was subdued, picking at the dinner Terrance served: oysters on the half-shell, consommé, breaded veal cutlets with zucchini and yellow squash, and Marlene's special iced pumpkin-ginger cake. Rachel was elegant in her black knit maternity dress and jacket, but beneath her eyes there were dark circles that worried me. After the coffee came, she got up, restless, to smoke a cigarette. I followed her to the other side of the patio. The torchlight glimmered in her eyes as though they were wet with tears.

"What's going on, Rachel? Is it Jack?" She rarely complained about Jack. He was slavishly devoted to her—the kind of man someone like Rachel required. But men often reacted strangely to pregnancy.

"What could possibly be wrong?" First cutting her eyes to Jack, who was listening carefully to something J.C. was saying over her wineglass, she looked back at me with a small, tight smile.

I knew when she was being sarcastic, but also knew better than to try to drag information out of her, particularly information about her feelings. She would proclaim them loudly or she wouldn't say anything at all.

As we watched, J.C. stood up from her chair and declared that she couldn't bear to sit any longer with Frank Sinatra singing "Night and Day," right there under the stars. She asked the men who might possibly be brave enough to dance with her.

Jack looked over his shoulder at Rachel, who stared back, impassive.

"He wouldn't. Not with J.C.," I whispered. "Jack would never do that to you."

Rachel gave a harsh little laugh. "Of course he wouldn't. Not our Jack. But he does look worried, doesn't he? Men are such bastards." She rested a hand on her belly. "Every one of them."

"You city girls," I heard Press say to J.C. "You can't sit still." But he didn't get up either.

"What a couple of mama's boys you are!" She turned abruptly and waggled a finger at Hugh. "I guess that means you win, Sheriff."

Hugh stood quickly, knocking over his folding chair with a loud clatter, and everyone laughed. I felt bad for him. It had seemed to me an odd invitation for Press to make to Hugh. We didn't often socialize with him. Because he had come to the house after Eva's death, I still felt awkward around him. But at least I liked and trusted him.

Before Hugh could pick up the chair, Terrance was there to do it, brushing off the seat with his ever-present white cloth. Then he stepped back through the terrace doors and into the dining room, where he waited. The glass hadn't yet been repaired, and the small panels of wood in one corner were a constant reminder to me of Olivia.

J.C. was tipsy and her steps were loose, compared to Hugh's careful moves as he tried to lead her. Rachel and I watched as she caressed the thick brown hair at the back of Hugh's head, and brought her mouth to his ear. When he finally leaned away from her a bit to look at her face, he laughed a laugh so clear and loud that Frank Sinatra's voice faded into the background. The album continued, and even after two more songs J.C. would not let Hugh go. Not even after Rachel went to Jack and put her hand on his shoulder to tell him that she was tired and they should leave. Hugh only managed to get in a wave *goodbye* while J.C. blew them a kiss.

I hugged Rachel close and whispered that I would call her, and inside I promised myself that I would. It was like her to be moody and somewhat cold—particularly with someone she disliked as much as J.C.—but not so subdued that she wouldn't eat.

As the lights of Rachel's Thunderbird swept over us, throwing our shadows and those of the Japanese maples tall against the house,

I went to sit beside Press, who had settled down again at the table while Terrance cleared the dessert plates and refilled the coffee cups. I finished my glass of wine.

"Champagne cognac, Terrance? Or some of that yummy plum port?" J.C. called over Hugh's shoulder. "You don't mind if I boss Terrance around a little, do you, Press, darling?"

Press nodded. "Whatever she wants, Terrance."

I put my hand on his arm. He was still mine, even if the woman who might try to take him from me was only a few feet away. Despite our distance and my guilt, I wasn't ready to give him up.

"It's getting chilly. Maybe we should go inside."

"Do you want my jacket?" Press started to take his jacket off, but I stopped him.

"No, I'm fine. We won't stay out much longer."

We sat another moment, quiet.

"Rachel doesn't seem well," I said.

"Rachel is Rachel."

"She certainly doesn't like J.C. very much."

Press laughed loudly enough for both Hugh and J.C. to glance our way. "She'll learn."

"Do you want to?" We hadn't danced since Olivia's New Year's Eve party, and I thought it wouldn't hurt to let J.C. see us together.

"What?"

"Dance?"

"Hell, no. You know I don't really like it. I only did it for as long as I did to get some pretty girl like you to marry me."

I smiled in spite of myself. I'd let myself drink two glasses of wine at dinner, knowing Michael was safe asleep upstairs with both the bathroom and nursery doors locked. I'd been self-conscious, particularly with Hugh there, but my discomfort faded as the wine did its work.

"Thank you."

"For what? Marrying you? That was my pleasure."

"No, silly. For changing your mind about the ballroom."

He turned his head to watch J.C. and Hugh. The Sinatra album had started over again, and Hugh was jokingly proclaiming that she was wearing him out.

"Did I change my mind?"

I squeezed his arm, feeling a tiny resurgence of the love I'd felt for him for so many years. Was it possible that it was still there? I wasn't sure. Remembering now, I'm certain that it was the wine. The wall was still there, warning me, protecting me. But at that moment I was hopeful.

"It means so much to me. I miss our life."

When he turned back to me, I believed I saw tenderness in his eyes.

Terrance, as though to encourage my wine-induced vulnerability, came outside with a tray of after-dinner drinks.

"Finally!" J.C. said. "We were about to turn into butter from spinning around out there. Hugh is a madman."

As the two thirsty dancers fell on the glasses of water and cognac Terrance had set out on the table, Press and I remained silent.

⌒

I closed and locked the nursery door softly behind me, leaving the key on the commode table just outside. Sometime during the night, Michael had climbed out of his crib to sleep on Eva's trundle bed. I wasn't ready for him to move permanently from his crib, but as I looked down on him, sleeping with one arm flung over the back of Eva's Lassie dog, I didn't have the heart to put him back. Before leaving the room, I pulled out the lower mattress in case he rolled off.

Moonlight streamed through the dome windows, brightening the stars on its surface and filling the well of the house with silver light. My feet were bare and cold on the gallery floor and I was about to hurry back to my room when I noticed that the door to the yellow guest room, J.C.'s room, was standing open.

How horrid a thing jealousy is! I couldn't help myself that my mind, rather than imagining that she'd gone down to the kitchen for something to eat or to the library for a book, went directly to the idea that she was in Press's room. I'd seen nothing untoward passed between them that evening; but as the wine had worn off, my suspicions reasserted themselves. The idea of J.C. in any sort of sexual situation with my husband or anyone was repugnant to me. Hers would be like the embrace of a particularly feminine, but ghoulish, spider.

So do not blame me when I tell you that I went to my husband's room as though I were being pulled there. I swear, I had no choice.

My hand trembled a bit as I touched the doorknob and rested my cheek against the wood. There was indeed a sound coming from the other side. As I turned the knob and let the door open of its own accord, I felt an overwhelming sense of relief. Press was snoring in the shadows of his tall bed. The shadows were familiar, too: he was alone.

With his door safely closed, I went to stand at the top of the front stairs to listen for any sound that might come from downstairs. But I heard only the grandfather clock.

I should have gone straight back to bed, ashamed of my suspicions, or at least comforted. But I was awake and curious. There had been another girl very like J.C. at Burton Hall: the same razor-sharp limbs and aggressive laugh. We rarely spoke and never shared a class, but she had caught me staring at her once, in the library. Before I could look away, she flicked her tongue from between her lips and ran it slowly across her large white teeth. It was a strange, sensuous thing for her to do, and I couldn't look away, and for a moment it was as though we were the only two people in the room. My breath caught in my chest. Then she turned back to her book, amusement plain in her callous smile, and the spell was broken.

Something about the stillness of the house, the heaviness of the air, made me give Olivia's doorway a wide berth as I passed. Olivia's room, like J.C., fascinated and repelled me at once. What other terrors waited inside for me? *But Eva. Don't forget Eva,* I told myself.

I knew I shouldn't go into the yellow room. I'm sure I gave myself some foolish excuse about her possibly being injured or too ill to close the door herself. And of course there was the possibility that she'd just wanted to leave the door open, tempting, suggesting, to someone that *he*—yes, of course he—should make his way inside.

I forced myself to breathe deeply to slow the beating of my heart. The anticipation I felt was inappropriate, surely, for a hostess who was only supposed to be checking on a guest's welfare.

The moon was high enough that the yellow room stood in deep shadow. I had stayed in this room more than once before Press and I were married, tucked up safely beside Olivia as though she might keep an eye on me there and keep Press away from me. Although Olivia called it the yellow room, its wallpaper was truly gold and silvery white. Large flowers traced in silver-white against a rich gold field caught the bit of moonlight and shone, iridescent. The far windows looked directly down on the garden maze. I'd sat in the window seat beneath them before, wondering what my life here in Bliss House would be like. That night, I wondered if J.C. had also been imagining what her life might be like if she were the mistress of Bliss House.

The bed was empty and in disarray, but there were smells in the air that told me she hadn't been gone too long. The peppery scent of *Caron Poivre* mixed strongly with flatulence and perhaps . . . what was it? Cognac.

There was light enough to see how her belongings lay about the room with surprising carelessness: yesterday's dress over the top of a chair, a stream of lingerie flowing from the suitcase on its stand to the floor, two pairs of shoes trailing along the middle of the carpet toward the far windows. The sight of the clutter reassured me, somehow. Press didn't like clutter, would comment even if the nursery were in too much disarray. He could never live with a woman like J.C.

I dipped my hand into the open suitcase, and its depths of silk and cotton and nylon released an invisible cloud of perfume. I lifted a slip to my cheek. It was fine silk, the lace at its bosom soft, not prickly, like the lace on so many of my undergarments. She, like Rachel, would pay attention to such things, I thought. The differences were often lost on me. How odd that the two women, so alike, disliked each other.

I heard a voice through the open window. The evening had cooled, and J.C. had gone on at dinner about how much she liked sleeping in a cool room *in the nude*, and then she had laughed at my reddening face. "Oh, Precious Bride. I *am* so bad, I know. It's age, I think. I have no reason to care what people know about me."

Still clutching the slip, I crossed the room to kneel on the window seat. (On the small table beside it was, indeed, a balloon glass with a splash of cognac in the bottom. Unfortunately, the glass was resting in a puddle of the stuff. How careless she was! But I didn't dare clean it up lest she realize someone had been in the room.) Sighing, I pressed my forehead against the glass. The view from this side of the house was remarkable in the daytime: the garden below, the woods, and then the distant purple ridge of mountains beyond. It was a vast, romantic view, and it made sense that the largest, grandest bedrooms were on this side of the house. Now the ridge was just a faint line against the horizon, but I could see the maze in the garden and three figures in the center of it quite clearly. Three, where there should just have been Hera, standing on her moss-grown pedestal, her peacock in her arms. Stunned, I squeezed my eyes shut for a second to clear them. When I opened them again, the figures were still there, etched in the same silver light as the flowers on the wallpaper.

"What are you doing in here?"

Hearing Press's husky whisper, I should have been chagrined. Ashamed of myself. But I couldn't look away.

"Charlotte!"

Without turning, I waved him toward the window.

"Why are you in here, Charlotte? Where's J.C.?"

I sat back on my heels, not knowing whether to laugh or cry out in indignation.

Press put his hand on my shoulder as he leaned forward to look. I watched his face, looking for the same shock that had taken hold of me. Instead, a sly smile came to his face.

I looked back down at the scene below. J.C. was on her knees in the white pea gravel surrounding the statue, just a foot or two away from one of the marble benches, her arms wrapped around the hips of the skeletally thin man standing in front of her, her face pressed into his groin. She wore a clinging robe, her head, back, and waist a trim, recognizable silhouette. The man's face was upturned to the clear night sky; his eyes were closed, a look of sublime pleasure softening his sharp features.

Terrance.

I put a hand against the window to steady myself.

Press looked down, still amused. "Poor Charlotte. Let's get you back to your bed where you belong."

"But we can't. They have to stop!"

"They're adults, Charlotte. This isn't any of our business."

"Of course it's our business. She may be a guest, but that man is at our table every day. He serves our food." I shuddered. "It's disgusting. And he's. . . ." I couldn't find the words.

"What are you talking about?" Press looked genuinely puzzled. "Hugh?"

I shook my head, continuing to whisper, afraid they'd hear even though we were many feet above them.

"It's not Hugh. Didn't you see? It's Terrance."

Press chuckled and rubbed my shoulder. "Honey, it's not Terrance. That's Hugh down there. Although I rather like the idea that she'd be a good sport and give Terrance a thrill."

"No. You're wrong."

"Am I? Look again."

God knows, I didn't want to look into the garden again; but Press seemed so confident, I had to see for myself. I leaned forward again, trying not to look at J.C. but at the man's face.

There was no doubt that it was Hugh. But I had definitely seen Terrance. I felt tricked somehow. Deceived. As Press led me from the room, I sensed a lightening of the heavy atmosphere I'd felt when I'd earlier crossed the gallery. It was as though the house were laughing at me.

Press helped me into my own bed and got in to spoon against me. He kissed me lightly on the back of my head as though I were a child and told me to just forget what I'd seen.

"She's a pistol, that J.C.; I'm sorry she shocked you."

I didn't think of myself as a prude, but I imagined what Olivia might have done. J.C. would surely have been quietly asked to leave.

"We can't have people like that around Michael. I don't want Hugh here anymore, either. What if Nonie had seen them? Or Marlene?" I didn't mention Terrance. A part of me was still certain that I'd really seen him, and I knew that he had witnessed—done!—far worse. But I wouldn't tell Press what I was thinking. What if he was a part of the deception? Though a part of me was very relieved that he hadn't been the man with her in the maze.

"They're adults, darling. It's not any of our business. And Nonie isn't here, is she?"

"You need to speak to Hugh."

"It didn't look like he was forcing himself on her. Did it look that way to you? What they were doing wasn't so bad. It's not like we've never done it."

I stiffened as he slid his hand over my hip and into the curve of my waist.

"What is it? Why won't you relax, Charlotte?" The evening growth of his beard was rough on my shoulder and his breath was warm. "Don't be upset with J.C. She had a lot to drink tonight. Would it have been better if she had invited Hugh into her room?"

"I didn't say that."

"Well, no one else saw them, so you don't have to worry about gossip. I know how you hate that. You and my mother. Two of a kind."

"What do you mean?" I shifted away, grateful to have my irritation as an excuse to no longer have his body touching mine.

"I mean you're like my mother in a lot of ways. You worry about what people will think. Who's to know besides us? And you *were* spying on them."

"I don't want to talk about it." Though I was secretly glad that he thought I was like Olivia.

He stroked my head. "My sweet, sweet Charlotte. Sometimes I think you're too good for this world." He said it softly, without a hint of irony. Within two minutes, he was snoring.

So it was decided. We would say nothing. But I couldn't stop thinking. Hugh was probably a temporary diversion. J.C. had spent the whole evening flirting with Hugh in front of Press. Either what she was doing in the garden was yet another bid to get Press's attention, or she was simply a well-dressed tramp.

Why was it that everything good and gentle seemed to have died with Eva? Everything around me had come to seem distastefully carnal: the slides, the things Olivia had shown me. The insinuations that I knew would be made about my father and Nonie. J.C. and Hugh/Terrance. Even Rachel seemed to be obsessed, complaining that Jack didn't want to have sex with her. It was too much.

I was worried about my father. Nonie would telephone if he weren't doing well, I knew. If everything were all right, she wouldn't spend the money on a long-distance call even though I had told her to reverse the charges. I envied her being back in the tidy house where I'd grown up. Two stories, four bedrooms, two easy sets of stairs: one in the front of the house and one in the kitchen. A fenced yard where Michael might roam safely. In contrast, Bliss House was endless. Unpredictable.

Then there was the chasm between Press and me that had everything to do with Eva. My guilt was certainly between us. Though we'd both lost Eva, it seemed now like I was the one who had lost more. He didn't miss Olivia, and I still felt like he didn't really miss Eva, no matter what he said. What kind of father didn't miss his dead child?

I saw the red fingers of dawn reflected in my dresser mirror before I finally fell asleep.

When I woke, Press was gone from the bed and it was after nine o'clock. My heart began to pound when I realized that Michael would have awakened by eight, and Nonie was not there to get him from the nursery. Any thoughts I had about the previous night were gone. Throwing on my robe, I hurried from the bedroom.

The nursery door stood ajar, and Michael's crib was empty. A wet diaper and soggy plastic pants lay on the changing table. As I left the nursery to go downstairs, I saw that J.C.'s door was open as well.

Chapter 21

Invitation

"Well, here's Precious Bride!"

I said *good morning* to both Press and J.C. and went straight to Michael, who was in his high chair, happily eating dry cereal from a bowl. I noticed the canned peaches in a second bowl. His fingers, which promptly grabbed for me as soon as I came near, were covered with both sticky peach syrup and flakes of cereal.

"Mama! Mama!"

"Yum, yum, yummy." When I kissed him on top of his head, I found that his hair was also sticky with syrup. He had been busy.

J.C. was wearing the silk robe I'd seen the night before, but I could see the outlines of a gown beneath it. A thick, peach-colored terrycloth turban was wrapped around her hair, so that her head looked too large to be supported by her reedy neck. The daylight made the fine lines at the corners of her eyes more pronounced, though without her makeup she looked five years younger than she had when she arrived.

Press cleared his throat. "Look, darling. Terrance has sausages."

Terrance stood behind J.C.'s chair with a platter, and I knew Press had been hoping for just that moment. He was determinedly straight-faced, but I felt myself coloring with embarrassment.

"Oh, my, yes. They are delicious. A marvel." J.C. stabbed a sausage link with a fork and held it out in front of her. "What did you say these were, Terrance? I keep forgetting."

"Venison sausage, Miss Jacquith."

Maybe I was carried away with relief that Michael was safe, but I suddenly also found Terrance and the sausages funny. I turned my head, trying to suppress a giggle. But when I couldn't, I pretended a small coughing fit.

"Precious, are you all right? Do you need me to slap you on the back?"

As J.C. pushed back her chair, I waved her away.

"Press, there's nothing funny at all about someone choking to death. What's wrong with you? You need to help her."

Press hurried over to pat me with exaggerated care. "Are you all right?" he whispered. I shook my head, unable to decide whether or not I was going to burst out laughing. Without looking at Press, I finally regained control of myself and was relieved to see that Terrance had taken the opportunity to move away from J.C. Sitting down, I told him that I would just have eggs and toast and juice. J.C. watched me intently from across the table.

Wanting to change the subject, I asked what everyone's plans were.

"I know my plans." J.C. lifted her hand. "Since the decorators have run off to work on some ridiculous emergency project. I mean, *who* has emergency decorating projects? Well, I guess that's not fair, because I actually have them all the time. Anyway, I was thinking I'd just laze about and read. I brought work with me—plans for a five-room pied-à-terre for a lesser Rockefeller who thinks heaven is paved with chintz—but with all this gray rain outside, I am *completely* unmotivated." She took a sip of coffee. "What about you, Press? You haven't said. Playing lord of the manor, or are you going out into the muck?"

Press laid his napkin beside his plate and took two cigarettes from his case. After tapping them, filter-end down, on the table, he gave one to J.C., who put it beside her own plate. "I'm going in to the office today. I was hoping you'd come with me. I want you to draw up something for my office and the other empty one in the building. It's pretty damn drab. Then maybe Charlotte could meet us for lunch."

Terrance appeared at Press's side with a burning lighter. As he held it to the end of Press's cigarette, I watched him carefully for some tell-tale sign of the transcendent pleasure I'd seen there the night before. There was only his usual passive, unreadable gaze, focused only on what he was doing at that moment. Had Press been right? Had my eyes fooled me? I'd seen Hugh, but I had seen Terrance just as clearly.

I realized that even if I had been mistaken, I didn't trust Terrance.

"Charlotte?"

Startled, I looked at Press. He and J.C. were both staring at me. "Did you hear me? I thought you could meet us for lunch in town."

For the second time that morning, I felt my face flush with heat. "No. I'm sorry. Lunch?"

J.C. perked up. "Oh, there's that cute little inn in town where your mother put me for the wedding. They did a nice breakfast."

"The inn?" Press shook his head. "The food hasn't been very good lately. There's a roadhouse restaurant about five miles down the highway. *Phil's,* I think it is. That could be an adventure." He looked more closely at me. "Are you all right, darling?"

Michael chose that moment to knock over his milk. "Up oh," he said. When I looked at him, he grinned.

"No." I quickly grabbed my napkin and pressed it onto the carpet to sop up the milk. "Michael, that was very naughty." When

169

the napkin was soaked, I reached for Press's. "You know I have Michael all day, now that Nonie's in Clareston. Michael is no fun at all in restaurants." As though to illustrate, Michael sent up an ear-piercing squeal, then loudly declaimed for more milk. I might have asked Shelley, the orchardkeeper's sister, in to babysit, but the last thing I wanted to do that afternoon was to go out to lunch with J.C. and Press. It was even difficult to look at her in the same robe she'd been wearing in the garden.

"What about Shelley?" Press asked. "She could watch Michael."

"It's short notice. She might be visiting her mother." At least I thought she had mentioned visiting her mother. If not, it made for yet another convenient lie.

"That's too bad." J.C. made a little moue of disappointment. "I was hoping we could spend some time together. In fact, I'd like to have you all to myself for an hour or so, Charlotte. There's something I want to talk with you about."

"Sounds mysterious." Press looked from J.C. to me and raised his eyebrows.

"You just hush. It's girl talk."

She was flippant, but when she looked at me I saw something in her eyes I hadn't seen before. Sincerity. She leaned forward. "Maybe the excellent Marlene could whip us up lunch tomorrow? We can eat something yummy here and have a good talk."

Michael banged his cup on the high-chair tray and shouted a word that vaguely resembled *yummy*. Then he began to laugh as though someone had just told a brilliant joke.

Chapter 22

Alone Again

The rain that had begun before breakfast showed no signs of stopping as lunchtime approached. Michael and I played with blocks and trains. We read books and sorted laundry for Marlene, who tempted Michael with a cookie she'd made that morning so he would stop trying to climb into the tub washer in the mudroom. It was a relief to have some normality in our day. He didn't even call out "Eva! Eva!" when we went into the nursery.

It hurt sometimes that he looked so much like her. Both fair and small-featured, neither of them particularly resembled Press. (Though by the time Michael was a teenager, he looked a bit more like his father.) Press had teased me that they were changeling children, that perhaps they weren't his at all. It had been a great joke between us because we both knew that I was as faithful as a dog.

It had never occurred to me to be unfaithful. Rachel teased and flirted with other men, but I was certain she'd never cheated on Jack.

Olivia had been forced to be with a man who wasn't her husband, and he had been forced to watch. My heart broke for them both. I still could hardly believe what I had seen. Was I going insane? Had what had happened to Eva pushed me into madness? I tried not to think about it as I played with Michael, but I couldn't help myself. I had been a witness, and to witness something like that was akin to participating. Olivia had had to live with it every day of her life, and who knew what had happened afterward. What if it had happened more than once?

I knew who the man was. His face was on many of the paintings on our walls, and in a few photographs in the stack of leather-bound photo albums in the library. What I didn't (couldn't? wouldn't?) force myself to think about was what it meant. Not then. Not yet.

At one o'clock, just after I put Michael down for his nap, Marlene let me know that Terrance was driving her into church in town, where she would dust and vacuum the sanctuary as she did every week. I wondered at her steadiness, her willingness to work in Bliss House. I knew she disdained talk of the supernatural beyond the Father, Son, and Holy Spirit (never the Holy Ghost, because she wasn't that sort of Christian). It was reassuring. She was the perfect complement to Terrance who, for all I knew, was Satan himself. (Of course I didn't really think he was Satan. But he was so unreadable that I might have believed anything about him.)

When they were gone, with the exception of Michael, I was alone in the house. What I wanted more than anything was to sleep, but I swore to myself that I would never again sleep when I was alone with Michael.

Chapter 23

Missing

"Terrance might have come back!"

J.C., Press, and I clustered in a half-circle in the front hall, watching Terrance in the kitchen doorway. At least I was watching Terrance. J.C. and Press were watching me as though I were raving. Which, perhaps, I was. I was as irrational as any mother might be whose child has disappeared from the bed where that child had been taking his afternoon nap, and was perspiring from running up and down the hallways, tearing apart rooms. Press and I had separated to look upstairs. Marlene and Terrance had scoured the downstairs, while J.C. went outside. Though none of us really believed, I think, that he had been able to open an outer door. We'd been looking for more than half an hour, and there had been no sign of Michael.

Terrance's face was impassive. How I hated that face. His hands, upturned at his thighs, were his only expression.

"You didn't hear him, Terrance?" Press said. "Maybe coming down the stairs?"

"Marlene and I only just returned a few minutes before you did, Mr. Press."

"For God's sake, Press. He could have come back earlier and left again. I don't think you know what kind of man he is. What he's responsible for. What he did to your mother!" I turned to Terrance. "Tell him what you did, you bastard."

Behind Terrance, I heard Marlene murmur "Oh, dear Lord."

Press took my arm and all but jerked me aside, pushing his face into mine. "You will not do this, Charlotte. You don't get to behave this way just because Michael got out of his room while you weren't paying attention."

"What are you saying?" No, it wasn't that I didn't understand what Press was saying. He was only saying what everyone else was thinking. What I was thinking.

The nursery had smelled slightly of urine from the diaper pail because Marlene didn't empty it until the evening. How used we women become to such smells, not minding what a man would find repellent because they come from our precious children.

After not seeing Michael in the crib, I had crossed the room quietly to the trundle bed's rumpled coverlet, expecting to find him snuggled beneath it. But the bed was empty except for the Lassie doll, which lay on the pillow where Michael's head might have been. I fell to my knees to run my hands over the rumpled sheets as though I would conjure Michael from them, but he was gone.

Would I have to tell them where I had been? I couldn't. No one would believe me.

"Charlotte! Stop this, and tell us where he is."

I broke away from Press and moved toward the telephone on the table a few feet away from Terrance. He didn't flinch, but only blinked slowly as I got closer. So still. He was always so still. Picking up the telephone's heavy black handset with one hand, I reached to dial "0" with the other.

"I'm calling the police. Anybody could've come in here and taken him." *And where were you, Mrs. Bliss? Had you been drinking, Mrs. Bliss? Were you upset with your son, Mrs. Bliss?*

Press strode over, but this time he had the sense not to grab at me. His voice was steady. Perhaps it could even have been called cajoling.

"Charlotte, stop. You'll just inconvenience them. By the time they get out here, he'll be safe in your arms. I used to disappear all the time. For hours. Then I'd turn up and find no one had even noticed I was gone. Let's not imagine the worst. We just haven't looked hard enough for him."

I hesitated. The police might not even keep looking for Michael if they thought I'd done something to him. My stomach clenched when I thought of him being hurt.

Another voice spoke up. It was J.C., her usual insouciant, playgirl manner gone and replaced with a serious tone.

"Tell us what happened, Charlotte. We all want to find your sweet boy. What happened while we were gone? You were alone?"

Alone? I'd been certain Michael and I were alone. I tried to make sure I was making eye contact with Press and J.C. so they would believe me as I told them how I'd been reading a magazine in the salon, the doors to the hall open, when I heard a sound out in the hallway like something soft hitting the floor. My heart had begun pounding with the fear that Michael had tried to come downstairs and had fallen.

But there had been nothing in the hall. I'd looked up to see that the nursery door was still closed. I had locked it myself. Unnerved, I went to the kitchen to make myself a cup of hot tea, putting on the kettle to boil.

"When I got home, it was boiled dry and the whistle had come loose," Marlene interrupted. "But it was on the lowest heat, or there might have been a fire."

From the kitchen, I'd heard a cry somewhere in the house—I thought from the servants' wing. God, it was a horrible, mournful sound, like something in pain. Not quite human, not quite animal. First, I'd rushed up the stairs off the dining-room hallway, to make sure Michael was all right; finding his door still closed, I'd started toward the back of the house. Then I saw the animal. At least I was sure right away it was an animal. What else might have made such a sound? (And here I did not tell them that I'd been terribly afraid it was an *unnatural* sound, and that I had experienced a huge sense of relief on seeing the creature's tail and two hind legs.)

Although I had no weapon, I followed after it, searching the servants' wing, but all the doors were closed. Was it a cat? I wasn't sure because it seemed too big. I went downstairs and searched every room.

The cry came again, reverberating in the hallway from above. This time so loud and long that I was sure it would wake Michael. I hurried up to the third floor, but the theater and ballroom doors were closed and it wasn't in the hallway or any other of the rooms. So I went back down to the servants' wing, and grabbed a broom to shoo whatever it was outside. I opened every door.

"Nothing?" J.C. looked concerned.

"For God sakes, Charlotte. This isn't helping us find Michael." Press ran his hand through his hair. "You must have fallen asleep."

"Of course I didn't fall asleep! I told you I was reading a magazine." Although I knew it was a fair assumption, it made me angry that he would accuse me.

I described how I had looked down into the hall again from the second-floor gallery to see a fox skirting the wall near the front door. As it trotted, it made a kind of hissing sound as though it were talking to itself, or calling to someone—something—else. Then it disappeared into the dining room. I started down the stairs, but I thought of Michael and I turned back. And when I reached the top, I started for the nursery.

Again, I hesitated. What I couldn't tell them was how it had seemed that time had slipped, just as it had when I was in the forsythia looking for the rabbit. Over an hour had been lost, but I knew that I hadn't been asleep.

"What did you see?" J.C. had come to stand very close to me. There was no skepticism on her face, as there was on Press's. Only concern.

"It ran into his room." Now my voice was almost a whisper. "The door was open, and it ran into his room, and when I got there, neither of them was inside."

No one else spoke for a moment.

"Jesus Christ." Press ran his hand down his face, covered his mouth.

J.C. touched my arm. I didn't move but only stared at her. "There's not time to explain, Charlotte. But I need you to trust me right now. Will you try?"

The stairway leading to the door to the roof was as claustrophobic as a dark, unwanted thought, and the air was heady with humidity from the rain on the other side of the door. I imagined Michael carefully climbing the deep wooden stairs, pressing his dimpled hand against the wall for balance. I could imagine it, but I didn't believe it. It seemed like madness.

Press turned the key in the lock one way, and then the other. The bolt clicked into place.

"It wasn't locked. How did you know?" Looking back at J.C., I heard the wonder in my own voice and all the horrible implications. Michael had never been in this stairwell, had never even been in the small room beside the theater where the stairs began—at least not with me. It was impossible.

"Let me by!" I didn't wait for J.C. to answer, but squeezed by Press to turn the key again myself, and pushed open the door.

Blinded by the brilliant sheen of silvery gray sky, I stumbled out onto the tar-covered roof. When I blinked, I could see the stark black outline of the dome, the two blocks of rooms, and the short iron railing around the edge of the roof. I squeezed my eyes shut until the shapes dissipated.

Press was behind me. "Terrance, you go on to the far south section. Charlotte, for God's sake, just wait here with J.C."

Ignoring Press's ridiculous admonition to stay where I was, I circled back around the odd little shelter that embraced the doorway, with Press calling after me.

"Dammit. Why won't you listen, Charlotte? Stop!"

"I'll go with her." J.C.'s footsteps followed behind me on the gritty rooftop.

The dome, with its circlet of narrow windows, rose in front of me to a height of about eight feet. The windows were not particularly clean but were spattered with bird droppings and grime, and streaked where the rain had come down hard against the glass. Though I hardly gave it a thought then, I wondered later at the state of the windows. From far below, the windows seemed clear as new glass, filling the hall with sunlight. But, then, who would come out to clean the windows? Much later, when I had time to think about it, I wondered why it hadn't bothered Olivia. Perhaps her vision hadn't been what it had used to be. Still, it seemed a strange oversight.

As I walked around the dome, I had the feeling that we were wasting time. Of course Michael wasn't up there! J.C. was still following, not saying a word, when I went to the front railing and looked out over the drive. Old Gate rested in the northern distance, oblivious to what was happening far above it. As I watched, the view shimmered with bands of moisture like some kind of mirage, the steeple of the Presbyterian church the only thing that seemed to remain firm and upright. Behind me, far on the other end of the roof, I could hear Press opening and shutting the creaking doors of the old storage sheds far beyond the dome and calling Michael's name.

"Michael," I whispered. "Where are you, baby?"

I forced myself to look down into the circle of the drive, moving my gaze cautiously closer to the house, which was where he would be if he'd fallen. Michael was a climber. Curious. He always wanted to be close to the things he was curious about: examining them intently, sticking them in his mouth if he could. Once, when Nonie had brought him into her room to watch a news program, he had crawled to the television cabinet and pulled himself up. Holding firmly to either side, he had pressed his face against the screen and made a loud humming noise, causing us to laugh. When he pulled away, he had left behind a wet, round smear on the glass.

Having once been close to the small sheds Press was searching, I didn't want to go near them again. He'd told me they were filled with paneling, old tools, furniture, and trunks. Who knew what the extremes of heat and cold had done to the contents? Everything was probably worthless by now. Worthless, but perhaps concealing a little boy. I turned back to look, but the dome was in the way.

I made my way back toward Press along the western edge of the roof, whose lines were unbroken except for the upright brick rectangles of yellow brick chimneys. The shallow wing's rooftop was a half dozen feet lower than the rooftop I was on now, and it held no strange dwellings or doorway shelters. Below were the garden and maze.

"Charlotte! J.C.!"

Press called from an open doorway in the farthest strip of rooms. I felt the new, constant pain in my stomach slip, lighten for the briefest second. The rush of hope propelled me toward his voice. J.C. was suddenly ahead of me.

But I saw movement in another direction. Something, perhaps an animal, had just disappeared around the curve of the dome. Dropping to one knee, I tried to peer through the windows, but the angle from where I was seemed all wrong, and the windows were too dirty. Yet there *was* something moving. And quickly.

Press called my name again, but I had to know what I'd seen. Brushing off a bit of loose, tarry gravel from my knee, I stood up. By now, the wetness of the roof had permeated the thin leather soles of my heels. Michael had been in bed barefoot and was too young to put on his own shoes, let alone tie them. What might the coarse rooftop do to *his* tender feet? (In a split second, I had a sudden memory of Eva as I'd seen her in the morning room. When she'd died, she been wearing the pink playsuit I'd put her down for her nap in, but why had she come to me wearing muddy sandals as well? And the ribbon. What about the hair ribbon?)

Ignoring Press, I hurried around the dome, staying close by the windows.

I called Michael's name. A clammy breeze picked at my hair and blew across my neck, giving me a chill; and with it came a certainty that the thing I had glimpsed was no animal, but Michael himself. Press called to me again, but the breeze carried his voice away. I heard it only as someone might hear from deep under water.

Yes! It was Michael!

Perhaps it was momentary joy that brightened the gray afternoon for me; but whatever it was, the light grew brilliant as a vast, newly stoked flame, and when my son stopped briefly and grinned back at me, naked as a cherub, he was the color of a golden peach.

I ran, but my feet were clumsy. My low heels weren't made for running, and I stumbled a second time, this time falling, falling, my arms reaching for Michael, my cheek scraping the crumbled tar.

I screamed Michael's name and pulled myself up onto my hands, mindless of the scrapes, to see him at the northern lip of the roof, squeezing his plump little body through the decorative iron trim. He didn't look back again, but disappeared over the edge of the roof without a sound.

Press shouted for me, but before he could reach me I was up, running for the edge of the roof. Was I screaming? Maybe. I do remember hearing the wind in my ears as I ran. Just as I reached the edge, two firm hands tried to pull me backwards from the waist. I couldn't see! Fighting him, holding hard to the iron trim, I strained to see the ground below.

Finally, for the briefest of seconds, the hands loosened and I collapsed over the railing so that I was staring at the ground. There, curled into a helpless crescent, was the body of a fox, the creamy-white tip of its tail stark against the stone of the patio below.

When I opened my eyes again, it was dusk, and the light of a single lamp groped pitifully in the overwhelming dark of the big room.

Oh, God. Was it happening again? It couldn't be.

I was afraid to turn my head, lest the person I sensed nearby turn out to be Rachel. Now Michael would be dead. I squeezed my eyes shut again. It was hard to think because my brain was fogged, but I knew enough to be afraid.

"Charlotte. Charlotte, you should wake up."

A woman's voice. I turned my head cautiously.

J.C. had pulled a chair up beside the sofa so that her angular body threw its shadow over me. "You'll never forgive yourself if you don't wake up. I've been waiting." The gloom made it difficult to see her face clearly. What I *could* see was her worry.

"Have they found him? Where is he?" I tried to sit up. Jack had promised that the shot he was going to give me would help me stay calm enough to keep searching for Michael without knocking me out. Clearly he had lied.

"I told Press it wasn't fair to you. Here's some water." She helped me sit up and gave me a tall glass of tepid water that I downed in just a few swallows. "Now that you're awake, we can both search for him."

When she took the glass back, and I thanked her, she sat back in her chair. "Does Press always treat you like this?"

My head ached. I wanted to get up and look for Michael, but I found it hard to move. "I don't know what you're talking about."

"You're not a stupid woman. And I don't think there's anything wrong with you."

"Is that what Press told you? That I'm crazy?"

"It doesn't matter what he's said to me, Charlotte. I've seen you with my own eyes. I'm no fool either."

"I thought I was 'Precious Bride' to you." I didn't bother to keep the sarcasm from my voice.

"That's just business, honey. We all play different roles, and it's never good to be serious all the time. You'll understand one day." She gave me a rueful smile. "Listen. I don't like what's going on here. There's too much pain." She glanced around the room as though pain were something one could see stuck to the walls or the ceiling, something to be disguised with a throw rug or a swath of paint. "I think Jonathan is afraid to contact me."

I stood up slowly, using the arm of the sofa for balance.

"I don't know who in the hell you're talking about. Where is everyone?"

J.C. followed me out of the salon. The chandelier was dark, and only a couple of lamps were on in the hall and along the upper galleries. I could hear voices coming from outside and the kitchen.

"The police and a lot of the neighbors' hired men are out searching the woods and orchards. I heard someone say there were extra lanterns out front. We can get one and go out and join them."

I didn't answer, but started for the front door. I'd only gone a few feet before I realized my legs and feet were bare, and the front of my skirt and blouse were streaked with dirt and tar. Not only had I been out of my mind with worry and panic, I looked like a madwoman. It wasn't any wonder that Jack had sedated me. Still, I wouldn't forgive him unless he walked through the front door carrying Michael.

He's gone! It's my fault. Again, my fault!

"I'm going to run upstairs to change and get a jacket." Without turning around, I asked J.C. if she had one warm enough for searching outside. I have no idea what led me to give her that consideration, except that she and I were alone.

"I do. I'll get it and meet you down here?"

We started up the stairs in silence, but when we reached the first landing I stopped.

"How did you know about the roof? Do you know where Michael is?"

"I don't know where he is. I swear to you I don't. Please don't think I'm cruel, Charlotte."

"I think you're worse than cruel."

J.C. briefly closed her eyes. "That's not fair. I just knew we had to go to the roof. But it wasn't a bad thing, don't you see? Nothing happened to Michael up there. We know that now."

"Why are you really here?"

"Do I really matter that much right now? Isn't the most important thing that we find Michael?"

From my darkened bedroom, I could see the driveway and the road leading to the orchards. There were several pickup trucks and a couple of sedans I thought I recognized parked in the driveway, but the dusk made it hard to make them out. Well beyond them, faint points of light bobbed through the trees, a many-eyed beast hunting for the slight, warm shape of my baby boy.

Alive. He had to be alive.

I quickly stripped out of my dress and stockings and grabbed a blouse, heavy sweater, dungarees, and tennis shoes from my closet. After using the bathroom, I splashed water on my face, smearing what little makeup hadn't worn off, and dabbed my face with a towel. Then I ran a quick brush through my hair. My wrist was sore from falling on it, but not sprained. Each action was automatic. Fast. When we found Michael, I wanted him to see a mommy he recognized. Not a pained, frightened mess.

Without the chandelier on, the gallery was heavily shadowed. I wondered about Terrance and Marlene. What were they doing? Had they joined the search?

I called out for J.C. "I'm going downstairs."

Hearing a familiar sound, I looked across the gallery at Olivia's room, which we had already searched several times. The door had certainly clicked shut.

"J.C.?"

There was no answer from J.C.'s room, though her door was open and the light was on. There was no light of any kind beneath Olivia's door. As I hurried over, I was thinking it might be a searcher who had decided to take advantage of the situation and explore places they weren't wanted.

I confess that when I put my hand on the doorknob, I hesitated, afraid that Olivia was going to show me something and I wouldn't be able to leave. But if she were there, wouldn't she want to help me? I went inside.

The sky outside Olivia's window was a dusky plum color, and the room was full of shadows. That the air smelled of roses— decaying roses—I tried to put down to my imagination.

"Olivia?"

I waited for what seemed like several minutes. The scent seemed to fade.

Disappointed, I turned to leave.

"Mama! Mamamamamama! Mama!"

Michael's voice. Above me.

I looked up. Michael's pale, happy face peered at me from behind the carved pediment of Olivia's seven-foot-tall French armoire. Seeing me notice him, he gave me another triumphant "Mama!" Then, "Michael down."

Chapter 24

Reunited

The front hall was filled with people, many of whom had been at the house after the funeral the week before, and the mood was light, as though they'd come by for an impromptu party. Marlene was handing around coffee, and Terrance had brought out a tub of bottled beer. I held Michael tightly in my arms as Press and I thanked everyone who had searched. It was mostly men, though there were a few wives too, mostly of the men who worked on nearby farms. Shelley, the cheerful, blond nineteen-year-old sister of the orchardkeeper, had even put on work boots to help with the search. I wouldn't have noticed, but she mentioned them, embarrassed that she was wearing them in the house.

"I had to come," she said. "My baby brother was lost for a day and a half when he was three, and we found him in an old well someone hadn't covered. It about killed my mother."

Michael shifted in my arms, wanting to get down, but I just held him more tightly. Relenting, he rested his head on my shoulder with a sigh, sucking on two of his fingers.

Shelley smiled. "She said there were years of leaves down there that broke his fall. He was just bruised, and very mad. Now he's training in the Navy to go on a submarine. You'd think he'd be afraid of dark small places after that happened, but he isn't." Shyly, she reached out to touch Michael's damp curls. "And where were you hiding, little one?"

Michael watched her intently for a moment, then grinned and turned his head away, shy.

Where had he been? I still wasn't certain.

After I'd shouted down the gallery to let J.C. know I'd found him, and asked her to find Press, I quickly changed his very full diaper and took him to the kitchen to feed him. Before everyone started gathering at the house to see Michael for themselves, I told Press and J.C. that I'd found him on top of the armoire. I saw the muscles in Press's jaw tense—a sign that he was either angry or trying to make a decision. Finally he said, "Well, he's a magician, this one." He rubbed Michael's head and kissed him. "But let's just tell everyone he fell asleep under his grandmama's bed and we missed him. It's not anyone's business."

J.C. and I had looked at each other, then nodded. It was the best answer.

I knew there was no way he'd gotten to the top of the armoire without help, and, given the number of times we'd looked in Olivia's bedroom, it seemed unlikely that he could have been up there, quiet, the entire time. But who would've put him up there? I still suspected Terrance, whom Press had assigned to hand out cigars to the men and was now making his way from group to group, holding open one of Press's smaller humidors. But I still couldn't answer the question *why*. It seemed like a prank—a dangerous, foolish prank. *Playfulness* did not seem to be in Terrance's dour personality. Then there was J.C., who might have done anything while I was knocked out and the others were searching. I silently cursed myself for giving in to Jack and his drugs. But Press had been holding me. I'd had no choice.

As Shelley continued to try to engage Michael, I looked across the hall to see Rachel talking to Hugh Walters, who wasn't in uniform but wore a denim work jacket and light brown moleskin trousers. Jack hadn't wanted Rachel around the stressful search, but had called her to come right over after Michael had been found. Seeing me, she blew me a kiss.

Michael, excited by the novelty of the crowd, began to wriggle again, and I recognized the signs of approaching hysteria. His eyes were rimmed in red, and he rubbed at them with his fist.

Having volunteered to help Marlene hand around drinks, J.C. finally came to stand beside me. After I introduced her to Shelley, Shelley said that she would try to find her brother, and excused herself.

J.C. had returned to wearing her very public smile, but toned it down when she stepped a little closer to gently pat Michael's back. He put his thumb in his mouth and rested his head on my shoulder.

"Looks like he's about to pass out."

"I really should get him upstairs. Have you seen Press?" I felt awkward and confused around her. Was she really having an affair with Press, and was she involved in Michael's disappearance? Or was I mistaken? Something about her made me want to trust her, but I couldn't make myself.

She said she thought she'd seen him go into the library. When I went in search of him, she drifted toward Hugh and Rachel. Recalling what I'd seen in the garden, I couldn't help but wonder how uncomfortable *that* conversation might be.

I found Press and Jack in the library, the smoke from their cigars clouding the room.

"There's my little man." Press rested his cigar in the nearby standing ashtray and rose to take Michael from me. I didn't want to let him go, but Michael had given a small grunt of delight on seeing his father and pulled away to reach for him.

"He needs to be in bed, Press. He's about to fall apart."

Michael rested his face against his father's cheek and patted his head as though it had been Press lost and in distress all afternoon. It was reassuring to see how comfortable the two of them were together. *Without Eva, we would all need each other that much more.*

Press sat back down in one of the broad, comfortable leather chairs, pulling Michael onto his lap. Olivia had bought the chairs on a trip she'd taken out West and had them sent back to Virginia. They weren't the kind of thing one saw in houses in Virginia, but perhaps in an elegant hunting lodge. But they suited the room, and suited the two attractive men resting in them.

Behind me, the library door opened with a murmur of voices from the hall.

"Here you all are. Why is everyone hiding in here?" Rachel waved a hand in front of her face. "Phew. Those stupid cigars. I thought I could at least get away from the smoke in here. *Will* somebody open a window before I die?" She held on to the couch's arm as well as her belly as she sank onto the cushions.

By "somebody," she obviously meant Jack, who quickly got up and opened the window beside the fireplace a few inches.

"So, are you going to tell me where he really was? I don't buy the whole hiding under the bed story. You can sell it to the hillbillies out there, but not me." She was looking at Press.

I also looked at Press, waiting to hear what he would say.

"I've already told Jack. Charlotte found him on top of the armoire in my mother's room. God knows how the tyke got up there. Somebody's idea of a practical joke."

Now Rachel looked at me, appraising. It was as though we had just been introduced and she was trying to determine what sort of person I was. I was puzzled at first, then realized she thought I had done it.

"You can't think I put my own son up there, Rachel!"

"Nobody said that." Jack shook the ice cube in his nearly empty glass, drawing Michael's attention. He drank down the final sip of whiskey. "No one is accusing you, Charlotte."

I remembered how Press had squeezed my shoulders so I would stay still while Jack injected me with the sedative. There had been a strange look of pleasure in Jack's eyes that I hadn't remembered until just then.

Rachel spoke quickly. "Everyone knows how horrible it's been for you, darling. Of course I don't think you did any such thing. I would defend you to the death. I swear on the tiny fiend in my belly." She tried a little laugh, but it fell flat in the silent room.

Press stood up.

"You were right, Charlotte. Michael does need to be in bed. You too." He brought Michael over to me and kissed my cheek. "You're exhausted."

I was still stung by the way Rachel had looked at me. But Michael returned to me without protest, and having him in my arms was a comfort. I told myself that what had happened with Eva had left a question in a lot of people's minds. Although I hoped Rachel would think better of me, I knew it was unfair of me to expect it. It would be a long time before anyone fully trusted me again.

I was asleep when Press came into the nursery. Michael had fallen asleep even as I'd changed his diaper. I'd been about to lift him into his crib, but instead I laid him on the lower mattress of the trundle bed, where he settled immediately, finding his thumb and pulling the sheet close to his face.

When the sudden light from the hall sliced through the darkness, I woke on the upper mattress of the trundle bed without any memory of falling asleep there. Turning over to rise up on my elbows, I saw Press silhouetted in the doorway.

"What is it?"

He left the door open just a few inches, letting some light in, and walked cautiously across the room to lean over the foot of the bed.

"How's he doing?" he whispered, putting a hand on the blanket covering my leg. It wasn't a terribly warm blanket. Had Eva ever lain here, cold in her own bed? The thought saddened me.

"Why don't you go back to your room?"

I sat up. "I want to be here if he wakes up tonight. He was so fretful." It would have been fruitless for me to be anywhere else. Away from him, I might not sleep at all. "What time is it?"

When Press bent toward me, he smelled of cigars and Scotch. "Just a few folks left. J.C. is still downstairs. Rachel and Jack, Hugh. They won't stay much longer. It's almost one."

I wanted to lie back down, to sleep and sleep until the heaviness in my chest dissipated. I wanted to drop my hand over the edge of the mattress to the trundle below and feel Michael's breath against my skin.

But Press leaned closer, steadying himself on one hand, and kissed me, hard, forcing his tongue into my sleep-clouded mouth. He hadn't shaved since early that morning (how long ago that seemed!), and his beard was harsh against my face. Before Eva died, he had made his way to my bedroom four or five nights a week, but I was surprised he'd come into the nursery with guests downstairs. With J.C. in the house.

His hand went to my breast. I'd been too tired to go to my room for pajamas and so wore only my bra and panties beneath the blanket; my clothes lay over the back of the rocking chair. It was strange to be there in the nursery, with Michael so close by, yet I felt myself responding to Press despite all that had happened. Grief and fear and, finally, elation had made me vulnerable. I'd ceased to trust him by then, and perhaps I'd even ceased to really love him. But desire has no need for love.

He climbed onto the bed, and was on his knees in front of me, hurriedly unbuckling his pants. As his pants fell, he took down his boxer shorts. I couldn't see much in the darkness, but the smell of him was musky, and he pressed himself against my face, my lips. His hands were in my hair, and he forcefully massaged the back of my head and my neck. Remembering that Michael was there below us, I pulled away. I whispered that we couldn't.

"Of course we can," he answered and tried again.

"I won't."

I pulled away again, whispering *no*. I had never told him no before.

With a grunt of frustration, he pushed me gently onto my back and quickly found my panties and began to remove them. The tension of Michael being so close caused me to tremble, and by the time Press entered me, I had to grind my teeth together in my mouth to stop their violent knocking. Our tender passion the afternoon that Eva died felt like it had happened a lifetime ago. The thought made me sad and I banished it, but it was quickly replaced by the memory of Terrance and J.C. in the garden. No, not Terrance. Hugh.

And through it all, I had the sensation that Press and I were being watched.

Press's face was buried against my neck, and the length of him was far inside me. I chanced a look at Michael, but he still lay sleeping, turned away from us. Despite the heat of Press's body, I felt a rush of cold and I looked beyond him to see a shadow on the ceiling, an ill-defined, darker spot in the darkness. As I watched, it gathered itself into a tight circle and slid across the ceiling to hang, suspended, for a few seconds before dropping in a long oily stream. I was startled by the sound of breaking glass, but Press was pushing into me with concentrated determination and wasn't disturbed. I squeezed my eyes shut. Waiting. Praying that what I'd seen was only a trick of the darkness. Whatever it had been had frozen every bit of my sudden desire, and I let Press finish without offering much in response, but he didn't seem to notice. He was quiet as he came inside me, shuddering to a stop to lie against me, heavy with sweat. When his breathing returned to normal, he rolled off me carefully—the bed was small, and Michael was still just a couple of feet away.

"Look what you do to me, you witch." He kissed me on the nose, his face shining with perspiration. There was no sign of the cruel Press, the deceitful Press. But whatever he saw on my face quelled his pleasure. "What's the matter? He's fine. He doesn't know a thing."

Whatever I might say about what I'd seen would surely sound mad, but I couldn't help thinking of Olivia. "What about everyone downstairs?"

His teeth were bright in the room's dim light. "I'll tell them the truth. That you seduced me."

Suddenly, I didn't want him to go. Turning onto my side, I wrapped an arm around his neck and pulled him to me, wishing, wishing that Olivia hadn't died. That Eva hadn't died. That he could be the same man I'd married and not a man of secrets. That I could close my eyes and open them a moment later to find that it was still early spring, and we were all happy and safe.

Finally he kissed my forehead. "They really will start chewing on the curtains if I don't get back to them. Try to go back to sleep."

He left the room, pulling the door softly closed behind him.

I lay back on my damp pillow. When Rachel and Jack were gone, would he go to J.C.? In that moment, I didn't really care. I had my son back, and that was all that mattered.

I dropped my hand to where Michael lay below me. Heat clung to him like a protective cloak. My poor boy.

Shivering, I pulled the discarded blanket all the way up to my shoulder and lay watching the place on the ceiling where I'd seen (or imagined I'd seen) the shadow. Before I finally fell asleep, I heard the distant chimes of the great clock in the hall ring two.

～

I dreamed.

The windows and doors of Bliss House were open and the winter cold was coming for me and there was no way for me to outrun it. Glittering ice covered the windows at the front of the house. I was naked, crouching close to the walls as I moved, trying to cover my genitalia because I felt someone was watching me. Not Press, but perhaps Marlene or Terrance. I was certain one of them might emerge from one of the rooms or come out from the back of the house. The paneling was so frigid that I knew if I paused too long in any one place, my skin would turn into a tough, frozen hide and I would become immobile like Hera in the garden. No, I had to keep moving.

Daylight, always at a premium in the deep interior of the house, streamed down from the narrow windows around the dome. I stretched out one hand toward the sunbeams' warmth, but they were freezing, too, like the walls.

Olivia's was the only closed door, and behind it was the only possible shelter in the massive house. To make my way there, I grabbed on to the railing, which was less cold, less dangerous than the tall paneled walls. As I pulled myself along them, every part of my body hurt, and I couldn't cover myself any longer because I knew I would be frozen if I slowed. With each crouching step I took, the sense that I was being watched intensified.

When I reached the top of the stairs, I had to drop to my belly, and the floor was cold against my breasts. My nipples caught on the tiny, age-filled grooves of the plank floor. All of the house's lovely furniture and carpets were gone, and its walls were bare. Bliss House had been abandoned. Or perhaps I was seeing it as it

193

had been when it was first raised out of the dirt, sculpted out of bricks from the local lime-rich clay.

Once I reached Olivia's door, I pressed my body against it to feel its heat, and I nearly swooned with relief so intense that it felt sexual. I opened the door carefully, worried that the frozen light shining in from the windows might cut me. But I needn't have worried. It looked as Olivia's room always looked. The papered walls were crowded with paintings, needlepoint samplers, and hangings done by Olivia's mother and aunts. The massive French armoire dominated the left side of the room, with Olivia's four-poster on the right. It wasn't until I was well inside the room that I noticed the smell. Covering my mouth, I tried to filter the fetid air by breathing from behind my hand. It was the smell of the slaughterhouse, or of the offal barrel behind the butcher shop a few doors down from my father's store on a July afternoon.

"Mamamamamamamama!"

How had I not seen him before?

Michael was on Olivia's bed, nestled in Olivia's arms. Rushing to them, my heart went cold. Yes, it was Olivia. Her long hair, which—since I'd met her—she'd pulled back into a tight, chic bun, rested in greasy strands on her shoulders. She wore a loose silk dressing gown covered with pale pink and white peonies, and her arms were wrapped tightly around Michael, who had begun to wriggle and whine.

"Mama! I want to get down. Make her let me go!" It was Michael's voice, but older. He held out his hands to me, clenching and unclenching his fists—a sure sign of his excitement.

Olivia, though, didn't move. Her eyes were fixed, the slack half-grin on her face showing only a sliver of her age-yellowed teeth.

"I'll take him, Olivia." My voice was flat and strange to my ears. "Let him go, Olivia."

Olivia didn't move, but continued to stare. Something flickered on her upper lip. A pair of flies lifted away and spun around each other for a brief moment, then landed at the corner of her left eye. She didn't blink.

I wanted to run away, but I wouldn't leave Michael. He didn't seem unhappy or even aware that the woman holding him was certainly dead.

"Come here, Michael," I said, as calmly as possible.

Michael tried to lurch forward, but only fell sideways into his grandmother's motionless lap, hanging over one of her arms.

"Mama!" He grabbed at her fingers, trying to peel them off of him, but the flesh began to break away and stuck to his hands. When he looked up at me, I saw the panic in his eyes.

Against all reason, I began to scream at Olivia for her to release him. Instead, more flies lifted from their resting places on her robe, in her hair, from the hollow of her neck, filling the putrid air with their ceaseless drone.

I woke, opening my eyes to find the sheet twisted around me and soaked with sweat, and Michael, his eyes wide and frightened in the faint blue light of the hour before dawn, standing on his trundle mattress, watching me.

"Eva." His eyes filled with tears that spilled onto me as he climbed up, into my arms.

Chapter 25

Respite

I was grateful for dawn.

Both J.C. and Michael slept most of the day. I sat in the nursery rocker, dozing or reading. There were no visitors and no workers, not even the painter in the ballroom—at least I didn't hear him, and the ballroom doors were closed. Had I really spoken to him only two days earlier? It seemed like a lifetime ago. Marlene cooked. Terrance served and polished silver. Even Bliss House seemed to rest after the excitement of the previous day.

Late in the morning, I called Nonie to check on my father, and to tell her about Michael disappearing. While I didn't exactly make light of it, neither did I tell her how panicked I'd truly been.

When I was finished, after a long silence, she said, "Why don't you come home to us, Charlotte? For a visit."

But I still couldn't leave. Though I hadn't seen Eva in days, nothing had changed, and the knowledge of what Terrance had done to Olivia was still there, but its urgency had faded. I wanted to forget what had happened to Michael. He had, after all, been found safe and unharmed inside the house.

And what if it really was me? What if I had done what everyone thought I had, taking Michael from his bed, putting him in Olivia's room? It was true that I hadn't been myself. Maybe the lost time, and the hallucinations—the fox, Olivia's rape, even Eva—meant that I really was insane.

"Not yet, Nonie. I'll come soon."

If I had listened to her, so many things might have been different.

I was in the nursery when I saw Press's Eldorado come up the driveway and stop in front of the house. The passenger door started to open, but then he quickly got out and hurried around to open it himself.

There was a bit of a fumble and laughter as he tried to help the woman in the passenger seat out of the car; once she was out, I saw that it was Shelley. I suspected that, young and inexperienced as she was, perhaps no man had ever before opened a car door for her. But the bigger question was why she was in Press's car at all.

She bent to take a small bag from the floor of the passenger seat. When the door was closed again, she stood looking up at the front of the house. If she saw me, she chose not to acknowledge it.

Press took a second, much larger suitcase from the trunk and guided Shelley, again laughing, to the front door.

I waited for him to find me to tell me what was going on.

⁓

I stood in the nursery doorway and watched as Terrance carried Shelley's bags to the bedroom directly across the gallery. When Shelley saw me, she smiled and waved, but looked too nervous or excited to speak. Press had followed them up the stairs, but came straight to the nursery.

Once inside, he closed the door. Michael smiled up at him from his circle of blocks and toys.

197

"I wanted to surprise you, darling. Shelley's going to be with us until Nonie gets back so you can get some rest." He bent down to Michael. "You like Shelley a lot, don't you, sport?"

Michael looked up quizzically, then he picked up a red block and held it out to Press. "Daddy, block."

"That's a good man." Press took the block and ruffled Michael's hair. "See? Michael agrees it's a great idea."

"You can't do this."

He stood up. I was in my stocking feet, and because he was wearing shoes, we stood eye to eye. But he seemed larger than ever to me right then, as though his mass had somehow doubled. I felt small. Worried.

"This is going to make everything easier. She'll have the room opposite, but she'll sleep in here with him at night. She's just a girl, but you know how responsible she is."

"Is this because of yesterday? You know I'm not the one who put Michael in your mother's room. You know that!"

Hearing my panicked voice, Michael stopped playing and came to my side. He held out his arms. "Up, Mommy! Up!"

"Do I know that? Does anybody really know that? You were here by yourself."

"You're lying. You had something to do with it. You and J.C.; I don't know what you're trying to do to me. Do you want to be with her? Is that it?" I was almost shouting now, and Michael was increasingly frantic. "Mommy! Up! Up!" I was shaking.

"That's beneath you, Charlotte. You need to calm down."

"Or what?" I bent to pick up Michael, who threw his arms around my neck and buried his face. "Look what you're doing to Michael."

"You'll adjust." Press's voice was cold. He didn't even look at Michael.

"I'll take him to my father's house. I'll take him home."

"I can't let you do that. It's not safe for Michael. Who knows what your father's involved in? Someone tried to kill him, didn't they?"

"How can you even think that? He was hit by some idiot driver." I almost laughed. "Are you sure we're talking about the same Roman Carter?"

"There are things in the world that you don't necessarily understand."

"You're implying that my father is some kind of criminal. And that's why you don't want me to take Michael to see him?" I shook my head. "That's a bizarre fantasy, and I don't understand why you would use my father like that."

He shrugged. "What would you rather hear? You need Shelley. You need rest. Rachel agrees."

"And I suppose Jack does, too?" Everyone in my life believed that I wasn't capable of taking care of my own children. And perhaps they believed something worse: that I was more of a danger than ever.

"This isn't about Jack. This isn't about anyone else but you, Charlotte."

"If I don't agree, what happens? Is the same thing that happened to your mother going to happen to me?"

As soon as the words were out of my mouth, I knew I'd made a mistake. My suspicions about Olivia's death had been buried so deep that I hadn't even really acknowledged them. I knew it was absurd to think that Press had had anything to do with his mother's death, but I wanted to wound him. From the shock on his face, I saw that I had.

We stood facing each other in silence, our child in my arms between us.

Then the look of shock dissolved into a mask of indifference.

"Be careful, my love. Don't ruin it." He touched Michael's hair with a gesture that was so tender, so untimely, that I could only take it as a threat.

Chapter 26

The Twin

The decorators returned early the next morning. J.C. was on her way to meet them right after breakfast, but stopped me before I could leave the dining room.

"Please, let's talk this afternoon. It's important."

Overhearing, Press had said, "It's going to be cool today. I'll have Terrance set up a table in the library and light a fire."

"Wonderful!" J.C. gave me one of her enormous smiles and hurried off to the third floor. Press followed after J.C., obviously still uninterested in talking with me directly.

The night before, I had pleaded a headache and spent dinner and the rest of the evening in my room. It didn't matter that Press was left all alone with J.C. He might have had sex with her on the carpet in the central hall, for all I cared about either of them. He seemed capable of it. For most of the night, I lay on my bed, wakeful, wondering why he would treat me so badly, why everything, including my son, was being taken from me. It had to be that he was simply finding more and more ways to punish me for Eva's death. There was nothing else I'd done.

⁓

After consulting with Marlene about the inevitable lunch, I went upstairs to Olivia's room, and then into the morning room. The Magic Lantern sat, cold, on its table. I spoke Olivia's name. I spoke Eva's name.

There was no enchantment left in either place. They felt as dead as their former residents.

(I am loath to mention the small voice that I did hear when I was in that room. It was the spirit of my own desperation, and it sounded much like Press's voice. *What would it matter if you were dead? You're not needed here any longer. Not wanted. Not needed. What use is it to live?*)

⁓

"They are going like gangbusters up there!" J.C. entered the library talking. "They'll be finished in a day or two." She pulled out the chair across from me at the table Terrance had set up. "This is so elegant, Charlotte. How kind you are. I know you don't really want to do this." When she surprised me by touching my hand, I withdrew it reflexively, then was embarrassed. But she didn't react, only unfolded her napkin and laid it over her lap.

"It seems I don't have anything else to do." It was a response that came as close to rudeness as I could allow myself. I had no friends in my own house, so why shouldn't I have lunch with someone who was probably my enemy? Now that I was alone with her again, and she was being serious, I realized just how much she intimidated me. At twenty-seven, I was not quite a generation younger than she. She could have been my much older, more successful sister.

Seated in front of a cheery fire, we genteelly dissected the two
tiny braised quail that Marlene had prepared. They rested in a nest
of stewed figs, and I found mine surprisingly delicious. There was
also a cold salad with radishes, fennel, and walnuts. J.C. ate without
self-consciousness, slathering warm butter on the homemade rolls,
drinking two glasses of wine to my single glass. How she stayed
so thin, I didn't know. There were girls at school who excused
themselves to the bathroom right after meals so they could purge
their stomachs. But J.C. sat, contented, when we were finished, and
smoked a cigarette. I suspected that she had the vibrating metabo-
lism of the mantis-like insect she resembled.

She kept the conversation light with stories about her time
studying design in Paris just before the war. Despite my mood, I
laughed aloud when she told me about finding herself naked in a
couturier's window after a curtain fell down as she was being fitted
for a gown.

After lunch, we moved to another part of the room to drink
the coffee Marlene had set up on a low table before clearing our
dishes. Strangely, I found myself relaxed and wanting another glass
of wine. But the wine was gone (perhaps I'd had more than one
glass, after all). There was cognac in the room's bar cabinet, but I
remembered the last time I'd been drunk in the afternoon.

No one cares if you drink, came the voice in my head. *No one cares
if you die.*

Distracted by my darkening thoughts, I wasn't prepared for the
direction she took our conversation.

"Has your daughter contacted you?"

J.C. was now sunk comfortably into one of the big leather chairs.
I sat in the other, my shoes off, my feet tucked beneath me. Until
that moment, I'd felt almost drowsy.

When I didn't answer—frankly, I was too stunned—she asked
me again.

"Your sweet Eva. Does she come and visit you?"

"Do you think you're being funny? Why would you ask something like that?"

Now she leaned forward. "I'm sure she's here. Don't you feel it? This house is. . . ." She let the sentence die.

"Don't tell me you believe Bliss House is haunted. Has someone been telling you stories?" I poured two cups of coffee, my hand shaking slightly. Something to do. Something to feel. She didn't know anything. The idea of J.C. seeing Eva, of being aware of Eva, set off a blaze of alarm inside me. Eva belonged to *me*.

"I've been trying to tell Press for years. You can't hide from what's here, Charlotte." She got up to take a cigarette from the box on the smoking table and used her dying cigarette to light it. Then she stabbed the end of the first cigarette into the ashtray and came to stand over me. Her soft, manicured fingertips found my cheek. "Don't be afraid, dearest. Why would you be afraid of your own child? I know she was the light of your lives. Press is devastated, but he doesn't have a mother's sensitivity." Before releasing my face, her fingertips brushed beneath my chin and I felt a disturbing shudder of pleasure pass through my body.

Was it that touch, that small seduction that led me to listen to her that afternoon? I was cautious—no, that's a lie. I wasn't cautious. My very being felt raw and exposed and, God help me, needful of someone to hear me. Here was a stranger, and not just a stranger, but someone who lived outside the boundaries of my every idea of propriety. She might have touched my husband in the same ways I had, moaned with pleasure at his touch just as I had. Was I so lonely? So desperate? I only know that I wasn't in my right mind.

She moved a hassock close to my chair and sat, her endless legs angled to the floor. I'd never seen gold eyes like hers. They were fiercely animated, as though she were seeing something wondrous and strange. She was watching me, but seeing something else.

"I had a brother. A twin brother, whose name was Jonathan Cortland. J.C., just like me. Though my mother hated that my

father called us both J.C." When she laughed, it sounded just as
artificial and forced as I'd always heard it, but I kept listening.
"Julianna Catherine. That's my name, though I'll deny it if you
tell anyone, yes?"

I nodded. Another secret. Like her tryst with Hugh (or Terrance? Dare I ask her?).

"He was such a pretty little boy. We looked alike. 'Girly' is what
people called him, because he looked so much like me. But he was
all boy, I'll tell you." She smiled at the memory. "He was tough.
And brave. Oh, my, was he brave. The morning it happened, we
were out riding our ponies across an empty cattle pasture, and
mine—well, Fancy wasn't at all as sweet as her name—was almost
dancing, as though she were trying to shake me off. The wasps
were bad that summer, and I thought maybe one had crawled up
under the saddle. And although I was twelve and had been riding
for years, my mother had made me put on some ridiculous loose
trousers and I didn't want to change before going out to ride. I
should've been able to calm her, or at least slide right off when I knew
she was out of control, but the stupid trousers caught, you see, and
Fancy was having a fit."

Her hands were like nervous alabaster birds. When she took a
long drag from her cigarette, she blew the smoke out forcefully, as
though in a terrible hurry. I'd never seen her so earnest, and it made
me wonder if I knew her at all. Did Press really know her? What did
he see in her? Perhaps it was her sophistication he craved. I knew,
at least, that she had no hesitation about performing a certain sex
act that I found tedious if not distasteful.

"Terrified. I was terrified. We weren't even at home, but were
spending the summer at my grandparents' farm in Arkansas. It was
beautiful, but it wasn't home, and I'm sure that's why Fancy was so
on edge. She just wouldn't stop bucking and crying. We were both
scared to death." One of her busy hands rested gently against one
ear as though she wanted to keep out the screams.

"John jumped off of King and threw himself at us. I had no idea what he was doing, and if I had I don't know that I could have stopped him. Hell, I didn't even really see him until he was right there. Right *there*."

"What happened?"

It was just a flash of a look in her eyes, but I was sure I saw cunning. How could that be? It was quickly gone, and the anxiety reasserted itself.

"He was killed, of course."

I put my hand to my mouth. "He was only twelve?"

"He didn't die right away. Fancy swung around and kicked him in the chest, puncturing his lung. She didn't mean it." Her cultured voice had slowly been sliding into a drawl as she spoke. "Our daddy wanted to put Fancy down right then and there, as soon as he heard."

I saw the boy lying in the green grass, broken and desperate for breath. Not knowing what the pony looked like, I imagined it cream-colored and squat, with a firm belly and short legs. Not elegant, but sturdy, its black lips pulled back in terror.

"Sometimes I remember those minutes, when I couldn't get off and Fancy had knocked him to the ground, and it was all I could do to hold on, praying that she wouldn't trample John."

"How did you stop?"

"I couldn't do anything. She just kept dodging, and then her legs gave out and she started to roll onto her side, which shook me loose. I hadn't done anything. John hadn't done anything. Fancy just ran off."

I waited, and J.C. took a couple more drags from her cigarette. She seemed to be thinking.

"It took him a week to die. They wouldn't let me see him."

It was hard to imagine the long-limbed, elegant woman sitting in front of me as a child. Even in her sorrow, there was nothing vulnerable about her. She stood up.

"What I wanted to tell you wasn't the story of John's dying."

"No?"

She bent over my chair, and as she spoke I smelled the menthol of her Salem cigarettes mixed with coffee on her breath.

"He's with me all the time, Charlotte. He talks to me. He tells me things. What it's like there."

"I don't understand."

Her shoulders sagged. "Oh, honey. Of course you do. You know exactly what I mean. I can see it in your pretty, pretty eyes." She touched my hair with the same hand in which her cigarette burned. "John can bring your baby to you. Eva is here, Charlotte, and we can bring her to you. Isn't that what you want? Isn't that what any mother would want?"

A log in the fireplace snapped, startling me, but J.C. didn't move.

Chapter 27

The Séance

Watching Press at the head of the dinner table, J.C. beside him, leaning conspiratorially on her elbow, her lips moving in a faint murmur, I saw how well they looked together. No one seeing them would doubt that, as lovers, they were perfectly suited.

A crescent of black hair slipped from the rhinestone (perhaps diamond?) clip at the side of her head and hung across her cheek. They were absorbed in conversation, laughing and teasing. Press's face was flushed with wine and his forehead wore the faintest sheen of perspiration. Once, if I had been as close to him as J.C. was, I might have touched my napkin to his head lightly, playfully, leading Jack to joke about my effect on my husband. Was it J.C.'s effect on Press, or the warmth of the fireplace behind him where a bank of not-quite-seasoned wood popped and spat, that made his ruddy face glow? He was smiling. So much smiling. I could hardly bear it. Their smiles were as sharp as knives.

Press had insisted that all the downstairs fireplaces be lighted, though it wasn't even quite cold enough to turn the central heating on. "Atmosphere," he'd said with a laugh. "If only we could order up a storm to encourage the family ghosts. Wouldn't Mother be scandalized if she knew we were going to have a séance?"

It had been J.C. who had broached the idea with him, telling him that it would give both him and me a sense of peace about Eva's *passing over.* I hated the phrase, but it did speak to me of a sense of Eva being in another, safer place.

I had made sure Shelley knew to keep Michael in the nursery. He was probably already asleep.

"Honey, are you absolutely, *completely* sure you want to do this?" Rachel covered my hand with hers. She'd insisted on sitting to my right even though a proper arrangement around the table would've meant that Hugh, who made up six at the table, should be there. "I know I said a long time ago that we should do a séance here, but I was joking, really. It's just too creepy, don't you think? I mean, Eva isn't going to come back, Charlotte. And Olivia coming back would be an even worse idea."

I couldn't tell her that they had both returned. I had been a witness.

Rachel, too, seemed to glow along with the candle- and fire-light. Everyone around me was vital and flushed. Even Hugh, who was usually so pale, with his light brown hair and boyish freckles. But I was cold, and felt as though all the life, all the blood had been sucked out of me. I sipped my wine, hoping to take on some of its red warmth.

"It's all in fun. Press says so." I glanced at Press, who, as though he'd heard me from far at the other end of the table, turned slightly from J.C. and winked—also conspiratorially. Were we all conspirators? And in what? I looked away from him.

"It just seems mean, somehow." Rachel also glanced toward the other end of the table, where Press had turned back to J.C.

"My mother consulted mediums all the time. She took me with her." Rachel and I both turned to Hugh, surprised.

"Really? Why?" I could hardly imagine Hugh, with his stiff collars and slightly too-wide ties, as a boy, let alone as a boy who visited mediums. He was a member of the theater group, but rarely appeared onstage, preferring to do lighting and staging. Though he'd lived in the U.S. since he was a teenager, his gentle Scots accent was still pronounced.

"Hugh seems very intuitive," J.C. had said when she suggested that he be invited. "I'm sure it comes from his Celtic roots."

"My mother was very jealous. My father died in the arms of another woman when I was just a boy. She was keeping tabs on him."

Rachel burst with laughter, but when I saw how serious his face was, I was immediately embarrassed for Rachel and him both.

"That must have been terrible for you."

Then he smiled. "Ah, the medium—Mrs. Strum—she cared nothing for my mother. Only her weekly money. To hear her tell it, my father was dallying with a new dead woman every month or so. I wish I could say it was harmless fun, but she was constantly distraught about it. Rachel is right to laugh. It was a strange deceit, but also cruel."

"So you're not a believer, then."

Hugh shrugged. "J.C. doesn't seem to be looking for any money. It can't hurt." He looked steadily into my eyes, making me feel self-conscious. "Are you expecting to talk to your little girl, then?"

"Is everything ready, Terrance?"

I confess I was relieved at J.C.'s interruption. She was looking in my direction; I turned to see Terrance standing just outside the dining room, in the hall.

He nodded.

We sat around the library's circular games table, which Press and Terrance had placed directly beneath the chandelier in the hall. J.C. had arranged half a dozen lighted candles near the walls, livening the faces in the surrounding portraits; a single candle flickered in the center of the table, washing the six of us in muted gold.

Rachel giggled and squeezed my hand. "We should be able to have wine while we're doing this."

"I think you've had enough wine." Jack said it quietly, but the openness of the hall magnified his voice. "That baby's going to be born with a cocktail glass in his hand."

Rachel started to argue, but J.C. shushed us, saying we needed to close our eyes and listen to her instructions. Press breathed a heavy sigh, and I wondered what he really thought of what we were doing. He had to be thinking of Eva. Would she speak to him? Would he ask her forgiveness?

It all felt so strange, as though we'd left Bliss House for some other place. Though the hall was immense, our world didn't extend beyond the weak light of the candle in front of me.

Then Press's lips were at my ear. He whispered, "It's going to be fine, Charlotte. I'm right here." When he kissed me on the cheek, it chilled me. It was as though he were in a play, acting a part.

How could I continue with him so close? I was no more sure of him than I was of the possibility that our dead daughter would return to us. There was Michael to worry about—I had almost lost *him* as well. And my father.

For the longest time, we sat, silent. J.C. told us to let our minds drift, to acknowledge any worries or sad thoughts and let them pass through us. At first it was uncomfortable to sit there holding Rachel's small, cool hand in one of mine, and to have Press's larger hand gripping my other. I could hear the sighs and swallows of everyone around the table. How intimate we were, and how awkward it felt. But soon, indeed, I forgot everyone else and no longer even felt my hands, but was lost in thoughts of my father.

Was he happy? Nonie would be with him at the hospital, making sure he was comfortable and that he had everything he needed. I thought of my old room in our house, with its white curtains and matching bedspread and how I would run my fingers over the spread, counting, counting the rows of tiny knots on its surface with my fingertips, and I was full of wanting for just a few minutes back in that room. How much did I want to run there and be surrounded by the morning smells of bacon and coffee that had reassured me that Nonie was there in the kitchen, waiting for me to come downstairs?

Breathing deeply, I could smell Rachel's *My Sin*, and I remembered the day we'd ridden the bus downtown to buy it for the first time, and how the saleswoman had sprayed it on both of our wrists, but Rachel was the one who wanted it, telling me that a woman had to have a signature scent, so I had to find my own perfume. The saleswoman had told me that I was a girl for *White Shoulders* if ever she'd seen one.

"Subtly innocent," she'd said. "In the very best way."

Rachel had smirked.

I hadn't worn perfume in weeks because it hadn't felt right. I'd awakened on the sofa, Rachel staring down at me, and smelled the last notes of the roses' scent floating through the open garden doors. That was the perfume I would never forget.

Somewhere outside my thoughts, J.C. began to hum tunelessly, but it was a comforting sound. A welcoming sound, like an alien lullaby. I had never imagined something so soft coming from J.C. The song floated through my thoughts, and I felt the tissue of my breasts begin to numb and tighten in the way they did when I was about to nurse one of my babies, and the feeling filled me with melancholy, and I was certain I would never suckle another child.

I can hardly express the depth of that sadness. It was different from the knowledge that I had lost Eva forever. It was like the death of the future. The death of hope.

When J.C. stopped humming, I held my breath.

I wanted to speak, to at least open my eyes, but I was afraid.

"Without opening your eyes, I want you to break the circle and reach for the paper and pencil in front of you. Pick up the pencil and begin to write, letting your subconscious and the spirit world guide your hand. Don't think of the words or the shapes, but just let the pencil move."

A part of me felt ridiculous, even in that heightened state of awareness. I was blind, and, except for the scratching of the pencils wielded by the others, I could imagine that I was alone in a very small room. No one could see what I was drawing on the paper. No one cared. I hadn't felt so free since the last time I'd painted, months before Michael was born. I imagined drawing and painting the animal figures on the ballroom walls, changing the strange and gloomy ballroom into a place of fun. As my hand moved across the page, my lips widened into a smile, and my heart lightened.

By the time I stopped writing, I felt excited and energized, dwelling in a state I hadn't known existed before. My heart warmed to J.C. and everyone that was close to me. I felt I might even be able to forgive Press. Eventually. I look back on it now and recognize it as the same flush of well-being that one gets from being drunk on good champagne. I have never felt that way again.

J.C. began to speak, asking Jonathan and any spirits who might be around us to be kind, to reach out to us and give comfort to the ones around the table who were in desperate need of it.

"I ask the newly dead to hear us, to take pity on those of us who are bereft, like pitiful children."

At the word *children*, I thought of course of Eva. Not the smiling girl I'd known, but the gaunt, wet waif who had visited me in Olivia's morning room. And, oddly, of the boy who had been Press's father. For he had, truly, seemed less like a husband than a sad, lost boy.

"Are you here, Zion? Helen? Who are the spirits who watch with us tonight?"

It was like St. Augustine's prayer: *Watch thou, dear Lord, with those who wake, or watch, or weep tonight, and give thine angels charge over those who sleep.*

Where were the angels watching over Eva?

I don't know how much time passed. Had the others opened their eyes? Would the hall be different? There was a kind of light now inside my eyelids, but I couldn't tell if it was coming from outside me or not.

"I can feel you here," J.C. said. "I can feel how strong you are. Is that you, Zion?"

In answer, there was no sound, but a powerful smell of something sharp and sulfurous. Beside me, Rachel coughed, then began to make small gagging sounds.

"Breathe, my dear." J.C.'s voice was reassuring, and calm. "Nothing will harm you."

She continued. "Zion, is someone with you? Helen, perhaps? Helen, please speak to us. Give us some sign that you are there as well."

We waited, but there was nothing. I felt none of the weakness or intense energy that I'd felt when I was in Olivia's presence.

Then I heard the voice from somewhere above us.

"Mama? Mama, are you here?"

Press took my hand again, but he couldn't have surprised me more than the sound of Eva's voice.

"Keep your eyes closed," J.C. said firmly. But there was excitement in her words. Eva's appearance was what she'd told me we should hope for. "Don't be alarmed."

Was it Eva's voice? Of course it had to be Eva's voice. It was a little girl's voice, and I was the only mama here.

"Eva, darling. Have you come to talk to your mummy and daddy?"

The voice had sounded so far away. I wasn't sure if it came from above me, or behind me. In that strange, bright world of nothingness behind my eyes, there was no such thing as direction.

"I'm sleepy, Mama. Tell me what to do, Mama. Why can't I see you?"

"Eva," Rachel whispered.

It *was* Eva's voice, Eva's delicate, childish lisp that Nonie had been working hard to sharpen. Press had found it distressing, and worried that she would become ridiculous as an adult, but I hadn't been concerned, believing she would grow out of it. Now it would never change.

"Tell her you're here." I knew J.C. was talking to me, but I found it hard to speak.

"It's all right," Press whispered. "She needs you."

"It hurts, Mama. The water hurts."

Unable to bear it any longer, I opened my eyes, and the brightness I had imagined was gone. The hall was still shadowed, though a curving rectangle of weak moonlight shone down from the dome and onto the wall beyond J.C.

Everyone else's eyes were open and they were staring at me. Waiting. What were they waiting for?

"Talk to her." J.C.'s voice was kind, but urgent. "They don't stay long."

"Mama." Now Eva began to whimper.

The sound was coming from above us. Up on the second-floor balcony, I saw her. My baby. She stood on tiptoe looking over the railing, just outside Olivia's room. That made sense, didn't it? There was a faint light behind her, flickering, brighter than candlelight. Her curls, thicker than I remembered, crowded her face, and she wore the long white nightgown that I had sent to the funeral home with Nonie. But even in the strange light, I could see that her face was as pale as a mask.

Press squeezed my hand. "Can you see her?"

"I'm here, baby." My voice was weak. Somehow it didn't feel right. What had I expected? God, I wanted to believe that it was her! There were all these people surrounding us, and she was so sad. So upset. If it was Eva, I could do nothing for her.

"Should I go to her?" Was I waiting for permission from someone? She had come to me, first, in the morning room. She had touched me.

"Ask her what she wants."

"She's told us what she wants. She wants me. She wants to know why I let this happen to her. What else could she want? She's not even five years old." I dug my fingernails into my palms in frustration.

"Eva, I'm sorry. Mama is so sorry. Mama loves you."

"That's good." J.C.'s voice was soothing. "Your mama loves you, Eva, darling. Can you rest now? We're all here for you, Eva."

"I'm scared, Mama. Help me."

The sulfurous smell had finally dispersed. Perhaps Zion had gone, or he had never been there at all. Maybe it was the smell of death. I prayed that it wasn't the smell of Hell, that my innocent Eva wasn't in torment.

Pushing back my chair, I rose. When I'd seen Eva in Olivia's room, she'd been so pitiful. Now she was my little girl again. Just sad. I didn't know what had changed, but I was hopeful. That I might be with her had occurred to me, but how would it happen? Certainly I would have to die to be with her. Perhaps just to touch her, to give her my life. It wouldn't bring her back, yet we would be together. My father had Nonie now. Michael would still have Press.

Press put a hand on my arm. "You shouldn't, my love. You can't really touch her."

"Don't be an ass," Rachel said. "Let her go. That's what we're here for."

I heard them, but I was focused on Eva. The light behind her had intensified and I couldn't see her face clearly.

As I passed him, Hugh also put out a hand to stop me, but I brushed him off.

"I'm coming, baby."

Eva turned her head so that I saw her in profile, though she was still so far away. It was such an easy, natural movement that my heart jumped in my chest. If only I could reach her, know that she was close to me! Then I would know what to do.

Behind me, the others were silent. I could feel them watching.

The light around Eva started to fade, and her outline with it.

"Wait for me, Eva! Wait!" I ran to the stairs through the shaft of moonlight, but the light around Eva continued to fade.

Taking my eyes from her for just a moment to steady myself on the stairs, I saw something pale and shining on the opposite side of the hall, at the railing of the third floor. Yes, I was losing Eva, but I couldn't look away. Taking a few more steps, I saw that it was a person. A man? I wasn't sure. The figure was slight, not very robust. Even in the faint light, I could see they were naked as they moved quickly, silently.

There was something fastened around the bottom of one of the railing's spindles, and as I watched, whoever it was climbed awkwardly—yes, naked—onto the railing.

When I saw the rope, fashioned into a noose, slip over the person's head, I cried out for them to stop, please stop!, but they kept on as though they hadn't heard. They didn't hesitate, and I knew I was going to see them die. But for just that moment I couldn't turn away. I stared, taking in every strange detail. I watched as they raised one leg and then the other to climb over the railing, the thick length of ropes curled against their body. They climbed over the railing and held on, arms extended behind, readying. Somewhere in the background, I heard chairs falling over and Press and the others calling for me. Eva screamed a terrified scream as well, and the sound echoed in the big hall. Understanding exactly what I was seeing, I closed my eyes and turned my head as the person let go of the railing and dropped, swinging, into the air.

But I wouldn't let myself faint. Even as Press and Hugh and Jack gathered around me, restraining me on the stairs, I wouldn't give up my consciousness or my sanity.

"Charlotte, darling. Speak to me." Press gripped my jaw, trying to get me to look into his eyes, but I strained to look beyond him. To listen.

Running footsteps on the gallery just above us. A child crying. Eva! But no. It couldn't be.

It hadn't been.

Above us, there was no body swaying at the end of a rope. There was no rope.

Downstairs, someone switched on the chandelier's light switch and the hall was flooded with light, blinding me as I looked upward.

Chapter 28

The Vision

I didn't answer their questions, nor did I succumb to Jack's insistence that he give me a sedative.

"You're pale, Charlotte. Let Press put you to bed, and I'll give you something."

Though I'd had two simultaneous shocks, I hadn't lost my wits. In fact, I felt better, clearer than I had in weeks. Standing on the stairs, I'd been overwhelmed for a few moments, and I'd gone to the brink—yes, a horrible, awful brink that felt strangely familiar to me. Maybe it was that my mother had been there before, and she had passed her vulnerability on to me. I don't know why she'd gone there, only that she had and couldn't stop herself from going over. But I had Michael, and, in some sense, Eva. I would not. I *could* not do what my mother had done and leave my child to be raised by his father. Alone. I had been terribly fortunate that my mother had chosen to marry a man who would be a good father. It wasn't clear to me that I had chosen as well.

No one in the house with me then would understand the other thing I'd seen—except, perhaps, Terrance.

"No. You're so kind, Jack. I don't need anything. It was shadows, up on the third floor. Only shadows."

"But we saw her." Rachel was adamant. "We all saw Eva. Right there up on the second floor."

Press was focused intently on me as I sipped the brandy he'd poured for me once we were all settled in the salon.

"I saw her. But she didn't frighten me. Eva could never frighten me. It was the shadows."

J.C. joined in the chorus, but I knew better than to trust her any longer.

"It was so sudden, Charlotte. Breaking that kind of psychic connection so quickly can be devastating. For you, and for. . . ." She didn't finish. Was she trying to tell me that Eva—dead Eva—might be damaged by my alarm? I wanted to laugh at her, but I didn't dare. They were all watching me too carefully.

Only Hugh stood silently in the background, looking out the night-blackened windows. I still wondered why he'd really decided to come. It had to be J.C., though there didn't seem to be anything more than a casual friendship between them. Of course, no one else was supposed to know that something more had happened. I was surrounded by so much deceit.

"I guess if there was ever any doubt that Bliss House is haunted, it's gone *now*." Rachel laughed nervously, and I saw Jack shoot her a look.

I held out my hand to her. "Maybe *you* need something, Rachel. All this excitement can't be good for the baby."

Rachel looked at me questioningly. Had she narrowed her eyes just the slightest bit? I wanted them all out of the house, including J.C. Odious J.C. I wanted her away from me most of all. What I suspected her of now was worse than being my husband's lover. She was a conspirator. Was Rachel the only one I could trust now?

"It's not a laughing matter," J.C. said sternly, looking at Rachel.

"Fuck you." Rachel turned her back on J.C. and missed the latter's look of serene disdain. The rest of us were used to Rachel's occasional profanity.

"Jack, I want to go home. I'm exhausted and this isn't fun anymore."

I was glad that she and Jack were leaving. Perhaps Hugh would take the hint. Jack looked at Press, eyebrows raised. Press gave a slight nod. I relaxed a little.

"Yes, I think we'd all better call it a night," Press said. He walked over to the bar table. "Quick one for the road, Jack?"

Rachel came to sit beside me. She started talking, but I missed most of what she said because I was watching Jack and Press at the bar.

When Press handed him his Scotch, Jack's hand slid gently over Press's and lingered there a moment before he took the glass. As Jack sipped, he watched Press closely as he talked, a look of comfortable pleasure on his handsome face.

"Charlotte? Are you listening? Do you want to come home with us, honey? You can go up and get Michael if it's all just too much to stay here. I know you must be devastated. Eva was *so close*. It was as though she could just come downstairs and climb up onto your lap, wasn't it? I don't know when I've seen anything so strange." She tilted her head, like a small bird. "Do you think she'd say anything else? I wonder if she knows what happened to her."

Now that I was paying attention, I saw that Rachel did look disturbed, even afraid, as though she truly believed we had all seen the real Eva.

I wonder if she knows what happened to her.

I felt my face go hot. Had Eva known she was dying? Dear God, was Rachel being cruel, or just her thoughtless self? I shook my head, not really caring what question she thought I was answering.

"If you change your mind, the car knows the way to the house." She called across the room to Hugh. "Hugh? It looks like Jack isn't finished drinking for the night, and it's not even nine o'clock. Do you want to come by?" Before he could answer, Rachel rose awkwardly from the sofa, one delicate hand on my knee for support.

Her emerald green dress hung artfully from its Empire waist, but she was far too pregnant for it to disguise her baby bump. She wore gold-heeled sandals that complemented the gold satin collar of the dress. I had tried to stay fashionable during both of my pregnancies, but I never came close to Rachel's precise style. She turned to call for Jack.

"Rachel." I kept my voice low.

"What is it? Is something wrong?"

"The back of your dress. Don't you feel it?"

Rachel twisted her head over her shoulder and pulled at the side of her dress to look. She laughed. "Oh, shit. Press! Jack! My water broke."

Now Rachel would have her own child. I knew then that I was completely alone.

Nonie was gone. Eva was gone. Press had put Shelley between Michael and me. I felt Eva's absence even more keenly, but I understood that the pathetic, dripping wraith that had come to visit me in Olivia's morning room was the real Eva. Not the child in the gallery who, I was certain, was flesh and blood. I had no friends around me. How odd that Olivia, whom I hadn't liked very much in life, was now the only one that I felt I could trust. And she was dead.

It had been some kind of miracle that the earlier screams hadn't woken Michael. As Press and Jack had led me back downstairs, I'd seen Shelley come to stand at the railing outside the nursery, but she had quickly gone back inside.

Before I went to bed, I needed to see Michael.

221

Shelley, sleeping on a cot in a corner of the room, didn't stir as I knelt by the trundle where Michael lay sleeping. In the light from the hall, I could see the flush of heat on his round cheeks. He'd pushed off his covers and lay in his sleep shirt and diaper. Though his diaper was wet, I didn't wake him to change him, but only pulled the covers up to his chest so he wouldn't wake, cold, during the night. Kneeling on the carpet beside him, I stroked his forehead.

"It's all going to be all right," I whispered. I felt it, even as I was saying it. I just wasn't exactly sure what was wrong, or how I was supposed to fix it.

While I knelt there, a shadow interrupted the narrow shaft of light coming from the hall, and I knew it was Press, waiting for me. I wasn't in any hurry.

Shelley stirred as I went out, but she didn't wake. She was so young. Only nineteen, she was almost a child herself. Although I knew she was the same sweet girl who, as a fifteen-year-old, had come to pet and admire Eva when she was a baby, I found myself not trusting her. Maybe if I had been the one to suggest that she come, I might have felt differently. All I knew at that moment was that she was sleeping in my son's bedroom and I was not.

"Are you sure you don't want me to drive you to the hospital? Don't you think Rachel needs her hand held?"

Across the gallery, the door to J.C.'s room was closed.

"Shhhhhhh." Moving quickly past Press, I left the nursery doorway. He followed. Reaching his bedroom door, I stopped but didn't go inside.

"You think I would leave Michael now?"

"You're upset."

"Rachel doesn't need me there. I called her mother. I'm sure she arrived even before Rachel and Jack."

He touched my hair, and I recoiled. The cold surprise in his eyes only lasted a moment, and the look of tender solicitude returned. I knew he was acting.

"We should go to bed. I wish you had let Jack give you something."

"We should talk about Eva."

He took my arm to try to lead me into his bedroom, but where once I would've followed, I jerked away.

"Don't lose your head over this, Charlotte. I don't want a scene."

It was my turn to be surprised.

"A scene? After what happened tonight, you're worried about me making a scene in my own house? Don't you think you should be more worried about what your good friend J.C. tried to do to us?"

Now he did pull me inside and shut the door. I knew that in a test of strength, I would lose.

"Or were you in charge of that little show? Maybe J.C. was just the hired help. Bravo to you both."

Press shook his head. "I don't know what you're talking about."

"She arranged for some little girl to come and pretend she was Eva. I heard her running away. For God's sake, Press. It didn't even look like Eva."

Press scoffed. "That's crazy. You know this house. You know what's possible. Why wouldn't Eva come back? She misses us."

"I don't know what to think anymore, Press. For years you've told me that nothing strange is happening here, and then you change your mind. I don't know what you believe or what you care about, except for your little group of theater friends. I don't even know if you loved Eva. I know for damned sure that you don't really love me."

I'd begun to shake and felt horribly cold with anger and worry. The shivering reached into my bones and I had to clench my jaw shut to keep my teeth from chattering.

I hated what was happening to me.

223

"Calm down."

"*You* calm down!" But I spoke from between clenched teeth.

It hurts, Mommy.

It didn't matter that the child had been a fraud. They were surely Eva's own words.

The water hurts.

"You're embarrassing yourself. You're not well. Everyone sees it. You haven't been yourself since you let Eva die."

For the first time in our marriage, I struck my husband. My arm and fist were stiff as I swung at him, and I wasn't strong, but when I made contact with the side of his face it put him off-balance and he stumbled sideways, surprised. His misstep was undignified and clumsy—mostly because I'd taken him off guard. Instead of striking me back as a less patient, less genteel man might have, he regarded me with a look of undisguised contempt.

Unwilling to continue with him, I ran through the door that joined our bedrooms and slammed it shut. I'd long ago lost the key, but I didn't hear him following me. I was fairly certain he wouldn't follow.

I collapsed on the floor against the door. Finally he had said it out loud—the thing that everyone around us, everyone around me was always thinking. I was responsible. Eva had died on my watch. I'd been passed out, drunk. No one blamed Press. Only me. He had simply moved on, grieving little, not changing his habits or appetites. I hadn't even been able to refuse his physical advances as I lay on the bed where my daughter had slept in the hour before she died. Where was my outrage over his complicity? My dignity? I had none. J.C. had taunted me. I was a joke in my own house.

Yet. . . .

Bliss House didn't hate me. Olivia was there, and the real Eva. Perhaps they were my real strength. Olivia had let me see her weakness and shame. And what I had seen in the hall, just that night. Olivia had trusted me with the truth. The world believed that Michael Searle Bliss had died from a ruptured appendix, but he had hanged himself. The world believed that Randolph Bliss was dead when Michael Searle was married, but he had been very much alive. I trusted the house to show me the truth. I wondered if Press knew the truth. Terrance had known. Had that been why Olivia kept him on after he'd witnessed her abuse and humiliation? Quiet Terrance. Blackmail was definitely a quiet man's game.

I couldn't—wouldn't—stay in my own room. It didn't feel safe. It didn't feel right. Bliss House was my home, and I wouldn't leave it, but neither could I bear to be near Press.

Still shaking a bit, I slipped off my shoes and went to the door. Downstairs, Terrance and Marlene were putting away the table and chairs we'd used for the séance. While they often worked together in silence, now I could hear the murmur of Marlene's voice, but I couldn't make out her words. She'd been helpful getting Rachel out the door, bringing towels, damp and dry, and a pillow so she could lie down in the back of the car. I wondered whose side Marlene was on. The answer *Press's, of course* came to me quickly, unbidden.

I couldn't sleep in the nursery because of Shelley. Across the hall, Olivia's door was still open. If only she were still there, still alive, so little of what had happened in the past few weeks would have happened. Eva would certainly still be alive as well.

There would have been no champagne, and no falling asleep. Press might have left the house, but the children wouldn't have been left alone with me.

I had to stop.

I quickly changed into a nightgown and robe and took my pillow from the bed. Remembering the icy chill of the morning room, I also took my bed's thick white coverlet.

With the door always shut, the morning room was colder than any other inhabited room in Bliss House, but it felt welcoming all the same. In the wan light from the windows I arranged my pillow and coverlet on the chaise and lay down, wakeful. Across the room, the sheet still hung across the wall and the Magic Lantern still sat on the table. Would I see Olivia again? Or perhaps Michael Searle? I kept my eyes open so I wouldn't see—again and again—that body hanging from the gallery. How terrifying it must have been to find it there. I wondered who the witnesses were. So many unanswered questions. Overwhelmed, I half-hoped Olivia would not show me anything else that night.

This was the rest of my life: a dead child, a living child, a husband I didn't know if I could trust. Ghosts. So many ghosts. I couldn't feel them at that moment, but I knew they were waiting. One day I might be one of those ghosts, trapped in death, as I was trapped in life.

After a few minutes beneath the warm blanket, my eyes closed, and I was watching Eva inside the playhouse as she mixed grass and leaves and tiny pebbles together in a bowl. "I'm making supper," she told me. "But you can't come in because you're too big. Only me. Only Michael."

At the mention of Michael's name, I looked around for my son, but he wasn't inside the playhouse or out. In the distance I heard angry voices and I looked toward the woods, which were glassy with frost. Men's or women's voices, I couldn't tell. Just a constant growl of argument. When I looked back into the playhouse, it had changed. Grown larger. Eva was grown larger, too, into a blowsy caricature of a little girl. But she was still Eva. The bowl had filled with water and her hand, swishing around the grass and debris, was bloated and white. I looked away.

In the far corner of the room—it seemed miles away—I saw Michael Searle, his face drawn and sad, perched on a chair like a bird. His voluminous white nightshirt billowed around him like a cloud.

I walked away, knowing Eva was safe.

Chapter 29

Contrition

I watched Shelley and Michael from the nursery window. It was a sunny, crisp day and even from a distance I could see how red Michael's cheeks were. As a baby, Eva had been slender—not too thin, but not a chubby baby either. Michael was all boy, with rounded elbows and cheeks and knees. In his chunky knitted sweater and corduroy pants, he looked like a ripe plum.

As Shelley stood by, Michael climbed in and out of the wagon. Every second or third time he got out, he would go to the back and try to push it forward before climbing back in again. He'd been such a compliant baby, but now he was becoming more certain of himself. More demanding. Still, he was good-natured and always loving. When he finally tired of the game, Shelley bent to pick him up, her shoulder-length brown hair falling forward, hiding her face, but I could tell she was confident and cheerful with him. With a pang of guilt, I realized that she was probably a better companion for an active toddler than Nonie.

I'd found a brief letter from Nonie on my breakfast tray, saying that my father was anxious to be back on his feet. The doctor wanted to keep him in bed as long as possible, but he'd been practicing all they would let him with his crutches. She said she'd found the house in good shape, and that the part-time housekeeper was doing a decent job, even if the kitchen curtains needed to be washed. I imagined Nonie in the kitchen, fussing with every detail. When I got to the line where she asked how I was doing, I knew she was really asking how I was doing without Eva, and I almost broke down. That wasn't a question I could answer easily. We had talked for just a few minutes only days before, but we had kept the conversation light. How I wished she were still at Bliss House, outside with Michael, instead of in a far corner of the state. She would've stopped any talk of a séance just by her presence. So much was different, and she'd only been gone a few days. I wondered how long it would be before I saw her again.

Satisfied that Michael was all right, I started back to my room to dress. Despite my sadness, I felt more rested than I'd felt in weeks. I'd awakened in daylight to the friendly laughter of the workmen on the outer stairs leading up to the theater. There had been no visitations in the night, no visions of Olivia or Michael Searle or Eva. Sleeping in the morning room had been the right choice.

Before I'd even passed the nursery, I heard the door to the yellow room open.

"Charlotte."

J.C. wore her dressing gown and her hair was brushed severely back from her face, which sagged with exhaustion.

"Please, Charlotte."

The way she glanced up and down the gallery after she called for me was almost comical. What lie was she going to tell me that she didn't want anyone else to hear?

Looking back, I wish I hadn't spoken to her so coldly. "Didn't you say the decorators would be finishing up tomorrow? Don't waste your time talking to me." Shaking a bit inside, I continued toward my room. Out of the corner of my eye, I saw her speed along the gallery, no doubt coming to confront me. But I wouldn't listen to her lies. I almost had the bedroom door shut when she pushed against it with surprising strength, forcing me backwards.

For a moment she looked stunned to have gained access to the room and to me, then hurried to shut the door behind herself. She looked around, perhaps performing some split-second professional appraisal of the room's details, or maybe just looking for Press. Satisfied, she grabbed me by the wrist and pulled me toward a chair.

We'd gone only a few feet when I jerked free and stopped. "Enough."

We faced each other.

"Jonathan was afraid. Do you know what it means when someone on the other side is afraid?"

"Why are you even here? You didn't need to be here for the stupid renovation. I know you're here for Press, whatever *that* means to the two of you. Have you had your little laugh over fooling the *precious bride*?"

J.C.'s panicked face tightened further, and I knew I had struck some truth. Before I could continue, she interrupted.

"Jonathan has never abandoned me when I've asked him to come. There were too many others here. Too much was disturbed. What do you know, Charlotte? What did you see? I know you saw something."

"I saw what you—or was it you and Press?—wanted me to see. Everyone saw the girl."

"I didn't want to be part of that. I swear I didn't. You don't know what he's like, Charlotte."

As shocked as I was to hear that I'd been right, I couldn't let her see it. "What I want to know is why, *Julianna*. You and Press were trying to—what? Frighten me? Make an ass out of me in front of Jack and Rachel and Hugh? I just want to know why."

J.C. shook her head violently. "No! Charlotte, you and Michael shouldn't stay here. Go to your father's house. Anywhere. There's nothing good for you here. Whatever you saw . . . whatever that was. *That* was real. Whatever is happening here is really happening. It's not part of any game."

She bit her bare lip as though she'd said too much.

"I don't believe that bullshit about your brother, either," I said, surprising myself with the profanity. "I've thought you were disgusting ever since Press introduced us. God knows what kind of people you spend your time with, and if you have a shred of decency, you'll get the hell out of this house so I don't have to look at you."

"You're wrong. I didn't come here to hurt you."

"Prove it."

J.C. dropped back a foot or so, and into the reflection of my vanity mirror. Even in her dressing gown, her edges were so sharply defined that she hardly looked like a woman.

Was she human? Had we all become less than human? I'd never been so cruel before.

"You have to let go of your guilt about Eva."

I moved toward her, wanting to shake her, to choke her. Anything to shut her up. "My God, you're unbelievable. You're not making any sense. You talk about my guilt when you don't even know me. Get the hell out of this house. I don't give a damn what Press thinks."

"It doesn't matter what you think of me. I'm trying to help you."

"I don't know why you hate me so much. If you really wanted to help me, you would start telling me the truth. But you obviously won't."

"There's a difference between wanting badly to do something and knowing that you can't."

Furious as I was, I was struck by the change in her demeanor from the previous days. It was almost as though she were a different person. She seemed resigned, if not contrite. Older. Her jowls sagged a bit and her shoulders slumped. We were two women separated by a small, fraught wedge of fear. Almost equals.

Yes, I was struck, but I refused to be moved.

She sighed. "It wasn't just the séance, Charlotte. He brought me here to get me close to you. This has been planned for a long, long time."

"What do you mean?"

"I told him you wouldn't understand. Ask him. I'm sure he'll be happy to tell you."

When she left the room, closing the door behind her, I had to work to control my breathing, my rabbiting heart.

~

She would be gone. I didn't have to think about her anymore.

I dressed and went downstairs to let Marlene know that it would be just the four of us, including Shelley, for dinner. She accepted the news in her usual calm manner, and when I asked if she could make up a small meal for Jack that I could drop by their house, she said she would have it ready in half an hour.

Grabbing a jacket from the mudroom, I went outside to spend a few minutes with Michael, my only respite.

Chapter 30

Seraphina

Sometimes I wonder at my younger self, unable to understand why I was so blind. I rarely questioned Press about what he was doing all those hours he was away from home. People told me how helpful he was to them as a lawyer, but to my knowledge he never did pro bono work for the poor, and I know he never presented a case to a jury. Now I think that I didn't really want to know what he was doing. I lived in a kind of fog, strangely secure in Bliss House. I know now that it's a world in itself, a world that exists on more than one level. But I could only perceive and understand one level in those early years.

Bliss House kept me from seeing the truth about what was going on around me. What Press was really like. What Terrance is—or was. Olivia showed me the truth about what she had endured. Surely no ill-intentioned spirit would try to make me more sympathetic to her than I already was. But perhaps I'm wrong. I lived for so long under one delusion that I may have been rendered unable to know when I'm living under a different one.

⌒

Rachel was still under some kind of sedation when I arrived at the hospital. It was common then, but not nearly as common now. All but the poorest of women were expected to remain in the hospital four days or more after childbirth, recovering. We weren't really delicate, though we were often plied with drugs to make us feel that way. But is it such a bad thing to put off the demands of children? We carry them for nine months, growing fatter and slower and worrying more and more, hearing nightmare stories from other women about the perils of breastfeeding and colic. How much nicer to have crisp young uniformed women and our own mothers (or friends) spoiling us for a bit. To delay that moment when the nurse puts your baby into your arms and says, "Off you go!" expecting you to understand that you're responsible for it forever. You can't give it back to her. It's yours for the rest of your life, unless death intervenes.

Jack had privileges at both the Lynchburg and Charlottesville hospitals, but Rachel had chosen an obstetrician in Charlottesville because she thought him prestigious. For everyone visiting her, it just meant a longer drive. I didn't mind being alone in the car for a while, but I couldn't stop thinking about Michael's birth, and how Eva had begged and begged to be allowed to come and visit the hospital. But Nonie was adamant that she stay home, and the hospitals had rules against child visitors.

While I felt a strange freedom being away from Bliss House, it remained in the back of my mind like a brooding shadow. Jonathan—if J.C. had ever truly had a brother named Jonathan—hadn't felt safe there. I didn't feel safe away from there.

Jack greeted me near the nurse's desk, his eyes glassy with lack of sleep, his shock of white hair flattened on one side as though he'd been sleeping on it. It was a careless look for someone who was usually so well groomed, but I didn't comment because he was sensitive to criticism.

"Rachel's hardly said a word. But she'll be glad you're here." He kissed me on the cheek and I caught a scent of a familiar after-shave and cigarettes. Grandma is in the room with her, but Dr. Daddy is apparently *persona non grata*. She's trying to talk Rachel into breastfeeding, but I think we all know that horse has already left the barn."

"Did everything go all right?"

"As far as I know. She apparently told the OB she'd cut his balls off if he let them give her an episiotomy. But then they knocked her out, so everyone survived."

I laughed, imagining Rachel threatening her nice old doctor.

"Are you okay?" Jack sounded almost shy. "Last night was strange."

I thought of how he'd touched Press's hand. That seemed strange to me, but I knew that wasn't what he meant. I didn't know what to think about Jack. I didn't hate him, but I understood he wasn't the person I had thought he was for so long. It made sense that Press had—*God help us all*—seduced him in some way, just as he had me, and J.C., and who knew who else.

One of the two nurses sitting at the nearby desk giggled, but I had no idea if it was directed at us. I had been out of the house so little that I hadn't thought about people recognizing me as the woman who had been responsible for her own child's death. Sud-denly I was even more self-conscious than usual. I drew my light coat more closely around myself.

"I want to hear about the baby. Does she have a name?"

He smiled and ran a hand through his hair.

"Damn. Don't know what's wrong with me." He took my arm. "The babies are down here."

The nursery was a few doors down a nearby corridor. On the other side of its enormous window, bassinets with babies in them were lined up in rows, each one bearing a sign with the baby's name, mother's name, and measurements. I found myself hanging a few inches behind Jack as he pointed to a bassinet far at the back. Rachel had been so very sure they'd have a boy. She hadn't rejected having a girl out of hand, but neither had she really entertained the possibility. Rachel didn't hide her feelings well, either. What would it be like to grow up having a mother like Rachel? A mother who had very clearly wanted a boy?

"Do you want to go in and hold her?" Jack asked. "I can get you in. You'll just have to wear a mask."

"Oh, no. I don't think so." Though I already felt pity for the poor child, I wasn't ready to hold her. I wasn't ready to watch her grow up, either, even though I was trying my best to be happy for them all. "What's her name?"

"Seraphina," Jack said, heading for the nursery. "Rachel didn't have any girl names picked out, and her mother suggested it. It was Rachel's great-grandmother's name. I'll bring her to the window."

She was precious, tightly swaddled in a pale pink flannel blanket with her very tiny, very red little face peeking out. Her eyelids twitched against the bright lights of the room and she began to work her rough, pink lips as though wanting food or succor. I've never understood why newborns are supposed to be able to sleep in rooms lit like operating theaters. Her coloring was newborn, and her lush hair was jet black. Her features were perfectly formed, almost like an adult's. She was a miniature of Rachel, but I saw nothing of Jack in her at all.

Forcing myself to smile and blow the baby a little kiss, I stepped back from the window while Jack put Seraphina back in her bassinet. Several of the other babies, disturbed by his presence, set up a righteous howl, and Jack left the nursery with the nurse on duty shaking her head behind him.

I met him in the hallway. "She's lovely, Jack."

"Seraphina? Yes, she is. She's quiet. Not like those other loud-mouth babies."

I looked closely at him to see if he was joking, calling the other babies "loudmouth." But his face held only irritation.

⌣

Holly Webb, Rachel's mother, looked up from the piece of fabric in her lap. Both she and Rachel were quite good at smocking—the artful embroidery that makes fabric stretch prettily. Rachel had done it in quiet times in our dorm room, surprising me with her skill. Her mother had decorated a large wicker fishing creel for her supplies, which Rachel still used.

"Don't make fun of me," she'd said. "It's the only thing I know how to do."

That wasn't true, of course. But it was the closest thing she did to any kind of art. Rachel, herself, preferred to be the decoration.

"Dear Charlotte," Holly whispered. She held her hand out to me.

I motioned for her not to rise, as her lap was covered with a pink swath of cloth that she'd obviously been working on for days. Rachel hadn't been joking when she'd said her mother had decided the baby would be a girl.

"You're so kind to come. She just went back to sleep. She's exhausted, poor thing."

"How long was her labor?" I kept my voice low to match Holly's, and sat down in the chair on the other side of Rachel's bed in the sparse, blank room. She'd managed to get a private one, which didn't surprise me, given Jack's association with the hospital.

"Nearly six hours. But as soon as she woke up the first time, she said she wanted to go home. And that was even before she'd seen the baby!"

I wondered if Holly knew how strange that sounded. From the smile on her face, I didn't think so.

"Isn't she adorable? Absolutely the perfect baby. I think she even looks a little like my own baby pictures. That will make Rachel's grandmother so happy."

Nodding, I looked at Rachel. Beneath the blankets her stomach was still distended, and her face was strained in sleep, her brow furrowed. I suspected they had given her morphine, although she didn't look as though it was giving her any peace. I didn't know when she would wake up again. I was happy that I'd seen the baby; but, sitting with Holly, I didn't have much to say. She was watching me watch Rachel. Of course, she had to be thinking about Eva. She'd been terribly fond of her, sending her sweets and buying her small presents whenever she and her husband traveled.

How much did she know? Had Rachel told her I'd been drinking that afternoon? She'd been at the funeral, of course, and had seen my hysterics. Everyone had seen.

"It was so lovely of Press to come by first thing, though I thought for sure he would've just come with you. He's so good to Rachel and Jack. Just like a brother."

Trying not to act surprised—*but was I so surprised?*—I said that he probably had business in Charlottesville and decided to drop by.

"Oh, do you think so?" She sounded as though she might disagree. If women were said to come to resemble their mothers as they aged, Rachel would continue to be stunning until the day she died. If anything, Holly Webb, with her striking brown eyes, full, well-shaped brows, and neat figure, was even more beautiful than her daughter. She arranged a demure blue cashmere cardigan over her thin shoulders.

"She never eats," Rachel had told me before I met Holly for the first time. "Watch her. She only pretends to, talks all through dinner, then has the housekeeper clear the plates away before anyone notices." And she'd been exactly right. I'd watched Holly do the same thing at every meal I ate at their house.

"Well, Press certainly came prepared, anyway." Holly, her hands busy, nodded to the shelf holding two bouquets of flowers—one quite compact and a little dull with yellow carnations and a lot of greenery, the other tall, with lilies, birds of paradise, and thick purple stock. "We both had Delmonico, at The Grange's florist, out of bed at the crack of dawn. Though they certainly are different in style, aren't they?" I wasn't sure what her smug grin implied.

It wasn't hard to guess which arrangement was from Press.

"Press does tend to go over the top sometimes." I tried to keep my tone light, but it was difficult to hide my embarrassment.

Holly rested her handwork in her lap. "Oh, the big one is from David and me. Press brought the carnations. Ours were delivered just a few minutes ago."

I was speechless. The small bouquet was like an insult compared to the other, and hardly suited to Rachel at all. I wondered if there had been some mistake. But Holly had said Press had brought it himself, first thing. I wondered that he'd even been allowed in so early. What did it mean? Perhaps nothing. It was just that everything seemed significant then, as though my life was strangely magnified.

"Are you well, dear? Rachel and I have been terribly worried about you. I can only imagine how devastated you are, but you look so thin. I have a prescription for iron pills from Jack. They might do you some good."

Was the woman so stupid? My best friend had just given birth to a baby girl, weeks after mine had died, horribly and suddenly. It was too much. Iron pills wouldn't bring Eva back. Why had I stayed as long as I had at the hospital? I had seen the baby: Seraphina. A seraph. An angel. But the baby didn't care that I was there, and Rachel wasn't even awake.

"Maybe you and Press should get away for a while. Sometimes a different setting can help. You won't be constantly. . . ." Her voice faded and her eyes left my face.

The busy chatter of the hospital staff floated in from the corridor.

"You need not have come, Charlotte. This must be so hard for you. You look tired."

The unexpected softness in her face, her voice, took me by surprise, and I felt tears threatening in the inner corners of my eyes. Of course I shouldn't have left the house.

I put on my gloves and fumbled for the wrapped gift I'd brought—an infant's pillow with an embroidered linen cover—and set it on the deep windowsill with the flowers. "I'll just leave this here. Please tell her I'll come by the house when she gets home."

Holly gave me a pitying smile. "Of course I will. Rachel will be so sorry she was sleeping, poor thing. I told her she needed to get more exercise while she was pregnant, that she'd be exhausted. But you know how she is."

By that point I was only half-listening. The car in the parking lot seemed so far away, and I wanted to get to it quickly. On another day (or was it in another life?) I might have gone over to The Grange for lunch and shopping, or stopped at the toyshop near the university and picked up a surprise for the children. But it didn't even occur to me then. I could only think of being back at the house.

Quietly pushing back the heavy wooden chair, I rose. Rachel sighed deeply in her sleep. She looked like a worried, sleeping princess.

"Before you go, would you look under the bag with Rachel's robe in it and hand me her notions basket? I thought she might get bored and want to work on something for the baby while she's waiting to go home. I've misplaced my needle threader, and I'm helpless without it."

No! I wanted to scream. *I want to get the hell away from here. Away from all of you!* But of course I put my handbag down on the chair, lifted the bag, and picked up the wicker notions basket by its handle. The basket was familiar, painted with the same cheerful red and yellow flowers—now chipped and faded—that had decorated it when Rachel first unpacked it in our dorm room at Burton Hall. I had envied that basket, and wished I had a mother who had taught me smocking and bought me dresses and sent me care packages with new gloves and cookies and expensive shampoo. Even though Rachel had joked about the basket being silly and childish-looking, it was obvious that it was one of her treasures, the sort of thing she might pass on to her own daughter.

Even through my gloves I felt the handle burning my fingers. (It was my imagination, of course. It was a perfectly normal wooden handle.) As I passed it over the bed, the brass catch loosened, and the basket gaped open, spilling some of its contents onto the bed.

Holly jumped up, gathering the ribbons and bits of cloth and spools of colorful thread as they rolled over Rachel's covered legs and across the bed or onto the floor. Nothing was heavy enough to disturb Rachel, but Holly still acted quickly.

"Charlotte," she whispered. "The lid. Close it?"

But I could only stare at the curl of Wedgwood blue velvet ribbon that clung over the edge of the bed like some lovely, poisonous snake.

Chapter 31

The Last Happy Afternoon

I don't remember much about the drive home. At some point I arrived back at Bliss House, and Terrance opened the car door for me. It had turned bitterly cold for October, and I had foolishly left the house without putting on a coat over my burgundy wool suit, but I stood on the front terrace for several minutes, watching the sky.

(I mention Terrance. It may seem confusing that I hadn't demanded that he leave. But what power did I have? In history, there have been men called "the king's men." Terrance was Press's man, a reality of Bliss House. I couldn't reveal what I'd learned about him without telling Press about Olivia's presence. And I would not give him more ammunition against me. You may be relieved to know that Terrance resolves the problem of Terrance without my help.)

As I fled the hospital room, Holly called after me, and Jack— where had Jack come from?—caught my arm, trying to stop me, saying Holly was signaling that Rachel was waking up. My head felt wild and I was breathless, all because of a length of ribbon. Wedgwood blue velvet ribbon. So delicate and sweet, something one might stitch onto the edge of a baby boy's smocked romper or coveralls.

But I recognized it as the same ribbon that Eva had been wearing when she first came to see me in the morning room. Where was that ribbon now, and why couldn't I remember her having it?

Eva had loved ribbons and hair bows and frilly dresses in a way that I never had, though I confess I had loved to indulge her whims. Like her mother, Rachel, too, had often given Eva little presents: a new rabbit fur muff, pairs of lace-trimmed panties and socks, real fawn leather gloves, and dear little hats. I'd once teased Rachel, telling her she was trying to outfit Eva like she was Bonnie Blue Butler from *Gone with the Wind*. It had been little Bonnie Blue's memorable death from a fall from a pony that had kept me from putting Eva on one, though Press had thought I was being silly.

My reaction to the ribbon—hurrying from Rachel's room like a dazed criminal—must have seemed bizarre to everyone who saw me there. Fuel to the rumors that were already being whispered.

I was confused. Olivia had appeared to me in many different kinds of clothes, not just what she'd been wearing when she died. But hadn't my visions of Eva been different? Eva had been so wet, always wearing the pink playsuit and ribbon and muddy sandals. Had Rachel brought the ribbon with her that evening and put it on Eva after she died, but before I'd been upstairs? And put shoes on her feet? No, it wasn't possible.

Perhaps I'd simply forgotten that Eva had brought back the ribbon from Rachel's house on another day. She wasn't quite at the age when she might acquire objects or words whose provenance was unknown to me. Children do eventually become connected to the world in ways we are not. Those first threads come slowly, but then new ones come, faster and faster, until our children are no longer exclusively ours. I felt another bit of Eva slip away.

I didn't yet know what the ribbon meant, but when I re-entered Bliss House, I was suddenly less troubled about it. Inside the preternaturally quiet hall, I felt my body relax, and I was finally warm. It would come to me.

I couldn't help my children or myself by worrying or being afraid. Not of Press. Not of the house. The worst thing that could happen to a mother had happened to me, and I had survived. But Michael was still with me and would be happy in Bliss House. He might go away to school for a while, and to work. Then he would perhaps come back with a family of his own and we would all live together.

I looked up to the gallery and saw what I expected: the door to the yellow room, where J.C. had been sleeping, was open. I couldn't be certain, but the house had a tangible emptiness that told me she was gone. There had been no cars or workmen's trucks in sight. Everything was finished. It was a huge relief to me—not just the absence of J.C., but the absence of strangers in my home.

It *was* my home, now. Press might bring any fool into it that he cared to, but I would be here to keep it safe for Eva and ready for when it became Michael's.

I looked into the kitchen, where Marlene was chopping vegetables for dinner.

"I'm going upstairs to rest for a while. Were there any calls?"

"No, Miss Charlotte. Shall I serve dinner at the usual time?"

"Six o'clock is fine. Are Shelley and Michael in the nursery?"

"She took him out to one of the farm ponds to see the geese. They've been making a terrible racket all day. I sent yesterday's bread with them."

"But it's so cold."

"They were bundled up."

With that, Marlene turned back to the vegetables and I knew our conversation was over.

Not really satisfied that Michael was sufficiently warm, I thought for a moment that I might follow them out to the pond.

But Nonie's voice in my head told me to stop being such a worrier. Michael was safe with Shelley, who, while not terribly bright, had lots of experience with toddlers and animals.

As I went upstairs, watched by all the expectant faces of the portraits lining the walls, I remembered that I'd missed another hair appointment. I had used a new round hairbrush and hairspray to keep my hair neat, and teased it, but perhaps it did need a trim. When I reached the second-floor gallery, I stopped at the gilt-framed Italian mirror that Olivia had sent home from one of her antique-shopping trips to New York.

Holly had been wrong. The face looking back at me in the mirror didn't look tired at all. My makeup was still fresh from the morning, and the area beneath my eyes held only a hint of a shadow. I liked the leaner lines of my face. Nonie had been gently harping at me for months to be more careful with my figure, and I guessed that now she might be satisfied.

As I continued to my room, I passed beneath the corner of the third-floor gallery where Press's father had hanged himself. I should have been horrified. Afraid. But I felt only pity.

I spent the next two hours—with an interruption to have a snack with a ruddy-cheeked Michael who'd been very excited by the geese—moving my clothes and other belongings into Olivia's room. It was where I belonged. Afterwards, I took Michael with me into the freshly painted ballroom while Shelley went to tidy the nursery.

Despite a brisk draft coming from right in front of the ballroom's generous fireplace, the ballroom was comfortable, and all the lights were working. I was relieved to see that the two brutal-looking metal eyes had been removed from the ceiling as I'd requested.

Michael laughed as he alternately stumbled and ran after the two large rubber balls I'd brought for him to play with. When he tired, he sprawled on my lap and I showed him the pictures of the animals I would paint for him on the walls: Peter Rabbit, Jemima

Puddleduck, Jeremy Fisher, naughty Tom Kitten. Though I'm not sure if he understood me as I explained to him what I was going to do, and how the ballroom would be a special place for him to play, he seemed happy, and finally drowsy. Content.

Because of the faint odor of paint in the room (are you wondering, as I did not at that moment, how the room had been transformed in so short a time? I had only engaged the painter three or four days earlier), I'd left the pocket doors open two feet or so. As Michael gently snored, I watched the sunlight fade on the theater doors across the hall and wondered how it must have changed since I'd last seen it. But I wasn't in any hurry to know.

It was the last truly happy afternoon Michael and I had together for a long, long time.

Chapter 32

Olivia Avenged

In the days after J.C. left, Press spent much of his time away from the house, which suited me very well. I spent two peaceful nights in Olivia's bed, but on the third night I awoke to a scent of roses so strong that it was like an assault.

Olivia was waiting for me.

Gathering the robe from the end of the bed, I rose anxiously and hurried into the morning room. Had it been she who had shown me the truth about Michael Searle's suicide? (I had no belief in J.C.'s supposed brother and felt the fool for being duped into the séance.) Was I the only one alive who knew? I doubted that Press knew the whole truth about his parents. If he did, might it not make him more compassionate? No. That was wrong. His father—the man I believed to be his true father—had been a monster. There had been no kindness in him, and Press was fast becoming like him. It was, I guessed, a case of *blood will out*. But was it that Press was only now exhibiting madness that had been handed down to him at his

246

birth, or was it that he was, God forbid, possessed by the spirit of the creature who had raped Olivia?

The sheet was hung once again in the morning room, though I knew it hadn't been earlier in the day. *Terrance*, I thought. Or, no. I certainly no longer needed rational explanations for what went on in Bliss House. I was far, far beyond that.

I waited. The Magic Lantern flared to life with its slight odor of hot metal and oil. With its light, the chilled room warmed. There was no more of the frost that had been there that first night, and I felt an odd sense of normality about it all. Except that Eva wasn't there. I feared that she had gone, driven away by Press and my own inability to help her.

The details of what Olivia showed me that night are shamefully sordid. Though God knows I have already related enough to alarm even the most jaded of listeners. I can only say that—even though at times I had to look away myself—it was a scene of such great passion and tenderness that I don't have the words to convey it.

Olivia was in her bed. She held out her arms to Michael Searle, who was now naked and finally unashamed; he lay down with her, kissing the bruises and hideous bite marks inflicted by the old man—his own hideous, desiccated father—on her pale, lovely skin. The moonlight streaming through the windows cast much of the room in stark relief, but the reflection from the well-stoked fire was gold and lively on their flesh. I will tell you that there was no true consummation between them, because consummation wasn't possible and had never been. But there was something more. There was an obvious, deep affection between them. Even, it might be said, love.

You may ask how such a thing is possible between two people such as they. I had seen Michael Searle clearly the night before, and my vision had confirmed a suspicion that I hadn't dared admit to myself. Michael Searle was a man, but, perhaps, also a woman. A hermaphrodite. His member was quite small, but his breasts were also gently developed. As he embraced Olivia with a languor that was both sensual and feminine, I could see that his body was nearly hairless, like a young girl's. There was no awkwardness, but only tenderness between them.

I felt no shock. Only pity. I saw the large corset lying over the chair, and I knew what pain Michael Searle must have endured every day of his life and why his chest was bruised and badly scarred. He had been forced to live completely as a man by the monster that was his own father—to hide his father's shame in him. Seeing such tenderness between the two of them, I understood that there was no shame between Olivia and Michael Searle.

My heart filled with feeling for them. For Olivia.

When the door to the bedroom up on the screen flew open, Olivia screamed and held fiercely to Michael Searle. Terrance entered, with the old man leaning heavily upon him.

Michael Searle pulled away from the clinging Olivia and, with a fierceness he hadn't shown the last time his father and Terrance had been in the room, flew at his father, Randolph, his hands reaching for the hideous wattled throat. But Terrance, who in the present I knew to be ponderously slow, was too fast for him and shoved Michael Searle hard so that he fell, his head hitting the massive blanket chest at the end of the bed. I—along with Olivia—waited for him to rise, but he did not. Because I had witnessed his later suicide, I knew that he wasn't dead, but I think Olivia did not know.

The old man did not react beyond giving his son a rheumy glance, but fixed his gaze on Olivia. She was an object to him. A property. Though his own body was decrepit and dangerously fragile, everything about his presence spoke of confident ownership.

Terrance turned from Michael Searle and went to steady the old man, who was speaking to Olivia. His words, like all the words spoken on that white screen, were unintelligible, but I had the impression that he spoke slowly. Their effect on Olivia was immediate. She looked from the old man to Terrance.

What was she saying? I moved closer to the screen, feeling the increase in heat from the Magic Lantern, as though it were burning hotter.

After speaking, Olivia closed her eyes for a moment and then nodded.

As Terrance helped the old man up the bed stairs, a retainer helping a demon king onto his throne, I saw Olivia feel for the drawer in the bedside table. She took out a handkerchief, along with something else that flashed green and blue in the firelight.

When the old man was finally on his knees over her—and I will not describe how he was readying himself because it makes me ill even to think of it—Olivia grimaced and swung the jewel-handled peacock knife into the side of his neck: once, twice, three times in quick succession.

The screen went blank, and I was grateful. I had seen enough.

How alone Olivia must have felt for the rest of her life! For a short time she had been loved, but then had to raise her son—perhaps the result of that first rape—alone. Bliss House had been thick with fear and hopelessness, and she had turned that hopelessness into some kind of strength. I had witnessed her strength and had thought it hauteur or disdain. What she had shown me horrified me. But I was also humbled.

Chapter 33

Press Revealed

There was no more sleep that night. I huddled beneath a third blanket from the chest at the foot of Olivia's bed, unable to get warm. In addition to turning on the bedside lamp, I also lighted a pair of candles, hoping for that much more heat. A book lay open beside me, but my mind was too filled with what I had seen.

"I saw your light on." Press hadn't bothered to knock.

Each of the preceding nights, I'd remembered to lock my door, and Press hadn't—to my knowledge—tried the doorknob. My own complacency had betrayed me. Though I'd known I couldn't put him off forever. In matters of sex, Press was rarely patient.

He tossed his robe onto a nearby chair and got into bed with me, wearing a comfortable smile.

I didn't yet hate him then, but I couldn't honestly say that I loved him anymore. How I wished there had been someone else to steal my affections. Someone gentle and kind and willing to take care of Michael and me.

When I tried to turn away, he pulled me close. He was naked, and I felt the heat of his skin and the prickling of his body hair through my gown.

"You know you can't leave me, Charlotte." He kissed my neck and rubbed his face against it, abrading it so that it stung. "You can't have Michael unless you have me."

"I never said I wanted to leave you."

"But you moved out of our suite. Locked your door. You've been an ice princess ever since J.C. left. And she could've been very, very nice to you, my love." He squeezed one of my nipples to punctuate his words, and I cried out softly. I couldn't bear the thought of Shelley hearing us. What he was implying about J.C. and me was probably meant to shock me, but she had told me herself, hadn't she? There was very little now that he could say that would shock me.

I was still cold, and I hated that he burned with warmth beside me. But it was as if he were a stranger. Worse than a stranger. My body refused to respond to him.

"You're breaking my heart, my love. You're not being a good wife, or a good mother. Everyone's saying you look so tired. So unhappy. Tell me you're not unhappy, my darling."

"I'm happy."

"You're going to have to work a little harder to convince me. You were so mean to J.C. that she left here in tears. It takes a lot to make an old warhorse like J.C. cry. What did you do to her?"

He continued to touch me gently, with his lips and his hands. I didn't resist when he edged my thighs apart, but neither did I make it particularly easy for him. I knew it was my duty to let him exercise his husband's privileges, but I wasn't so naïve as to think what he was doing was right. It's so hard to describe the change in him. In a matter of a few months, he'd gone from being my generous but slightly arrogant husband to a manipulative stranger. Yet the only things that had changed in our lives were the deaths of Olivia and Eva.

"Didn't you like J.C.? Is there someone you would like better?"

I turned my face further into the pillow, which made him laugh. The sound of it was too close. Disheartening. We were utterly alone. In the nursery, not so many days ago (though it felt like a lifetime), I had at least felt someone else there, watching us. God knew it wasn't right, but I preferred the presence of some unseen entity to that of my husband.

"Oh, Charlotte, Charlotte. How precious you are. Promise you'll always stay like this. So beautiful."

I lay there, waiting. Enduring. Thinking that Olivia had endured much worse. It hurt, but only because I couldn't make myself respond. The things that had once brought me so much pleasure were like ancient rituals that had to be endured. There was no shame in them. Only sadness.

When he finished, he used the pristine bedsheets—his mother's sheets—to wipe himself clean. I tried to turn over so I didn't have to look at him, but he grabbed my shoulder and jerked me back. It was the closest he'd ever come to touching me with violence.

"I can play this game as long as you like. Just know that you are here for me until I decide I don't need you anymore."

"I don't understand. I don't understand any of this."

"We've had a wonderful time, haven't we? No one could ever say I haven't treated you like a queen."

"If you're going to treat me like *this*, why in God's name won't you divorce me? Let me leave. It's like you want to humiliate me. Are you going to continue to punish me for Eva?"

"You can leave anytime. I won't stop you."

"I don't want anything from you. Just let me take Michael. Then you can have any woman you want. In your mother's bed. Anywhere. I'm sure J.C. would be happy to come back and take my place."

Press sighed. "I don't think so. Michael stays."

"You can't keep us here. My father will take me in."

"And break his Roman Catholic heart? He wouldn't put up with a divorce, my dear. He's such a traditionalist. Divorce isn't the way we do things. You don't have any grounds."

While I suspected he badly overestimated my father's desire for me to remain married to him, I knew he was right about there not being any grounds on which I could divorce him. There was nothing that I could prove. I had no bruises and no real evidence that he'd cheated. In movies and books, people hired private detectives all the time, but right now he was watching me too closely. I was cut off. There was no one to hire. All our friends were Press's friends. And Rachel? Even then, I think I understood that I couldn't count on Rachel. I'd heard of two women from our Burton Hall class who had divorced, and neither of them had come out of it well. They'd had to leave behind their friends, and, in one sad case, their children.

While I stared off, thinking, wishing he weren't so close to me, I could feel him watching me. But his gaze felt unfamiliar. Where had my husband gone?

Finally he lay back heavily on the bed a foot or so away from me. He stroked my arm, and I felt goosebumps rise.

"Even if you did try to divorce me, I'm afraid you wouldn't get very far. I have two men who will swear you've been throwing yourself at them for months, begging for sex. Even after my mother's funeral. You've shown the most appalling taste. So unbecoming for a young mother."

I was speechless.

"It's not going to come to that, though. You wouldn't put Michael or yourself through that kind of humiliation. Everyone knows you're unstable. Hiding Michael away in my mother's bedroom. Disappearing into the morning room. Wandering the house at night and running like a criminal from the hospital. You don't want to push it. You know how people can be."

No, I hadn't really known how people could be. But I was learning. God help me, I was learning.

The same voice that had tried to persuade me to kill myself the night of the séance reminded me about the knife hiding in Olivia's jewelry box. (How odd that it sounded so much like Press's voice!) If I let him fall asleep beside me, I could reach it easily. But I refused to be a murderer. I couldn't leave Michael and let him grow up knowing his mother had killed his father and died in the electric chair. Randolph Bliss was believed to be long dead and buried when Olivia killed him. He'd obviously faked his own funeral and hidden himself from the world. His wife was dead. (She'd been found in the woods, and there had been no investigation. Had he arranged her death, as well?) There had been no arrest for the murder of Randolph Bliss. No scandal. Only Terrance knew. And he would again be a kind of witness if I killed Press. Like Olivia, I would be blackmailed and have to live with Terrance, whatever his demands. There was no choice. I was no murderer.

"Why did you marry me? What did I do to make you hate me so much?"

He rolled over onto one elbow. I could smell Scotch on his breath, but I knew he wasn't drunk. "Hate you? My God, Charlotte. You're one of only two women in my life I've ever come close to loving. Haven't I given you everything you wanted? Security. Position. Have I ever said *no* to any little thing—or big thing—you've wanted? Now you have my mother's jewelry, half of this house, plenty of money. No one will ever take your place here unless you make it happen."

I waited for more.

"I *protected* you. Do you think that anyone else's wife would have escaped punishment for getting drunk and letting her daughter drown in the bathtub while she slept it off? You're a very, very lucky woman. I treasure you, just like my father treasured my mother. Just like *his* father treasured my grandmother."

My gut went cold remembering what I'd seen happen in this very bed. There had been worse suffering than mine in this house.

"I know about your father."

"Everyone knows about my father. It's hardly news that he died."

"That's not what I'm talking about."

"What?"

I had his attention now, more than ever, and I felt something new grow inside me. It felt horrible. Disgusting. But it felt right. I had almost pitied him because of what I'd learned about Olivia, and the rape. What Michael Searle had been forced to watch. I knew Michael Searle wasn't his father, but did Press know it?

I didn't go on. He deserved to keep wondering. I had no pity for this man, and I was done loving him. Still, a part of me was convinced that the man lying beside me wasn't really Press. The man I had known as my husband had disappeared in the days after Olivia died. Even if this man, this Preston Bliss had shown some glimmer of compassion that night, I didn't know that I wanted him back. The place in my heart that had been full of him for so long was full of something else now.

It was a dark, fearsome something else, and I didn't want to look too closely at it, because I was afraid it might kill us both.

Chapter 34

Running

What do you do when you realize that life as you once knew it is over forever?

My life had ended once already—in that same, very strange month of October—the day that Eva died.

Press had woken me. No, that's not precisely right. I had awoken to find him standing over me, holding a tearful Michael, looking horrified. He had looked at me as though I were some stranger who had wandered into his house and done something unspeakable.

I had done the unspeakable. I had let our daughter die.

"What is it?"

When I'd held out my arms for Michael, Press had taken a step back, reluctant. Who would give their precious son to a stranger?

Why hadn't I felt something the moment that Eva had fallen into the tub, hitting her head? A mother should feel something when her child's life slips away into the water, or into the air—a sudden

absence in the universe. But no. I had felt nothing. Sensed nothing.
I hadn't even been awake.

～

The next day, I did the only thing I could do. Press was wrong
about my father. I was certain that he and Nonie would stand
behind me. They had to. Michael was too precious to risk, and I
knew that if I stayed with Press, he would do something to hurt
Michael or twist him in some way. Bliss House was where we
belonged, but not if Press was in it. I'd rejected the idea of killing
him, but I now knew where I really stood. Michael and I were
prisoners, and Press valued life far less than I did. I could only trust
that Olivia would be there for Eva if I couldn't be. But Michael was
alive, and I had to protect him. So I ran away.

I thought it would be difficult not to give myself away. But I
was better at lying than I knew.

When I went down to the kitchen, I found Press, Marlene,
and Terrance seated at the table. Press stopped talking, and he and
Marlene looked at me, but Terrance started to rise. I put out my
hand to stop him.

"That's all right, Terrance. I just came to speak with Marlene
about dinner, but I'll come back." Perhaps I should have made an
effort to speak to Press. I confess I knew it would embarrass him in
front of Marlene—if not Terrance—when I ignored him. But the
loathing I felt, along with my pride, wouldn't let me. How much
had my pride cost me already? I turned to leave, but Marlene spoke.

"The side of beef from our order was stocked in the freezer
yesterday, Miss Charlotte. I thought maybe steaks with autumn
vegetables, and bread?"

"That's fine. Is there mail?" Glancing at the table, I saw that a
stack of mail rested at Preston's right. An envelope with Nonie's
handwriting sat on top.

"I'll bring it to you when I've been through it, darling." Press smiled. *Darling*. Had I ever really been his darling? Somehow I knew he would never give me the letter.

"We're doing the memorial tomorrow night. I'm just finalizing plans with Marlene and Terrance. It's a light menu, though God knows that crowd can eat! Just think. We'll christen the new theater in style. Helen would've loved it, don't you think?" He turned to Marlene. "Twelve people, plus Miss Charlotte. Terrance will serve and take care of cleaning up. It will go rather late, so there's no need for you not to retire at your usual time."

"It's no trouble, Mr. Preston."

Terrance shook his head. Press just smiled. It was decided.

Thursday. Halloween. It seemed appropriate, given the secretive, dramatic natures of both Helen and Zion. The secretive, dramatic nature of my husband.

I turned to leave again, and Press said, "Don't worry about a costume. I have it all arranged."

Holding my breath so I wouldn't be tempted to shriek at him, I hurried toward the stairs between the kitchen and dining room. By the time I reached the second floor, I was panting.

As I left the small hallway where the stairs were located, I nearly ran into Shelley, who was leading Michael by the hand. Shelley looked startled and, worse, there were gray shadows beneath her eyes.

"I'm sorry, Mrs. Bliss. I didn't hear you." She let go of Michael's hand and he toddled toward me. I picked him up and held him close—so very close—to feel the softness of his fine blond curls on my cheek.

"Where are you two off to?"

"It's so nice outside, I thought we'd walk out to the springhouse and maybe play in the playhouse for a little while. I was going to stop in the kitchen to get a snack to take with us." She hesitated. "That's all right, isn't it?"

Of course, she'd hesitated because the playhouse had been Eva's. I smiled to reassure her. "Just keep him away from the pool."

"Oh, I definitely will. We won't even go in the woods. I promise."

I kissed Michael and set him down. "You be good for Shelley."

He seemed to have bonded with her quickly, and I was—mostly—grateful. He would miss her. But he would have Nonie and my father, as well as me, if everything went the way I hoped it would.

"I think I'm going to stay in his room tonight, Shelley. I've missed him, and he doesn't sleep very well in bed with me. You can even go home for the night if you want to. Why don't you do that? Come back in the morning."

She looked reluctant, but finally nodded. "I'll stay here. I like to be here when he wakes up. He's the most cheerful boy I've ever seen in the morning!" She picked him up as he started to break for the stairs, and he giggled.

When they were gone, I waited in my room until I saw Terrance bring Press's Eldorado from the garage.

I packed a few of Michael's things in the single suitcase I would take to my father's house. Two changes of clothes, a few diapers, pins, and plastic pants, his winter jacket (he was wearing a sweater outside), shoes and socks. His favorite toy—a stuffed Winnie the Pooh bear—I left in his crib, and told myself I would remember it when we were ready to leave. There was already a change of clothes for me in the case, along with a framed picture of Eva, and the hundred dollars I kept in my jewelry box for an emergency. This certainly qualified as an emergency.

I thought of going over to Rachel's, if not to say good-bye then to at least see her and the baby again before I left. But I knew myself too well, even then. I was used to telling Rachel everything, and while I wanted to believe that she wouldn't betray me to Press, I couldn't take the chance.

Dinner and the hour in the library with Press after dinner was a puppet show of politeness. He was uncharacteristically affectionate with Michael, which I found a little alarming. And although we were alone, he didn't mention J.C. again. I wondered if she would dare to return for the memorial. She had known Helen and Zion, though I didn't think terribly well. When Marlene had cleaned her room, she'd found her bottle of *Caron Poivre* sitting on the dresser and brought it to me. It was an odd thing for her to have left behind. I told Marlene that she could keep it if she wanted, that J.C. probably had more than one bottle. It was a mean and small thing for me to do, but I felt no regret.

Press spoke to Michael, who was on his lap. "Do you think we should tell Mommy what her costume is, or should we let it be a surprise?"

I tried hard to sound curious. "What is it?"

He grinned. "Why, it's Brunhild, of course! Don't you remember? Helen thought you'd make a wonderful Brunhild."

"Ah." I nodded. The idea of putting on a costume for all of Press's friends repelled me. Though I took comfort in the fact that I would be gone that night and wouldn't actually have to.

"But can you sing, my dear?" His eyes gleamed with amusement.

Yes, I remembered. For my own preservation, I smiled. "I don't have to wear horns, do I?"

He played at looking hurt. "Not if you don't want to, I suppose. Maybe just golden wings on the sides of your helmet."

Picking up Michael (I really didn't want to go near Press, but I had no choice), I said "Time for bed, sleepy boy."

Michael snuggled onto my shoulder, not at all reluctant to leave Press.

"I'll probably come in to see you tonight. I think you should sleep in your own bed." It was obviously an order. Not a suggestion.

"Oh, Press. Shelley had Michael out for so long today. Didn't you notice how warm he is? I want to sleep in his room tonight in case he feels bad. It wouldn't be right to disturb him if he's sick."

Press made a kind of grudging, grunting noise. My heart was pounding as I left the room, and I held Michael closer as though I could muffle the sound.

Press's bedroom windows overlooked the short driveway leading to the carriage house, so I paused outside his door before gathering Michael to make sure I heard him snoring. There was no question that he was inside his room and asleep. Michael barely woke when I picked him up out of his crib, and we managed to get down the kitchen stairs without making any noise at all. The doors onto the patio from the dining room opened easily, and the *click* of their latch was lost in the constant chirp of a lone, late-season cricket in the nearby bushes. It seemed that Bliss House was going to let us go.

Walking across the patio in the moonlight with Michael draped in his favorite blanket and drowsing against my shoulder, I was both anxious and fairly confident that we would get away. At the last moment before leaving my room, I had put Olivia's jeweled peacock knife in the pocket of my coat. I felt as though she were blessing our escape.

The moon was high, so we weren't in the house's shadow for very long. Reaching the driveway, I tiptoed carefully, worried that my shoes would be too noisy, and when I reached the other side, I stayed in the grass all the way to the carriage house.

I hadn't driven in days, and when I'd looked in the box on the wall in the butler's pantry for my car keys after Terrance and

Marlene had gone to bed, I'd seen that both sets of keys to both cars were gone. My heart sank as I realized that Press was thinking ahead of me, and I knew we were in more danger than I'd first imagined. The Jeep keys were there, but it would've been foolish to try to sneak away in the growling, topless Jeep. It was as though he'd left its keys there to taunt me.

Panic set in for a moment, and then I remembered that he had ordered a third key for the Eldorado Brougham that had been delivered a few weeks after Olivia died. A key that he kept hidden in his golf bag in the garage. I prayed that he had forgotten about it.

I nearly wept when I found the single key in the bottom pocket of the golf bag.

Michael began to fret as I worked to strap him in the passenger seat. He was still far too small for the seatbelt, but he was much too big for the infant basket. "Shhhh. We're going to see Grandpapa and Nonie. You want to see Nonie, don't you? Look. I've brought Bear for you." I tucked the bear against him, and he wrapped an arm around it, somewhat comforted. I didn't have a plan for driving away with a screaming toddler, and had no idea what I would do if he didn't sleep most of the way. Every other time we'd traveled, Nonie or Eva had been there to entertain him.

Headlights off, I drove the quietly rumbling Cadillac across the expanse of grass that met up with the driveway at the beginning of the lane's line of trees. My heart seemed to skip a beat when I pressed on the gas pedal a bit too forcefully so that the tires skipped and spun as they finally met the gravel.

Good-bye, my darling Eva.

I dared not look in the rearview mirror as I continued, slowly, down the lane to the county road that led to town.

As we entered town, I couldn't help but smile. I would be at my father's house—home—in a matter of hours. By dawn. And twenty-four hours from that moment, I would be in the bed I'd slept in for more than half of my life. I knew I would be welcome there, but I had no idea what would happen with Press. He would no doubt come after us, probably showing up on my father's front porch, looking serious. What would he tell my father?

What would *I* tell my father? I had no proof. Only suspicions. I'd never given him reason not to trust me, had I? I prayed that he'd take me in his arms and tell me, "I'm glad you've left that worrisome place, Lottie."

Chapter 35

Helen

So lost was I in my thoughts that when I noticed the red lights in my mirror, I suspected they had been there for an unconscionably long time. In the late 1950s, Old Gate was even smaller than it is now, and I never imagined that the county sheriff's deputies would bother patrolling in the middle of the night. It wasn't as though Old Gate was on the way to anywhere. The town's two service stations even closed at 8:30 in the evening.

But, yes, the red lights were following me, so a half-mile from the two-lane highway that would take us to Highway 60 and closer to my father's house and safety, I pulled to the shoulder. It was the second time in a month I'd been pulled over, and only the second time in my life. Michael didn't stir.

As the patrol car pulled up behind me, the Cadillac filled with pulsing red light the color of a carnival candy apple. I couldn't imagine why I was being stopped. I'd been careful coming through town, and definitely hadn't been speeding despite being desperate to get to the highway.

I waited for what seemed like ten minutes before a man, silhouetted by the patrol car's blazing headlights, appeared in my side mirror and then at my window.

Relieved to see Dennis Mueller's attractive young face, I rolled down my window.

"Why, Dennis, we really have to stop meeting like this!" I tried to sound gay and charming, but my words came out in a staccato rush.

Dennis leaned forward and peered into the car. Seeing Michael, who was slumped over, asleep, he straightened again.

"I'll need to see your license and registration, Mrs. Bliss. Please." I wondered at his anxious formality.

"Is something wrong? I don't think I was speeding."

"Just your license and registration, please."

As I looked up at him, another car—a Mercury coupe—passed us slowly. A woman's face stared boldly from the passenger window, and they drove on.

"I don't understand." But I hurriedly took my driver's license from my wallet and felt for the leather folder in the glove box that held the car's registration. It surely couldn't matter that the car was registered in Press's name. I handed them to Dennis, whose lips pressed into a hard, narrow line as he shone his flashlight on them to read.

"I'll need to keep these, Mrs. Bliss. I'm sure there's some mistake, but this car was reported stolen yesterday, and the department has to take possession of it."

I laughed nervously. "Of course there's a mistake, Dennis. This is my husband's car, and we certainly didn't report it stolen." My voice was raised, and Michael complained with a quick bleat of alarm and dropped back to sleep. "You must give those back to me. This car is obviously not stolen."

"Ma'am, I can radio back to the station to have someone come and pick you up, but I can't let you take the car. Your name isn't on the registration, and I can't let you drive it away."

He was growing more agitated, his tightly controlled voice getting higher.

"That's ridiculous. No one needs to call anyone." My hands gripped the steering wheel so tightly, I could feel the ridges of it pressing into the pads of my palms. I couldn't let anyone call Press. I wanted to believe that it had all been a stupid mistake, but in my heart I knew better.

"I don't want to take you into custody, Mrs. Bliss. Your little boy, neither."

But I wasn't listening. I'd made a decision. Jerking the car into DRIVE, I pushed down the gas pedal and veered onto the road. I had an impression of Dennis Mueller reaching out after me, and, glancing in my mirror, saw him stumble and fall into the road. That he might have been seriously injured never occurred to me. My mind was blank with fear.

Moments later, the red lights behind me had disappeared, and I was nearly to the intersection that would take me out to Highway 29 toward Charlottesville.

"It's going to be all right. It's going to be all right," I whispered to myself under my breath, grateful that Michael hadn't woken up. Reaching the intersection, I stopped and looked in my rearview mirror. Dennis Mueller hadn't followed me. There was no light at the intersection—just a stop sign. I turned. Accelerated. But I hadn't driven more than a few hundred feet when I saw the woman in the road. She was barely dressed in a sagging satin bathing suit or leotard, her hair wild about her chalky face, across which was a slash of bright red lipstick or, perhaps, blood. Her legs were short and heavily fleshed, her feet bare. She turned her head as I stomped the brakes, and I saw that the side of her scalp was torn away, bloody. It was Helen Heaster.

The Eldorado's brakes locked and we fishtailed so that I lost control. I cried out as the car left the shoulder and hurtled, bumping and sliding, down the brush-clogged slope.

Chapter 36

The Truth

I was unconscious for such a short amount of time that Michael's cries hadn't quite turned into full-blown screams. My head ached, but my first panicked thought was for him. I fumbled for my seat-belt; but as I shifted, I realized my left foot was caught beneath the seat, and I felt a terrible pain as I pulled it free.

"It's okay, baby. You're fine. Just fine." I spoke to calm him, but I had no idea if he was actually fine. The seatbelt had loosened and twisted with the rolling of the car, and I found him sideways, the belt squeezing his small torso in two. "You're okay. You'll be all right."

Ignoring the voice in my head that wanted to shout for help—to scream in horror of what I might have just done to my second and only child—I struggled to release him. The buckle was caught up beneath his arm, and my heart broke for him when he began to cry harder as I squeezed it that much tighter to loosen it. But in a few seconds the buckle released and he dropped, free, into my hands.

Heedless of any injuries that I couldn't see in the dark, I pulled him close and kissed his soft hair and his cheek that was wet with tears. He was free and he was breathing. That was all that mattered.

Except that I knew we had to get out of that car. We had to get away.

The car had stopped just short of the bottom of the hill, but hadn't rolled, thank God. I was able to open the passenger door easily and pull Michael out. I tried to put him down for a moment so I could get my purse, which lay on the floor of the back seat, but he clung to me, crying and terrified. I felt cruel, but I had to wrest him from my neck. When I set him on the weeds outside the car, he screamed louder.

"It's okay, Michael. It's all right. I just have to get my purse."

He wasn't hearing me. I bent back into the car to grab the handle of my purse, but when I jerked it from beneath the seat, something popped out with it. Even with the car's dome light on, the floor was in shadow, so I pulled up both the purse and the thing beside it so I could see it in the light.

It was a small, mud-encrusted sandal. A sandal that, beneath the mud, had once been white leather. Eva's sandal.

When had I seen it last? My head was pounding and Michael was screaming. When? Why was it in Press's car?

Picking up Michael again, I had the presence of mind to shut the door and carefully climb around to the driver's side and shut the car and headlights off. All the while, I was thinking about the sandal.

My leg hurt, and I had the worst headache of my life, but I didn't think either one of us was bleeding. The night was quiet except for the sound of the occasional car up on the highway. No one was stopped above us. No one had found us, yet. I had to find a way out of town, but I knew I couldn't go back up to the highway. The police would be looking for us.

"We have to run, darling. And I need you to be very quiet." But Michael was crying harder.

We entered the woods at the bottom of the hill. The night was chilly, and my leg was stiff, but I walked as quickly as I could. I had to think.

The woods were sparse, revealing the lights of houses on the eastern edge of Old Gate. I had no plan except to get Michael somewhere warm that wasn't the police station. I didn't like heading back into town, and I racked my brain trying to think of people I knew on this side of town. In my fearful fantasies, I imagined every door being shut against us. My father and Nonie were the only people I could trust, and I had to find a way to call them. Shamefully, a part of me was even a little embarrassed that we were in such distress. The Bliss name wasn't a particularly popular one, and Eva's death had added to the air of scandal around it.

After a few minutes, still unable to hear any voices or footsteps behind us, I slowed—but not too much. I knew that if I stopped, my injured leg might keep me from starting again.

We were another half mile from Father Aaron and the church, where we might be safe, and I knew I couldn't make it. Michael had quieted but was shivering in my arms.

"Soon. Soon we'll be warm, baby."

It was his shivering that made me remember: Eva—or Eva's ghost—standing in front of me in the morning room, wearing the Wedgwood blue ribbon. Drenched. Water running into her muddy sandals.

Eva had died wearing her sandals and a ribbon that she'd gotten from Rachel. She wouldn't have had either on if she'd been trying to take a bath. It was unthinkable. Eva hadn't died in the house, and she hadn't been alone.

"Oh, Michael. Your poor sister."

Finally we reached the outermost road circling the town, and as I crossed a back yard littered with children's toys, a swing set, and a rusting car, a dog I hadn't noticed when I entered the yard lunged at us, barking madly. Michael screamed, terrified. He had little experience of dogs because Press didn't like them. Frightened that the dog would attack us, I began to run, but the barking didn't get closer. When we passed close to the house, I saw that the dog was chained to a shed in a corner of the yard. I was so grateful.

No lights came on in the house, and I hurried on, finally deciding exactly where we might go.

Chapter 37

No Quarter

"*Someone* needs to look at Michael, Charlotte. If you don't let David call Jack, then I have no choice but to call the hospital for an ambulance."

Finally, Michael and I were both warm. Rachel's father, David, had poked up the waning fire in the family room, and Holly had brought me tea and a cup of warm milk that I was letting Michael sip in my lap. There had been no use in lying about the wreck. The bruises on my face and the mud on my now-ruined loafers sitting by the front door told a large part of the story. They had answered the door together, Holly looking apprehensive and David irritated. He was like Rachel in that he didn't suffer fools or interruptions patiently, and given that it was nearly three A.M., our arrival had certainly interrupted his sleep. Now he stood at the entrance to the family room watching us silently. I knew that Holly didn't care much for Press, but I had no idea how David felt.

"We're both just tired. Don't you see?" I knew I was being unreasonable. "David looked us both over." But David didn't let me finish.

"I told you that army field training from fifteen years ago doesn't make me qualified to pass judgment on automobile accident injuries now." Then he continued, more kindly, "I think Michael is all right, but I still believe you may have a concussion. You should both see a doctor."

"There's an eight-twenty morning train from Lynchburg, or you could drive us up to Charlottesville. We could be in Clareston before supper. I promise we'll go by the hospital just as soon as we get there." I could hear the panic rising in my voice, and knew I sounded insane to them. Holly had listened sympathetically when I told her that it was more than a small argument that I'd had with Press, and that I needed to get to my father's house, or at least call him and let him know we needed to come home. But I couldn't be certain they believed me. I took several deep breaths to calm myself. Michael, too, was upset, restless and fretful in my arms.

"Let me take him, Charlotte." Holly held out her hands for him. "I'll give him back whenever you like."

"Please. Can't I use the phone?"

"Just let me take Michael. Let me help calm him down."

I didn't want to let him go, but Holly seemed sincere enough, and I thought it might buy some time and sympathy.

"Come to Holly, sweet boy." She smiled brightly at Michael, who didn't seem afraid of her. "Let's look at the toys I've got here." She took him to the large basket of infant toys she had for Seraphina, who wouldn't be ready for them for months.

I sank back into the comfortable chair, telling myself I wouldn't fall asleep. I had to persuade them to let us get to Clareston and my father and Nonie. I thought about Eva, but I knew I didn't dare tell them what I suspected about Rachel.

"You said the policeman pursued you?" David came all the way into the room. "Something about the car being stolen?"

"It has to be a misunderstanding, doesn't it?" I tried a smile. Of course I knew it was nothing of the sort, but I didn't want to complicate things. "My car has never been stolen."

"But why would someone report it, then?"

I didn't like the way David was looking at me at all—as though I were a teenager prone to lying. I hadn't lied. Everything I had told them was the truth, but I had seen in their faces that they weren't sure what to think. I had been an idiot to come to them. They weren't really my friends. Complete strangers would have been better. I wasn't thinking straight, and now I couldn't stop the flood of panic inside me.

Holly had Michael, and I was going to have to try to get him from her without them becoming suspicious. If I had to walk all the way to Clareston, I would get Michael to safety and my father's house. Why had I come to this town? Press had fooled me in some horrible way. I imagined then that Holly and David were a part of it all, that they had been involved in Press's duplicity. Olivia had never truly warmed to them. What if it hadn't been because of her dislike of Jewish people? Perhaps she knew something about the Webbs the way she knew something about Press. But Olivia wasn't there to protect either Michael or me. I had to be smart.

"Use your head, Lottie." Nonie was always trying to make me be sensible, and I was, most of the time. God, how I wished she were with us.

Michael yawned, making Holly smile.

"Press hasn't been himself since Eva died. Can't you see he blames me? He can't forgive me? This is just one way he's trying to hurt me. Surely you can understand how hard it's been."

I thought I saw sympathy in David's eyes, but I wasn't sure. Bringing up Eva might have been a mistake. I imagined then that the world was divided into two groups of people: those who believed Eva's death was my fault and blamed me; and those who believed I was responsible, but pitied me. My hope was that David Webb was in the second group.

"You can't just take a man's son away from him, Charlotte. Especially if the boy's injured."

"He's fine. Can't you see he's fine? Look at him. He's just exhausted."

David glanced at Michael, then back at me.

"I'm calling Jack." When I started to protest, he said, "It's either Jack or the hospital, Charlotte. You're not a child. You know what's right, here."

"Then stop treating me like a child." Getting up, I bent to take Michael from Holly's arms, but she held fast to him. I tugged, trying to pull him away. He called out for me, sounding frightened.

"You can't. David, we can't let her leave here with him."

"Then just let me use the phone. It's in the kitchen, yes?" It was the best chance I had to reach my father.

Before I knew what was happening, David took ahold of my shoulders and pulled me backwards so that I fell back against him. Even though he was nearly two inches shorter than I, he had control.

"Listen to yourself, Charlotte. Listen." He turned me around to face him. "Do you want to hurt your son, too?"

Stunned and sickened into silence, I could only look down at the room's expensive wall-to-wall carpet. Michael continued to cry for me, but I couldn't bear to look at him.

Half an hour later, I was resting on the beige velvet sofa, stroking Michael's hair as he slept in my arms. My badly bruised leg was extended over the cushions. They had argued that calling my father—who was still recovering from the hit-and-run accident—in the middle of the night would unnecessarily alarm him. I knew they were wrong, but I didn't have the energy to disagree. But they had promised to tell Jack that he was to come alone, without Press. Yet when Jack arrived, his face creased with concern, Press was close behind.

I would be back at Bliss House, a prisoner, before the sun rose.

Chapter 38

Upstairs, Upstairs

Press returned me to Olivia's room, knowing I wouldn't try to leave again without Michael. And he made sure I knew that Michael was no longer in the house. I was in a state of drug-induced sluggishness, but I remember everything that happened after I woke in Olivia's bed later that day.

There was a glass of water and a cup of tepid tisane on the bedside table, and, squinting to keep the strong afternoon light streaming in the windows out of my eyes, I drank both quickly and fell back on the pillows. I wanted to search for Michael, but couldn't force myself from the bed because any movement was painful: not only my head, but my neck and injured leg. Feeling for the bell beside the bed that would ring in the kitchen, I found it, but decided not to ring it. Would Terrance or Marlene even bother to come? Barely able to complete any train of thought, I gave up and went back to sleep.

Though I slept fitfully that second time, I woke in the early evening from another dream of Olivia and Eva in the kitchen.

Again Eva stood on the stool, close beside Olivia, but now water dropped from her body in a hundred endless rivulets and pooled on the floor. But this time Olivia gestured me forward so I could also watch over her shoulder. There was a small goose, flopping and honking in the enormous kitchen sink as Olivia forced it down, again and again, to keep it from escaping. Eva watched the goose as well, her face blank and unemotional even though the scene was violent and horrifying in the extreme.

"Don't look," I said to Eva, wanting to take her in my arms. But I didn't try to touch her. Even in my dream, I knew she wouldn't really be there.

The light around us was the filtered golden amber of an autumn afternoon, and I ached for the days I had walked in the lane beneath the trees with Eva and Michael. As we stood there, the kitchen seemed to grow and stretch so that the floor and the walls got so far away that they disappeared, and we were left—sink and stool, and now-screaming goose—standing in a broad pasture, with Bliss House at a distance behind us, its windows bathed in the amber light. Finally, Eva looked up at me. The velvet ribbon that had been in her hair now hung loosely around her neck, and a fine goose feather was caught in her curls.

"Go upstairs, upstairs, Mommy."

But how could I? *Upstairs, upstairs* was her name for the third floor. There was no upstairs to go to out here. I looked over my shoulder at the house.

"Come with me. Don't stay here, baby."

Eva stared past me toward the house and, in that moment, I saw how she might have looked as an adult: favoring Press only slightly, with delicate cheekbones and a curve to her brow that spoke not just of intelligence, but of cheerfulness too. She was my daughter, and would always be my daughter. Press might not have treasured her the way he should have, might even have stopped thinking of her, but I would never stop.

As the dream faded, I felt my consciousness returning, the pain returning, and I fought it as hard as I could.

Someone was moving in the bedroom. I heard the faint clinking of china in the direction of the bedside table.

"I'm sorry I disturbed you, Miss Charlotte."

Marlene *did* look sorry, but was otherwise her collected sensible self. With the cooling of the weather, she had switched to a long-sleeved black dress. In the darkness of the room, her pale head and hands seemed almost disembodied. But she was, indeed, whole and human.

I clutched her knobby wrist.

"Don't lock me in here, Marlene. Please, don't. I need to see Michael." My headache had lessened some, but the words still hurt coming out. I could almost see them, dark green and sharp, glinting in the faint moonlight.

I could also see the surprise on her face. "Lock you in? Why would anyone do that?"

Embarrassed by my panic, I let go of her wrist. "Where's Terrance?"

"Mr. Preston said he thought that you'd prefer that I serve you while you're ill." She hesitated. "Shall I bring you some soup? I've brought more tisane. It's chamomile and valerian, for your nerves."

In that moment I might have wept but for my desire to see Michael. I felt terribly alone.

I whispered. "Marlene, please help me out to the telephone. I have to call someone."

She seemed not to have heard me as she poured tea into the cup on the bedside table. "I'll be right back up with some soup and crackers for you, unless you think you could eat something more."

"The telephone. Please." I tried to sit upright. My head still hurt, but I felt like I might be able to get out of bed. Before I did anything else, I needed to use the bathroom.

"I'll tell Mr. Preston you're awake. I'll be back in a few minutes with your soup, but you can ring if you need anything else."

She started out of the room with the tray that held the teapot and water pitcher.

"Why won't you help me use the telephone? Help me, Marlene." Now tears threatened, welling in my eyes.

She stopped and turned. Her words were kind but held no apology.

"Mr. Preston had the upstairs, hall, and kitchen telephones removed, Miss Charlotte. There's only the one in the library now."

"What about Michael? Have you seen him? Is he with Shelley?"

"I'm sorry. You'll have to ask Mr. Preston."

When she was gone, I sat in the waning light, wanting to leave the room but somehow afraid of what I would find. Olivia's room was like a kind of island in the house. Michael was out there. Somewhere. But I had to be strong to find him.

Chapter 39

More than a Bastard

I didn't have to wait long for Press. It was he who brought my soup and crackers, looking like a contrite, caring husband. Such a superb actor. His actions were completely unironic: the way he closed the door, softly, with his elbow, as though he didn't wish to disturb me, the solicitous *let's turn on a small light, it's so dark you might spill your soup* and *how is your head? Better?*

My husband. My jailer. Though I had not heard a key in the lock, as Marlene had promised. He knew only too well that I would not leave without Michael.

Jack had given me an injection against the pain, whispering that I shouldn't make a scene in front of Holly and David, promising that it wouldn't hurt me. The pain had, indeed, gone for a while. I didn't know if he had called Press after David had first called him, or if David had called Press directly. But I knew it didn't matter. I was lost. Michael was lost to me. Press had come into the Webbs' living room with exclamations of gratitude to David and Holly,

280

but he had approached me cautiously, as one might a violent child. Or a madwoman.

I didn't make a scene.

Even when Press took Michael from my arms so Jack could tend to me, I didn't protest. I knew no one would hear a word I had to say against Press. Really, what was there to say? He hadn't injured me. There were no witnesses to his threats. He was a man who had lost a daughter, and his wife had gone a little mad with grief.

By the time we got out to Jack's car, I was shuffling with weariness brought on by the drugs, and I only just remember seeing Shelley's anxious face in the passenger window of my sedan. The last thought I had before we drove away was that Michael would at least be taken care of on the way home.

I hadn't had the presence of mind to think that Press might take him from the house right away. I was too tired, too drugged to worry.

I would be lying if I said I didn't find the tiniest bit of solace being back in Bliss House. It wasn't a good thing, but at least it was familiar. Better the devil you know.

"I want to see Michael."

"What kind of greeting is that? Of course you want to see him, but you're not in any shape to see him yet. You don't think I would do anything to hurt him, do you? If so, you're doing me a huge injustice, my love. Give me credit for at least a small amount of humanity."

I turned away. I hated looking at his smug, not-quite-handsome face. He looked very different to me now. Something about his eyes wasn't right. I thought again about the jewel-handled knife. Was it still in my clothes? But if I killed him and he *had* done something with Michael, then I might never find Michael again.

"I hope you're ready for the memorial tonight. There won't be a lot of people, but you know almost everyone. They'll understand, of course, if you're not yourself." He set the tray on the side of the bed. The smell of the soup made me salivate. I couldn't remember the last time I'd eaten.

"I know you must be hungry."

The soup was too compelling. Turning my head, I saw it was Marlene's vegetable soup. Beside it, she had put very thin slices of her special rye bread on one of the Minton dragon plates.

Unable to bear looking at him, or at the food, I turned over again to face the short wall with the dresser and jewelry box.

"Go away. You're a bastard."

"Something more than a bastard, my love. Much more."

I felt him move away from the bed.

"You might as well eat. You're only hurting yourself."

"Should I just assume you've drugged the food?"

When he laughed, he sounded so satisfied. Genuinely amused.

"Assume whatever you like. Would it really matter? You may be a martyr, but no one sets out to like pain, Charlotte. Pain is an acquired taste. If I were you, I wouldn't work too hard to acquire it. You're likely to get what you want, and I don't think it really suits you. You're not as fragile as you think you are. I think you've held up very well, considering that you killed your own daughter. Not many women could survive that."

Quickly turning over so that it felt as though knives were shooting through my head, I flung the steaming soup bowl at him, and watched with satisfaction as the carrots and potatoes and bits of celery tumbled down his shirtfront.

"I didn't kill her, and we both know it."

Press didn't move, didn't change expression.

"You've shamed yourself, Charlotte. Remember that."

Chapter 40

A Clever Trick

"Go upstairs, upstairs, Mommy."

Even with Press's threats, I couldn't get Eva's words out of my head. She meant for me to confront Press in the theater, I was certain. I didn't know what she wanted me to do, but I decided I would know when I went inside. Above my head, I could hear people walking around. Voices in the hall, bright laughter on the stairs that echoed in the dome and filled Bliss House with an air of celebration. For the first time in years, there were people invited upstairs and into the theater.

"You know almost everyone," Press had said.

Yes, I would be there.

Aching, and lightheaded from hunger—I hadn't trusted the soup, but had retrieved the bread from the floor—I went to the wardrobe and found the costume that Press had provided. It was, indeed, a Brunhild costume, complete with a braided gold corset and flowing ivory skirt. Resting on the floor of the wardrobe was a kind of helmet decorated on either side with eagles' feathers. A molded half-face mask lay beside it. So like Press. I could imagine how the others looked. Press loved a masquerade, but he was never who he pretended to be.

Pushing the ridiculous costume aside, I found a clean pair of loose wool slacks and took a tunic sweater from the drawer. My progress was slow as I washed and dressed. The anniversary clock on the mantel chimed ten-thirty. I found my coat, dirty and torn (I must have looked quite strange to the Webbs), lying over a chair, and transferred its contents into my sweater pockets. I didn't know what was going to happen—if I would find Michael with Press, or somewhere in the house. I was acting completely on my faith in a dream, and in my dead daughter.

When I reached the third floor, I started for the closed theater doors. Above me, the dome was alive with bright stars as it was every night. I could hear music, not loud but strange and foreign, coming from the theater. Press had had new chandeliers hung inside, but the light showing beneath the door was as gold and wavering as firelight. Even in the gallery the air was pungent with sharply scented incense that was nothing like what Father Aaron burned at church on high holy days.

I reached for the handle of one of the doors, but I heard light, running footsteps behind me. Unmistakably Eva's footsteps.

"Eva." I whispered her name. "Eva, come back."

The footsteps paused for a moment, then continued up and down the other side of the gallery in front of the ballroom, getting louder and louder, heavier and more frantic. Eva, running until she was exhausted. How many times had I watched her run from the nursery door to the back stairs, or around the gallery on a rainy day? Sinking onto one of the tall armchairs resting along the wall when she got tired. I sensed that she had stopped at the armchair outside the ballroom, perhaps to rest. But then the running began again, footfalls thundering until I had to cover my ears. Certain that everyone else in the house must be hearing it too, I ran across the gallery to where I thought she was.

"Eva. Stop."

Finally, as I stood in front of the ballroom doors, they did stop. I could feel Eva—or something—breathing heavily beside me.

Did she want me to go into the ballroom? I put my hand on the inset handle of one of the doors. As I slid it open, it rumbled lazily in its overhead track.

I've never been able to explain what I did—or rather didn't—see that night. It might have been the result of some drug or unconscious hypnosis. What I mean to say is that what I'd seen in the ballroom prior to that day must have been the result of some trick or enchantment.

The room in which I'd played with Michael just a few days before now looked exactly as it had before I'd had it painted. There were the same hundreds—or maybe thousands—of delicate Japanese women and gruff-looking men painted onto the walls. I groped for the button light switch and pressed it. A few of the wall sconces came on, and I saw the glint of light on the metal rings attached to the ceiling.

Shocked, I spun around to look out to the hallway. Nothing there had changed. But when I looked again, I knew I wasn't deceived. The room had not changed. There was no faint odor of paint, not a single drop cloth or tool on the floor. Something brushed past me and I heard the footsteps again, running, running, running, playful.

I was, I confess, afraid, despite the presence of my daughter. Nothing was right, and my mind raced for an explanation. Stepping into the room, I could no longer hear the music from across the gallery, so deep was the quiet of the windowless ballroom. It was another trick of this house, which had enchanted me for so many years, hiding its true nature, hiding the true nature of my husband.

Standing in the unchanged room, I suddenly understood that I had been seeing only what I had wanted to see. The house, the strange man I'd "hired" to paint—they had all been just what I wanted. What had Michael seen when he was in the room with me? How had the house affected him?

Looking out the doors, I saw the railing from which Michael Searle had hanged himself. He'd committed suicide rather than live with what his father and Terrance had done to Olivia. Done to him. Surely I hadn't invented that.

It was what my own mother had chosen, rather than live with me.

What sort of person was I, really?

"Help me. Someone help. Please."

The voice came from inside the ballroom. I turned around but didn't see anyone.

But it hadn't been a ghostly sort of voice, and it was coming from the fireplace. Afraid, but also afraid not to respond, I went to the fireplace and saw that the flowered panel beside it was a few inches out of place.

"Who's there? Please, help me."

It was J.C.'s voice. The sound of it was so piteous that any animosity I had for her was completely overwhelmed. I couldn't ignore her—and hadn't Eva led me to find her?

Between the two of us, we got the stubborn panel open.

The woman who stumbled out of the hidden passage was nothing like the woman who had swanned into Bliss House the previous week, her clothes perfect, her confidence intimidating and annoying. Now her skirt and blouse were torn and stained brown with—*dear God*, it was blood. One of her eyes squinted shut, a mass of purple and black bruising. The other was blood-red, the cheek below it dramatically swollen as though badly broken.

When I instinctively reached out to steady her, she flinched but didn't turn away.

"There are rooms down there. He's an animal." Her shoulders hunched, her voice was a raw whisper. "It's not Press anymore. Whatever he is, he's going to kill me. Do you understand? We have to get away from here. I told you! Didn't I tell you? And you wouldn't listen, Charlotte!" She began to weep. Great, heaving sobs.

"Were you hiding? What's in there?" Later she would describe the strange warren of rooms far beneath the house. I didn't want to see them, but I eventually did.

Choking on her sobs, J.C. sank to the floor. I was going to have to get her to a hospital, but I couldn't let Press know that I had seen her.

I had to think of Michael first.

Whatever I did to help her might lead to Press punishing me by keeping Michael from me forever. I knew it was a selfish thought, but I couldn't help myself.

The sobbing suddenly abated, and she gripped my arm with fingers whose nails were torn and filthy with dirt and blood. "He told me about Eva. It wasn't you, Charlotte. He thinks he's going to kill me, so he told me."

"Told you? What did he tell you?" I knelt beside her on the floor. "Tell me about Eva!" I took her by the shoulders. If her head hadn't turned a fraction of an inch, looking past me, transfixed, I might have shaken her.

I swung around.

Terrance.

Chapter 41

Roses

"Hello, stranger."

I heard Rachel's voice but could only see her in my peripheral vision. Turning my head, slowly, I knew I should be afraid, knew I should be moved to action, but I couldn't make myself do anything. My breath was short and I had the horrible feeling that I might die at any moment.

Press and Terrance and a man in a rubber clown mask had led us into the theater. I hadn't seen Rachel at first, but there were several other women, all also wearing bizarre masks: a rabbit, a man's mustached face (though the body below was decidedly female), a mouse, even a pig. Jack, with his silver-blond hair, was Mercury, silver wings like layered sickle blades protruding from his back. The other men were costumed as well. I was sure that the man in the featureless black gauze mask was Hugh Walters, the sheriff. Press had fitted himself with a dark mustache and tidy oiled beard. It, along with the oxblood Victorian waistcoat, proclaimed him to be Faust. When he was close enough for me to whisper, I told him he looked like a fool.

Once the doors were closed behind us, I had recklessly announced that they should look at J.C. to see what kind of man had brought them all here.

When everyone stopped to stare at us, I realized how many of them were scantily dressed. Two women, wearing only masks and swathes of pastel tulle on their rather robust bodies, had been interrupted while dancing to the waltz playing on the stereo. A Pulcinella, his blousy pants loosened, his member exposed, had turned away from a shepherdess seated on a lounge in front of one of the room's tall windows.

The realization of what was happening—what *had been happening*—among these people, under the thin guise of play readings and literary conversation and, now, a funeral memorial, swept over me.

I had been the fool.

Someone laughed and the party resumed. Press held my arm, and Jack grabbed my elbow to hold me still and stuck me with a needle. Within a few agonizing minutes in which I swore at Press, calling him names I didn't even remember knowing, I was drowsy, but fought sleep as hard as I could.

When I woke, it was to Rachel's voice.

I lay on a cushioned table or platform of some kind, and my head was raised so that I had a view of the transformed room: the thick carpets and plush velvet curtains. There were modern lamps, standing and on tables, and a number of candelabra filled with lighted candles that smoked faintly in the big room. I smelled burning wax and perfume. Rachel's *My Sin*, but there were other scents as well. Laughter and murmuring voices came to me from all directions. Above my head were the theater's new twin chandeliers. All was comfort, richness. The refinished paneled walls had a silken glow. It should have been beautiful. But it was not. It was pure evil.

"I bet you feel a little funny." Rachel looked far different from how she'd looked when I'd seen her at the hospital. Her hair was swept up and sleek against her head, not full and lush as I was used to seeing it. She didn't need a mask like the others, because she wore exaggerated, Kabuki-like makeup. It made her look unusually childish, like an expensive doll. Her cheeks were heavily rouged as though to contradict the deathly pale ivory foundation beneath it, her eyes lined to freakish roundness, the lids painted a brighter white than the foundation. But there was something else unfamiliar about her. Her eyes were reddened from some drug or alcohol—in fact, she held a goblet (one of Olivia's jewel-toned goblets from the butler's pantry) full of wine—but there was also an edge to her voice. It was clipped and precise as though it pained her to speak.

It all led me to wonder if maybe I wasn't in a dream after all. The Rachel I knew loved to dress up in costume, but only if it was flattering.

"Not to worry. It's not permanent." She gave a little giggle. "At least Jack and Press say it's not. We trust them, don't we? You just have to be very still for a while. Jack says you probably won't even remember."

I tried to speak, but my tongue felt thick and useless. What if my lungs stopped working and I couldn't breathe?

"Shhhh. Shhhh." Seeing panic in my eyes, Rachel patted my arm. I could feel her hand on me, but why couldn't I push her away?

"Before anything happens, we must have a talk. Just you and me." She glanced around. Satisfied, she said, "I have a secret to tell you, darling. I'm afraid it's a secret you're not going to like very much."

I couldn't stop her. God help me, I didn't want to know any secrets from her. There had been enough secrets. Far too many secrets.

"Listen." Rachel came even closer and traced a finger over my cheek. "Eva was at my house that day, while you were sleeping off your indiscretion with the champagne. You know how much she loved the geese."

Eva! She was talking about Eva. She was going to tell me this thing, and I couldn't stop her. I could barely move my head.

I tried to say *no*, but it came out as an animal grunt.

She touched my hair.

"I was glad when you cut your hair. You're not as pretty with short hair, Charlotte. Your jaw is too square. It's too mannish." When she glanced away, I knew she was looking at—or for— Press. Always Press. How had I not seen? She turned back to me, her painted lips a small moue of dissatisfaction. "I couldn't deny her the chance to feed the geese, and she'd asked so nicely. She had such lovely manners for a little girl. That made you happy, didn't it? Perfect little girl for perfect you." Now her face was very close to mine, and I could smell the sour wine on her breath. Her lipstick was smeared and her false eyelashes untidy. I imagined her face pressed into one of the enormous pillows that lay strewn about the room, unspeakable things being done to her, her face hot against the silk. I felt as though I might retch.

"Darling, what's wrong? Are you thirsty? No one ever goes dry here, you know." She held the glass of wine to my lips, and the thick bouquet of grapes made my stomach turn. I turned my head from it as far as I could and felt the wine slide down my chin.

"You always were a baby about wine. Remember that time you puked all over your shoes the night before Easter break? You were all upset because Nonie had sent you the shoes from Richmond. Fucking Nonie. Fucking in-everyone's-business Nonie. You know your father was fucking her all along, yes? Everyone knew but you. We used to laugh about it, Press and Jack and I. Couldn't stop."

It was fine that she was insulting me. These words didn't sting so much. If she was talking about Nonie and my father, she wasn't talking about Eva. I hated to hear Eva's name come out of her mouth.

As though our minds were one, it was the next word she said.
"Eva." She repeated my daughter's name again and again, as
though tasting it. Taking it for her own. "Eva, Eva, Eva." Shaking
her forefinger at me, she scolded. "You coddled her, you know.
You needed to let her be more independent. She liked coming to
my house when you weren't with us. I'd let her sit at my dressing
table, and I'd comb her hair and let her put on my jewelry. *Mama
doesn't let me play with her jewels,* she said. *Nonie brushes my hair.
Mama hurts my hair when she brushes me.* That cute little lisp. I loved
that cute little lisp!" She shook her head with eloquent dismay. "I
was a better mother than you were. Press would sit with us and tell
us how pretty we were together. Salt and pepper. And she would
put her tiny hand on my cheek and pat it, and then she'd kiss me.
She always smiled, Charlotte, when she was with me. With us."
Her face turned pensive.

The music stopped for a few moments and the sounds of the room
washed over me: quiet moans, grunts. If it hadn't been for the low
laughter, we might have been in a barn instead of the candlelit theater. What was happening to J.C.? Where was Press? He'd left me
to Rachel. Rachel in her costume with madness in her eyes. Why
hadn't I seen it before? But I knew the answer. I had loved her. I
had thought I knew her, but I'd been so horribly wrong.

"I used to think about you dying. I asked Press why you couldn't
just die, but he would never talk about it. He loves you, you know.
In his own way. Not the way he loves me, of course. But I think
he grew fond of you, Charlotte. You're like some great yellow dog:
obedient and friendly and cheerful. I hate how cheerful you are."
She mocked me. "You have to make the best of it, Rachel. You'll
have a baby in time, Rachel. Be nice to your mother, Rachel. Not
all of us are so lucky, Rachel." She shuddered. "I wanted to slap the
smug little smile off your face. I had to watch you—watch Olivia
make a fuss over you with your pretty blue eyes and your stupid
pedigree. She didn't really like you either, you know. She was as

fake as she could be, but you ate it up. Poor, dumb Charlotte. She was just using you. Press was just using you as a brood mare. What did it feel like, brood mare? He almost left you when you had Eva first, you know." She paused to take a sip of her wine, then put it aside. "'Girls should be drowned at birth,' he said." Then she laughed, imagining her own joke.

I tried to edge away as she climbed onto the cushion beside me, her warm body pressing against mine. Now it wasn't just her breath that overwhelmed me, but the cloying scent of recent sex. Rachel smelled like sex. Rachel *was* sex. And I suddenly understood why Press had wanted her. What man wouldn't want Rachel? Now that she'd given birth, she was fecund. Ripe. It was no use trying to get away from her. She pressed herself against my hip and laughed.

"Press used to tell me about fucking you. He said it was like fucking a mannequin the first few times." She pressed her lips against my ear, and her breath made gooseflesh run down my side. "Didn't I teach you anything, Charlotte? I should have come into your bed. All those nights we were alone. So close. It was my duty to get you ready for Press, but I let him down, poor thing, because I don't really care for girls." I felt her teeth bite lightly down on the edge of my ear. "He told me you learned to give good head, though. It made me a little jealous when he told me about it. But do you know what he was doing when he told me about it? He was touching me here. . . ." She cupped my breast in her hand, running her forefinger slowly over the nipple, but I could hardly feel it. My head filled with the sound of a thousand bees—some horrible humming that rose in pitch, and then I realized it was a sound that I was making or trying to make, willing her away from me. I squeezed my eyes shut, wishing her away.

"Jesus, Charlotte. Are you crying?" She took her hand away. "Aw. You poor thing. Am I scaring you? Did you think I was going to do something terrible to you? You poor stick." She moved away slightly. "Don't worry. Nobody wants you. Don't you understand that now? Press didn't want you from the beginning. He just got used to fucking you. And he wanted your stupid babies."

She climbed down from the pedestal. "No. Not your babies. Just sons."

I couldn't move, but in that moment I'm sure I felt my heart stop. *Eva.* Press hadn't wanted Eva. In my head, I screamed his name. Where was he? Why was he letting Rachel tell me these lies? But I knew the answer, didn't I? They weren't lies, and I had known it for a long, long time. It was in the way he looked at Michael. It was in the way Eva had followed after him, climbed onto his lap, begged for his attention. She had been so desperate. Deep down, she had known he didn't love her.

He'd taken her from the nursery, surely telling her they were going on a special adventure—just the two of them. Leaving Michael and me behind. A trip to Auntie Rachel's and Uncle Jack's. Off to feed the geese and enjoy whatever other pleasures Rachel had planned. When I had taken her there, Rachel had given her ice cream for lunch and teased her that Nonie and I probably only gave her nasty vegetables. I had laughed! How easily I had believed that Rachel was only being indulgent.

Oh, God. Had they done things to her? We lived then in a world where few people—certainly not I—imagined that anyone would touch a child in a sexual way. It had been beyond my darkest, most suspicious thoughts. But I suddenly understood that it was a possibility. Looking into Rachel's now-cold eyes, I knew she was capable of anything. What about Jack? Surely not a doctor. Who knew what these people were capable of? They had all become strangers to me.

Michael? Where was Michael?

Rachel was drinking more wine. A man wearing a horse mask and a white dinner jacket and red bow tie came up behind her. The wine in Rachel's glass sloshed a bit as he pressed himself against her back and wrapped an arm about her waist. She wavered, but then pushed him away, nonplussed. She had no time for him.

"I should let him have *you*." She grinned wickedly. "He's pretty good. Not Press good, but pretty good." Then she was suddenly somber. The music had changed again. It was no longer classical music, but some sort of strange drumming. Behind Rachel, a kind of collective shout went up.

"Everyone's happy tonight. Do you know why? Because Press is in charge now instead of that old letch Zion. Everybody loves Press. Did you know that? Everyone loves Press, everyone wants Press. It's this house, too. We belong here, Charlotte, because this is where Press belongs. He's a part of us, and we're a part of him."

There was a satisfaction in Rachel's eyes that sickened me. When, God, would I be released from this horror? What had Jack done to me? My eyes were so dry, I felt they might wither in my head. Was Michael sleeping somewhere else in the house? Was he with Shelley? How seamlessly she'd fit into our life after Nonie's departure. I prayed that they hadn't hurt her as well. She was hardly a child, but she was so young and vulnerable, with no one but her brother to look out for her. Like me, she was alone. And at that moment, I felt alone in a way I'd never felt before. I had nothing. Not even Michael. How could I protect him? The truth was that I couldn't.

The tears began again. This time they slid down both temples and I felt them work their way into my hair.

"Darling, darling, darling." Rachel kissed my forehead and stroked my arm. "Eva didn't cry, darling. Did you know that? She was such a brave little thing. Bold, even. She marched down to the pond with her bag of crumbs for the geese. So proud of herself. You would have been proud of her too. Like a little angel out among the geese. They're obnoxious bastards sometimes, but at first I had the real sense that they were being careful with her. Isn't that funny? Perhaps because she was so tiny—not much bigger than they were." There was a faraway look in her reddened eyes. "I promise I told her to be careful. Those geese can bite. Well, you remember how that one nipped at her that last time you both came over. She knew better than to tease them with the crumbs. I mean, she was throwing them right at them. I don't know. Maybe she accidentally hit one in the face? It was hard to tell from the porch."

I could see Eva at the water's edge in her pink playsuit, hair pulled back with the blue velvet ribbon that Rachel had tied around her head, surrounded by hungry geese. Geese that snapped at her and honked. She'd stuck close by me the day she'd been nipped. I knew she was afraid of the geese, had wanted me to come with her to feed them. And I knew Rachel was lying. She'd made Eva go down to the pond alone. Afraid.

"I shouted for her to get back from them, and she tried, bless her heart. She really tried. But those mean old geese were just determined to get at that bag, and she just wouldn't let go. But she wouldn't run away either! She was stubborn, Charlotte, just like you. If only she'd let go, they would've taken it and left her alone."

She was alone. My baby was alone by the water. Harried. Afraid.

"You might ask where Press was during all this. Well, I called for him, and I called for Jack. I'm sure I did. But those two. . . ." She paused dramatically and whispered. "You don't know what those two can get up to sometimes. They just don't hear a thing, those boys, so it's really not my fault, Charlotte. You didn't think Jack was actually up to making a baby with me, did you?" She shook her head. "You don't know how many times I wanted you to know, my dear. You're almost too precious to live, you know that?"

I hadn't missed the lascivious look in Rachel's eyes when she'd teased about what Press and Jack might "get up to." It was all too much. Seraphina was Press's child. Another girl. It explained the pitiful flowers in the hospital. They were a statement of his disappointment in her. No wonder she had looked unhappy, even in sleep.

If only I could've closed my eyes to shut it all out. I couldn't bear to hear any more. The drums played on, not quite drowning out the voices and the other hideous sounds beneath them. The drumbeat was in my head, thudding through my body, growing stronger.

"They chased her right into that water and she fell. It was comical, really. You might have laughed. I almost did. I mean, I wasn't afraid for her or anything like that. She was a big girl, and the water wasn't all that deep."

Stop! Why couldn't I stop her talking?

"I finally went down there myself, and, oh, Charlotte, I was so big. So slow. You understand. I was huge!"

With a vain touch, she smoothed her stomach, which was much smaller now. She wasn't her old svelte self by any means, but she would have her figure back soon enough.

Please, God, make her stop talking. Please, please, please!

"Those birds!" Rachel's face filled my vision. Tiny sprays of her saliva dotted my face. "I couldn't chase them away. They were all over her, splashing and squawking. There was absolutely *nothing* I could do. Water was flying everywhere! Finally she let go of that stupid bag, though I'm sure there was nothing left by then. It was all wet and falling apart. But they went after it, every single one of those stupid birds."

I knew that water. I had even imagined Eva falling into it, a less dramatic fall, with me right there to stand her up again and warn her about getting too close to the pond. The kind of tiny drama that plays out in the heads of all mothers who see their children near passive dangers. But not this. Not this terror.

Rachel closed her eyes, her sour breath spreading over my face. Her mascara was so thick that her false lashes clung together in fan-like arcs below her eyes. When she opened them, I saw madness.

"It was so easy, my Charlotte. She was just as big as a minute, and such a polite child. She hardly fought at all. All the fight had gone out of her from wrangling with those silly birds."

I saw the water closing over my precious baby's face. I'd imagined it a hundred times or more happening in the bathtub. But now the water was flecked with green and streaked with sunlight and the water far beneath her was as black as night. Rachel's hand was spread over her chest. Pushing. Pushing down, until Eva closed her eyes forever.

"Press raced like the devil to get her home and in the tub before you woke up." Rachel sighed deeply as though expelling her own life's breath. "I almost wish you could've been there. She was so peaceful. Because everything was okay after that. What's that phrase they used to use in chapel at school? 'The peace of God, which passeth all understanding.' That's what she has now."

No. There was no peace for Eva.

Chapter 42

Revenant

Before leaving me, Rachel wetted my lips with a finger-smear of wine and kissed my cheek with an exaggerated fondness. The small taste of that wine made me want to retch.

Around the room, bodies moved in shadow: touching, writhing, creating strange silhouettes that will be forever burned into my mind. I watched, but after a while it all became oddly distant, like the scenes that Olivia had shown me. It was happening to someone else.

For a long time, no one came near me. No one touched me, and I could imagine that I wasn't really there. I didn't want to close my eyes, because I would see Eva's face. Eva's vacant, water-ruined face, just as I'd been seeing it for weeks. Only now, Rachel would be there too. No matter how much I wanted to, I couldn't save Eva's life. She was gone. Maybe I could set her free from whatever haunted purgatory she was living in with Olivia, but I could do nothing beyond that. But Michael I could save. I was certain of it. Less certain, though, was I of my own survival.

While I was grateful that no one had come near me, I felt as though I were waiting for something. In my heart, I understood that that thing—that person—was Press. Or whoever he had become.

I must have slept, or at least I have no memory of someone putting me into darkness. No, not total darkness. I could see faint shapes beyond whatever piece of incense-fragrant fabric lay over me. The theater—if that was still where I was—had gone silent.

Was I afraid? I was afraid for Michael but not for myself. He was my only reason for living. My father had Nonie. I had lost Rachel, or rather I had never had Rachel. She had caused me the worst pain that I could imagine. Perhaps I should have felt some relief knowing that I hadn't been responsible for Eva's death, but I got no comfort from the fact. And Press. I hadn't really had him either. He had belonged to Rachel. But a part of me didn't wholly believe that. Rachel, in her hubris, imagined that Press would never use her in the way he had used me. Press wanted something from her, and I assume it was the same thing he wanted from me. She had given him a daughter, but maybe she would try to give him a son. Like me, Rachel was a womb.

There was too much stillness, given the number of people I knew were in the room. Would they kill me? Kill J.C.? I didn't know where she was. It had been easy enough for Press to fake the circumstances of Eva's death. How much easier would it be to excuse my death? Poor, mad, careless Charlotte who had let her daughter die. Did all these other people know that Rachel had killed Eva? What did Press really know?

Slowly, slowly the drape was pulled from my body.

"Charlotte."

How often had that voice called my name? From the hallway. From the other side of my bed. Sensuous in its depth. Even now I hear it, long after I last saw Press.

"Charlotte."

Even from the new depths of my loathing for him, my body, my treacherous body responded.

He walked into my view.

Press was naked. He seemed broader, taller than he had ever seemed before, and the black hair on his chest and groin was opaque in the dim light. I recognized my husband even though he, too, was wearing a half-mask. How foolish and strange. But my life was so strange. Why shouldn't everyone around me have been wearing masks? Only Rachel had shown her face. That was like her. She would want everyone to see her. It was her lifeblood to be seen.

Somewhere behind Press, someone was pounding a stick, a walking stick perhaps, on the floor. Slowly, at first, but then the tempo increased.

The intense lethargy that had been like a weight over my entire body was beginning to abate. Whatever Jack had injected me with was wearing off.

I had witnessed Olivia's rape. Her ultimate humiliation. My terror lay in wondering if Press would be the only man, the only person to use me that night. I felt the force of the masked stares. I had witnessed their debasement. But as long as they kept on their masks, I would try my hardest to forget, to erase them from my mind. If I survived.

"Charlotte."

Three times. The third time Press spoke my name, it sounded different. Final.

The stick continued its beat, reverberating in my body. The anticipation of the circle gathered around me was a palpable, hungry thing. Rachel, however, looked unhappy. Even in my fear, I felt some small satisfaction in that.

Press climbed a stair to reach me. What was there in him that was compelling him to do this in front of all these people?

I closed my eyes, unwilling to witness my own humiliation. As he entered me, the onlookers were silent, but I'm certain I felt the house shudder beneath me.

My husband had made love to me many times, but never with such slow deliberation. His breath quickened, and the breath of the circle of people quickened along with it.

Then something in the air changed. I opened my eyes. The room turned viciously cold and one of the women cried out as the air around us crystallized into something like snow—not falling, but simply hanging midair around us. The crystals stung, clinging to our skin. Press, apparently unaffected, continued. My body was now frozen inside and out. The pounding of the stick faltered only for a moment, then also kept on.

People began to fall away, alarmed. Only Rachel stayed. Her eyes had widened in her bizarrely made-up face, and her look of displeasure had turned to fascination.

The house shuddered again with a tremendous groan, and the walls of the theater bowed inward, creating a web of cracks across the long ceiling and causing the chandeliers to swing wildly. Now there were more cries from the others in the room, frightened exclamations that the doors couldn't be opened. Press's breath was hot in my ear and I knew he wouldn't last much longer. Rachel leaned forward, rapt. Over her shoulder I could see Jack, his mask insufficient to hide his crown of white hair. It was Jack who held the stick. Jack who was keeping time despite the chaos around him. The trusses above the ceiling shrieked with strain.

Then it was no longer Press laboring over me, and I felt a sharp pain deep inside. The man wore the same mask, but the hand that gripped my shoulder so violently felt icy and thin. Thinner than that of any other human on earth. Below the mask, the face was mottled and scarred. The lips were nothing but two faded, cracked lines of gray flesh.

Behind the mask, the eyeholes were empty. There was no life there, no humanity. There was nothing. I opened my mouth and screamed.

I retreated inside myself as deeply as I could in that lifetime of minutes. Far, far back to a time that was made up mostly of stories I told myself about my mother. I was in her bedroom, lying on her bed, playing with the cat that had been hers when she married my father. What was the name? The name? The sounds, the pain were bleeding through and I tried to remember the cat. Fredo? Frederick? No, it was Alfredo. Creamy white with azure marble eyes and a tail nearly as long as my arm. My mother kneeling near the bed, petting the cat, talking to it, telling it to be gentle with me. And another day, the cat had scratched me, and I heard my father's voice, loud, as he pitched it across the room, angry. No, not that day. I needed another day to block out the sounds and the hideous smell of the grave.

So much pain! Those eyes, the empty eyes stared back at me, even when my eyelids were closed. I would see them forever. I tried to think of the back yard, playing in the grass, waiting for my mother, the sun on my face, the rough surface of the patio bricks beneath my small hands. Looking toward the driveway and the garage. The garage door was open. No!

There was no safe place for me. No escape from the thing that had been Press ill-using my body. Digging into my shoulder, splitting open the inside of me as though he would stab me until I bled.

I opened my eyes once again.

The thing's mouth was slack beneath the mask, its putrid breath a fog between us in the frigid room, and I finally recognized it.

My tongue worked inside my mouth, dry and thick. I thought of water. Clear water.

My voice came, but it was only a whisper.

"Olivia. Please, Olivia."

The creature didn't seem to hear when the house groaned again. (I knew what it was. Who it was. I had seen him/it before, hadn't

I? He was worse now. More decayed, barely more than articulated bones hung with rotted flesh. He was no longer human, if he had ever been.)

My shoulder ached where he gripped me and my insides felt as though they were on fire.

Then came the scent of roses. *Olivia.*

I had never had a truly murderous thought until that moment. It was a thought wrapped in the heavy, languid scent of early June roses, the bower of white and red and yellow of Olivia's garden. With the scent, I felt the blood flowing back into my limbs, and my revulsion for the creature panting above me grew, and I stopped being afraid.

At the edges of my vision, I saw climbing rose vines chasing from the pedestal where I lay. They ran over the carpets, blooming, blooming, blooming, their petals a violent white against their thick green leaves and snaking vines. They ran to the corners, crowding, fighting to cover the walls, the windows, the floors. They were my hope: both innocence and death. I knew they meant death as well as salvation. Finally the room was engulfed, the scent overpowering. It was only then that I realized that the vines were coming from my own hands—a strange and terrifying gift.

As the roses grew, the demon above me flickered and faded away and there was only Press. The grimace on his face, though, was nearly as hideous as the creature's. Perhaps it had been Press all along, and in my fear I had hallucinated Randolph/the creature.

If God is truly merciful, He will someday let me forget the moment I chose to kill my husband. To punish him for letting our daughter die, and for every act of cruelty he'd committed since Olivia had died. With my blood freed from whatever numbing drug that Jack had used, I could lift my hands, and they were no longer my hands, but leafy vines studded with thorns. While my husband stared, horrified, into my eyes, I raised my hands to his powerful neck and pressed them against his skin. At that moment there *was* mercy, for I felt nothing as I did it—neither the piercing of the thorns nor the pain of killing someone I loved. As he screamed, the light in the eyes behind the mask flared, then dimmed. Blood erupted from him, raining down on me.

I might have dropped my hands at that, but I found myself filled with a sense of something—someone—who was not me. Neither was it Olivia or Eva. *Something to do with the ballroom, the hundreds of images of Japanese women. No. Just one woman, over and over. And the strange, sharp scent of chrysanthemums. Why chrysanthemums? There were cherry blossoms on the ballroom walls.* Whoever it was overwhelmed me with their rage, and that rage flew from me, propelling Press across the big room and crushing his body high against the wall of thorn-covered vines.

He fell.

As I watched, the vines covering the room melted away like snow under the noon sun. Press lay slumped on the floor, unmoving.

Chapter 43

One More Funeral

One more death, one more funeral. No one in Old Gate was surprised. October had become November, frigid with rare early snow that fell on our hats and coats as we stood by Press's open grave. I had considered making the service private, but everyone in town would have come anyway. Afterwards, they filed up our drive in their cars and trucks, led by the sheriff's cruiser, ready for their fill of funeral meats. Only there was no Terrance, stiff and formal and alarming to strangers in the way of church bishops and Boris Karloff, to greet them and serve them sweetened iced tea. After he and Press and the other man took me into the theater, I didn't see him again. He hadn't been in costume, and I was certain he wasn't one of the partygoers. After Press's body was taken away, I discovered he'd slipped away from Bliss House like a thief in the night. His room was empty of every belonging, the surfaces thick with undisturbed layers of dust that might have been there for decades.

No one ever tried to find him. No one cared. I asked Marlene, who had slept two rooms away from him and worked beside him for over ten years, if she knew where he might have gone. There was a moment—not even a second long—when she seemed not to know who I was talking about. She blinked.

"Did you ever see him eat?" she asked. Puzzled, I told her that I hadn't. "Every time he sat down, it was as though he was afraid he would never have another meal. I've never seen the like in a grown man. Then he would do his dishes and get on with his job. I hope that wherever he's gone, there's someone to feed him." That single, astonishing thing was all she had to say about him.

She stayed with us for another year, until she married a man from her church who owned the butcher shop in town. I couldn't blame her for anything Press had done, or what she had believed of him. She seemed unaffected by the strange things that happened in the house. I envied her that.

"No sherry, no Scotch," I told her as we made plans for the funeral. "It will just make people stay longer."

But after the guests began to arrive I changed my mind, and had her put out sherry, Scotch, and other liquor as well. If anyone thought it was suspiciously like a celebration rather than a wake, I didn't care. Bliss House had been a place of sadness for too long. It was time to open the house up and let other influences in. We had all had enough of Press and his dark hand over our lives.

I had Michael back. (Later that terrible night, I had found him safely asleep at the orchardkeeper's house, with a confused and upset Shelley.) Nonie had returned with my father, though he remained ensconced in a chair in the library during the funeral service, his casted leg resting on an ottoman. I had turned the library into a temporary bedroom so he didn't have to use the stairs.

Bliss House was mine, as much as it could belong to anybody.

"He's dead." Hugh Walters had gently lifted the half-mask from Press's face and closed his eyes. It was a peculiar thing to do, given that he was a policeman and Press was a victim, but it sent a signal that he knew Press's death couldn't be handled as a regular crime. Hugh's pleasant face looked bewildered. I had liked him, and almost felt sorry for him until I remembered how many crimes he must have covered up for Press. How he had stood by like the others while I lay drugged and exposed.

J.C. spoke from halfway across the room, where she stood against a wall, her hands pressed behind her as though she were ready to launch herself into one of the windows opposite. Her voice was now clear, despite the injuries to her face.

"Obviously, he had a terrible accident."

Rachel, who was clinging to Jack, gasped.

"That's insane. She killed him." She pointed at me. "She's got a goddamn knife. Look at her!"

I looked down. The jeweled peacock knife was in my right hand. Both the blade and my hand were covered with blood. A later glance at one of the tall, elaborately framed mirrors standing against the walls would reveal that my tunic sweater and bare legs were also bloody.

"You bitch!"

Jack held Rachel by the arms while she screamed unrepeatable profanities at me.

It was the roses I remembered. Not the knife. I knew that I was somehow responsible for the blood covering my husband and my own body. Had the roses been my own delusion? Certainly the shaking of the house had not. It had driven everyone else from the room and out of the house. Both the pocket door to the hall and the door to the outer stairway stood open—one to the distant light of the chandelier, the other to the night.

It certainly hadn't been I who had propelled him across the room.

"That's not what I saw," J.C. said, calmly. "I saw him fall off the stage, drunk, onto one of the tools the workmen left behind."

I could have wept with relief at her words. If only I had trusted her before it had become too late.

Now Rachel turned her attention to J.C. But before she could get a word out, Jack jerked her backwards.

"Be quiet, Rachel. Just shut up!"

He looked like a teenager playing dress-up in his silver leotard and tights. His wings were still stiff and cartoonish. There was something more than anger in his face. There was fear. Press was no longer there to protect them.

Hugh stood up.

"Yes. That's exactly right." He walked toward Jack and Rachel. "You need to get her under control, Jack. In fact, just take a quick look at him." Here, he inclined his head toward Press. "Call the death. We'll get a certificate later. Let's get this place cleaned up and I'll get the coroner and the funeral-home people here."

"The coroner?" J.C. had crossed the room to come and stand beside me. When she touched my back, I felt myself shaking beneath her hand. I wasn't sure I would ever stop shaking.

"It won't be a problem." Hugh's voice was low. Not quite ashamed, but neither was it triumphant. "If that sounds good to you, Charlotte."

I nodded. Press was dead, and yet his influence was still making sure that everything would be taken care of. No one who had been there that night would want it known that they'd been there—or what they'd been up to with Press and, earlier, Zion Heaster. They would want to keep their secrets and, in return, would keep mine.

⌒

After the wake, J.C. found me alone in the kitchen, sitting at the table in the butler's pantry. There had been a frost the night before, and all of the more tender-leafed herbs in the garden outside the window had succumbed. The wilted plants were like slender, ruined creatures fighting to stay upright. I'd been thinking of Beatrix Potter and Peter Rabbit and the animals I'd planned to paint on the walls of the ballroom. I wouldn't bother to try to have it painted again. The house obviously didn't want the room to change. Whatever—whoever—was attached to it would never let it.

J.C. put a glass of Scotch along with a small glass of sherry on the table, and touched me on the shoulder as she sat down. Her makeup was heavy, but the swelling had abated so that her cheek and lips looked almost normal again. She kept her voice low. "I know we've said just about everything, Charlotte. Thank you for forgiving me."

I nodded. We had said enough the night before as we sat talking in the morning room until nearly two A.M. She was ashamed of her affair with Press but had the dignity not to try to excuse it in light of the bizarre changes that had come over him during the past months. He'd brought her down, secretly, from the hotel a couple of times for the "parties" in Rachel and Jack's barn, which explained Rachel's animosity toward her. Of course Rachel would have been jealous. Hearing that, I confessed that I was rather glad she had pretended not to remember Rachel's name during our chance meeting at The Grange (had it only been the week before?). At that point, anything that made Rachel miserable was fine with me.

But it wasn't until she told me that Press had hinted that he was going to eventually kill me that I understood how much J.C. had risked. When she told him he was going too far, that it all needed to stop, he had beaten her up and, with Terrance's help, taken her to the rooms below the house. I never learned the details of what he'd done to her down there over those two days. The distant, guarded look in her eyes told me enough. When I asked how she'd broken free, she said that she believed Olivia had somehow helped her to escape. Knowing all that Olivia had done for me, how could I doubt her?

"Everything's packed. The car from The Grange will pick me up at two." J.C. looked at her watch. "Are you sure you and Michael don't want to get away for a while? The offer's still open if you want to stay at my cottage on the hotel grounds. I'll be back in New York in two days. No one will bother you."

"Thank you. We're going to stay here with my father and Nonie. Michael's been through enough these past few months. And now Press is gone. I can't take him away. He doesn't really know anywhere else."

She slid the glass of sherry in front of me.

"I think you should have several of these."

I shook my head.

"You didn't eat any breakfast either, did you? At least it's something."

Marlene had come from the dining room into the other end of the kitchen with a tray full of dishes. I lowered my voice so she wouldn't hear me, but it didn't really matter. I wouldn't be able to hide it much longer, anyway. "Just the smell of wine turns my stomach. I think I'm pregnant."

J.C. covered her mouth. "Oh, God, Charlotte. How is that possible? Not. . . ."

"No. At least two months. That's when I started getting sick with both Eva and Michael. I wasn't paying any attention to the dates. I guess I assumed the stress had affected my—you know. My cycle."

"What will you do?"

"Michael will be happy. He's missed Eva so much. Maybe it will be a boy. He'd like that."

When she leaned forward, I saw a glimmer of the old, cynical J.C. in her eyes. "Will you name him after Press?"

I laughed. It seemed like such a peculiar question to ask so early. But people would want to know.

"Randolph."

"You can't! That's . . . I don't know. It sounds insane, Charlotte. Why would you do that?"

"I'm staying here, aren't I? It's only fair that if I'm to stay and try to heal this house, heal my family—or what's left of it—then another Randolph might help make it right."

"I don't think you should do this to yourself."

"I'm not doing anything to myself. I'm going to live my life and raise my children here, where they belong. It would take a hell of a lot to drive me away now." And I meant it.

⁓

Michael and I watched from the front door as the driver helped J.C. into the long black Lincoln that would take her back to The Grange. She turned to wave from the back window as they headed down the drive. Michael blew her a kiss. The only time I ever saw her again was at The Grange when we both chanced to be there at the same time. She had said she would visit us, but I couldn't blame her for not wanting to come back to Bliss House.

The day after she left, Nonie and I went down the hidden staircase to the rooms below. I was trembling. Nonie was silent.

The rooms told a vile story. There were magazines and books and photographs and drawings—filthy things. Much of it was even older than Press. But he'd clearly spent a lot of time there. There was evidence of women besides J.C., too. Or at least one. I suspected it was Rachel.

The rooms could be reached from the outside by a tunnel that began behind a door hidden in a wall of the springhouse. I sealed it up myself, not wanting to trust the job to anyone else. Then I closed the panel beside the fireplace and locked the ballroom doors.

No one is allowed in the ballroom at all. The boys, teenagers now, know this. We have rules. Rules to keep them safe.

You will wonder about Rachel, of course.

Old Gate is a small town, so we get in each other's way sometimes. But we've developed the skill of not actually seeing each
other even when we're in the same store or restaurant. I'm not sure
what she tells people if they ask about our friendship. I just pretend
I haven't heard and change the subject.

That following spring, I saw Holly at a garden party. She was
showing another woman a picture of Seraphina, and exclaiming
what a wonderful mother Rachel was becoming.

Something rose inside me, a desperate desire to tell her to
remind Rachel to keep her little girl away from the geese that
settled so prettily beside her pond. I wanted to imagine the sick fear
in Rachel's eyes. Does she love Seraphina now? Is Seraphina precious to her, now that she will never have another child for Press?
Somehow I doubt it. Rachel is Rachel.

We hold each other at bay: a murder for a murder. It would
always be so.

But does she ever wonder about Press? Where he is?

I have no need to wonder. I know he is here. With me. With us.

Epilogue

The May sun beats upon the roof and windows and solid outer walls, and I can feel it all. But the sun and the heat can't harm me. It may weather the brick and fade the gray tiles, but that is nothing. I am here inside the house. I am one with this house.

I feel the car approaching, the flattening of the shells and stones in the drive. My sense of them is faint at first; but as the car comes closer, I can smell the heated exhaust, the odor of disinfectant, of a wet diaper, of Charlotte's hairspray and her favorite hand lotion. I can smell my child, new and alive. They are driving carefully with their precious cargo, as I would have them. Charlotte comes to me scented and lovely and cruel, as I always knew she might be. Did she imagine that I thought her helpless? I feel her strength as she approaches, the strength that threatened me, that took my life. But I am not interested in you now, my faithless wife.

I watch as that filthy saint, Roman Carter, limps to open the car door for her, and my anger swells. Can he feel it? See how complacent he is, smiling at my wife and new son. His sanctimony smells of dried ink and stale coffee. Jack, my dearest Jack should

315

have killed him with that car. My hatred makes me want to tear loose an arrow of ironwork from an upper floor and shoot it into his heart. Let him collapse on my step, his eyes open to the thing that killed him, understanding. Finally understanding. But I will do nothing now. He will wait, as I have waited.

Now she puts that lovely leg out of the car. Still, I would touch that leg, wrap it in mine, and press naked against that yielding ivory skin. I might whisper in her ear, telling her what I was about to do so I could see the terror in her once-adoring eyes, then tear at the curve of her proud neck with my teeth, rending her flesh, exposing her lying throat to the flies.

But I am patient. I have no need of that sort of violence. Once I needed a stage, but now my breaths, my words are the creaking of a door and a draft in the great hall where I once loved to play. My sighs are the glinting of the stars covering the dome. My audience is every thing, every person who lives and has died here. And there are the others. The ones who have never lived but are welcome in this place.

Look how carefully she cradles my newborn son, tucking the corners of the blanket around him despite the heat rising in waves from the hood of the ticking car and the patio stones. So precious to her. Precious to me.

I can sense my father smiling at his name.

There's so much I need to show my son. So much I need to teach him, as I was taught. My need to touch him swells, pushing against the inner walls of the house, causing even the paintings to shudder with my frustration. For an eternity I have kept my peace, waiting for him. Even now, there is no one inside to hear. Everyone is outside, anxious to greet him.

Charlotte, look what you have stolen from me! I would be there beside you, but you were selfish. Like my mother, who plagues me still. Yes, she is here with me. With Eva.

Hold my son just so, Charlotte. Will you give me that? I want to see his eyes, and he's hiding them from the brutal sun. He will have my eyes. He will have my strength because I will give it to him. You will not stop me.

Finally, finally! The odious Roman opens the front door. Can you hear me, my son? Can you hear me welcoming you? Can you hear the chorus of voices welcoming you home? Now that you are inside me, I will sigh, cooling you with my breath.

Welcome, my son. Welcome, Randolph.

Acknowledgments

Charlotte's Story comes into the world borne by so many lovely people who deserve far more than my grateful thanks.

Susan Raihofer, my most wonderful agent from the David Black Literary Agency. We've grown into this business together, and I couldn't have a better partner in literary crime. Sometimes we even talk about work when she calls.

Maggie Daniel Caldwell, the friend of my heart, who tells me tales of the beach and life and love, and always makes me laugh.

J.T. Ellison, who keeps me sane and wondering how she has time to do all the amazing things she does while also being the perfect friend, therapist, and publishing mentor.

Carolyn Haines, who has the best stories, a generous heart, and a contagious enthusiasm that overwhelms even my darkest moods.

The brilliant group at Pegasus, especially my thoughtful editor, Jessica Case, who made my dream of a haunted house full of stories come true, and always makes the stories better. Also, publisher Claiborne Hancock and marketing maven/editor Iris Blasi.

Henry Sene Yee has produced yet another cover that haunts me in just the same way that *Bliss House* does. Maria Fernandez created the elegant interior design.

Living the life of a country mom and writer, I don't get out much. My days are always enriched by the delightful women who give me so much online and handwritten encouragement, including Elizabeth "Lyzz" Pickle, Sue Spina, Leta Sontag, Judy Daniel, Lauren Winters O'Brien, Brandee Crisp, and my dearest Jen Talty.

All hail the Nashville literary crew: editor Blake Leyers, and writers Paige Crutcher, and Ariel Lawhon, who crack me up every time.

Jennifer Jordan, editor, writer, and encourager, who keeps me cheered with all manner of critter cuteness and reminded me that Emily D. always has just the right words.

Writer Ashley Malick, who cleverly named the town of Clareston.

My parents, Judy and Jerry Philpot, who cheer me on and inspire me every day.

Ann and Cleve Benedict, whose Virginia/Other Virginia love story always makes me smile.

My sisters, Teresa McGrath and Monica Wilmsen, who—after years of my tormenting them with big-sister advice—still tolerate me and take my calls. Thank God for them both.

Cleveland Benedict II fills my day with joy and jokes. Plus, he still gives me hugs, though he wouldn't want me to tell you that.

Nora Benedict is the music in my life. Play on, sweet girl.

There would be no books without my dearest Pinckney. No sunshine, either. He has all my love.

Coming from Pegasus Books in 2016

The Abandoned Heart

A BLISS HOUSE NOVEL

LAURA BENEDICT

PEGASUS CRIME
NEW YORK LONDON

Three women.
One troubled man, and a cursed house.
Generations of lives at stake.

It's 1899, the cusp of a new century, and Bliss House, the proud creation of Randolph Hasbrouck Bliss, has stood for twenty years, casting its unsettling shadow over Old Gate, Virginia. Already the house has a reputation for trouble, but there are those who can't keep away, drawn by rumors of strange goings on beyond the public entertainments—traveling troupes, preachers, spiritualists, and musicians—that take place in the house's third floor theater.

Now Randolph has a new wife, Lucy, a rebellious daughter of Old Gate society who defied her family by marrying him in secret. She's made a blithe promise to him that she will give him the legitimate son he has always wished for, without understanding what it will cost her. Randolph is a man of peculiar—even hellish—appetites that leave their mark on everything and everyone around him. This is especially true for Lucy and the other women he has pulled into his orbit, promising them stability, wealth, and freedom.

Lucy soon comes to realize that she is simply his latest conquest. Quiet, plain Amelia, Randolph's first wife, and the very young Kiku, who was virtually unknown in Old Gate—both came to Bliss House long before her, and left their own marks.

For Bliss House never forgets what happens within its walls, and nothing that dies there can ever leave.